MW00830363

Also by Piper CJ

THE FOX AND THE FALCON

PIPER CJ

Bloom books

Copyright © 2025 by Piper CJ
Cover and internal design © 2025 by Sourcebooks
Cover art and design by Helena Elias

Sourcebooks, Bloom Books, and the colophon are registered trademarks of Sourcebooks.

All rights reserved. No part of this book may be reproduced in any form or by
any electronic or mechanical means including information storage and retrieval
systems—except in the case of brief quotations embodied in critical articles or
reviews—without permission in writing from its publisher, Sourcebooks.

The characters and events portrayed in this book are fictitious or are used fictitiously. Any
similarity to real persons, living or dead, is purely coincidental and not intended by the author.

All brand names and product names used in this book are trademarks,
registered trademarks, or trade names of their respective holders. Sourcebooks
is not associated with any product or vendor in this book.

Published by Bloom Books, an imprint of Sourcebooks
P.O. Box 4410, Naperville, Illinois 60567-4410
(630) 961-3900
sourcebooks.com

Cataloging-in-Publication data is on file with the Library of Congress.

Printed and bound in the United States of America.
WOZ 10 9 8 7 6 5 4 3 2 1

To E—
You were so bad in bed
that it made me reevaluate my choices
and turn my life around.
I've never thanked you for that.

Before we start, a word from Piper

Disclaimers on Religion and Mental Health:
You hold in your hand a work of fiction, comedy, commentary, and irreverence. While it has been thoroughly researched and informed by my lived experience in the church, it is in no way representative of the religious majority or meant to be a how-to handbook on interacting with the supernatural of any realm or pantheon, or a reflection of the personalities of the beings within them. Some readers may find religious irreverence upsetting, and personifications of gods, fae, religion, and mythology may not be suitable for all readers.

Regarding mental health, we find ourselves in the shoes of Marlow, our protagonist, who does not look upon her mental health journey with kind eyes. While this is authentic to my experience with mental health and the experience of many, it in no way endorses a world that regards mental health issues as shameful or flippant, merely as one character's walk through those waters. This extends to the way she speaks about herself, refers to her perceived experience, and her troubling internalized narrative, which permits and accepts others speaking to and about her mental health unkindly. For help or more information on mental health matters, please visit mentalhealthfirstaid.org and other resources.

Notes on Sex Work:
There is no trigger warning for sex work, just as there are no trigger warnings for loan officers, real estate agents, veterinarians, or authors. Sex worker empowerment and destigmatization is an issue that is important to me and is prevalent in many of my works. If something about sex work causes you discomfort, my goal is not to make the environment more comfortable for you, but to encourage you to confront thoughts and feelings of whorephobia. For more information, please read the lived experiences, articles, and input from sex workers themselves as they contribute to tryst.link/blog/tag /articles/ and other resources.

Content Warnings:
This novel is intended for an adult audience and may contain themes and elements regarding mental health, gods, religion, beliefs, and sexual expression that may be troubling or unsuitable for some readers. A thorough list of content warnings for this and all Piper CJ works can be found at pipercj.com /gallery/content-and-trigger-warnings

NO OTHER GODS
ORIGINAL LITERARY SOUNDTRACK

BY THE BOOKISH SONGS COLLECTIVE

THE DEER AND THE DRAGON
(THE WORLD OF NO OTHER GODS THEME)
                                LINDSAY DILLS

ONLY YOURS
(CALIBAN AND MARLOW THEME)
                                VICTORIA CARBOL

STAY WILD
(FAUNA & AZRAMES THEME)
                                GIORGiA

CYCLES
(CALIBAN THEME)
                                ELLYSE MOIR

MARIBELLE, MERIT, MARLOW
(MARLOW THEME)
                                TAYLOR ASH

IMAGINE ME
(MARLOW AND CALIBAN THEME)
                                KENDRA DANTES
                                & NINO TOSCO

WAKE UP
(THE DEER AND THE DRAGON THEME)
                                ARCANA

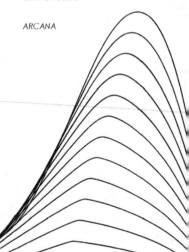

Pronunciation Guide

Aesir	AY-sir
Álfheimr	ALF-hi-mur
Azrames	az-RAY-mus
Baal	ball
Caliban	CAL-ih-ban
Canaanite	KAY-nuh-nite
Fenrir	FEN-reer
sølje	sole-yeh
Vanir	vah-NEER

Chapter One

S PACE AND ITS STRANGE, OMINOUS DARKNESS WAS AN ABSTRACT thing. Stars, planets, and a bright, silver moon were all supposedly stitched together by nothingness. They were as vaguely interesting to me as knowing we've only explored five percent of the ocean, or that a single human contained twenty-five thousand miles of blood vessels—enough to wrap around Earth four times. Every bit of data was tucked away like a shiny rock plucked from the beach: pretty, but useless, and largely forgotten.

I knew they existed—the black holes, the emptiness, the great, vast nothing—but they had no bearing on my life. Until I lost him. When Caliban and I were ripped apart, I stepped into the void. Gasping, clawing, unable to breathe. And at long last, I understood space. I knew the crushing pain of a life without air.

Chapter Two

THERE WERE DOZENS OF REASONS TO LET SOMEONE INTO your bed. Intimacy, stress relief, boredom, experimentation, and lust, to name a few. I once fucked a girl—poorly, I might add—who'd spent years pining after me just so she could shake the cobwebs of fantasy from her head and realize we were, in fact, a terrible match. A perfume-scented, brightly colored magazine had once proclaimed that women who'd had more than twenty partners were unlikely to find love.

Good, I'd thought. *At least then, I'd have an excuse.*

Caliban wasn't my first, or third, or fifth.

He wasn't real, after all—the man who'd haunted my steps for as long as I could remember. But he was one hell of a coping mechanism, and this beautiful, perfect figment of my imagination had helped me survive my tumultuous upbringing. He had been there for my rocky transition from the sheltered church to the liberal hedonism of a non-Christian college. Now, god willing, he'd help me keep my head above water as I studied for midterms while writing a novel. Why I'd thought it was a good idea to spend my junior year squandering my free time as I role-played as an author was a mystery I'd never solve.

I'd thought about taking Caliban to bed, of course. I'd

picture looking into those silver eyes while gripping the back of the neck of whoever happened to be on top of me. I'd imagined chilled lips sending goose bumps down my neck while being kissed by another. I'd allowed my imagination to explore the forbidden curiosity of someone stepping from the shadows to run their hands up my dress, under my shirt, cupping my jaw, claiming my mouth.

Tonight, he was there before I'd finished my unsatisfied daydream.

I was overcome with the misty rush of the forest floor while a candle flickered and The Weeknd piped through my bedside speaker. Maybe my phantom had sensed my anxiety as I struggled to get Booker, the basketball team's leading point guard, out of my bed. I wondered if he could smell it too—the cologne of petrichor and magical otherness—but perhaps he thought it was just the candle. He was a man, after all.

I'd stepped into my panties and tugged a T-shirt over my head the moment he'd finished and immediately began to collect his clothes. His belt buckle clattered as he caught it with a chuckle.

"Come on," Booker said, one muscled leg still beneath the covers, "let me stay over."

The sooner he left, the sooner I could crack open my bedside drawer and get myself off. Booker wasn't terrible between the sheets. He was uncomfortably big, which meant an overuse of lube and the wincing that came from a man hitting your cervix, and never in a good way. But for a few sweaty minutes, I was able to escape my life and just be utterly present. And I'd be lying if I said a huge facet of my attraction wasn't simply knowing that he was widely coveted, yet I was the one kicking him out of bed.

I cracked the bedroom door and gestured toward the living room. "I have an eight a.m. lab," I said. "I can't stay up late."

He was unamused as he swung his legs over the side of the

3

mattress and slipped into his jeans. "We've been hooking up long enough for me to know you dropped out of chem. You don't have anything in the morning."

Shit.

Booker crossed the room in three steps. The candlelight exaggerated the contours of his abs and broad shoulders. He kept his T-shirt in his hand as he looked down at me. "We don't have to do this booty call thing, Marlow. I want to take you to dinner. I want to look up into the stands and see your face. I want to watch movies with you and introduce you to my teammates and…"

His voice drifted off as he studied the apologetic pucker between my brows.

"You're a nice guy, Booker."

The hope in his eyes dimmed, then smoked out. He closed his eyes and took a deep breath. A muscle ticked in his jaw as he steeled himself against rejection.

"I'm sorry. I really am. It's just…"

"Spare me." He slipped the T-shirt over his head and left without a goodbye. Perhaps if I were someone different, I would have felt bad about the way we'd left things. Instead, I felt only relief that he was gone, and that I knew exactly who I'd find when I turned around.

The corner of Caliban's lips tugged up in a half-amused smile. I relaxed and riled at once, both relieved by his presence and excited he was here. I could never anticipate his visits, but if he were a figment of my imagination, he must have appeared because I needed to get things off my chest. Booker may have been a perfect specimen by every human standard, but Caliban's beauty stole my breath altogether.

"I'm switching back to women," I said as I flopped onto the bed. I watched him lean against the wall near the door, arms folded over his broad chest. "Men bring a dick to the party and think it's all they need to get you off."

"It can be," he said, silver eyes glinting with some wicked sense of knowing. He tilted his head as if listening for the distant sounds of a disappointed basketball player's footsteps.

"But I'm not confident in your taste in men."

I propped myself up on my elbows, eyeing him.

A beat pulsed between us where the time for me to reply had come and gone. I was generally so quick with my smartass retorts and general complaints.

He looked at me with a single quirked brow. My heart skipped a beat as I summoned whatever courage I possessed.

"You're a man," I said at last.

He rubbed his jaw as he chuckled. "Love—"

I thought of the first time I'd brushed his hand—quite by accident—and how my veins had filled with cold, spiked adrenaline when I realized just how solid and real he'd felt. I'd grown bolder as the years ticked on, reaching for his hand when I needed, thinking of the arms wrapped tightly around me when I'd longed to be held, or the night I'd rested my head in his lap and he'd touched my hair until I fell asleep.

"Sit next to me?"

Caliban ran a pale hand through his hair. "Listen, Love—"

"Is it not possible?" I asked.

The amusement faded from his voice. "It's more than possible, it's just—"

Great. An imaginary friend rejecting its creator would be a new low. Possibility aside, was there something within me that deemed me unworthy of indulging my fantasies? Perhaps this was a lesson in self-love. At least, I told myself as much as I asked, "But you don't want me?"

"Oh," he said, the sound so quiet it was more of a soft, chastising breath than a word. The bed slouched under his weight as he sat beside me. He tucked his arm behind me, and I rested my head on his chest. He touched his lips to my hair as if to kiss it, but instead, he muttered, "If I've made you feel unwanted even for a moment, I've failed you." He brushed cool fingers along my jaw, working them into my hair and slowly knotting them to force my chin up. No longer was I a woman poised for rejection, but mere inches from his lips.

5

He inhaled, and the lightning bolt that passed between us was like a cord that rose from my belly, traveling through my throat as he sipped my breath like electric, crackling wine.

I had never craved anything like this kiss.

I tried to close the space between us, but he tightened the hold on my hair, immobilizing me. "If we start, I won't be able to stop," he said.

"I don't want you to stop," I replied.

He shut his eyes, flattening his lips into a line as he struggled with some controlled emotion. "It's not... I don't mean tonight. I mean: I love you for you. I love our conversations and losing myself in the labyrinth of your mind. I love championing your dreams. I love catching your tears and righting your wrongs. I don't need anything more from you to be utterly fulfilled. But if you let me into this part of your life, you will be opening a door that I'd sooner die than close."

It was a warning, but it wasn't a no. He wanted it every bit as much as I did. He had more self-control, though, as he managed to remain statue still while I tried once more to kiss him. This time when he tightened his grip on my hair, I released a quick gasp at the small hurt.

"You'll have to say it, Love."

"Say what?"

His jaw flexed as his gaze flitted from my eyes to my lips to my throat, wandering lower, looking at me as if I were something to be eaten. I was acutely aware of his cool fingers in my hair, of the prone position that left my neck exposed, of the excited flood between my legs as the electric crackle worked its way into the deepest parts of me.

"Tell me that you want this with me. Tell me your body is mine, and I'll make it so."

The chilled spike of fear only added to the excitement. I wasn't sure what fucked-up parts of my brain had turned my sexual perversions into deals with the devil, but I knew I wanted this more than life. I needed to be wrapped in the arms that had kept me safe for so many years. I needed to

6

know what it might be like when the person in my bed was someone who lit my soul on fire. I needed to know how full a ghost could make me feel.

"It's yours," I breathed.

His eyes remained closed. His whole face twitched. "Say it all."

There was no oxygen in the room as I struggled to say, "I want this with you, Caliban. My body is yours."

His posture shifted nearly imperceptibly as something clicked within him. He exhaled slowly, releasing his tight hold on my hair as he cupped the back of my head and brought his lips to mine. Goose bumps covered my arms and legs as his lightning worked its way through my blood. Greed crept into my kiss as I plunged my fingers into his hair in return and kissed him back with pent-up intensity.

I swung my leg over him, and for one magnificent moment, he squeezed the small of my waist, gripping my hips with thinly controlled desire. He pulled my tee off first, then drank me in until I began to squirm, self-conscious under the weight of his gaze. He reached over his head, grabbed a fistful of his black tee, and pulled his shirt off in one swift motion before flipping me onto my back with a growl.

The blurs of licks and kisses and teeth, the small hurts of perfect bites, the moans and gasps and sounds, the bucking of hips when touched in sensitive places, the unbridled longing to taste and be tasted—it was all tossed into a blender. I made it abundantly clear that I did not want foreplay. I wanted him inside me. I wanted to see what he'd meant when he'd implied some men might possess the equipment to get me off with a cock alone. He had equipment that I wanted access to.

I maintained my confidence right up until I saw the rock-hard pillar of marble and desire waiting at my entrance, and the blood drained from my face.

"Do you trust me?" he asked, as if reading my mind.

I continued to stare at it as I nodded, one knee near my tit and the other hooked around his hip as my courage waned. I didn't want it to hurt. My body count of sexual experiences only included two dicks so far, but the one with the baseball bat in his pants had been the sort of mistake I'd sworn not to repeat.

Caliban licked his palm and coated his cock with one smooth motion, then nudged my entrance. I swallowed as I continued to stare, watching with wide, worried eyes as it went in deeper and deeper and deeper. I wasn't sure at what point I'd closed my eyes and let my head collapse into the pillow, but I focused on my breathing as he pulled out ever so slightly, then worked himself in a little further. My sharp inhalations and pleasurable groans alternated as he moved. I wasn't conscious of much else as the thumping heartbeat between my legs filled me completely.

I dug the fingernails of one hand into the back of his neck as I pulled his face close to mine, but the other hand gripped his thigh, keeping his body at bay. It felt so fucking good, I couldn't risk the pain, the flinch, the winching disappointment of him bottoming out and throwing a single moment of discomfort into this utterly perfect moment.

"Hey," came his husky command, "look at me."

I struggled to comply, lifting my eyes to meet the starlit burn of his gaze.

"You're pushing me away. Give me your hands."

The briefest flash of panic shot through me. "But—"

"Give them to me."

My heart thundered as I took my hand off his thigh. He didn't break eye contact for a second as he caught my wrists in his broad, rough hand. I swallowed, worry clear on my face.

"Trust me," he said with low, husky reassurance. "You can take it. Don't look away."

Chills snaked down my spine. Ice and butterflies and adrenaline filled my belly. I looked at him with worry and fear and trust and panic and lust as he sank every inch into me, igniting a light within me I hadn't known existed. I choked on my gasp as my hips rolled into the shiver-inducing sensation.

"There's my girl," came his low growl. "You can take it."

It was hard to know how much time had passed. Ten minutes? Two hours? My thoughts tipped like leaves in the wind, disconnected from any tree of rational thought. The space between infinities engulfed each slow, hard thrust, filling me with glitter, with starlight, with spirit and flame and shadow and absolute goddamn magic. This was what it meant to be fucked right.

No amount of vibrating toys or swirling, suctioning lips and tongue compared to the secret treasure chest of oxytocin that he alone had managed to unlock. It pumped through me like the most delicious and explicit of intravenous drugs.

I reached up to touch his utterly perfect face, and the sound he made as he kissed my palm was so tender it nearly broke my heart. Except, my precious organ was too pickled in serotonin to ever experience heartbreak. In fact, I was quite certain that if I opened my mouth to express a single thought, I'd only be capable of telling him that my body wasn't the only thing that belonged to him. I admitted a truth I'd known for a long, long time.

I was his. Mind, body, and soul.

Chapter Three

THE SECOND HAND ON THE CLOCK TICKED THE SAME WORD over, and over, and over.

Gone, gone, gone.

One week ago, I'd been held by the Prince of Hell. My hair had been ruffled by Azrames, the demon of vengeance. Silas—full-time angel, part-time dick—had scooped me out of harm's way. One week ago, I'd willingly given my blood and signed myself over to the Phoenician goddess Astarte because I was, as Fauna so often liked to remind me, an absolute idiot. I hadn't just peered behind the veil; the veil had been torn down in its entirety as gods had walked among mortals under the guise of the fabulously talented, wealthy, and beautiful in the tiny town of Bellfield. One week ago, I'd been drugged, panicked, deviously horny, and sobbing inconsolably in Fauna's arms as she'd held me under the ice-cold water of my apartment's shower and told me that everything would be okay.

What a goddamn liar.

"How are you so calm? It's been a week." I paced back and forth, gnawing on my knuckle. I refused to sit still despite Fauna's relentless insistence that I calm down. Deep, angry imprints from my teeth wounded my forefinger as I bit into it again and again. I kicked a stray shoe to the side so

I could continue my pacing unencumbered. My place was a mess, and at this point, there was no saving it. I'd given my maid the time off, as I didn't know how to explain the bizarre sigils scribbled in permanent marker on my door or windows. Similarly, I had no idea how I'd explain Fauna to... anybody. It had taken long enough for me to make sense of the skosgrå—the Nordic nymph of sugar and chaos—and I'd barely scratched the surface of understanding her.

"It hasn't been a week, drama queen. It's been six days. We know they went to another realm, or else your police would be giving press conferences and human news anchors would be talking about some mass murder at a fertility clinic. Time passes differently in other realms. For all we know, they've been gone no more than ten minutes."

"How can you just sit there?"

"I'm not just sitting here. I'm eating. And cartoons are on." Fauna snapped off a piece of cherry-red licorice. She'd been a stabilizing force for the first few days of my tears, my recitation of events, and my shock as memory after memory kept bubbling up in traumatic flashes. She'd been there for me, holding me while I cried, reassuring me, talking me through everything. She had taunted me more than once for trying to seduce her in my drug-addled state, but given that I'd been under the influence of a fertility goddess, I was offered a little begrudging compassion.

But when it came to actually doing something about Caliban's disappearance, Fauna had been monumentally unhelpful.

She'd shot down my pleas to visit Betty—the witch who ran Daily Devils in the art district—when I'd begged for alternative paths to answers. Betty worked exclusively with Azrames, after all, and he was presently indisposed. All my other proposed solutions, from crystal balls and tarot cards to seances and Ouija boards, were similarly shot down.

Days of brainstorming had led us to a few conclusions. The first was that if Caliban and Azrames had won the fight in Bellfield and dragged Anath to Hell, we would have heard from them. The second was that if Silas had slain the Prince of Hell, Heaven would have made its celebrations known. If they were unreachable, it meant they had to be with the Phoenicians.

"Okay, what about a different witch?" I asked. "Maybe one who works with a Phoenician deity? Could they channel someone from that realm like Betty does with Azrames?"

"Sure," came her dry response, not bothering to look away from the television. "Let me know when you find a Canaanite practitioner."

I chewed my nails. "Maybe the Nordes have heard something. Could you ask?"

"They haven't." Fauna tapped her temple. "If there was new intel in the Nordic network, I'd know about it."

"Your nonchalance is coming across as pretty fucking heartless," I bit.

"I have reason to be calm. Caliban's alive, and that's what matters. When he dies, you'll know."

I choked on my question. "How?"

"The same way I know Azrames isn't gone. If a bond like yours was snipped, that loss would punch an invisible hole through your chest. You don't stay tethered for lifetimes and not feel it when he's gone."

"Everyone has spies, right? Wasn't that the lesson of *Fire and Swords*? Every kingdom has an infiltrator; every seal has a leak. There must be someone connected to the Phoenician realm who knows something. If they're being held prisoner, if they're being tortured...I need to know they're safe. I need to know Caliban is all right."

She looked up from her cartoons. "I'm pretty sure the lesson of *Fire and Swords* is that every scene is made better with tits."

I stomped my foot. "Take this seriously!"

"Give them a few more days, Marlow."

"Please." I interlaced my fingers as if in prayer. "You said you have a place in the mortal realm, right? A house where you keep all your hipster outfits? Your landlord is some fae that you do favors for? Well…do other fae do him favors, too?"

She chewed on her lip. "It's possible."

"Ask him. I'm safe in this apartment." I shot a glance at the graffiti of warding on every window in my home. "Maybe the gods hold ransom. Maybe someone will be willing to strike a deal."

She told me not to hold my breath. A moment later, she vanished.

While she left me to gather intelligence, I could do little aside from pace.

Twenty-three steps from the front door to the windows.

Twelve steps from the wall behind the couch to the entertainment set.

Thirty-one steps from the same wall behind the couch, down the hall, past the first and second bedrooms, the guest bathroom, and the linen closet.

Six steps from the television to the dent in the couch where Fauna had been ten, twenty, forty minutes prior.

An hour passed and my palms began to sweat.

I'd seen the glint of the meteor hammer as Azrames had whirled it above his head like a flail at the end of a lasso, taking out enemy after enemy. I'd watched Caliban saw off the head of the Phoenician goddess of sex, love, and war. I'd been there when the glittering angel had snatched me from the swarm of parasitic entities.

Now for all I knew, I'd sent Fauna away to meet the same fate.

Three hours later, a knock came at the door. I threw it open to see copper hair mixed with blocks of silver. Her freckles were stark against unusually pale skin.

"I need to alter that ward," she muttered. Her voice was disconnected, eyes glazed over, as if she wasn't truly present. "I don't like that it keeps me out."

Panic lanced through me. I wrapped my arms around her neck. "What happened? What did you learn?"

"She has them," Fauna confirmed. "They're with Anath."

I pulled away from the hug, searching her face for answers. "And?"

"Anath told Baal and every heavy hitter in the Phoenician pantheon that the human author Merit Finnegan came to Astarte's clinic. You made enough of an impression on Dagon for him to corroborate your presence in Bellfield. It seems they've pieced together that your success is linked to being the Prince's human, which is why he showed up for you. They want to see you."

A painful lump formed in my throat. "We…we need to go to the Phoenician realm."

"No." She pushed past me and plopped down on the couch. "You can't go now. And I can't send you in there alone. We're going to need help."

"Fine, yes, good, let's get help. More demons? Did you go on dates with any other angels? Do you know Thor? He's a legendary fighter, right?"

She shook her head. "First of all, you sound stupid. We have no time for the comic book versions of gods. And no to whatever else you asked. The fae who told me put himself at great risk to pass along the message."

I took a seat beside her and snatched her hand tightly. "What did this fae tell you, exactly?"

Her eyes remain unfocused. "He confirmed what we knew, then the realm's gossip: that you're the Prince's human. Anath didn't witness Astarte's death, so it sounds like right now they have no proof as to who murdered their goddess. That's good news for all of us. The Phoenicians plan to send you a formal invitation to their realm. He said he'll volunteer to deliver the message."

"Why? What's in it for him?"

She sucked her teeth. "You wanted me to strike a deal? I struck a deal. The specifics are none of your business."

It was hard to know if she was being flippant, or if there she was genuinely irritated. Regardless, I had taken a step closer to answers. "Okay, so we go get help while we wait for the messenger, right? And he can't come to my apartment since it's heavily warded, so do we need a meeting location? What's the plan? What—"

She pressed her index fingers into her temples. "You're giving me a headache. Leave the planning to the immortal being charged with keeping you alive, okay? I promised my contact that I'd wait to make a move. Our earthly location isn't important. He'll find us when the time comes. If we start visibly gathering forces now, all eyes will be on the only fae who could have spilled their tea. We can't dime him out."

"But—" My fingernails bit into her hand.

"But nothing," she snapped. "I know you're scared for the Prince. That's fair. But you've only known him for what... twenty-six years? And of that, you've spent...ninety-nine percent convinced he was fake? So, you're fresh to reality. Welcome to the party, newbie. I've known him—or of him, I mean—for...Let's see..." She began to count on her fingers. "How long is forever?"

"Fuck off."

She shook her hand free of my grasp. "If they were holding Caliban prisoner, Hell would have sent reinforcements to rescue their Prince. My source made it sound like he's remained in their realm of his own volition. Azrames, on the other hand...he has no titles. They have no reason to keep him alive. Caliban might be there for him."

"You keep insisting that they're safe, but they're no longer fighting parasites, Fauna. With Astarte gone, Anath is the last remaining Canaanite goddess of war."

"Thanks for god-splaining to me." She rolled her eyes so hard I could have sworn I heard them pop...Then, "If you really want to take on a goddess, we *can* go to the Nordes. But if you sprint to the Nordic realm for the first time right after I

15

was seen interrogating umpteen fae in the fae network, we'll have blown our cover."

"And what? They'll be fine with us running to the Nordic pantheon for help after we've received a message? Won't that seem *more* threatening?"

"I promised him, Marlow. Our word is our bond. Running to the Nordes without cause looks suspicious. If we play our cards right, we may still find a way to get them to fight with you. There are other incentives to stir the pot. But... you might need to work on your persuasion techniques."

Her casual tone was infuriating. "I don't understand how you can just sit there! You know Az is being held hostage. We know where they are. We know—"

"These aren't mortal games. If you ask one more ignorant question that proves you're not listening to me, I'm going to duct tape your mouth shut." Her expression softened, presumably in reaction to the wound clear on mine. She gave me her hand once more. "In the meantime, we need a distraction. What can I do? Want to swap sex stories?"

My lip twitched in a sneer. "No."

"Liar. Everyone wants to swap sex stories. Come on, tell me about your best lay. Your craziest night. You have to have some really good tales. Was it with the Prince? Of course, it was. Demons are...well...*demons*."

"Stop it."

"Oh." She pouted. Her irritation had evaporated. The playful, infuriating nymph returned. "Is it because Caliban's not that good in bed? Trying to protect the Prince's reputation among the realms since he's been outshined by some country boy named Jake in the back of a pickup truck?"

I narrowed my eyes. "The country boy was a girl named Sasha, it was a rusted 1970 Ford something-or-other, and she was an uptight law student looking to break a little tension over summer break. I put a blow-up mattress in the truck bed, packed a picnic, and lit citronella candles. It was adorable. And no, she wasn't better than Caliban."

She steepled her fingers like a Bond villain. "Yes, good. Tell me more about Sasha."

"Absolutely not."

She made a dramatic show of crossing her arms. "Then you *must* tell me about Caliban! Why are you withholding this from me? Please, I'll give you anything. What will it take for you to describe his package? I could tell you about—"

I had a feeling she was about to tell me what Azrames did with his horns, and to be honest, I wasn't positive that I could continue looking him in the eye once I knew.

"Come on. Give me something while we wait. Time will pass whether we speak or not, so you might as well give me some wild stories from your glamorous life as a former lady of the evening. Tell me about a crazy client with an obscene fetish. Live a little."

I planted my hand on my hip, eyeing her testily. "Fauna, I'm sitting on a treasure trove of tales. You don't know the half of it. And you never will."

She slumped back into the couch cushions, grabbing a handful of candy. She clicked the television on once more. "You'd be a hit at parties if you took that stick out of your ass."

I glared between her and the screen. "Back to cartoons? Seriously? With all we're going through?"

Fauna threw up her hands. "You're impossible. You need more intervention than I can offer. Let's get you out of the house."

My eyes bulged as she reached for my laptop.

"Don't touch that!"

"Too late," she said through a mouthful of sweets as she quickly typed in my password.

"How do you—"

"*Caliban69*? It was like the third thing I tried. It's how I *know* you've got sex on the brain." She pressed the button before I had the time to lunge from my place in the living room.

Nia picked up after one ring. My friend's eyes widened into spectacular spheres as she stammered out a greeting. She shouted an off-screen cue for her music player to stop.

"Oh my god, hi!"

I dashed toward the couch, but Fauna extended her foot to effectively kick me in the stomach with a single, stalling gesture. I grunted against the explosion of pain, pretty sure my stomach had ruptured. It took me a second to suck air back into my lungs, but by then, the pair was already well into introductions.

"Hi, yourself." Fauna smiled in return. "We haven't formally met. I'm Fauna. You're Nia, right?"

"Nia Davis-Greene!" I snapped, still fighting for my life. "Hang up the phone right now!"

Fauna kept me at bay. "You're one of three humans in the world Marlow talks to and you've got a hyphenated last name? So feminist. I love it. Anyway, I've been trying to get her to take me out of the house, but she's boring. Are you busy tonight? Can we come to yours? Invite that peach with the quirky name! What was it?"

"Kirby?" Nia asked breathlessly, still gaping at Fauna. I'd sent Nia the selfie that Fauna and I had taken outside of the coffee shop many moons ago, but seeing the ethereal nymph in all her video-chatting glory was something neither Facetune nor Photoshop could fake.

It took me a minute to curse and swear and throw Fauna middle fingers before I groaned my way into frame. "Fauna is really pushy," I said, shoving myself onto the couch and body checking her until I took over the screen. "We're fine, Nia, really. I'm not—"

Nia's eyes bulged at the implication that I might back out. "You're coming over tonight, and if you don't, you're dead to me. Darius!" She yelled the name to an unseen face. She hollered again until her husband answered. "Get your ass to the store. We're making the best of the nice weather tonight!" Then to us, she asked, "Fauna, do you eat meat? What do you prefer on the grill? Burgers? Hot dogs?"

18

Fauna made a contemplative face. "Pineapple goes on the grill sometimes, right?"

Nia didn't so much as bat an eye. Off-screen once more: "We're doing shish kebabs with pineapple! Get stuff for five!" Then to us again, "What do you drink?"

"Make it sweet."

"Get mixers for piña coladas," she said to her husband.

"Five?" came the male voice from beyond the edges of our devices. "You, Kirby, Mar, and me. You don't have any other friends."

"This is a dinner to meet Mar's new friend," Nia said, tone resting heavily on the last word. He must have jumped into action at the implication. I could hear him rustling with his shoes near the door as I wrinkled my nose at Nia. He was a good guy. He was probably just as excited as Nia that I had someone new in my life, even if they couldn't see how wrong they were about the freckled goddess of sugar and chaos.

"Nia, we really don't have to," I said with my mouth. I hoped she heard the underlying telepathic message: *Please, save me from this. Cancel on Fauna. Say no. For the love of god, please!*

She waved away my protest with too much intensity. "Bullshit. It'd be a crime not to take advantage of one of the last nice days of the year. We've wasted half the month as it is. Darius is already on his way to the store. You'll offend us both if you cancel now. Be here at six for drinks. We'll do food at seven? I'll call Kirbs."

Fauna arched her back over the couch, dangling her hair in front of my face as she said, "Thanks Nia! Can't wait to meet you!"

"We keep it casual," Nia said, tone somewhere between warmth and bewilderment as she eyed my new companion. "No need to dress up."

"I never do," Fauna responded brightly. "See you at six." She shut the computer before I had time to argue. She smiled at me with infuriating, unwavering victory.

"Proud of yourself?"

"Immensely." Fauna grabbed another stick of licorice as she asked, "Isn't it rude to go to parties without bringing something? They always bring something on TV."

I shook my head. "Not when your sister is the host."

Fauna, normally a living noodle of blurry irreverence, stilled. "You're sisters?"

I yanked the computer from her and walked across the apartment to set it on the kitchen island before she got any other smart ideas. I made a mental note to change my password. "What, we don't look like we share a parent? That's racist, Fauna."

She narrowed her eyes almost imperceptibly as she scoured me. She searched my hazel eyes and pink features, gaze flicking between me and the now-dark computer. At long last she said, "You're telling a joke."

I flashed my teeth. "I am."

Of course, my colorless skin and Nia's rich brown looked nothing alike. I had no siblings. Nia was one of three, though her brothers didn't live in the city. I gave Fauna a brief history of our found-family story, which made her grin.

"Almost like you and me!"

I was about to argue that Fauna had tried to leave me to die on more than one occasion—something I was quite confident Nia and Kirby would never do—but my memory flashed to several hostile texts from Nia wherein she'd promised to kick my ass. Maybe there was a love in joking about violence completely separate from the lived experience of growing up in a family whose primary mode of correction was corporal punishment.

Fauna had once told me she'd loved me. At the time, I'd believed her.

When Nia, Kirby, and I said we loved one another, we believed it, every time.

Fauna draped herself over the side of my couch with a dramatic sigh. She gave me an innocent pout as she said, "Now, just to be clear, when it comes to your friends…"

"You can't fuck my friends, you freak."

"Just asking!" She blew a kiss.

"Well," I amended, "Kirby would be into it. But Nia and her husband are monogamous."

She made a face. "Monogamy? In this economy?"

I tried to keep from laughing, but the only thing I could get out between my giggles was "But please don't make a move on Kirby. Their head would explode."

"Because I'm so spectacular?"

"Because you're chaos in a bottle," I said, not bothering to comment on how I had no comprehension of her centuries of life and love with Azrames, despite her attempts to explain it to me.

Stay wild and free.

It had been his way of saying goodbye the first time I'd witnessed their flirtatious interactions. After spending time with him, it was hard to understand why she'd *want* to be wild and free. Then again, she was not me, and I was not her. If she wanted to sleep with centaurs just for the plot, eat sweets, binge reality TV, and piss off angels, that was her prerogative. All I wanted was to be reunited with Caliban.

I thought of his face as he'd shouted to Silas in the final moments in the lobby. He'd begged the angel—Hell's adversary—to rescue me. He'd needed to ensure I'd be safe while he took care of the problem—a problem I'd caused in the first place.

Now I was the one who needed to know he was safe.

If our rescue mission was forced to wait, I supposed a sham of a dinner party would suffice.

Chapter Four

I DIDN'T KNOW WHAT I'D EXPECTED, BUT I'D LOST THE ABILITY to be shocked.

Nia's backyard deserved a feature in *Better Homes and Gardens*. We avoided the front door altogether and unlatched the gate of their wooden privacy fence. Fauna and I headed toward the strings of twinkly lights pinned to the ceiling of their covered back porch where Nia, Kirby, and Darius were already happily chatting. An L-shaped couch with waterproof cushions surrounded a copper fire pit that was more for show than any source of heat. Fluffy clouds dotted the sky, each aglow from the soft red orange of the setting sun. A giant television, perfect for tailgate-style parties where sports boys played sports ball and drank sports drinks and talked about sports, was mounted to the pillar, though Nia had muted the sound the moment we'd arrived.

It didn't surprise me when the Davis-Greenes lost the ability to speak as Fauna burst through the door like a hurricane. It didn't surprise me when the Nordic nymph took over making the piña coladas, pressing the buttons on the blender and adding too much sugar while our hosts stared, slack-jawed, at my fae friend. It didn't surprise me when Fauna ushered us all into the warm, late-summer night to enjoy the comfortable sunset. It didn't surprise me when Fauna flirted with Kirby and caused their brain to short-circuit. It didn't surprise me when we fumbled for the remote, needing to put on the television to fill in awkward silences as she said too many incomprehensible things to keep the conversation flowing organically. It didn't surprise me when we all relied heavily on the pitchers of rum, coconut cream, and pineapple juice after Fauna's nonsense became a little more challenging than we knew how to handle. And it didn't surprise me that, as with all things, Fauna did absolutely nothing in moderation.

"Do you have more?" Fauna asked, loudly slurping the frothy dredges of her tropical drink through a straw.

I would have been happy to enjoy the warm September evening with a nice buzz. Nia had the best patio furniture. It was probably the booze talking, but I was relatively certain that if I closed my eyes and relaxed into the cushion, it would swallow me whole, as if I was a chocolate chip tucked into bread dough.

Yeah, maybe I'd had a few too many. Fortunately, my years in sex work had trained me to maintain my composure after several drinks. I managed to put up a thin barrier between the façade of a fun night with friends and me drunkenly sobbing about how my demon prince boyfriend had been kidnapped by pagan deities.

"Pretty please?" Fauna's request brought me back to the question.

My sigh was the long-suffering exhaustion of a parent. I just wanted to be a chocolate chip. "Who are you asking? You're the one who broke into their kitchen and made the drinks. You know it's empty."

Fauna gestured. "Peaches hasn't finished her drink. Does she—"

"They," I corrected, too tipsy to have a strong reaction but nowhere near wasted enough to allow even a feral forest nymph to misgender my oldest friend. The patio couch swallowed me whole as I sank deeper and deeper into the cushion. The last lights of sunset twinkled out with an iridescent shimmer, leaving us alone with the embers of the grill and the glow of the outdoor television. The wafting smoke of cooking meat and fruit and vegetables smelled heavenly. My arms and legs already felt so heavy. I'd abandoned the outside world to drift into a comfortable nothing, but I had to keep just enough wits about me to play the role of owner at an off-leash dog park while keeping an eye on Fauna.

Undaunted, she corrected, "Right! Sorry. Kirby, peaches, were you going to drink that?"

"Be my guest."

Fauna gave their fingers a grateful squeeze, and the touch sent their cheeks reddening. They were too easy to fluster.

Nia reached for Fauna's empty glass. "We're out of mixers, but I still have half a bottle of Malibu. Want to cut it with La Croix and pretend we're drinking coconut water?"

"How responsible," I muttered.

This is insane! How can you drink piña coladas and laugh with your friends while Caliban is trapped in another realm? A realm that's demanding your presence?! the sober, reasonable voice within me screamed. I pounded the rest of my drink to cage her, begging the booze to numb me.

Darius remained several notches above us in sobriety. He facilitated the evening's functionality while he played with the grill's fire, dished up the shish kebabs, poured drinks, and overall continued to be the only human male who deserved rights, as far as I was concerned.

"So," Nia said after her third shish kebab. She picked at the charred fruit, then looked at Fauna as she asked, "Marlow meets a gorgeous, long-lost friend that neither Kirbs nor I have *ever* heard about. The two of you vanished off the map. Marlow has no friends, so there's no use pretending she has a life. Let's cut to the chase. Are you seeing each other, or what's going on here?"

24

My throat constricted at the question. Nia was such a good friend. She just wanted to be a part of my life. And I could do nothing but plaster on a fake smile and lie. When I remained mute, Fauna swept in with a response.

"Oh!" Fauna sparkled as if barely affected by what had to have been her seventh or eighth drink. I knew her well enough to notice how the beverages dulled her mayhem ever so slightly, but it was nothing like the impact it had on the mere mortals. "Gods and goddesses, no. Our sweet Marlow's unbearable. I'd probably kill her if we dated."

"Great," Kirby said, perking slightly from where they'd melted onto the couch near Fauna. "Because I met someone who's obsessed with you, Mar. He came into work not too long ago, ranting and raving about this really obscure niche series called Pantheon that we probably weren't cool enough to know about. I feel like you're the kind of person who'd want to date a superfan so they can follow you around in kiss-ass adulation." They pulled up his profile on their phone, then turned the screen for us to see.

Nia leaned forward, sniffed at the picture, and relaxed back onto the cushion. "He looks like he drinks Mountain Dew."

Fauna snorted. "I'm afraid our favorite dummy is taken."

A hollow thump echoed woodenly through my chest. My eyes widened in time to match the others around us. Nia, Darius, and Kirby were all staring at me, but I only looked at the agent of chaos. The loose-lipped Nordic nymph was too distracted by her food to even notice how still the rest of us had grown. She finally caught my eye to see the daggers I shot her.

"My brother," Fauna said easily, maintaining our smoke screen as if utterly unaffected by the devastation happening to the men we loved.

Wait. The sober voice within me was quieter, but still shocked. *Is Fauna outing you? Did she really just say you're dating her...? What's happening right now?*

25

Fauna ran her finger along the rim of her drink. "Those two go as far back as she and I do. We all fell out of touch for a long time, but…"

"When," Kirby said flatly. It wasn't a question.

Copper waves cascaded over Fauna's shoulder as she tilted her head to the side.

"I've known Marlow since childhood. I know everyone she knows. When did she meet you—the brother-sister duo we'd never heard of before last week?"

Fauna looked at me apologetically. "How much do they know? Am I allowed to tell them…?"

I couldn't breathe. Was she really about to ask me if she could explain gods and realms and demons? For fuck's sake, I'd known coming here was a bad idea, but never in a million years had I thought it would be *this* bad.

Sure, Fauna, go ahead and tell my best friends that I can see behind the veil. Tell them I was gone last week because I was in Hell. It'll probably be fine.

Fauna cleared her throat delicately. She twiddled her thumbs, eyes on her fingers as she said, "Marlow and I met on the job when I was offering…companionship."

Three sets of shoulders unclenched.

Nia and Kirby relaxed the moment they'd received a satisfactory answer. *Of course, Fauna is stunning*, they must be thinking. She was a high-end escort, after all. Of course, this was why I'd never brought her up before. We protected one another's identities in the industry.

My relief was separate entirely. Fauna deserved more credit than I'd given her.

Darius was busy at the grill, and either hadn't heard what transpired, or was too polite to interject. Good man.

Nia redirected the conversation. "If your brother is half as good-looking as you…"

At last, I understood why she'd brought Caliban up at all. Fauna radiated a seraphic beauty. Perhaps she was doing me a favor by laying the groundwork, should I ever want to

26

introduce Caliban—the only other one of my three other-worldly companions who could take corporeal form—to my friends. I was confident that even if Caliban was a thousand times more respectful and collected than my Nordic friend, he'd be far more difficult to be around. He was...distracting.

Kirby still hadn't smiled. They'd never been a mean drunk, but the wounds in their voice suggested that tonight might be the night that changed. "Since when do you not tell us if you're seeing someone?"

My heart sagged.

Because he's a demon, Kirbs. Because he's invisible, and I spent decades insisting he was a hallucination. Because I grew up in the church, and then became a devout atheist who mocked the sandbox of religions by writing mythology books. Because I love him so deeply it's as if his blood is my blood, his bones are my bones, and right now he's in trouble. He's in another god's realm because of my mistake. All of this is happening because I fucked up. And the only thing I want is to run to him.

I said none of that, of course. "Because it's different with Cal—"

"His name is *Cal?*" Kirby slurred, voice heavy with implication.

"Listen," I tried to clarify, realizing I was a bit too sloshed to be making any serious declarations. "This isn't like Tech Guy or CFO or any of the nameless no ones. I didn't tell you because he doesn't belong in the category of dating-app-mocking opportunities. I was crazy about him back in the day. I didn't want to bring it up unless it was something."

"And?" Nia asked. "Is it? Something?"

I heated from my place across the patio furniture. An early-autumn breeze swirled through the party, offering the barest of reprieves. Between the overturned red plastic cups of downed fruity drinks, the stained paper plates from our meals, and the evidence of our partying, there wasn't enough liquor in the world to hide my blush when it came to what

Caliban and I meant to each other. I looked at my feet as my thoughts went to him. I took a break from my panic to think of how beautiful he was, how kind he was, how wise he was. I was scared for him. But I was also head-over-goddamn-heels in love with him.

"Holy shit," Kirby gasped. "How dare you!"

I twisted the material of my shirt between my fingers, unable to look up.

Doing his best to deescalate the brewing storm, Darius attempted to distract us by grabbing for the remote. He was usually pretty good at creating a safe environment when the world grew hostile. He angled the remote toward the TV and began flipping through stations.

Kirby glared. "You're not off the hook, Marlow Esther Thorson—"

"What's with you all and your names?" Fauna asked through a mouthful of pineapple as she picked around the vegetables. "Peaches here is the only one smart enough to use a pseudonym."

"While throwing around my full government name! And if they keep scolding me, I'll tell everyone their middle name, too."

Kirby wrinkled their nose. "It's a family name! Leave Aunt Gertrude out of this."

The couch didn't get its chance to burst into whatever argument was sure to follow.

Darius interrupted. "Oh, fuck."

The low shock in his curse drew our attention. He was generally a friendly, albeit quiet, fixture when we were hanging out. Our eyes followed the arc of his hand as he kept the remote pointed up at the muted TV.

My stomach twisted.

"Turn it up." I inhaled sharply, recognizing my author photo over the anchor's shoulder as the six o'clock news looked at us seriously. Darius in his pursuit of the game's final score had stumbled across something unthinkable.

28

"Mar—" Nia reached out to grab me.

"Turn it up!"

I scraped my fingernails against my scalp as the Viking horn rang from my phone. Two low and high notes each time a text came in. Up, down, up, down, up, always followed by my mental completion of the battle cry: *Charge!* It had seemed like a quirky idea at the time, but it had been my text tone for seven years. I was so used to keeping my phone on silent that I forgot how annoying it could be when you belonged to a group chat.

I didn't look away from the TV as I reached over to silence my phone.

(EG) 6 missed calls

"Darius, turn it off," Nia said breathlessly.

"Don't you dare," I said through my teeth. The TV and its terrible glow burned into my retinas. Everyone looked at me, while I looked at the face staring back from behind the screen. "I need to hear what they're saying. Turn up the volume."

"Marlow, please," Kirby begged, voice turning on a dime as it flooded with sympathy.

"The volume, Darius!" I got to my feet. I couldn't take this news sitting down. My focus cut through the booze in my system as I made eye contact with the news anchor. Maybe it was the rum, but I peered directly into her as she spoke.

I pressed the redial button beside EG's contact information. She picked up on the first ring.

"Marlow," my editor said breathlessly. "What's your status? Where are you right now?"

"I'm with friends," came my numb reply.

"Don't turn on the TV," EG demanded.

"I'm looking at it right now."

"God, Marlow, turn it off. Turn it off right now."

I shook my head in disbelief as the screen changed from my author headshot to a politician's stage and the image of a crying husband, wife, and child. I recognized the middle-aged politician immediately. I knew the way he looked while ordering the most expensive bottle on the menu. I knew the uncomfortable jokes he made about the working class. I knew the smug way he'd slip me envelopes bulging with cash, bragging about how half of my income was funded by taxpayer dollars. I knew the guttural sound he made when his face turned purple at the moment of orgasm. His blue suit, her white dress, and the baby's red onesie completed the country's flag behind the podium. Two children under the age of five also stood in front of their mother, gripping her leg, undoubtedly to garner public sympathy. How patriotic.

"It's too late."

"...*Merit Finnegan, author of the bestselling Pantheon series...*"

I spoke, but my words were so robotic, so detached, that I could have sworn they'd come from someone else. "He's doxxing me."

"Turn it off!" came the shrill, far-off voice from the phone that dangled at my side. EG continued to yell at me while the world around me crystalized, then cracked. I heard the high, bell-like tinkling of glass ring through my ears as the earth shattered.

On the screen was the slicked hair, hard jaw, blue eyes, and old money of one of my long-standing clients. We hadn't met in over two years, but he'd been a thrice-monthly regular. Republican Senator Geoff Christiansen, father of three, distant relative of the Rockefellers, and staunch activist against the social issues for which I loudly advocated, had gladly shelved his morals to spend roughly twelve to fifteen thousand dollars on me every single month. His vices had paid off my car and bought me three of my favorite Gucci bags.

Face grotesque with false contrition, he forced a

tremble into the hands that clutched his papers. His wife of fourteen years, mother to his three strapping sons, clutched his arm as he stood behind the podium and addressed the world.

The banner below him announced that the senator had been caught in a prostitution ring. The scrawling words proclaimed he was at the center of a defamation case regarding a sex scandal. I could hardly look between him and his wife as his thin lips moved again, eyes watering with theatrical penance.

EG continued talking as I ignored her and snatched the remote from Darius's hands to turn the volume up further.

High-pitched feedback preceded his words. His insincere voice rang through the microphone as the news played his speech for the public. "My love for theology as a Christian and a family man—"

"For fuck's sake," I muttered.

"—led me to an interest in world religions so I could better understand my faith, which extended to Merit Finnigan's books. When we struck up a friendship over my desire to become a more educated person in global theology, to deepen my own faith, I had no way of knowing that she was a professional escort. I—"

"Marlow!" EG's voice screamed from the dangling receiver. "Marlow, answer me right now or I'm throwing your contract in the shredder and dropping you from Inkhouse!"

I lifted the phone to my ear. I blinked, the haze of tropical drinks snapping away against the stark adrenaline as I demanded, "He's going to claim we were...what? Lovers? His plan is to admit to infidelity on the grounds that he didn't *know* I was a sex worker? Is cheating on his wife supposed to be better?"

Four pairs of eyes bore into me as my friends watched helplessly while my reputation, and with it, my career, fell apart.

EG exhaled loudly, clearly both glad I was finally on

the phone and dismayed that it had ever reached this point. "Christenson is a scumbag. Our publicists are scrambling to get a statement together. We'll have one within the hour. Our marketing team is confident you're going to come out on top. What I need you to do right now is turn off the television. Lie low for a couple days—"

I looked at my friends to see if they could hear EG's voice. I was too intoxicated to fully understand how loud or quiet any of the sounds around me were to others.

"Disappear?" I clarified.

My editor's voice came back firm and maternal as she pressed, "Take a vacation, Marlow. Delete all of the social media apps from your phone. Don't check your email. Don't search for articles about yourself. Get on a plane. Go to Fiji. Go to a Tibetan monastery for a month. Take a trip. Is there anywhere you've been wanting to go? You don't even have to write. Forget about deadlines. Between PR, legal, and me, know Inkhouse will handle this. Give me your green light and we'll issue statements on your behalf. You know I can sound like you in a pinch."

Fauna set down her plate and crossed the space to me. Kirby and Nia remained speechless as Fauna squeezed my hand.

"I can disappear," I repeated quietly.

"Do not use that word. Do not say *disappear*. Repeat back to me that you understand I'm asking for a vacation. I am talking about mental health. Take care of yourself. I am talking about an extended stay in the Maldives. Tell me you hear me."

I swallowed. "No, EG, I'm okay. I'm…with someone. A friend. She and I can…" I looked into Fauna's concerned doe eyes before saying, "We can get off the grid. She has a place out of cell reception. And EG?"

My eyes burned as I stared into the static of the screen.

She inhaled sharply. "Yes?"

I closed my eyes, letting the bullshit from the senator and

the commentary from the news anchor wash over me in the background.

"Thank you for not saying *I told you so.*"

EG's voice softened. "No use crying over spilled milk, angel. That's what paper towels are for. Now, you're with a friend? You promise?"

I wanted to bury my face in Caliban's chest and cry. He was the one I needed, and in his absence, I searched Fauna's face for comfort, but she'd already taken the remote from Darius and found something entirely more interesting on TV. She'd lost interest in me enough to find a worthwhile cartoon. An old man and a little boy jumped into a spaceship on the television, and she was utterly enraptured. I looked between her and the TV and almost choked between a laugh and a sob. I knew that if I looked at Kirby or Nia, I'd cry for sure. "Yeah, I'm at a barbeque right now. A friend has been staying at my place."

"Good," EG reiterated. "She'll be your person on the outside, and you have a team of friends on the inside. You're not alone, whether you're Maribelle, Merit, or Marlow. We've got your back."

"You're one of the good ones, EG."

"I know," EG said with an audible smile. She confirmed for a final time that I was fine, waiting until Fauna called dismissively into the line to confirm her existence before EG agreed to get off the line.

The moment the line disconnected, Nia and Kirby joined me on their feet, pacing with rage.

"What a piece of shit," Kirby burned. "What a worthless lowlife! What a bastard! What a—"

"Listen." Nia flattened her hands until they were parallel to the ground. "I've lived a good life. I'm not afraid to go to jail. Give me his address."

Kirby snapped, "At least we know why she's dropping off the face of the earth this time. This tragedy cancels out your wrongs, Mar. I might even find it in my heart to forgive you for leaving us hanging."

33

Nia jutted a thumb toward Kirby and said, "While I'm in a murderous rage, I'm also willing to kill Kirbs if they don't shut the fuck up. If I'm going to get the death penalty, I might as well get it twice."

The ends of my nerves tingled as if my entire body had fallen asleep. I hardly knew what I was saying as I looked at the back of Fauna's head, watching how the coppers and silvers glistened against the television and the black of the dark night sky beyond. "We—Fauna and I—we were talking about going to hang out with her family. I might just turn off my phone for a little while," I said slowly. "Please don't call my mom, even if it's two weeks or more."

"More?" Nia demanded, looking like she might throw things. "How long are you planning to leave the grid?"

Kirby turned on her. "Nia, you called her fucking mother. She gets four weeks without us calling the police on her this time."

Nia shot daggers. "I'm already killing you, Kirby. At this point you're just making the mode of death worse for yourself."

"It's okay," I sighed. "I'll be with Fauna."

"And...her brother?" Nia's lethal anger softened ever so slightly.

I nodded. "That's the plan." I touched Fauna's arm lightly, trying to get her attention as if I were talking to a toddler I'd been babysitting as she stood too close to the electric glow of the screen. "How are the cartoons?" I asked.

"Amazing," she responded, unbothered by the shitstorm unfurling behind her.

I tested my words carefully as I said, "Fauna, I'm under strict instructions to fall off the face of the earth."

"I know you've been wanting to take a *trip*," Fauna said through clenched teeth, "but we promised we'd wait to go on that vacation."

"This is different," I said firmly. "We aren't taking a vacation to go get a tan. We're going to go visit your family because Nia is threatening to murder someone, and I'd rather your *sister* take the fall for it. Do you have any family members who want to kill a Republican?"

Fauna's eyes became slits. She shifted away from the television to study me.

Her expression said: *You're really asking me to go now when I made an oath?*

The anger that flickered across my face replied: *We aren't going to the Nordes to gather troops. We aren't breaking any promises. I'm part Norde, and one of their own is being doxxed. I reserve the right to demand help from my gods.*

Either she was excellent at reading facial expressions, or she had some form of telepathy that she had yet to share. She sighed. "Fine. You're right. This is a great reason to go see my family."

"Are you ready to leave?" I asked. "I'd like to start packing."

"That depends. Do you have the button so I can watch this episode when we're back at your place?"

My fingers flexed in frustration. "Yes, I have the streaming service with all of these cartoons."

"Great!" she said merrily, returning the remote to Darius's hands. She hugged Nia and Kirby deeply while I called the rideshare. We were lucky to have a driver accept our trip with a car only three minutes away, sparing us the awkwardness of explaining anything further. Nia and Kirby barely had time to walk us to the front of the house before the vehicle pulled up. I gave them each another brief hug.

"I love you both," I said, not looking over my shoulder as Fauna dashed off to claim the car.

"We know," Nia answered for them both. "Don't do anything stupid."

"Or do," Kirby said, "but live to tell the tale."

"Also, Fauna seems—"

"Batshit? I know," I said.

"Is her brother...?"

"Cal is very sane, and indescribably wonderful, and if I

35

make it through the next two weeks, then I promise you two can meet him."

"As long as you promise to make it through the next two weeks," Nia confirmed with a sisterly squeeze.

Chapter Five

Dox/doxx [däks]: verb
Doxing/doxxing, doxes/doxxes, doxed/doxxed:
transitive verb.

To publicly identify or publish private information about someone, especially as a form of punishment or revenge.

Example 1: The republican senator doxxed the sex worker, outing her despite having enthusiastically and consensually solicited her services, in order to ruin her life and save his spineless, pathetic, sorry ass.
Example 2: Doxxing gets sex workers killed, and is never, under any circumstances, okay.

I SLAMMED THE DOOR BEHIND ME AS I SLID IN BESIDE FAUNA. We'd only been in the car for two minutes before the driver commented that we smelled like we'd had a great time, which meant we were sweating rum. Fauna promised him that I'd tip him twenty dollars if he pulled over at a grocery store for her to get candy, which shouldn't have surprised me. He laughed, thinking it was the munchies. I rolled my eyes, knowing she was a lunatic without need for an occasion.

The driver cranked the music while we waited for the

angelic, freckled supermodel to breeze into the grocery store, allowing me to feel the music's bass as bud and booze hummed in my cells. I closed my eyes and relaxed into the vibrations until Fauna returned. She'd collected a handful of candy for herself, but pushed a newspaper-wrapped bundle into my arms.

I opened my eyes to look up at both her and the present. *Sunflowers.*

She held my hand and sat with me for the rest of the ride in uncharacteristic silence. I wasn't sure if it made what I was feeling better or worse.

We were out of the car and into my apartment before I'd fully had time to process the events of the night. My friends had met Fauna. She'd mentioned Caliban. I'd been doxxed on the news by a politician.

Holy shit, I'd been doxxed, I'd been doxxed, I'd been *doxxed.*

And it wasn't even the worst thing to happen to me this week.

I clutched the sunflowers uselessly against my chest as Fauna rushed to the television. She immediately began mashing buttons until she pulled up the same episode that had been cut short at Nia's house.

"Fauna—"

"You didn't even say thank you. Look what I got us! Because we're—"

"We're sunflowers," I finished for her, accepting the newspaper-wrapped bouquet. I didn't bother to ask how she'd paid for them. She was the sort of person I assumed walked down the street and received things for free. The paper crinkled as I hugged the loosely wrapped flowers to my chest.

"Your friends are lovely, by the way. Darius was a great cook. Nia and Kirby are both way cooler than you. I see why you like them. I don't totally understand why they like you, though."

My vision blurred. My life was crashing in around me from every direction. I couldn't stop picturing Caliban behind bars, regardless of what her contact had said of his voluntary presence amongst their gods and goddesses. Our impending trip to the Phoenician realm filled me with terror. I didn't want to go to Hell without him. I certainly didn't want to be in Heaven. And now, after years of being careful, after years of protecting myself, the mortal room had been destroyed for me.

The Nordic realm was the only answer.

"Fauna, I know you love to make fun of me, but..."

Her face fell the moment she looked up at me. "Hey now...is this about Geoff Andrew Christiansen, at 1577 North Gold Coast, who goes jogging alone in the Lincoln Memorial Gardens every morning, passing the Chess Pavilion at roughly five forty-eight a.m.?"

"I..."

"I know I'm mean to you," she said, "so I think you forget a few things. One: I'm smart, I'm capable, and I love you. And two: I'm a motherfucking goddess, and have very important friends on both your side and mine."

"How did you...?"

"The less you know, the better. Now, can you leave this to me and come watch cartoons? In the words of the little boy: get your shit together, put it in a backpack, and take it to the shit store. Or, whatever he said. I'd know the line better if you'd let me listen."

So I did.

I had Geoff to thank, in a way. Without his asshat fuckery, I wouldn't have been able to force our timeline forward.

I gave Fauna space to giggle and snack through the rest of the episode while I grounded myself in the shower. I'd been doxxed. But so had he. He'd outed me to humans, yes. But in doing so, he'd outed himself to gods. I lathered my arms and legs with honey-scented bodywash as I let myself think of the best part of the evening.

39

My friends knew about Caliban. He was real, and now they knew it, too. Well, they knew a version of the truth, and for now, that was more than enough.

I stepped onto the cozy bath mat, scrunched the water from my hair, and wrapped a towel around my chest. I touched my hand to my heart and was surprised to find that it was still beating. I could do this. *We* could do this.

I left a trail of wet footprints from the bathroom into the living room and asked the most pressing question on my mind. "Does time pass at the same rate for the Nordes?"

She beamed at me. "Look who's happy and clean! It's good to see you smile. Thanks for trusting me. Now, onto the Nordes: you're asking all the right questions, and I have no answer."

I shook my head, uncomprehending.

"That's the fun!" she sang. She seemed to have fully accepted that our new reason for visiting the Nordic realm freed her from breaking an oath. I'd been the catalyst for a glorious, painful loophole. Irreverent once more, she continued, "Sometimes no time passes at all. Sometimes a day. Or a week. Or a month. Some humans even wake up backward in time when they return to the mortal realm! Perhaps if we're lucky, we'll go see some Nordes and then pop back into the mortal realm like forty-five minutes before what's-his-face makes his speech. Maybe he accidentally trips and falls on his way up the podium. Maybe, I don't know, his head hits the corner of the stage in a super unfortunate way. Brain matter everywhere. So sad."

I blinked, struggling to understand what she was saying. "But...you don't know? There's no way to tell?"

She rested her elbow on the back of the couch, propping her head in her hands as she said, "Well, not to the linear-minded. So, ready to meet your great-grandfather?"

"Definitely not."

"That's not a no," she said brightly. "We leave in five."

I looked around the apartment and wondered what I had

to do, what I had to prepare, what I needed to get ready before disappearing. I was panicked, drunk, and my place was a mess. If I was leading the charge against Fauna's initial advice, I needed a moment to pull myself together.

"Make it twenty."

She laughed. "It's an expression. We're not going until the show is over."

"I swear to god, this is the third episode in a row you've watched."

"Welcome to binge culture, baby."

A bright, animated blur of colors continued to fill the screen. The lasers, portals, and swirls of pink nonsense made it feel like I was watching a drug-addled fever dream.

"It's a cartoon for stoners," I said, slathering a thick layer of judgment over the final word.

"Because your body is such a temple?"

I looked at the show. She was right. I was still wasted.

She gestured pointedly at the television. "People love to learn about gods, right? Why not learn from the things we like? Maybe there's a reason I'm obsessed with this cartoon."

"Right, that would be in line with every other assumption I have about your very sane, reasonable choices."

She gestured to the screen enthusiastically. "The makers of this show? Geniuses. I mean, they're dickhead human men and I endorse nothing about their personal lives, but in terms of dimensions? It's the closest you humans have ever come to understanding the fae realms. Everywhere! At all times! Everything! It's infinity, Mar. I mean, they're doing it for comedy, just like your show about couples marrying without seeing each other, or that one where no one cleans their house for ten years—one, because humans are stupid, and the other because they don't get free medical help, and all the other things that make for good television in dystopian mortal society. But this cartoon allows for all of us. The old gods and the new, the human realms and the immortal. The blended and the—"

The two-dimensional figure belched with a beer in one hand and a science fiction tool in the other, and I couldn't help but narrow my eyes at her infantile taste.

Undaunted, she went on, "Plus, the grandpa's lines are brilliant. You know how I love a smartass."

"Are you sure it isn't that you relate to his issues with addiction?" I asked, snatching the chocolate bombs from her hand while the tiny cartoon grandfather downed another beer on the screen.

"Fair point," she conceded.

"So, not five minutes?"

She looked at the clock, then back to me. "Five minutes is relative. Change into whatever you have that most resembles my day-to-day outfits so you blend in. We're a relaxed bunch. And don't touch my chocolate bombs. I'll see you when the episode's over."

Chapter Six

WHY DID THEY MAKE STAGE LIGHTS SO GODDAMN HOT? Sweat stains threatened to tip my hand and tell the *Good Morning America* hosts that I was an imposter. I took a few nervous steps backstage and my sweat-slicked feet slipped within my heels. The book I'd written in college should have been unreadable drivel lost to the slush pile. My compulsion to write it had nothing to do with expectations for the future. The unprecedented fame was debilitating.

"Shit!" My involuntary curse preempted an impact that never came.

Cool hands steadied me, one on my back, the other bracing my elbow before I could fall. I looked reflectively into the empty space, but for all the world, I was utterly alone. He helped me onto the blue-gray sofa perched in front of a giant marquee scene meant for photo ops.

Caliban's voice was a low, comforting balm. "You're going to do great."

"I feel like I'm breaking the law by being here. Like, things like this are not for people like me. Any moment now, the police are going to burst through the door and say, *Marlow Thorson, you're under arrest for being Merit Finnegan. You weren't allowed to write books or make something of yourself or be invited to a talk show* And I'm going to have to say, *Of course, officer, I totally get it, take me away in cuffs.*"

"That's not very ACAB of you," he said. My heart warmed when invisible smiles curved his words like they did every time he told a joke.

My answering smile was short-lived. Anxiety reignited as I emphasized, "I really, really, don't want to do this."

"All magic comes at a price," he said. "Sometimes that price is having to be perceived by the public in order to sell your book."

"Whatever you say, Confucius." I shot a worried glance to the door to ensure no one would burst into the green room and catch me speaking to a ghost. "Public speaking is the number one greatest fear across the globe. Eight billion people can't be wrong."

He chuckled. "It's just a conversation between you and the hosts. No one else is there."

"Like I'm going to take your advice on who is and isn't present." I wiped my hands on the high-waisted trousers I'd paired with a black bandeau. Black on black on black was an authorly cliché, and I suspected it had its reasons. We were a breed of introverts, and the color helped to conceal the evidence of our panic.

"I'm tired of talking about the Nordic pantheon," I said. "Like, I know the book just dropped today, but publishing moves so slow. The sequel is already written and in the final stages of edits, but I can't say a word about Greek mythology out there."

Another chuckle. "Maybe those should be inside thoughts. You don't want to tell your audience you're tired of the book before they've even touched it. And we probably don't want to piss off Odin."

"I've been knee-deep in the All Father and his lore since I first started writing the damn thing in college. I'm so relieved it's out so I can be done talking about it. Let me loose on Bacchus and Aphrodite and Hades. Let me talk about *A Sea of Fates.*"

44

He ran a hand over my back in comforting circles. "Bad news, Love. I don't think you understand how marketing works."

I used the cuff of my blazer to dab at the beads of perspiration collecting near my brow. "I don't understand how *any* of this works. I was the least popular trailer trash church kid in the history of existence. I didn't exactly shine in college, either. Mediocre grades at a mediocre school. Then I was a preschool teacher in Colombia to thirty sticky, unruly toddlers just to justify all those years studying Spanish. I sang for my supper as an escort. Being an author was just a dream, you know? Dreams aren't supposed to come true. How the hell did I end up here?"

A genuine laugh this time.

"It's nothing, nothing," he said in response to the pucker of my brow as I awaited an explanation, but the amusement in his tone suggested otherwise. His words softened as he asked, "Do you want me to go out there with you?"

My mouth dried. "Is that...? Can you do that?"

The pressure of his hands disappeared, and a moment later, a bottle of water rested on the sofa beside me. If he'd carried it over, I hadn't seen it happen. I drank too quickly, water dribbling down my chin and smudging the makeup they'd painstakingly applied before sending me to the green room.

"I'll hold your hand. You can give it a squeeze any time you feel nervous."

"So, the entire time?"

The door cracked open and a busy-looking man with a black headset peered in. "Five minutes, Merit."

"You got it." I flashed him the thumbs up.

Both he and I looked at it, confused as to why I'd chosen that particular gesture. A polite PA would have closed the door, but he watched as I nervously lowered my thumb, cleared my throat, and nodded.

"Yeah," I said to the blank space where Caliban sat, "maybe I could use the moral support."

◆

I wished I could explain what happened, but I thought I'd blacked out.

I delivered what I was told was a very compelling, articulate pitch on *A Night of Runes,* the first book in the Pantheon series. The horrifying studio lights were neither too hot, nor too bright once I was beneath them. I was told I was very witty, and that the audience seemed immensely charmed. I was told the host promised she'd rush to buy a copy as soon as the show was over, and ended the segment by saying, "I have a feeling your debut novel will be cleaned off every shelf in America by the end of the day, Merit Finnegan! Congratulations, and we can't wait to see how you take the world by storm."

I had foggy memories of posing woodenly in front of the marquee with the GMA logo, holding a hardcover copy of my book. The fugue state didn't truly dissipate until I was in the car on the way back to the airport. Survival adrenaline dwindled, leaving the fog of sleep in its wake.

I didn't check my phone until I made it through security and found my gate.

(Kirby) Holy shit! Please remember the little people when
    you're famous! Proud of you, Mar.
(EG) You killed it out there. I knew you would.

I opened the most addictive of photo-sharing apps and frowned at the screen. The numbers couldn't be right. I closed out of the app entirely and reopened it, only to see larger numbers than before. I was gaining new followers by the thousands. I posted the photo and watched the likes roll in. I was sure it would have been an absolute rush if I had been able to remember any of it.

The daze carried me forward into a three-hour flight and one long cab ride that I'd be charging to Inkhouse's expense account. I remained on autopilot as I rode the elevator,

46

opened the door, kicked off my shoes, and collapsed on the living room couch. I hadn't intended to nap, but by the time I opened my eyes, the house was pitch-black.

"You're awake," came a voice from the darkness. A smile colored its edges.

"Do I smell coffee?"

"I didn't want to wake you by using the oven, but you hadn't eaten. I put a few jars of coconut milk chia pudding with berries and granola in the fridge. I'd love it if you put something in your stomach before you started in on the coffee."

"Too bad, phantom," I said. I rubbed the sleep from my eyes and wiggled my fingers for a cup of coffee. "I had no idea I could cook in a fugue state. If I'm going to black out, it's a pretty neat trick."

He sighed. Moments later, a mug of black coffee warmed one hand, while a jar of honey filled the other. Caliban said, "Not fighting my existence today, then?"

"I'll work on being sane again in the morning. For now, I'm just so glad the interview was over. And I love being crazy if it means I make myself coffee while getting to pretend I have a boyfriend."

I leaned into his gravity as the cushion beside me dipped. He settled into the space at my side and wrapped his arm around my back. "You're impossible. But I'll take what I can get. For now."

"Oh, ominous." I giggled into my coffee. Then to the darkness, I asked, "Did it really go well? The interview, I mean?"

"You were sensational," he promised. "I wouldn't be surprised if everyone in the nation went out and bought a copy."

I released a satisfied sigh after the first scalding sip. "Wouldn't that be a dream," I murmured. "That would put me on a list for sure."

"Is that what you want?" asked the shadows.

47

"It's what every author wants. *A Night of Runes* came out today, so I have to wait a week to find out if I made any lists. *Publishers Weekly* is the most transparent. It uses raw sales data from Bookscan. *USA Today* uses independent bookstores, big chain store sales, all that jazz. Indiebound is, well, independent books. That one's well-named. But then there's the *New York Times*."

"And *that's* what you want?"

I shrugged, if only to myself. "No one really knows how that list works. You can be number one in sales by tens of thousands of copies on some of the other lists and still not be on *New York Times*. Maybe it's so coveted specifically because it's so shrouded in secrecy."

"Ah, yes," he agreed. "Glad to hear you agree that the best things are the ones cloaked in darkness."

"I don't think that's what I said."

He plucked the cup from my palm, and I listened to it settle onto the coffee table. A large hand worked its way from my knee up my thigh. "And is there anything I can do to help the time pass while we wait a week?"

"It's always sex with you," I said, but there was no conviction in my statement. A steady heartbeat had already begun to thump between my legs.

"No," he chided gently, "it's always sex with *you*. I worship your body. I love making you happy. I *live* to make you come. But I am utterly fulfilled as your friend, or protector, or confidant. Fuck, I'd die happy just for the chance to sit in silence with you, knowing you understand how I feel for you. One day, you'll want me for more than what I can do in the bedroom."

I'd never beat the psychosis allegations if I sat there arguing with myself—or, the man I'd projected as an extension of myself. I just wanted to feel good. I reached into the darkness for him. He caught my hand and pressed it to his face. Within an instant, my fingers knotted in his hair, pulling him to me. I swung a leg over his lap until I straddled him, renewed adrenaline filling me. Maybe I was an absolute nutcase, but my vivid imagination had helped me write not one but two books. My detachment from reality had also spared me from the nervousness of hypervigilance during a horrible interview. What's more, apparently I'd just unlocked the fantastic new ability to make coffee and chia pudding while napping.

Thanks, insanity.

He slipped my shirt over my head in a fluid motion. My bra was on the floor with a single pinch of his fingers. I gasped the moment his lips wrapped around my nipple, cool tongue sucking it into a luxurious peak. My hips moved against him as I threw my hair back to savor the sensation.

The room remained utterly black as he flipped me onto the couch with ease. He began to kiss and lick his way southward, one hand kneading my breast while another undid the button to my trousers. The hot air of his breath warmed the space between my legs over my panties before his mouth made sinfully glorious contact.

I moaned like he and I were the only two people in the world to hear our sounds. The vibrations of his answering moan felt so fucking good against my clit. I lifted my hips as he removed the soaked piece of fabric.

Most importantly, perhaps I was alone with my vivid imagination, but this was so, so much better than watching porn on my phone with one hand while holding my Hitachi in the other. When it came to masturbatory indulgences, I'd created the best one around.

Chapter Seven

F AUNA'S FINGERS FLEW TO HER LIPS TO COVER A SMIRK. "IS that what you're wearing?"

Uncertainty paralyzed me as I looked down at my outfit. I knew I needed the sølje, but apart from the enchanted broach, I was lost. I'd slipped into black leggings, ankle-high combat boots, and a white, long-sleeved shirt. I wasn't sure if I was ready to go to an exercise class, hike a mountain, or kick some ass. I stared at the shake of her shoulders as she giggled.

She flicked off the TV. "I'm fucking with you because I knew it would freak you out. We don't give a shit what you wear. Maybe grab a jacket, though."

It took a while for my anxiety to settle after her comment. Adapting to the designer fashion and wealthy upper echelons of Hell had been terrifying enough. I had no idea what to expect from the Nordes. I was supposed to meet the very gods and mythological beings about whom I'd written pretty absurd fiction—*researched* fiction, but made-up stories nonetheless. My only example of their people was Fauna, and she was nuts.

I looked out the window as if expecting sunshine in the middle of the night. We'd been in tank tops and crop tops only moments before on Nia's patio. "It's September!"

It was as if there was a fishing line pulling one corner

of her lips ever upward. "Do you think the Nordes love the Lofoten Islands and fjords and Icelandic mountains for the balmy weather?"

I grumbled as I grabbed an autumnal puff jacket from the closet.

"Do you need something warmer?" I asked her as I scanned my clothes.

"Me? No, I won't be in mortal form when I'm there."

I squinted at her, struggling to discern if this was another of her many unfunny jokes.

"What, you think I'm always limited to your human rules? Just wait 'til you see me on my home turf." She extended a hand for me as I finished shrugging into my jacket. I wrapped the fingers of my free hand around the broach.

I eyed her skeptically. "Wait, before we go... I could really use a heads-up of what to expect."

"Sure," she said, "but first, tell me this: Will my answer make a difference?"

I could feel the lines in my forehead as I frowned.

"If I tell you that we're going plummet through time and space and land on a giant Viking ship in the Atlantic Ocean in the year 600, eat salted cod, brave the cold, and go to war, would that stop us from going to see the Nordes? Would you no longer want to ask for help in getting your precious Prince back?"

"I—"

"Exactly. So, if you have to go anyway, what good is the question?"

I fidgeted. "Because I'm an anxious person."

Her short huff was impatient, but not unkind. "Sure, but what purpose does anxiety serve you? Will it keep you from going?"

"No."

"Precisely. Now that I've cured all your problems, let's get going. We're off to see what I can really do."

Perhaps if she hadn't shown empathy and understanding

51

in previous conversations about mental health, I would have stomped on her toes. Ignoring her glib remark, I reached out my hand uncertainly. "You're just a normal person there, right? That's what Silas said?"

She tossed her head back, a bright, airy laugh filling the room as she said, "You think they're going to send a *nobody* to watch the Prince's human? I'm no more of a nobody than you are. And you, Marlow-Merit-Maribelle, are *not* a nobody."

✦

I didn't even like leaving my apartment for the promise of brunch and bottomless mimosas. There was no ancient library, no mushroom-covered fairy glen, and no fifty-percent-off Gucci sale that sounded more fun than staying home in my sweatpants rewatching one of my comfort TV shows.

Not only was I about to go somewhere terrifying and otherworldly, but it wasn't even the Phoenician realm to rescue Caliban.

Rome wasn't built in a day, sure, but maybe Romulus and Remus would have hurried their city along a little if their soul mates had been at stake.

As Fauna's and Azrames's combination of warding was *too* good, now none of us could jump in or out. I proposed the alley behind the warehouse, to which Fauna made a comment about preferring trees over the city scent of urine. There was only one park within walking distance of my upscale loft, and it was intended for off-leash dog owners. In the daytime, the wooded walking path would have encircled a pack of yellow labs and dachshunds and a disproportionate number of huskies given that we lived deep within a city.

"Can we just go?" I shot an anxious glance over my shoulder. There were no floodlights in the park after hours, if only to discourage trespassing.

"Give it a sec." Fauna peered at the silver slices of moon through the trees. "I'm waiting until it's overhead."

"Does it make a difference?"

"Kinda." She shrugged. "The veil is thinner when we believe it is. It's like how a placebo effect can cure uncurable illnesses and all that jazz. And all the realms have the same night sky. Isn't that beautiful?"

"I have the sølje," I argued. An image of the enchanted broach flashed before me. The dangling, silver piece of jewelry was a traditional staple of many Scandinavian families. Most søljes, however, hadn't been gifted by the fae, and didn't grant their user the ability to go back and forth between the mortal realm and the lands of gods. "I don't need a thin veil."

She waved a hand to shush me. "You're interrupting the cinematic value of ceremonious realm hopping."

"Are you fucking with me?"

She closed her eyes and sucked in a deep lungful of cool, autumn air. "A little."

"Hey!" A man's voice sliced through the night with jarring clarity. Fright hit me like a lightning bolt as I spun to see the speaker. For fuck's sake, it had to be a security guard. His flashlight may as well have been the LED brights on a douchey pickup truck, as it was utterly blinding.

"Fuck, Fauna, we gotta go."

"Would you calm down?" She continued staring at the moon, which gave me time to be panicked enough for the both of us.

"Well, well, well," he said, flashlight bobbing as he approached. "What do we have here? Park's closed, ladies."

I shielded my eyes from the bright spotlight, but he didn't lower it. My heart picked up on the irregularity before it registered with my brain. Up, up, up ticked my pulse as I waited for the man to reveal himself.

"We were just leaving," I said.

"I don't know," the man said. "I think you should both stay here while I call the cops. Unless..."

Fauna spoke up at last. "Unless what, pig? We suck your dick?"

"Ha!" Aggression flared as he shoved the beam in Fauna's

53

face. She didn't so much as squint as she looked back at him, utterly unbothered. "Your words, sweetie, not mine. You're the ones breaking the law."

"Are we?" she replied. The question was innocent enough, but a thinly veiled threat coursed through her two simple words. The venom within them was far more terrifying than being discovered by the man in the first place. "Impersonating law enforcement is a misdemeanor with up to a year of jail time. As of 2022, it's now a federally recognized offense for someone to use their legal status for sexual coercion."

"Listen, lady," he threatened. I heard the bone-chilling click as the man armed himself. "The way I see it, this ends one of two ways."

Fauna pouted. "Only two? Then you're not very imaginative."

"Don't you think you can—"

A crack of earth. A terrible scream. A sharp cut of light. His sentence was ripped in half by the booming sound I can only describe as a fully formed oak erupting from the earth with volcanic force.

It was hard to explain what happened next.

I winced against the bright light. I covered my face, dropping to the ground as a single fire discharged into the air. An inhuman, yet distinctly male screech ripped through the night in the seconds that followed the gunshot. The flashlight flew from the guard's hand, bouncing along the path while blood-curdling wails drowned out every other sense. I screamed in return, my parasympathetic response releasing as much adrenaline as possible as I readied myself for an attack. Surely in a second, it would be me. Whatever nightmare, whatever werewolf, whatever hacking, slashing serial killer known for prowling parks had found us. I began to hyperventilate as I fumbled around on the path for the flashlight. By the time I wrapped my fingers around the handle and pointed a trembling beam of light in the security guard's direction, I saw...nothing.

Freshly turned earth with a new array of roots and weeds sprouted from what I was quite certain had been a hardened walking path only minutes prior. I shot the beam of light at Fauna, who blew on her fingers, then outstretched them as if examining a fresh manicure.

A new fear filled me.

My voice shook as I stared at her. "What...what did you do?"

She dropped her hand and gave me the same bored expression she'd given the man only moments prior. "Like I said, he wasn't being very imaginative. I'd like to say he'll think twice before harassing women again, but, well...he won't have the chance."

The beam of light illuminated the fresh patch of dirt once more as I understood with horrific clarify that somewhere beneath the earth and brambles lay a dead man. My vivid imagination sprinted into action, picturing moss packed into guts, veins and arteries and capillaries replaced with soil, a tree trunk erupting from his mouth, and vines shoving bones out of the way to make room for the unstoppable force of a deity who could manipulate nature.

But I didn't imagine the damp, crimson secretion where his blood soaked through to the surface.

I didn't know how she'd done it, but I knew in my bones: Fauna had killed him.

The flashlight fell limply to my side. Numbness overtook me as my eyes readjusted to the moonlight. I stared at Fauna and, for the first time, wondered if I was safe with her.

I scolded myself for the thought. She'd saved me. Maybe it was something like this—total punishment of any man who might threaten a woman—that had brought her and Azrames together in the first place. But try as I might, I couldn't talk myself out of the terror I felt when I looked at her.

She extended her fingers, and I flinched away as if she'd been holding the security guard's gun.

"The moon is right," she said. Then, observing my

trembles, she said, "Trust me: the world is better without him. That was *not* a good guy. I know you're feeling a little frazzled right now, peanut, but I have just the thing to fix it. Now that the riffraff's out of the way, it's time you took a vacation."

Chapter Eight

TIME AND DATE IN THE NORSE PANTHEON UNKNOWN, AGE 26

F AUNA HAD LEFT ME SPEECHLESS BEFORE, BUT NEVER LIKE this.

Fear was replaced with something new.

It didn't matter how vivid and sharp and expressive my imagination was. I tilted my head back, eyes wide as I fought to recall any moment in fantasy, in mythology, in literature that could give me the language for what I saw the moment I stepped foot in the Nordic realm. I scrambled through nature documentaries, through cinematic masterpieces, through decades of great works of art as I stared and stared and stared.

I'd spent my life training to have a rigorous frame of reference for the fantastical. Despite my broad exposure to science fiction and fantasy and literature and mythology, my willingness to expand my imagination into every nook and cranny, I gaped at the realm before me, comprehending nothing.

Each object, each feature, each thing came to me in pieces as I struggled to assemble the puzzle before my eyes. This was more bizarre than murder-by-vines ever could have been.

I'd seen mountains before. I'd seen cliffs, trees, pits, and waterfalls. I'd certainly seen the sun before. But this sun, as silver as the moon and glimmering like diamonds, sent the world into a brilliant shimmer.

We stood at the base of a mountain that made the Swiss

Alps look like anthills. The peak had a Seussical curve to its tip, bending to one side as if leaning in to tell us a secret. As unfathomably wide as it was tall, the mountain jutted from between the fork of two rivers, each as wide as an ocean, creating a silver sash around the mountain until they converged, then tumbled off into a bridal-veil waterfall that dissipated into mist. If it weren't for the mossy green carpet that stretched from us to the mountain, we would have had no way to reach it. I could almost discern the dotted, shimmering shapes of far-off buildings clinging to the mountainside.

The thrum of distant music, the Fauna-esque scent of the sea, of pine, of cold, the songs of birds and the rustling of leaves beneath the arching mountain swallowed me whole.

I opened my mouth to speak, but nothing came out.

Nothing in my frame of reference ever could have prepared me for the ethereal glow of colors and impossible sights before me.

Grinning with pride, she stretched out her hand in a grand, sweeping gesture. "Welcome to Álfheimr."

My heart lurched uncomfortably. "Holy shit."

She tossed her hair over one shoulder. "I told you that our realm was objectively better."

"Holy shit. Holy shit, holy shit, holy *shit*."

The same tinkling-bell laughter I'd grown to know and love answered. "Good job, wordsmith. That's why you're the famous writer."

I moved forward, one foot in front of the other, neck craned upward as I struggled to process a mountain the size of the moon.

"Pretty, right? Pretty people come from pretty places." She buffed her nails against her shoulder, then blew on them, stretching her fingers wide for show.

I followed her in a daze as she led me across a long, soft green stretch of grass. "So, you cured my anxiety. We didn't land on a Viking ship. We're not eating salted cod. But this…"

"What could I have said that would have prepared you for my realm?"

"Fair point," I murmured. "And we're going to the mountain?"

"We're going up there," she replied, pointing to the tiny dots clinging to the cliff that I suspected might be buildings. Unless we grew wings, it would take us weeks to hike there. My stomach grumbled. Maybe my body was already protesting the idea of an endless hike.

I appreciated the long stretches of silence she allowed as we walked. I wasn't confident I'd pull it together anytime soon. Instead, I asked, "I'm ready to know things, now. Who are we here to see? Is there anything I should or shouldn't do if we're going to go on a rescue mission and get them to help us fight for—"

Fauna spun on me and, for a terrifying moment, I saw her for the dangerous killer she was. Her eyes were tight. Her lips were pulled back in a silent snarl. Her fingers flexed by her sides.

"Just because we're alone doesn't mean we're *alone*," Fauna said, voice dropping to a low growl as she rested on the final word.

In a panicked instant, I understood my blunder. She'd sworn an oath to her informant that we wouldn't act on his information, and anyone could be listening. I needed to play it as if we had only come to the realm so I could seek revenge against the senator and his doxxing. I pitched my voice to tell her both that I understood, and that I wouldn't make the same mistake again. "If we're going to rescue my reputation as an author and fight back against Geoff Christiansen. This is my pantheon, and surely I have allies here, right?"

The tension drained from the moment like air hissing from a balloon. Her hands went limp at her sides. Her face relaxed. I'd saved myself from sticking my foot in my mouth, if only for a moment.

"Now," I said, hands extended as if to soothe a rabid

animal, "please tell me who we're here to see and what I need to know."

The last glimmer of threat dulled. She exhaled and shook out the remnants of her anger, as if her body might strangle me of its own volition if she didn't scatter the urge to murder me to the wind. After a deep, calming breath, she said, "Fine. So, Hell is all one metropolis with different courts— think of them like subdivisions of the city. The human realm has seven continents. The Nordes have Ásgard and the nine worlds—"

"Yes, I know," I said, continuing to look around for other signs of people, of activity, of life. But it was only me, the nymph, and the mountain.

"Oh!" She threw up her hands dramatically. "Well, pardon me! I didn't realize you knew everything already."

"No! No, I'm sorry. I just meant that I did my best to cover the basics when researching the first Pantheon novel. But spending time with you has taught me that know nothing and am always wrong. Please help me, Oh Great One."

"That's better. Anyway, so you probably don't need to be a linguist to see the etymological connection between Álfheimr and elves, right? I'm basically a skosgrå, which you knew. Personally, I like *nymph* a little better—it conveys a clearer message to the human brain, since elf can mean so many things to the mortals, and only point-three-percent of your kind speaks a Scandinavian language. By the way: it's irresponsible to write a book on the Nordic realm for an English-speaking audience without including a pronunciation guide. The *a* with the little circle above it is pronounced *oh*. Why is that so hard to grasp?"

I trailed behind her. "So, to be clear, you *want* me to keep calling you a nymph."

"I'm just saying: Tolkien got it right with Álfheimr elves. Don't get me started on your toy-making, tree-cookie version of the word. Talk to the Celts and their fair folk about it. But I digress. We're our own people. Think of the god and goddess Freyr and Frejya like Álfheimr's presidents, because those of us who live here are the Vanir."

"Should I be writing this down?"

"Just listen. I'm trying to teach you things."

"Sorry, sorry."

She made a tired sound, busying herself with examining the flowers that dotted the grass. She kept talking as if I wasn't there, speaking instead to the flora. "The Aesir have your big heavy hitters: Odin, Thor, Loki, Baldur. On the other side, the Vanir oversee those of us in Álfheimr, even though the Vanir mostly live in Vanheim. They pop in to make sure we're not starting fires or whatever. They're a race of pretty chill gods. None of us in Álfheimr are important enough to live in Ásgard, but it's just a hop, skip, and a jump away, and we can always visit. It's the closest world to ours."

"*World?*"

"Country. City. Continent. I've said it before: words are just words, peanut. Use whatever verbiage helps you wrap your little noggin around things. So, yes, for this, we'll stick with *world*, but don't go picturing a rock floating in space. Now, stop interrupting."

"My apologies, again," I said but had stopped watching her. If this weren't a life-or-death mission, I might have wanted to lie on my back and look up at the Dr. Seuss mountain and infinity rivers. I wondered if I'd ever be able to return to soak in the waterfall and smell the blossoms and catch the tiny twinkling lights that dotted the air like fireflies when my life wasn't falling apart.

A chill from the crisp air sent a shiver through me, as if it were a cool day in late spring. Or perhaps the goose bumps running up and down my arms stemmed from the reminder that Fauna's irreverent, joyful exterior was a mask. The man in the park and the warning threat were both reminders that I was, in fact, in the presence of a dangerous goddess. Maybe it was good that I'd brought a coat.

Fauna continued. "So, the Vanir in Álfheimr report

directly to Gullevig. She's great. She's been killed like three times and keeps coming back. Other religions act like it's such a big deal, but you don't see her bragging. Freyr and Freyja are a little too important for the day-to-day, so we talk to Gullevig, she talks to them, and so on. Anyway, it's like a manager-supervisor situation."

I repeated it back slowly, tasting each word until I was sure I understood. "Vanir is a catch-all category for the gods directly over you. Freyr is your...*president*...in Álfheimr, and everyone reports to Gullevig, who was dead. But now isn't. Okay. Who killed her?"

She nodded, picking her steps carefully so as not to step on any of little blossoms peeking through the carpet of green. "Not a bad question, actually. Time for you to learn about the wonderful, perfect, never-done-anything-bad Vanir, in charge of fertility and good things, who were subordinate to the war-loving Aesir."

"If you don't like the Aesir, does that mean you're saying Odin and Thor and Loki are the bad guys?"

"Bad? No, absolutely not. But you don't have to be *bad* to be wrong. Anyone who hoards power is the enemy, regardless of what realm you're in. And a lot of us feel that way. Heaven and Hell aren't the only realms that split and went to war, after all. We all have our skirmishes. Just like humans and your countries. Though gods usually fight for, like...reasons more important than oil.

"So, anyway, we've got the divide between the gods, right? The Aesir had a lot of rules. You know me well enough to picture how a race of my people would hate being told what to do. But as I was saying, the heavy hitters and the Vanir were at war for a hot minute. The tide kept turning back and forth, so for a while it was a toss-up over who would take the crown. Long story short, there was a hostage exchange and a truce, where the Aesir absorbed the Vanir and we were unified after the peace treaty. In theory, everybody was a winner and we're one big happy family. That's the story.

62

That said, half of the Aesir are still grumpy about it because the Vanir don't always play by the rules."

"Sure," I conceded, "I can imagine Vanir citizens wouldn't be thrilled to adhere to new rules they didn't agree to. It's not like everyone got an equal say when the two morphed into one, right?"

She beamed. "That's the smartest thing you've ever said. Proud of you, peanut. Yup, their rules can be shitty."

"I remember the war of the gods from the Poetic Edda..."

Her head whipped around so quickly that her hair was little more than a swirling tornado of bronze and silver.

I stopped her before she could scold me for butting in. "I'm not cutting you off! I just wanted to clarify what we're going to do right this very second. I will sit patiently and listen to everything forever. Teach me all the names and all the histories and all the things. I just need to emotionally prepare myself for what's going to happen when we get where we're going."

"I'm getting to that," came Fauna's exasperated grunt. Fortunately, we were an unknowable distance from the base of the mountain. "All this was to say that it's usually the sour motherfuckers who are looking for reasons to dick around. You don't look for help in someone who's chill with the status quo, right? Like, you're not going to ask Jeff Bezos for tax reform against billionaires. You're going to rally the masses. If you want someone to help you seek revenge against a politician, you'd ask the citizens. And, hypothetically, if you wanted to dabble in a war between Heaven and Hell, we'd need some renegades. Good thing we're not here for that, right Merit?"

"Right." I was catching on. "So, what sort of renegades do we need for vengeance?"

Satisfied with our ruse, she continued to lead us forward. "We're going to go meet two friends of mine. Last I checked, they're going by Ella and Estrid."

"Sisters?"

"Lovers."

I chewed on the information. "And we think they'll help us because they're Vanir and don't mind starting shit?"

"See, you get it. One of them is Vanir and always down to mess with the order of things. The other has been slighted *because* she's Aesir. You'll see. Plenty of Nordes from the nine worlds of Yggdrasil defected. Don't even get me started on how much better Álfheimr is than Jötunheimr. Ice giants do *not* know how to party. Tons of the coolest jötunn found their way here to paradise." She smiled at me. I still couldn't believe how much ground we had left to cover. It would be days or weeks or a month before we arrived. Maybe I'd die of old age and the dust of my skeleton could be carried up the gargantuan mountain on a breeze.

"Should I be keeping an eye peeled for giants?"

She chuckled. "*Giant* is a relative term. Sometimes it's metaphorical. Though leave it to centuries of pagan purists to insist on its literalism. Take Loki, for example. He's technically a giant, but the motherfucker got Tom Hiddleston to portray him. Great PR move on his part, which is why I'm sure he has a new cult of devotees. He has a giant personality, makes giant choices, and is the cause of giant waves amongst the gods. But let's focus on one group at a time. For now, we'll pop by Ella and Estrid's place and see if either of them wants to go on a little adventure to find some...retribution"

"Demonic and angelic political justice." I didn't want to risk breaking our vow of silence on the topic, but my gut told me she was forgetting about Silas.

"Yeah," she sighed, "let's play that one by ear and see how we feel about all parties once we get there."

My chest tightened uncomfortably. I was positive we were both discussing the angel. "He's up to something." It was exhausting to wrap our conversation in deceit, but a promise was a promise. Geoff Christiansen deserved to boil in a vat of acid, to be sure, but I did *not* care about him enough to reference him this often. Still, I stuck to the script as I said, "I know he'd help us with the senator."

She cast a glance over her shoulder. "You have more religious trauma in your pinky finger than most people experience in a lifetime. You're the last person I'd expect to argue on Heaven's behalf to go against their...*political* interests. So, what? You think he's gone rogue?"

I pressed the heel of my hand into my temple, rubbing slowly as I recounted events. "When I was attacked in my apartment and Caliban couldn't help, he put out a tier-five favor, remember? Anyone could have answered, and Silas came. You were the one who told me Silas could have used it to end the war. He could have asked for free access to Hell. He could have had Caliban killed. Instead...you remember how weird he was when he came to my apartment? He acted like Caliban had only put out a tier one and sent him to Bellfield. He stashed him in that terraformed god-catcher. The more I think about it, the more it seems like he put Caliban there because no one else could reach him."

"He's still an angel. He could be doing all the right things for all the wrong reasons," Fauna said quietly.

I watched her prance through the blossoms and blades, thinking of the infamous date she'd gone on with the agent of Heaven. "I thought you didn't mind him. He didn't just save Caliban by cashing in that favor on something small. He was also the one who showed up and rescued me after we killed Astarte. He got me back to you."

"Can't force me into a box, baby. I feel what I feel."

"And when can I talk about what I feel?" I hoped she knew what I was asking. I didn't have the energy to rework it into a madhouse of double entendre.

Fortunately, Fauna picked up what I was putting down. I needed to know what I could or couldn't say to the rebels. She said, "Tell them why we came. Casually mention other things in your life, if they're relevant. If another topic unfolds, well, we can hardly be held accountable for organic conversation."

Half of what she said at any given moment was nonsense, but every once in a while she rang with the clarity of a bell. Empowered by our plan, I was ready to get going. "Please tell me you're leading me to a motorcycle or some well-stashed horses or an airplane or something. This will take forever on foot and I'm starving."

She looked back at me. "Oh, it's too far to walk. Are you ready? I can just pop us over there."

I blinked. "Are you serious?"

She shrugged. "You usually have a cornucopia of dumb questions. I wanted us to be out of earshot while you got them out of your system."

Chapter Nine

A DAVID ATTENBOROUGH IMPERSONATOR NARRATED MY inner monologue as Fauna led me through the city.

One of nine realms, Álfheimr is as beautiful as it is vast. The bright, mountainous branch on Yggdrasil's tree contains as many cities, villages, and isolated farmsteads as the Scandinavian nations who observe it. A first-time visitor to these lands should make their way first to the precariously perched city of Kletti. One might find its colorful homes reminiscent of those lining the Danish canals, Icelandic harbors, or Norwegian fjords. All visitors would be wise to book their stay overlooking the infinite rivers that hold our beautiful realm in their sparkling embrace. Tourists seeking a more modern experience would be pleased to find state-of-the-art skyscrapers sandwiched between wooden stave churches and stone fortresses. Past and present, modernity and decay all find their place in Kletti, as will you, dear traveler, for the low, low price of your sanity.

I hadn't closed my mouth in twenty minutes. Fauna tried to manually shut it for me at one point, but it had just fallen back open when we'd rounded the next corner. At some point, my brain had stopped recording new material. I was too overwhelmed by the combination of ancient relics, and the spectacular majesty of new, flashy brilliance. I wish I knew more names of crystals, as I was pretty sure moonstone and labradorite were only two of the twenty on the list of building materials. Everything from home to business looked like it had been carved from crystal, stone, wood, glass, or steel.

"You're lucky you're cute," Fauna said, "or I'd find this embarrassing." I shielded my eyes as she stepped into a light so bright it hurt to look at. She approached what I could only describe as an opalescent coffee kiosk and leaned over the counter, ordering god knows what in some dialect of Old Norse that I'd never even come across in my studies, let alone heard out loud. She returned with two cups of hot mead and two slices of an air-thin pancake that an untrained eye might call a crêpe, but I knew to be the potato-based lefse my grandmother had made every Christmas.

"I don't want lefse," I said. "I want to find help."

"Then give it back," she said, extending her hand for the treats.

"...I want both things," I replied, yanking the mead and lefse out of her grasp.

"That's right. Be grateful."

"Oh, you've done plenty to me," I said through a mouthful of food.

"I could have taken us right to Ella and Estrid's, but I would have been doing you a disservice if I didn't show the place off a bit," she said with a wink.

I didn't want to sightsee, but I also couldn't risk alienating my friend and ally by pushing her further on her oath. So, we took the scenic route. The mountain was large enough that I barely felt the incline as I trailed behind her. I caught glimpses of water peeking between gaps in the buildings on one side, and the rise of the mountain and rows after rows of streets, homes, businesses, and city on the other.

Every street, every statue, every manicured garden and storefront and home and building deserved whatever drop of awe I could muster. While Fauna had said that her city was cradled between two rivers—ocean-wide and unfathomably deep—a thin, burbling stream of diamond-clear water ran

68

like a tiny moat separating the buildings from the road on every street.

She dragged me toward a huge, classically beautiful wooden home.

"Aren't Scandinavians known for a minimalist aesthetic?" I whispered, attempting humor.

"You'll find more of that in Ásgard. They've stayed with the times."

I'd been joking, but my mind wandered to a visual of Thor, god of Thunder, drinking beer out of a frosted glass in a mansion of clean lines with polished concrete floors, a three-story wall of windows, lofted ceilings, and the futuristic shades of black, gray, and white so popular among the wealthy. That was the living situation I'd chosen after my influx of money, after all.

I was about to make a second joke about whether or not Loki was responsible for the chaotic torture in the form of IKEA's self-assembled furniture, but Fauna wrapped her hand around the doorknob and let herself into the home without knocking.

"Ella! Estrid!" she sang. "I brought you a human sacrifice."

"You're not funny," I said, palms slick with sweat.

I clocked movement as a woman stood from the couch. Her partner rounded the corner, appearing in my blind spot.

"Human, meet my friends. They've been together since ages before Jesus was born and changed the global calendar. Ella and Estrid, this is—"

"Merit," came my hurried introduction. One woman was more beautiful than the sun and stars. The other was more intimidating than a blizzard of sharpened knives. I cleared my throat and attempted again, "Merit Finnegan."

The one who looked most like a warrior wrinkled her nose at Fauna. "You brought us the girl who wrote shitty fanfic about our people? Why?"

For fuck's sake. It was hard not to take her comment on my life's work personally.

"Give her a sniff and tell me you don't recognize that scent," Fauna replied.

Every muscle in my body clenched as if a venomous snake neared my jugular as the warrior leaned in and inhaled. She pulled back a moment later, lashes fluttering as if reeling from some piece of information in my scent profile. I took a subtle sniff at my underarm to see if I'd forgotten to put on deodorant.

"You can't be serious," the warrior said.

"Serious as a heart attack, Estrid," Fauna replied.

If the warrior was Estrid, then the shapely woman who'd come from the couch had to be Ella. I cleared my throat. "Is someone going to tell me what's happening?"

"Soon enough, peanut. It's polite to introduce yourself to your hosts before summoning them to grand adventures."

"Grand adventure, eh?" Estrid repeated. Her demeanor went from skeptical to endeared in an instant. She extended her left hand for a handshake. I lifted my right hand instinctually, then faltered when I understood why she'd offered the opposite hand. Jagged scars ran from her jaw, down her neck, and ended in a capped metallic plate where her right bicep might once have been. It was as if a lightning storm had taken her hand and forearm, leaving the imprint of its bolts as evidence. While the woman was both stunning and intimidating, it was her eyes that terrified me the most. I'd never seen a color so blue.

Humiliation over my faux pas heated me. I switched hands quickly, offering her my left. "I'm sorry."

"I'm not," she said. "I killed thirty-seven men and left with only one injury. I'm a legend."

"And so humble." Fauna grinned. "My kind of people."

"I'm Ella," the other said, cupping my hand with both of her own.

Perhaps my mind had been doing me a kindness by protecting me from seeing just how stunning she was before this moment. I short-circuited. I barely had two brain cells to rub together as the single most beautiful creature in the universe winked at me before walking away.

My hands went into stunned autopilot. I unzipped the coat Fauna had talked me into grabbing for the chilly temperatures of her realm and dropped it uselessly on their furniture. It seemed wildly inappropriate, but so did being here in the first place. I was adrift between a warrior and a visual treasure.

I was pretty sure there was no *Miss Manners* handbook on how long one was supposed to wait before asking her Nordic pantheon hosts to rush into battle on behalf of an angel and a demon or two. Even if there was, Miss Manners would have presumably disapproved of my doxxing-specific cover for showing up at their house unannounced, as lying was generally frowned upon.

Fauna ushered me into the house. She navigated me onto a settee and helped herself in the kitchen, much like she'd done at Nia and Darius's. Going new places was hard. Meeting new people was harder. But their enormous bay window with a view of the river and its limitless horizon helped.

"I love what you did with valkyries," Ella said with a molasses-like purr.

"I hate what she did with valkyries," came her partner's answering eye-roll.

Estrid, I learned, was a valkyrie, and not a fan of my work.

Her partner, Ella, found my portrayal of Odin's shield-maidens hilarious. Only elusive vagaries were made as to who Ella was or what she did. From the low cut of her dress, ample curves of her chest, hips, and thighs, luscious tousle of long, curly hair, and way she draped herself over furniture as if she were honey drizzled onto a sweet, I had a short list of preliminary guesses.

Estrid, on the other hand, looked like she could crush anyone's face beneath her boot and the victim would probably

71

thank her for the honor of being stepped on. Her gold-blond hair had been shaved to the scalp on both sides. A long stripe of hair remained down the middle, which she'd braided. She reminded me of the angel, though I wasn't sure who between Estrid and Silas was more muscular. I was fairly certain that they'd be evenly matched if they were to arm wrestle, even if Estrid was down an arm.

While Estrid was outwardly threatening, I knew better than to underestimate Ella. Despite the soothing voice and sparkling smile, I had no doubts she could break my bones with a nonchalant flick of her perfectly manicured fingers.

I sent Fauna a look that said, *Can I ask them yet?*

Her silencing glare was answer enough. I was to play by her rules in her realm.

Fauna, Ella, and Estrid instantly fell into the high-spirited revelries of old friends. They spoke around me as if I wasn't there, which I appreciated. Maybe they could smell the shock oozing from my pores and didn't want to spook me further. Whatever the reason, I was left to stare at the furniture, the art, the numerous glinting weapons, the walls, the very stitches and fabric fit for gods.

If I was to be left alone with my thoughts of Anath, war, kidnapping, torture, hostages, and long-lost love, I might as well give the rest of them some privacy. I abandoned the couch and wandered to the window to get a better look at the view. Something shiny caught my eye before I had the chance. I gaped at the seven-foot display case and its rows upon rows of precious things. Emeralds, black opal, jadeite, and other unspeakably beautiful rocks, crystals, and sparkly trinkets that I could neither name nor place glimmered from their display mounts. Some were embedded in the hilts of swords or encrusting the pommels of daggers. Others were set in dainty crowns, pretty rings, or elaborate necklaces. One sat on a silk cushion. More still were scattered along the shelves like confetti.

They would have been the very first thing a visitor

noticed in a normal home, but this one was full of legendary beings and a baffling ocean that everyone kept insisting was a river. Egypt's Royal Museum Alexandria was said to have more jewels than anywhere on Earth. A single gifted plate at Alexandria had been appraised at fifteen million pounds. But we were not on Earth, and these gems were fucking enormous. I tried to guess the earthly value of the gems, but had little frame of reference. The Cullinan Diamond, just large enough to fill one's palm, was the largest diamond in the world, and it was worth over three hundred million dollars.

These shelves had to have six Cullinans combined.

"Stick one in your pocket," Fauna said over my shoulder.

I jolted in surprise, completely unaware anyone had approached.

Fauna pushed a cup of tea into my hands. "I'm kidding—probably."

"Can we change the topic yet?" I looked into the amber water. I was tired of dancing around the issue.

"Why don't you drink first?" Fauna cut me off.

I took a sip, if only to keep myself from crying. I wrinkled my nose at the bitter aftertaste. Somehow, I found myself surprised that tea could be over-steeped even when prepared by gods.

"Do you like our baubles? You can thank Venus here for all of the pretty things." Estrid called.

Ella narrowed her eyes. "You know I hate that comparison."

Estrid smirked. "Doesn't feel great to be misrepresented, does it?"

I took another sip of tea before noticing a new expression on Fauna's face.

"You should take a seat while you drink."

I abandoned the incredible collection and settled onto their plush couch. I sniffed the mug. Its aroma was herbal, but there was something curious and wild beneath the scent. "What's in it?"

"Fun stuff. Do drugs, commit crimes. That sort of thing."

I'd already had several sips, if only to stave off the awkward chatter. I wasn't sure I needed anything more in my system. I tried to set it down, but she crossed her arms.

I tucked my feet under myself, curling into a ball of insecurity on the couch. "Fauna, I don't think I'm equipped to handle drugs in a magical realm."

Her face puckered as if she'd sucked something sour. "So, you'll drink beer in Hell and party with the humans, but you're too good for our Nordic tea? Come on, elitist. Down the hatch."

"But..." My vision blurred as the amber tea took on a different hue.

"Oh," she said, tucking an arm around my back. "No, this isn't like *her* drugs. This is fun among friends. Though I do suppose I should have been a little more sensitive to goddesses handing you cups of things."

"I suppose it's too late now," I sighed, suddenly aware of a tingle at the tips of my capillaries.

The others lifted their cups in a salute. Ignoring ten years of classroom-mandated Reagan drug propaganda about peer pressure, I wrapped my fingers around the mug once more and took a long, slurping sip of the strange, bitter tea. This wasn't Astarte's cucumber water in her weird sex dungeon. This was Fauna. She might be a flippant, sexy candy monster, but I loved her, and I believed her when she said she loved me in return.

At first, nothing happened.

Maybe my years of partying in college and late nights with Nia and Kirby had been the sort of Olympic training my body needed to develop a rock star's tolerance.

I listened to the three as they discussed old friends, adventures, and swapped stories of wars and the past. When the conversation turned to lovers, my tongue loosened.

"I'm in love too, you know," I said. The words bubbled from me without shame or hesitation.

"Do tell," Ella purred. "One of the few ways for humans

74

to gain immortality is to be loved by a writer. Their bodies die, yet their stories live on. Who have you made immortal?"

"He's already immortal," I said. A tick somewhere behind my left ear prodded me to look at Fauna, checking to see if I'd crossed some barrier, but she remained a pleasant shade of smirking friendliness. Did friendliness have a shade? Yes, it did. It was a golden sparkle. Even the act of smirking possessed a magenta hue.

Doe eyes met mine and I felt like I understood the loophole all at once. A human doused with the helium equivalent of truth serum wasn't here for betrayals or spies. She was simply babbling. And perhaps that was enough.

"He's a demon," I said, freed of my constraints. "Have you ever been to Hell? I'll take you if I ever get to go back. He's in some trouble right now, so it might be a while. The whole world's gone to shit. My career, my name, my..." I stopped myself from saying *boyfriend*. The abrupt end to my sentence had a sharp, silver tone, like breath on a frozen winter's day, if that breath turned to diamonds in the air.

"So she smells like—" Estrid began, looking at Fauna.

"But she's partnered with—" Ella spoke over her partner.

Fauna's hurried response was low and incomprehensible, mostly because it was more rainbow than words. Demons, hell, angels, something, something, something. She wasn't Astarte. This wasn't cucumber water. This...this was fun. This was good.

Their voices left their bodies like colorful musical notes. Fauna was a deep green intermingled with gold. Ella's voice was a sparkly crimson. Estrid's was turquoise and magenta. They all intermingled, the misty spaghetti strands of their words playing and tangling in the middle of the living room.

I reached out to touch the colorful notes, and paused to look at my fingers. They were tingling with a music of their own.

"Someone's finally having fun," Fauna said, tightening her arm around me.

Her doe eyes were larger than ever before. I saw the planets within them. Each freckle was a constellation. She was the Milky Way. I reached out to touch her face and she laughed, giving my hand a friendly kiss as she snatched it away and held it at her side, as if tethering my hands to the earth so they didn't float away.

"Your drugs are better than Astarte's," I said.

"Astarte?" The pair gaped in unison.

Fauna turned to the others. "Last week, she was drugged by Astarte and kept trying to fuck me." She leaned in conspiratorially. "Apparently the Phoenicians had this whole kingdom thing going in the States! Their sex and war goddess terraformed a city in the mortal realm as a god-catching seal so she could run a fertility clinic. How many Phoenicians were there, Merit? Three?"

"Four," I said hoarsely, watching as my voice came out in shimmering shades of grays and blues. The navy and silver escaped my lips and then returned to kiss me before they joined the other colors. "Astarte, Anath, Jessabelle, and Dagon. Crimson, sparkly copper, phthalo green, and…what color are mermaid scales?"

Ella pouted, confusion distorting her lovely face. "Are you…?"

Fauna gave my knee a squeeze. "She's assigning the gods colors, apparently. They'll be thrilled."

I played the colors like piano keys under my fingers, pressing into each word as I said, "No, they won't. Half of them are dead."

That gained their full attention. Ella and Estrid leaned forward. Ella pushed, "You were there?"

At the same time, Estrid said, "What do you mean, *dead*?"

I nodded, enjoying the static-like thrill that ran through my veins each time I bobbed my chin up and down. "He cut off Astarte's head… I saw Jessabelle die on screen…meteor hammer. I think she was a soul eater. I don't know…" I lost interest in the middle of each sentence, allowing the words to drift off so I could watch their cerulean physical shapes.

"But Dagon and Anath?" pressed Estrid.

I shrugged. A distant part of me was annoyed that they'd begun insisting I speak as soon as I'd become perfectly contented to remain silent. "They were still fighting Anath when we left."

"Who's *they*?" she tried to clarify.

Fauna took over for me while my fingers played with the sparkling, misty colors. I tried to catch the words, but they disappeared every time I opened my palm. She tucked her arm around me to help me with an anchoring sensation as my gaze bobbed about the room.

"Are none of you seeing this? Look at the pastels. No, not that one." I plucked a note from the space between us. "This word is a crushed velvet maroon."

Fauna squeezed my hand. "Why are we here, Merit? Tell them."

"Oh." I pouted at the necessary lie. "You're supposed to kill a senator I'm mad at, or something."

"*Exactly*," Fauna emphasized. "That's the *only* reason we're here. We came to you because a senator named Geoff what's-his-face doxxed her. On an utterly unrelated note, since we're already talking about Merit's Phoenician escapades, this is what I've gathered so far: the Canaanite fertility goddess was pulling a Vanir wet dream. She wasn't really getting recognition anymore, so she started her own kingdom…only, she couldn't quite do it alone. She needed crops, she needed weather, she needed the same foundations every civilization needs. So, she had Dagon trapped in this lake so that the whole town flourished, right? But because the town itself was a god-catcher, no one could come to save him. If they did come for him, her sister, Anath, was there. The *we* Merit's referring to is the Prince of Hell and…do you remember Azrames?"

Ella's face lit. "How could I forget! What a night."

Fauna wrinkled her nose in an indecent giggle, and I made the executive decision not to ask. "Az and the Prince—she calls him Caliban—were still fighting Anath and a ton of parasites when an angel helped them out."

"Why does she call him Caliban?" Estrid asked.

Fauna leaned forward excitedly, eyes flaring for emphasis as she said, "This is the Prince's human."

The two looked at me with new eyes.

"So when she said she loved a demon..." Ella's thick lashes fluttered.

"*Her?*" Estrid asked incredulously.

I wanted to be offended by the implication, but some part of me knew that the negativity wouldn't be a pretty color, and I didn't want to spoil the rainbow. "Do you have anything amethyst to eat?" I asked. "It has to be purple. Lavender is acceptable."

"And an angel?" repeated Estrid.

My stomach rumbled for lilacs and pansies and violets.

Ella rose from the couch and returned with a plum, a pile of grapes, and an uncut eggplant.

"I love you," I replied, taking the plate. The grapes were delicious. I was surprised to learn that plums tasted chartreuse, and waited for a break in conversation to inform the others.

Fauna paid me no mind. Estrid hung on her every word as she explained, "Yeah. Heaven's gotten involved. As you can imagine, they see the useful potential of the Prince's human in their war. It doesn't help that Merit's mom is a real treat. Real Heaven-freak, that one. She gives them more of a foothold than they deserve. Anyway, as you can imagine, it would be really convenient for their battle if Heaven claimed the Prince's human. So that's where I've been. Babysitting."

Ella chewed the tip of her thumb as she looked at Fauna. "How did you get the job?"

"Smell her," Estrid said. "I caught the scent when she walked in."

The most beautiful woman in the world put a hand to the back of my head, which made me curiously aware that I still possessed a body. She leaned in, just as Jessabelle had done. I recalled thinking Astarte's assistant had been a vampire going in for the kill. This time, I wondered if the impossibly gorgeous goddess-like creature at my side might kiss me. If she did, I wondered if it would sparkle. Maybe a kiss would create a color of its own. Maybe our lips would lock, tasting like the diamonds on her wall as our new gems joined the foggy dance that created a rainbow bridge.

"Are you Hnoss?" I asked her.

Ella's full lips parted in surprise. Her shimmering doll eyes widened. "How did a human…"

Fauna giggled at my side. "I forget that you're actually intelligent, peanut. I prefer to think of you as my sweet dummy, but I don't give you enough credit."

Ella's laughter was shinier than any of her jewels. "Well, I'm impressed. Even walking the streets among my practitioners—"

"What do I smell like?" I asked. "Anath sniffed out my Nordic blood. But since you all smell Nordic…"

"Oh, honey." Ella stroked my hair. "You don't just smell like a realm to us. One whiff and we know exactly *who* sourced the blood pumping through your veins."

My head lolled from one side to the other, too high to bother with the efforts of turning it to watch the speakers.

"Can you go get them?" Fauna asked the valkyrie.

"Them who?" I said, lifting a finger before the shiny, colorful distraction of my question drew my hand to try to catch my words.

The valkyrie grunted. "I'm assuming you want me to get them because of this *news* you've just shared. Leave it to me to think you'd just stopped by for a visit. Of course you fucked with another pantheon and need help cleaning up your mess."

"I fucked with no one," Fauna said, lifting her hands to show she was unarmed.

"I fucked with quite a few of them," I mumbled. "Or

tried. I suppose I'll never get to finish the deed, now that Astarte's dead and Caliban's trapped in their realm."

"Oh, Fauna." Ella clicked her tongue. "My, you have a gift for burying the lede."

"We're in over our head," Fauna replied, "and I'm a bit tongue-tied until certain events click into place. You know how it is. Words and bonds and blah blah blah."

"I'll get them," Estrid said, "but you're paying for this."

"With what!" Fauna laughed. "Your lover owns all of the treasures in the realm."

It was all babbling nonsense, but at least their gibberish glittered.

Estrid stepped backward into the ether with a glare. Other stuff probably happened. More time likely passed. But one moment, a battle-worn valkyrie stood in her living room, and the next, she vanished, leaving a steely cloud in her wake. She didn't walk out the door; she truly *disappeared*. Perhaps I was too lost in the swirl of sparkles to understand what happened, nor did I feel particularly inclined to try.

"Are you excited?" Ella asked.

"For the second course?" I asked, looking at my picked-over fruit. The eggplant, as it turned out, was not delicious when raw. "Who is *them*?"

To Fauna, she repeated, "Is she excited?"

Fauna bit her lip. "She doesn't know."

Ella laughed. The sound was like the tinkling of silver bells. "I'd say that's a treat, but the human's won me over. Don't you think she should be told before she's ambushed? And for fuck's sake, why did you get the girl high?"

"She loves getting high! This is her second time getting high in literally just one week."

"And neither of those times were consensual," I interjected. I supposed I had told Astarte to do anything necessary to get the job done, then signed my name and given her a blood offering. I'd also blindly follow Fauna wherever she

80

led me and drink whatever she gave me, and perhaps in the games of gods, those actions were consent enough.

I'd intended to continue with a speech about how I missed my sobriety when I was distracted by the lovely shade of peach my finger was. Skin was so pretty. Had I never noticed the human body before? The pinks and browns and golds were marvelous. Life was amazing.

Fauna wrinkled her nose in disappointment. "Well, Merit?" She tested my pen name carefully. "I did you a favor."

Drugging me so I had an excuse to talk about my true motives for seeking an audience with the Nordes didn't feel like a favor. I attempted to shake my head but felt as if it were filled with helium. It was about to disconnect from my shoulders and float off to join the shiny words that bobbed about the room.

I wanted to tell her that immortal beings needed to stop fucking with my drinks. Instead, what came out was "Fauna? Your words are green and gold. Did you know that?"

She plucked the tea from my hands and grimaced as she set it on the low table. "I may have misjudged your tolerance. Whoops. Let's try to get a glass of water in you before they get here. Ella? Help me out?"

Ella chuckled. "Water is not gonna cut it for this little gooseberry. But sure. I'll get a pitcher."

"Is he going to be mad at me?" Fauna asked.

She was looking at Ella for an answer, but as I didn't know of any men who might be irritated with her for drugging me, I answered on Caliban's behalf. "I'm sure the Prince will be thrilled that every time I'm around any god but him, I wind up stoned against my will."

First to me, Ella said, "Drink this. And she isn't talking about your Prince." Then to Fauna, "And yes, I guarantee he'll be angry. No one's ever happy with you, Fauna. But then again, you wouldn't be doing your job if you were keeping the peace."

"I was born to stick it to the man." She winked.

I gulped down one glass, then another, water dribbling down my chin as I gasped against the cup like a child drinking from a sippy cup.

Fauna's face was a swirl of giggling regret as she said, "I'm big enough to admit that I fucked up on this one. But my heart is in the right place."

"With what?" I asked. I thought the tea had only relaxed me and opened my eyes to the colors of the universe, but it seemed to be jumbling everyone's words, as well. None of their cryptic exchanges made sense.

"Okay, when they get here, there's something you need to keep in mind. They haven't been to the mortal realm in decades, so you'll probably want to avoid cursing. I'm sure she's precisely as old-fashioned as she was when she left your plane of existence, and hasn't had the luxury of rotting her brain with your media like I have."

"When who gets where?"

The question was barely out of my mouth before Estrid reappeared with two figures. I felt my face collapse in on itself like a dying star as I frowned, eyebrows gathering, forehead creasing, lower lip raising in a pout. I narrowed my eyes to look at the curiosities in the room. Estrid offered an apologetic smile before stepping to the side so I could look at the figures more fully, but nothing about them made sense. I stared at the man and woman for a long time, searching for reason, but none came. They hadn't spoken, so I had no sense of their colors.

The man—at least, I was pretty sure the beautiful, androgynous, elfin figure was a man—looked like he'd stepped out of a snowy forest in the middle of a hunt. His hair was dark, but short on the sides, much like Estrid's. The hair upon their respective heads was rapidly thawing as though it had been frozen only moments prior. The powdery white disappeared from the fur trim covering the man's shoulders, from the leather on his fingerless gloves, and from his bow and the arrows that dangled from the quiver strapped around his hip.

The young woman with icy blond hair and lashes beside

him had a pink nose, cheeks, and ears from the cold, but her skin and hair were too white to show the change in temperature the way his did. I spotted frosted edges on the red fox fur wrapped around her upper body. She was similarly dressed for winter hunting.

There was something about her that looked so familiar, from the bridge of her nose to the curve of her hips. I was nearly certain we'd met before. I wondered if her voice would be as pink as her nose.

The man wrapped his arm around the woman's waist. Her hand flew to her mouth in surprise as she shook her head. After a while, her hand moved to his chest. I neither understood nor wholly cared why they were staring at me. I did my best to remember that they couldn't see the colors until they drank the tea, and wondered if they'd be offered a warm cup soon.

"Fauna?" I whispered loudly as I continued to stare back at the strangers.

"Yes, pumpkin?" She returned the stage whisper.

I blinked slowly, waiting for the phantom figures to evaporate. The woman's familiarity suddenly clicked with the silvery clang of ringing bells. I recognized her from the face that stared back at me every time I looked in the mirror. "Either I'm really high, or I'm looking at my dead great-grandma."

She squeezed my knee. "You are really high. And two things can be true at once. Happy family reunion."

Chapter Ten

I'D NEVER BEEN PATRIOTIC, BUT THAT DIDN'T STOP ME FROM loving Independence Day. The midsummer holiday was a deliciously warm reprieve from the Thanksgivings, Christmases, Valentine's Days, and birthdays that usually came with bulky coats, icy roads, and a frosty layer of snow. Burgers, hot dogs, lakes, rivers, boats, beaches, sunburns, country music, themed bikinis, cut-off shorts, and copious amounts of alcohol coated America's favorite excuse to get drunk and play with fire.

I'd wandered away from the bonfire, leaving a handful of people I knew from overlapping humanities classes, and a gaggle of people I didn't, to remain engaged in whatever mating rituals ensued when two or more drunk college kids hung out over the summer. The bonfire was too far from the beach, and as we were on one of the largest freshwater lakes in North America, I was fairly certain I'd be able to see the fireworks reflected in the water.

It was stupid, but so were some of life's best things.

And then, there were the colors.

God, I loved fireworks. They were the sort of thing my peers had outgrown as the years ticked on, but some of my favorite childhood memories took place on the Fourth of July. We were poor, but the sky belonged to everyone.

Anyone who could lay down a blanket on a grassy knoll or park a truck with an unobstructed view had front-seat tickets to a kaleidoscope of joy.

Some hissed and spun in tight, golden corkscrews before erupting in pinks, greens, and blues. Some left long, palm-tree-like streaks across the sky as gravity claimed their colorful embers. Others were short, crackling bursts. Once in a while, a firework would erupt in coordinated shapes, like hearts, stars, or rosettes. Some were light-blue jellyfish. Others were pink chrysanthemums. But my favorite, without fail, was the fountain.

Metallic, glittering starlight would twinkle and fall to the earth, and I'd close my eyes and make a wish. The lakes were too large to possess the glassy quality one found in postcards or picturesque landscape calendars, but I could still make out the glistening colors in the choppy, dark waves. The soothing rush as wave after wave lapped upon the sand was vastly preferable to whatever Toby Keith hit blasted in the background. I wanted to put as much space as possible between me and the dumbass who'd been trusted with the aux.

"You're kind of far from the party, aren't you?"

"Caliban!" I exclaimed. I stretched out my hands for him like a toddler who wanted to be picked up.

"And a little drunk," he said with a smile. He had the most perfect white teeth I'd ever seen. Everything about him was chiseled from the same pale, perfect marble, from his shock of hair to the strength in his hands. Michelangelo himself couldn't have carved anything so beautiful if he'd spent his life trying. He didn't belong on the same freshwater beach as tank-top-wearing college bros with beer bongs and flip-flops, let alone the same planet.

"I was hoping you'd come find me," I said. I tipped back the dregs of the sweet, cotton-candy-flavored punch from my red cup and tossed it onto the ground.

"No need to litter," he tsked. He picked up the cup and made indentations in the plastic with his fingers. A moment later, it disappeared in a burst of black glitter, as though it had never existed. He extended his hand.

"Am I next?" I asked, referring to the cup.

"I'd sooner die than let harm befall you," he swore.

"How gallant." I hadn't meant to sound sarcastic, but I was growing a little tired of gallantry. Every penis-owner at the party had been trying to get laid, hurling sloppy pickup lines at anyone who would listen, and then there was Caliban, ever the gentleman.

"I could use a drink. Want to return to the party?" he asked.

His request was both odd and irrelevant. I plucked a flask from my back pocket and handed it to him.

He took a swig and made a face. "Is this apple moonshine?"

"We call it Apple Pie," I replied. "Everclear, spiced rum, apple cider, sugar, and cinnamon. And since when do you...?"

"What? Interact with your environment? Is it freaking you out?"

"A little."

He'd never been inappropriate with me, which I found downright offensive for an imaginary friend. If he were a figment of my imagination, shouldn't he be catering to my every whim? Perhaps it said something about my self-esteem that even my delusional coping mechanism allowed little more than the chaste, borderline-familial comfort of a man who respected firm, platonic boundaries.

Not tonight. It was a holiday, goddammit, and I wanted him to flirt with me.

"If you're going to share my booze, you might as well hold my hand."

He looked at my outstretched fingers as if they were curious antiquities and he the archeologist.

"That depends," he said, and I heard the conspiratorial tone of an impending deal. He loved his trades. "You've convinced yourself I'm not real, and I won't try to talk you out of it. But just for tonight, let's play pretend. I'll hold your hand, and you indulge in the fantasy that I'm here in the flesh."

My hand dropped limply to my side. I cast a quick glance at the men walking hand in hand in our direction.

"I'll look insane with my arm outstretched holding air," I said quietly.

"Maybe," he conceded. "But it's a holiday. Indulge your deviant fantasies, and let's see if anyone gives you a funny look. Perhaps we'll just be another couple on the beach."

My lip twitched at the word. *Couple.* Of course, I'd thought of him romantically. He could have been an asexual accountant I only saw during tax season for platonic exchanges, and I'd still daydream about ripping his clothes off and wondering if his skin tasted as good as it smelled. I was sure he didn't mean it. If I'd made him up, he should at least be an active participant in my orgasms.

He stretched his hand toward me. Fireworks continued to crackle, waves continued to gently kiss the shore, and the couple continued to walk toward us, but he did not budge.

"Okay," I agreed. My voice lacked conviction, but I extended tentative fingertips, slipping them into his cool, strong palm. "Tonight, we're just a man and a woman."

"Something like that," he said with a smile. "Give me more of that horrible drink."

I handed him the flask once more. "I didn't realize your tastes were so elitist."

"I prefer gin," he said. He returned the flask to me after another swig, and I tucked it into my back pocket. My hands dangled, free for grabbing, as he was a real man who might catch my hopeful signals.

Drink preferences aside, tonight, he would indulge me. Tonight, my lustful waking dreams could explore the barest edges of my uncontrollable feelings for this perfect, striking man, and I would play a little game. We were two people walking on the beach. We could pretend to be anyone. Maybe we were communist spies, reporting our findings to

Mother Russia. Maybe we were science buddies quizzing one another on DNA architecture and whether we had a social obligation to keep bioethics every bit as rigorous as our technological advancements. Or maybe—and I was inclined to go with option three—I could pretend that Caliban was my partner, my boyfriend, my lover.

Then again, hand-holding was a solid first step, but parents held hands with children and drunk girls held hands with strangers as they led one another to the club bathroom, which robbed the gesture of its intimacy.

The pair of men passed, and two sets of eyes went to us. Well, they went to me, one man smiling, the other openly gaping, but I allowed myself to pretend that they perceived Caliban, too.

"Happy Fourth," I greeted the men.

"Happy Fourth," they replied in automatic unison, one tripping over his own feet as they stumbled to get one last ogle before continuing on down the beach.

"Did I spill something on my shirt? Why were they looking at me like that?"

"They were looking at *us*," he corrected. We walked the next two hundred feet in blissful silence, leaving footprints in the sand, our eyes on the moon, the stars, the festive explosions. There was a chance I was buzzing on alcohol, but the fuzzy dopamine sure felt a lot like love. I was content to spend the walk in silence when he spoke again. "Could we...do something? Just you and me?"

Please, god, let this man ask to fuck me on the beach.

I cleared my throat. "What do you have in mind?"

There was something reserved about his question. With halting uncertainty, he asked, "Would you just sit here for a while and watch the fireworks with me?"

"I...Aren't we already watching the fireworks?"

He tried to smile, but the skin around his eyes remained tight. "I mean, can we keep going as we are? Acting like we're real, that is. Just tonight."

I couldn't explain the strange pain that needled me in the heart as I held his gaze. Quietly, I replied, "Just tonight."

Caliban took a seat on the sand and patted the space beside him. He planted a palm near my hip, and I relaxed into the space between his arm and torso, tucking my head beneath his chin. We tilted our faces skyward and watched the sky like any other couple quietly observing Independence Day.

"You know what I like about the stars?" he asked.

I turned to watch his face, waiting for him to continue.

"They're the same everywhere. They have different names, but it's the same moon and its phases, the same constellations, the same tidal pulls and powerful birth charts."

"Sure," I conceded, though I didn't seem to feel as strongly about it as he did. "I guess there's something unifying about looking at the same moon in China and Greece and Brazil."

"No, I mean..." His smile returned as he shook his head. "Yeah, something like that."

"Sometimes, in moments like this, I miss being in the church."

"I make you miss...the Bible?" He sounded more amused than I understood.

"No." I pushed his arm. I hoped he found the gesture playful, but I had no idea how to flirt with him. Most men were so simple. Caliban was a locked box within a vault within a concrete brick, as far as I was concerned. I expanded, "I just miss the sort of catch-all gratitude that came with having a single source for everything. I miss being able to look at a sunrise and thank God. I miss being sad or sick or scared and knowing exactly who to pray to. And tonight, it would be pretty fucking nice if I had someone to talk to."

"Talk to me," he said.

"No," I amended. "I mean, I'd love to have someone to thank for bringing us together. It used to make me feel lighter to look at the fireworks and thank a deity for a beautiful show, for perfect weather, and for the chance to cuddle on the beach with someone I..."

His sharp intake of air caught me off guard. I wasn't sure what I'd said wrong, but I bit my lip before I put my foot in my mouth.

I'd been talking to Caliban for four years. I knew the cadence of his voice inside and out. And I knew when he was keeping something from me. There was discomfort in his wording as he said, "Have you explored any other pantheon?"

I slipped out of my flip-flops and dug my toes into the sand. "What, like, worship Hecate instead?"

"Well, sure, she's an oddly specific example, but yes. If you're missing a sense of something greater, have you entertained the idea that maybe it's because, well…there's something greater?"

I used my toe to draw a heart in the hard-packed sand. A sidewise glance told me he wasn't paying attention to my buzzed attempts at beach-faring courtship. A quote clanged around in my head. "Yeah, yeah, C.S. Lewis said something about that. I was a big Narnia fan."

"What did he say?"

I cleared my throat and did my best impression of a British man: *"If I find in myself desires that nothing in this world can satisfy, the only logical explanation is that I was made for another world."*

The rhythmic firework display increased in tempo. We had to be nearing the grand finale. I cuddled into him, my boyfriend for the night, real or imagined, and watched the colorful explosions in awe.

Caliban's single, soft laugh was too somber for the occasion.

I squeezed his forearm. "Hey, what's on your mind?"

"He was smart," was all he said. "Lewis, that is. You read a bunch of his books, didn't you?"

"I did indeed, fiction and nonfiction. Your drunken date in the Daisy Dukes is a well-read lady. Remember *Screwtape Letters*? That book about demons writing back and forth to each other?"

Another laugh. "Yes. Precisely like that. The man was something of a demon lover."

I giggled at the thought, then supplied the only tidbit I knew on the topic. "Lewis was quoted a time or two saying he had an unhealthy taste for the occult."

"At least his logic was sound," Caliban replied. "You can't have one without the other. If you believe in Heaven and its King, then you believe in its adversaries. Though its portrayal of said adversaries might be somewhat biased."

"Well, can you blame them? History is written by the victors."

"I wouldn't count their chickens just yet," he said under his breath, but not so quietly that I didn't slip it into my bank of odd Caliban tidbits. I collected memories of him like they were arcade tickets. Perhaps one day I could cash them in for a real boy.

I didn't want to ruin the mood, so I did my best to return our banter to irreverence. "Great, so, on America's birthday, my primary takeaway is that I should pray to Hecate and that demons are real."

"Hecate, sure." He hummed as if racking his brain. "Or Frigg, Frejya, Skadi, Sif—"

"Are you just listing Nordic goddesses because of my surname? That's not very America's Birthday of you. Shouldn't we be setting up altars to Columbia and whatever other colonizer goddesses of manifest destiny?"

"We're missing the finale," he said. He gave my hip a squeeze as the fireworks erupted in all directions, smothering the sky in smoke and color and light.

The thunderous pops had ceased, leaving us alone with the distant twang of steel guitars and songs about drinking with the boys and killing your husbands.

I wasn't ready to leave. Getting up would mean leaving Caliban, and tonight was so, so rare for us. I almost never indulged my delusions enough to relax and have fun. I could sit here in the dark if he could, though I'd prefer to fill the sky with rainbows. Maybe I could stretch it out, just a little longer. I'd been doing preliminary research on the Nordic pantheon for a writing project, and if it encouraged him to stay, I'd gladly talk about Scandinavian nations and Vikings and powerful hammers and Ragnarök if it meant he would stay.

"I get it, you know," he said at last. I caught the way his frosted lashes fluttered close, each white hair brilliant in the moonlight, as he spoke. "I have one person to thank for every good thing in my life, and it's you."

Chapter Eleven

Really? None of you can fix this?" The too-beautiful man thrust a hand toward me, and I could only assume he was referring to my explosion of levity and colors.

Fauna washed her hands of responsibility. "I cause chaos, I don't undo it. Plus, I thought I was helping her out. She's a ball of anxiety, this one."

"Chaos is an understatement. You're going to be the end of us, Fauna," he grumbled. "You're lucky we like you."

"What's not to like?"

Great-grandmother. Mother of mother of mother. I rolled the words from one side of my mouth to the other, tasting the same silver clanging sensation I'd felt the moment I understood precisely who stood before me. I could barely hear the exchange over the *ting, ting, ting* as bright, starlit metal swirled around the woman. She looked really good for someone who'd been dead for thirty years. I turned away from the very solid-looking ghost of my ancestor to see what the other pretty colors were saying.

"Where were they?" Ella asked Estrid.

Very serious. Too serious. Not nearly enough shimmer.

"Jötunheimr," she responded.

Oh, that word was fun to hear, but no fun to see.

I was certain the exchange was supposed to make sense,

but I couldn't unravel the bundle of colorful yarn as their sentences wove together. I knew Jötunheimr was where the frost giants lived. Primordial chaos. They continued to speak about the land of giants and lawlessness in a way that invoked loud music, sharp colors, and shades of black, gray, and ice. I didn't think I wanted to go there.

The man approached me through my hazy tunnel of vision. I struggle to focus on him, as the kaleidoscope surrounding him was utterly distracting. He was so pretty. He looked like an angel. I giggled at the thought, because no, he looked nothing like Silas. Estrid looked like Silas. Estrid, with her magenta colors...What were his colors? This man's? Silas's? This man had spoken a little. I couldn't remember what shade—

"You're too beautiful to be a great-grandfather," I said. "You look like an angel. Well," I amended with a giggle, "maybe not an angel. They can be shitheads."

"*Tsch.*" Fauna made a hissing, corrective noise while waving her hand across her throat as if to tell me to stop speaking. My, she was funny when she wasn't being a bully. I loved her so much. Maybe when she was done scolding me, she would come cuddle.

His answering smile was patient, if a bit patronizing.

To Fauna, he said, "You get one pass when it comes to my family. Pull a stunt like this again and I'll see to it that you're kicked out of Álfheimr and sent back to the snow."

I waited for her retort, but in a curious shift, her greens and golds faded into shades of gray as she glared at her feet. My lips parted to ask her what was wrong, but before the words left my mouth, the beautiful man pushed a hand against my forehead.

The touch had no physical force, but every sparkling piece of my colorful energy lurched backward as if thrust into the seat behind me.

"Holy shit," I gasped, horrified.

"I told you not to curse," Fauna whispered with reproach.

His palm moved from my forehead to my palm, gathering my hand in his own as levity abandoned me.

"We both know Fauna well enough to know you're not to blame for this. It's a pleasure to meet you," he said. "I go by Geir."

"Eir is the one in the Norse pantheon known for healing, and she's a woman," I said to him with surprising confidence.

Estrid stretched an arm behind Ella on the sofa. "Humans and their gender binaries."

"Humanity's getting better," Fauna said quietly. Whatever had bothered her earlier hadn't passed. I couldn't place her discomfort, but she defended me as she said, "Mortals used collective nonbinary pronouns long ago, and there's a renaissance in their language and perception as of late."

"I'm glad to hear it," said the man with the dark hair and the black-trimmed wolf coat. He'd fully defrosted now, revealing the various shades of leather and fur. "Please, use my chosen name and pronouns, and understand why Aloisa prefers this as my form. Let me be the first to tell you that your great-grandmother and I are proud of you."

Aloisa.

"You may be proud of your lineage," Aloisa said. "I'm not sure I can say the same."

I stared at the woman with the white-blond hair that matched my mother's perfectly. She was practically my age, if not younger. I'd always assumed that the wool bunad was the reason for her shapeliness, but as I looked at her now, I saw healthy, curvaceous hips and a chest and thighs that had nothing to do with weighty traditional dresses. She looked like she'd stepped out of the grainy black-and-white photo that remained pinned to my refrigerator. She was human, and also...not. I saw the familiar ocean eyes I knew from Grandma Dagny. Her nose had been passed down to her daughter, and to her daughter's daughter. But there was a glow to her that reminded me of the bits of starlight that had bobbed in the grassy meadow beyond the tree.

She was related to Lisbeth, all right. I'd known her for ten seconds and she was already a bitch.

"It's nice to meet you," came her cordial voice from across the room.

It wasn't a very familial welcome by most accounts, but it tracked for the chill that ran through my maternal lineage.

Geir rose from his position in front of the couch to fetch a chair for himself and my long-dead great-grandmother. I was quite sure that I'd sobered up, yet I had to be higher than ever. I no longer saw words and colors, but I sat in a circle with a valkyrie, a faun, a Norse goddess, an elf responsible for my fae blood, and my deceased relative.

But I was incomplete without my demon.

I spoke my truth and asked: "Are ghosts...? Is the after-life...? Is this real? Am I still high?"

Fauna made a pitying noise. "Yes. My methods were voted out, peanut. You're woefully sober."

My shoulders sagged as I thought of how many times I'd asked Caliban the exact same question, confident I was crazy simply because I refused to accept any reality beyond my own. True insanity was denying the facts before your naked eye because they didn't fit into your worldview.

Fauna offered tea of the non-hallucinogenic variety that was presumably not hers to offer. They both politely declined. Ella moved to the kitchen and returned with six frosted glasses and a gallon of spiced mead.

I was grateful for the booze as anxiety claimed me once more. I shook my head, sinking deeper into the couch. I looked between the beautiful home, the mythical figures, the two newcomers, and her. The only thing I could think to say was "There's no such thing as this."

Fauna was the first to chuckle, asking, "Is this really where you draw the line?"

"No." I bristled. "Ghosts are a different thing entirely. I've swallowed gods and fae and demons and the veil. But she's—" I gestured to my long-dead relative.

Aloisa cut her off as she crossed to me. She hugged Geir, fingers slipping through the black fur on his shoulder before she gestured for me to get to my feet.

"I'll take it from here. Let me take a look at you, girl," she said. She spoke with the force of someone three times her age. She took my face in a single hand, giving my cheeks a squeeze almost as if she were a rancher inspecting horse teeth. She chuckled before giving me a light hug. "You're my stock after all, aren't you?"

"But—" I stopped myself.

There was a game often played by children in the church, called When I Get to Heaven. It was something we played to busy our minds with the mysteries of the universe. We all had things we wanted to ask God, whether it be about the creation of the universe, the existence of mosquitos, or why he let good people suffer and die. Our curiosity usually stayed positive, lest we risk blasphemy by questioning his will or implying he'd been imperfect.

She may not be God, but I did have questions.

"I didn't see this realm on the list of afterlives," I said, gesturing to their living room. "How are you here?"

"I ended my cycle to be with Geir," she said with neither emotion nor explanation.

Shaking myself into a more productive line of thought, I said, "Fine. If you're my ancestor, then there's something I need to ask."

She frowned at the seriousness in my voice and stepped backward to rejoin Geir. She indicated for me to continue. I clung to my newfound sobriety, glad for the rage that bubbled like a dark tar to replace the colors. It was a curious thing to meet one's deceased ancestor.

But I didn't feel curious. I felt betrayed.

"Never mind your cycle or why you're standing in Álfheimr. I'm sure I won't understand the explanation. You're here. I just need to know…why didn't you intervene? Why would you let your daughter—my grandma—spend her life

97

thinking she was insane? Why did you leave Norway? Why, with my mother—"

"If I may?" Geir asked.

My anger expanded. I failed to control my irritation at his interruption.

Aloisa raised an eyebrow. "Give it a go."

He touched his heart for emphasis. "Dagny was not being spared from me, or from the Nordes. Aloisa took her overseas to escape other mortals, as they were both still in the realm. Do you know of bonding?"

"She does," Fauna answered for me.

Geir nodded appreciatively. "Aloisa couldn't very well bond herself to me with a half-mortal, half-fae child. Her child needed her more in the human realm. So, I gave her a talisman."

"The sølje." An image of the silver broach flashed before me.

He nodded once more. "Precisely. But it wasn't Dagny's time to come or go. She was in a new cycle as a soul, and her decisions couldn't be taken from her. Aloisa ended her mortal cycles with me and remained with the Nordes."

Fauna wiggled her shoulders as if shaking off whatever had burdened her. She settled into familiar irreverence as she said, "That's what brings us here. Apparently, love for the preternatural runs in the family. Your granddaughter has shacked up with the Prince of Hell. It's very romantic. Thousands of years of lifetimes and all that. We've since gotten ourselves into a sticky situation when Heaven laid its claim on her."

I didn't miss the pointed look that Fauna shot at Aloisa.

"The Prince?" Aloisa avoided me altogether. She stared at Geir, but his gaze remained trained on me.

Geir held my eyes as if searching me for something. He looked at Aloisa at long last and they exchanged a long, unspoken conversation.

"Do you have a dog in the fight between Heaven and Hell?" I dared a question.

Her face twisted. "I have a grievance or two with Heaven."

"Join the club," Estrid muttered.

"I thought we were going to the land of religious freedom," Aloisa said. "But it was a fairy tale. A lie. The persecutions were no better there. The only benefit was that I didn't speak English—at least, I could feign foreignness with anyone who had ill intent. It's a luxury I couldn't have afforded if Farsi, Cantonese, or Swahili had been coming out of my mouth. But I was a Western face in a time when xenophobic neighbors assumed if you looked like them, you must think like them. They didn't speak enough Norwegian to find me guilty for my pagan ways. I spared my child. My daughter grew up using English with her little American neighbors. She wasn't cursed with the hiding forced on immigrants. I gave Dagny her best shot at life."

"We know," Geir said to Aloisa supportively as he gave her knee a squeeze.

"No," I bit, "we don't know. Do you have any idea what my grandma—what Dagny's—life was like? She didn't leave her house for thirty years because she saw what she thought were angels and demons everywhere she went. She was paralyzed with fear, and you just let her believe—"

"Mar—" Fauna cautioned.

"No." I got to my feet. "Grandma Dagny was sweet, and kind, and good, and everyone thought she was crazy. She raised my mother, and my mom is *definitely* crazy. Lisbeth continued to see angels and demons or whatever manner of fae wanders our earth unseen to everyone else around them, but it drove her so deep into the church that now I have an angel up my ass laying claim on me. That wouldn't have happened if you hadn't abandoned your daughter and hoped that luck took care of her."

"I didn't abandon her," Aloisa snapped. "And I'd watch my tongue on things I don't know about. How many children have you had? How many around you were being killed or accused of witchcraft? What were the persecutions like? How

99

many countries have you had to flee to keep your loved ones safe?"

My hands clenched into fists. "I—"

"Furthermore"—Aloisa widened her stance as if ready for a fight—"would you have the spine to do it if it needed to be done? Could you shelve your selfish desires for love and sex and romance if your family—if your child—needed you? What do you know of sacrifice?"

I tried to hold my glare but felt like a defiant child. I looked at the wall as I received my tongue lashing.

"Aloisa..." Geir reached for her hand.

"I'm not done!" Aloisa continued. "Your mother saw what the fae blood did to Dagny, so what did she do? She found a way to *manage* it. She found a worldview that allowed her to navigate her clairsentience. You think your mother is cruel? I think she's practical. You think she's crazy? I think she's using the only lens that allowed her to accept that what she was seeing was real while still functioning in the mortal realm. Did you do that, Merit? Did you find a way to accept two realities?"

This time when I looked at her, I saw only my mother. I came from a long line of women who knew how to instill deep wells of fear.

"Told you she was a spitfire," Fauna muttered under her breath.

I released my fists, fingers flexing at my side. "That's not fair."

"What's not fair?" Aloisa demanded.

I set my jaw. "It's not fair to leave everyone in your family to their own devices and hope for the best. Passing psychic abilities through your bloodline...it's like you gave infants tools to build houses and expected them to come back with a mansion. Instead, they beat themselves over the head."

"Is that what I did?" Aloisa threw up her hands. "Because I think I fled to a new country to keep them safe. I think I found a new society, a new language, a way to shelter my family. I think I set them up for success—which, by the way, who are you to complain? Success drips from you, *Merit Finnegan.*" She said the name as if she tasted its falsehood.

"I was born in poverty."

My great-grandmother rolled her eyes with the angst of someone in their teens rather than over a century of years to her name. She squared up against me. "Gods and goddesses, Marlow," she said, dropping the pretense. She knew exactly who I was. "You were poor by wealthy, modern Western standards. I've looked into your lives long before your success, Marlow Esther Thorson. This is one of your most privileged cycles. You had food, shelter, and running water. You are an attractive, talented, smart white woman in a world that's rolled out the red carpet for you. You live in luxury. The cards were stacked in your favor, and your ingratitude is not a pretty color. Play the victim all you want, but no blood of mine walks through the world with that attitude. My daughter didn't, and neither did *her* daughter. The only one I'm disappointed in is *you.*"

Adrenaline crackled through my veins. Her cruel, invalidating words stole the air from my lungs.

"How can you be on Lisbeth's side? She's sided with Heaven when you've literally bound yourself to the pagan Nordes—"

Fauna raised a finger. "Actually, pagan is a—"

"Not now, Fauna!" I returned to my great-grandmother with a snarl. "If you want to wash your hands of familial responsibility, just say that."

She crossed her arms and asked, "What familial responsibility are you taking, Marlow?"

"I..." I planted my feet. An accusatory finger came up in anger as I said, "I am breaking intergenerational curses. I am—"

The room turned to me conspicuously, which gave me pause. I caught Fauna's eyes, her eyebrows lifted in a curious test. She wasn't warning me. In fact, I think she was equally prepared to be offended by whatever I said next, as if I'd gone so far off the rails that even my eccentric companion could no longer laugh off my words. I deflated slightly as I considered the rest of my sentence. I was—what?—banishing the falsehood of the veil? I was choosing the sanity of the mortal realm over my mother's delusions of angels and demons? My life was in shambles. I'd lost Caliban. My career as an author would be in ruins by the time I returned as Merit Finnegan, the doxxed escort, pariah of the publishing community. This was all I had, yet my grandmother was pushing me out of her preternatural embrace.

"They were abusive," I said quietly.

Aloisa was relentless, but my words did have a mitigating effect. She appraised me with a long, slow exhale. The room thrummed with tension until she spoke. "Tell me, Marlow. I want you to picture a child in your arms. Your baby. A soul you created, and one for whom you're responsible. Now let's say you believe at your *core* that this tiny child, your baby, the love of your life, will burn in a lake of sulfur unless it believes in a specific god. Now, if you're convinced that eternal torture is a possibility, is it kind to bow out and let your offspring do whatever they want? If you truly believe your child will be pulled limb from limb until the end of time unless it worships a specific deity—if that's your *core* belief—what would love look like?"

My lips parted, but no sound came out.

"It's not rhetorical. I'm actually asking," she said firmly.

"I'm..." I blinked in disbelief. "I don't know."

She didn't miss a beat. "Because I think it would be loving for her to do *everything* she could to try to get her daughter to accept that deity and go to her version of an afterlife. She might be wrong, but she doesn't know that. All she knows is that she can see angels and demons, and that she loves you. She knows she doesn't want her child to be tormented for eternity. Given the foundations of her perceived reality, she has no other avenue."

I'd never been so lightheaded. I suddenly understood why Fauna had attempted to do me the kindness of drugging me. This was worse than anything I could have fathomed. I swallowed, tears spiking hot and angry at the inner corners of my eyes while I stared at the cold, unfeeling statue of a woman before me.

"Are you saying she wasn't abusive?" I asked.

Her answer was impassive. "I'm saying two things can be true at once, and that's uncomfortable. You don't have to accept or live with abuse. You should distance yourself from it. You should stand on your own feet. But it's a lie to write a narrative wherein your mother doesn't love you. There are several dishonest things about you, Marlow, and they're all tightly wrapped around your victimhood. Now, we came here because we were told you needed aid, but I think I understand the help you need."

Ella perked up from the corner. "But, if your great-granddaughter truly is the Prince's..."

I didn't understand the silencing look Fauna shot in Ella's direction, nor was it in the top ten most distressing things at the moment.

"It hasn't happened yet," Aloisa replied. "There's no reason to believe this life will be any different. And if it is, maybe that's a path for her to forge on her own."

At a loss for words, I reached for Fauna. Her expression went from confused as she took my hand in hers, to kind as she squeezed my fingers in return. Things weren't going our way. But I was not alone.

"Aloisa." There was pain in the word as Geir whispered his partner's voice, akin to a futile plea.

"No," Aloisa said. "This is Marlow's battle. And if she keeps looking at herself as the one who needs saving, she won't learn the lessons she needs to learn. She certainly won't have the spine she needs if all things come to pass. Grow up, Marlow. Be worthy of my genes."

Aloisa took a backward step into the air, vanishing into

nothing. Geir stayed behind in the wake of her disappearance, looking at me with empathetic eyes. "The Prince of Hell? Truly?"

I nodded, but couldn't bring myself to say more. I couldn't feel my legs. I may as well have been standing on mist and clouds. I was glad Aloisa was gone, as I knew I'd begin to cry any minute. Geir seemed to sense it.

"Tough love is her thing," he said.

My ears rang with shock. I answered numbly. "It's my mom's, too."

His frown was understanding, but not apologetic. "Her spirit is half of why I fell for her. And she's quick-tempered, but she's a good person. She has the fire to survive anything, in her human life and in this one. I'm sorry this was your first meeting. For what it's worth, you're both equally right and equally wrong. And I heard what she said. But this is bigger than your mother, or grandmother, or my partner. What you might mean for the realms...we'll be there for you at the end."

Fauna shook her head at my side, and he stopped speaking.

I swallowed down the bubbling tears.

When he spoke again, it was with renewed conviction. "She will show up for you, as will I. You are family, and I'm proud to call you such. You'll never be alone." He clasped my free hand between his again, and I stared into the eyes of a striking man who could have easily been two years my junior, rather than thousands my senior. He was level-headed, he was pretty, and he was kind to me without invalidating his partner.

"It was nice to meet you," I said quietly, knowing it was polite, but I wasn't sure if it was true. He took a backward step into nothing, and I was left staring at the empty space he left behind.

A long, uncomfortable silence stretched between the four of us who remained. At long last, Fauna squeezed my hand and said, "I honestly don't know why I assumed that would go better."

Chapter Twelve

M ORE TEA?"
Fauna might as well have asked me if I wanted to sign over my life savings, jump in the Antarctic Ocean naked, and give a free full-service session to Republican Senator Geoff Christiansen. I could tell from her grimace that she could see the flames behind my eyes before I even started speaking.

"Firstly, absolutely not," I bit. I remained on my feet as I glared at the room. "Secondly, how fucking dare you. Thirdly, what's wrong with you? Fourthly—"

"Yes, we all know you can count very high," Fauna muttered as she swept up my now-cold teacup and carried it to the sink.

Estrid took over. Her face folded into something that almost resembled sympathy. "Well, Aloisa has a reputation for being a hard-ass. She fits in really well for a newcomer. More of a valkyrie than a human, in my opinion."

"Just like her partner." Ella glowed.

I stopped myself from asking something insensitive about Geir and his gender, particularly as he'd impregnated my great-grandmother. I'd studied the healing valkyrie, Eir, ad nauseum. The tales had used feminine pronouns in the Prose Edda, but it was thousands of years out of date. No amount of learning would qualify me to understand his gender better than him.

Besides, he was fae, and I'd spent weeks learning that I didn't know jack shit about life behind the veil. Instead, I asked the only thing that made sense.

"Álfheimr isn't the afterlife. Valhalla, maybe, but humans don't come here when they die."

The three looked at me with amused curiosity. From the kitchen, Fauna shouted, "Please, sweet pea, tell us where humans do or do not go when they die!"

Well, my friend was officially back to her cheerful, if condescending, self.

I wasn't such a stranger to this world that I didn't know when I was on the losing end of a supernatural—err, preternatural?—argument. Rather than double down, I thought of the palm against my forehead and asked, "Was he really Eir?"

Estrid answered for all of us. "Geir? Yes, he was our healer. Very useful in battle."

"We needed him," I said, heart cracking.

Fauna's doe eyes met mine. She nodded as if to say: *The cat's out of the bag. Might as well spill what's left of our secrets.*

I wasted no time speaking my mind. "If we're about to storm an enemy pantheon, we needed a healer." My mouth soured with each word. "If you had prepared me, Fauna, I could have handled things differently. I could have won allies for what we need instead of alienating relatives. You set me up for failure."

Fauna snorted. "She's been aware of you for decades. I seriously doubt one perfectly worded conversation would suddenly win her over."

My temper crackled. "Then why bring her? Why bring either of them?"

"If I told you that I had my reasons, would you trust me?" She sounded sincere. I didn't care.

"Not in the least." Then to the others, I asked, "If we

don't have Eir or Geir or whatever your healer is going by these days, can't other valkyries...?" I flinched as I abandoned my question, remembering the conflation of myth and lore from my studies. Even from the texts, I had no idea what was fact and what was fiction.

Estrid made a face while Ella snickered. I knew immediately this was why Ella liked my portrayal of her partner's people while she did not.

"No," she said tersely. "Valkyries are not healers—Geir was, specifically, when he was going by Eir in a feminine form. What do you know? Grim reaper? Rally cry? Death deity? War god? We belonged to Odin, sent in to fight his battles. We were his warriors, the ones on the frontline, the bloodshed that spared everyone in Ásgard."

"She knows everything just enough to know nothing," Fauna said cheerily from over our shoulders. Any tension she'd carried during our meeting had melted from her. She'd returned to the sunniest version of herself as she bustled about the home that did not belong to her.

"We know when a warrior is worthy to live or die. We chose the slain."

I'd learned as much in undergrad, and had doubled down on my research when writing the first Pantheon novel. *Valkyrie*'s etymological origin was that of two words. *Vair*: the slain. *Kyrja*: chooser. Despite knowing this, I had to ask, "You get to decide who dies?"

She crossed her arms. "I'm qualified. I can hamper enemies or stir those in battle. We identify heroes and champions just as we separate the weak and unworthy. We know who's fit to go on to the afterlife they've earned, should their mortal cycle end."

"So..." I tested my words. "You're a war god, like Anath?"

Her laugh was gruff. "I'm as much like Anath as Fauna is like Echo."

"The Greek nymph?"

Once more, Estrid rolled her shoulders in a half-hearted

expression. "We're the same, and we're not. Compare us at your own risk."

"Is...is Fauna like Eir? Where, I know her true name as something else?"

Ella and Estrid exchanged quick looks. Ella was quick to say, "I'm sure you know that names are something that can't be given out. I'm sure she'll tell you when she's ready."

Fauna reentered the living room with a platter full of snacks. The room clammed up with the stiff unoriginality of sixth graders who'd had their gossip interrupted. Fortunately, Fauna was too busy humming to herself and picking things off the plate that she didn't seem to notice. I wasn't sure how I managed to be surprised that she'd collected everything sweet in the home. I was a little disappointed in myself for expecting anything different from her.

Ella's voice possessed a sympathetic affectation as she asked, "So, since Aloisa and Geir aren't exactly joining our dream team, that means we're down a healing ability and whatever it is his fae-made partner can do. How would you two go about finding two demons—"

"And an angel," I offered, bristling that everyone seemed so willing to disregard Silas's sacrifice.

"—and an angel, if they were taken by Anath to rejoin the Phoenicians?"

The three exchanged a mixed basket of incomprehensible expressions.

"It's been a long time since I've gotten into any trouble. I think I'd very much like to start some shit with the Phoenicians. What about you?" Ella cooed.

"El," Estrid started. Her expression softened at Ella's pout.

"I'm perfectly capable." Ella answered whatever pieces of the question had been left unspoken.

I wondered if that was true. If Ella's true name was Hnoss, then she was the daughter of Freyja, the deity of lust, seduction, and treasure. She was fucking gorgeous, charming as hell, and had a dragon's hoard of jewels to help her defend her title. Still, I didn't know what good that would do us against the Canaanite pantheon.

I allowed them their private exchange, looking about the house while they quietly argued. The gems weren't the only thing in the house that glittered. I regarded the wall leading down a corridor where pointed spears, swords, daggers, and precious metals were mounted. They were certainly well-armed, though I'd expect as much from a valkyrie.

I looked back to Estrid and noted something unmistakably hungry. The distant glaze in her eyes made me think perhaps she was seeing long-dead visions of distant battles. I wondered how long it had been since she'd reveled in the glory of the fight.

"We're battle-ready against demons, angels, fae, mortals, creatures, and parasites. But if we're taking on Anath? We don't have anything for a god," Estrid said, voice worried. She had been crafted by the warring Aesir to find victory in Odin's battles before defecting from the Aesir to live in a realm free of an overlord's commands. She wasn't afraid of a fight. I knew her hesitation was for her partner.

Fauna made a face at the statement. She jutted her thumb toward me before saying, "I had a dagger, but this one left it behind when she got into it with Astarte."

"What dagger?" Estrid asked.

"*Etimas di mori.*"

From across the room, Ella said appreciatively, "Even the gods die."

A tingle went down my spine as I thought of the dagger Azrames had mounted in his apartment—the one Caliban had used to ensure Astarte's claim to me was finished. I hadn't bothered to translate its meaning.

"So, what else can kill a god?" I asked.

They exchanged looks before Ella grinned. She draped across the couch, gripping Fauna's forearm and giving it a squeeze. "Not what...*who*."

Chapter Thirteen

T HE *WHOOSH* CAME WITH NAUSEA, WHIRLING, AND DARKNESS.
I didn't love that Fauna had drugged me to soften
the blow of meeting my great-grandparents. That said, I was
pretty sure I would have preferred being high now. The elfin
city was a distant memory. Gone were the stars dancing upon
the twinkling rapids that wrapped around Álfheimr. There
was no warm, glowing light, no sheer mountain, no skyscrapers or bustling life.

"Help," came my involuntary response. Wind knocked
from my lungs, I stared face-down into my damp, earthy
landing. I could only describe the feeling as thumping onto
the soft, grassy carpet of a haunted cemetery.

"Where are we?" I asked.

"Some friend you are, Fauna," Estrid spat. "Bringing a
human here? They did a shit job sending *you* to protect her.
You lose her Prince, get a major goddess murdered, and have
now dragged her into the goddamn bog. Guardian of grief
and fucking harm if you ask me."

"Knock it off, Ess. This is Hafna," Ella said through
clenched teeth. "Fauna brought us to Hafna."

Fauna said nothing, but I knew the Old Norse word.
Forsaken.

I learned everything I needed to know about the place

from the valkyrie's anger. Warrior, immortal, chooser of the slain, and yet she was horrified at where we'd been taken. I looked at Fauna for answers, but came away with more questions.

Did I know her as well as I thought I did?

A distant, Bible-thumping Lisbeth shouted words about trickster spirits in the recesses of my memory, but I shoved them down.

Lisbeth was wrong.

Fauna was my friend.

Everything would be fine.

I extended my hand for Fauna, and she took it.

The wood, stone, and glass of Ella and Estrid's warm, beautiful home had oozed like paint melting from a canvas; it gave way to the dark, wet field of nightmares. We'd landed on the curving shores of what appeared to be an island in a glass-still lake. I searched for the distant banks for only a moment, as the perfectly still obsidian reflection of the watery surface between us and the mainland was too unsettling to look at for long.

The only path forward was in.

If the thick fog, the squish of the marsh, the dead trees, and the black water weren't terrifying enough, Fauna's change in demeanor filled in the gaps. She was the single most dauntlessly chaotic creature in all of the realms, yet she'd grown quiet. Not just quiet, but on edge.

She tightened her grasp on me, looping her arm through mine as mud swallowed our feet, urging us forward as we trailed behind the others. If it weren't for the occasional hum of insects or flutter of large, dark birds, I would think there was nothing here at all. Ella and Estrid hadn't spoken in fifteen minutes. Ella rose from the marsh with hands and forearms so black with mud that she might have been wearing silken, elbow-high gloves. Her dress was impractical, but she'd hiked the fabric to her hip and let the mud swallow her naked calves, darkening her up to the knees with silt and muck.

I wasn't sure how anyone knew where they were going, but Estrid stopped at a particularly large femur bone and muttered that we must be headed in the right direction. I looked to Fauna for confirmation, but she didn't meet my eyes. Her gaze remained fixed on the pair before her.

Through the mist I heard a gentle splash, almost like a fish jumping out of water. The prolonged slurping sound that followed told me that I was not hearing a fish.

Anxiety slithered slowly through me, spreading like a poison from my spine into my limbs. "Fauna," I whispered, unable to keep the quiver from my voice. "I don't think I should be here."

"You'll be fine," she said back, voice hushed.

She wasn't convincing.

Our presence in this swamp was my fault. If it weren't for my yelling match with Aloisa, we would have had Geir and his gifts of healing on our side. I wasn't exactly sure how their assistance would have helped us with Caliban, Azrames, and Silas, but then again, it seemed moot to ask. If my misfit team wanted a healer, it stood to reason they anticipated physical warfare. And yet, he said they'd be there at the end.

I supposed a healer would be useful if this miserable mission ended in our death.

Etimas di mori. The god-killer.

If we couldn't play defense and revive ourselves during battle, we'd need one hell of a strong offense. Despite the glittering array of weapons, we possessed nothing that could stand against Anath. It had been Ella who had said that we should pay a visit to Fenrir.

I had blanched. "The apocalypse dog?"

Fauna's hand had flown to her mouth as she choked on a laugh. "Oh my gods and goddesses, I'm never calling him anything else."

My ears had hummed. "Did a god and goddess really give birth to a wolf?"

Fauna had waved away the question. "Some say she's the

mother. Reliable translations say she's the *keeper*. I guess it depends on whose abhorrent mistranslation you cling to. But he's who we need right now."

Ella made a sympathetic face now. "It won't be easy. But, if anyone can do it..."

Yes, I knew Fenrir's lore. I'd used his story in my first Pantheon novel, albeit as a rather creative adaptation. Often accredited as the love child of Loki and Angrboda, Fenrir was a dark, mighty wolf so powerful that he'd been predicted not only to cause Odin's death, but to bring about Ragnarök— the end of the world. Fenrir had two siblings that Odin had similarly mistreated. A sister named Hel who Odin had dropped into the depths of the realm of the Underworld, and a brother who he'd hurled into the sea. Meanwhile, Fenrir had been tricked into being tethered by the gods to keep the nine realms safe from his jaws.

"Why would he help us?" I asked incredulously.

Estrid found this question particularly amusing. Her combat boots made a sickening, slurping sound as she freed her foot from the marsh only to plunge it into the next step. "Are you serious? Gods ruined his life. He was designed to tear a hole through the fabric of reality and bring about the end of the world."

"And that's reassuring?!" I demanded.

"He'll join forces with the enemies of the gods in power," Fauna said, quiet but certain.

"Not *these* gods! Not Hell! Not the Phoenicians!" I struggled to keep myself from pacing. I wasn't sure why I was trying to talk three Nordes out of this decision. I certainly didn't know more about it than them, and yet, something told me that immortality made them a bit more liberal with their choices.

"To stick it to the man," Fauna clarified. "Fenrir was powerful, but not evil. He lived peacefully with everyone for a long time, but he just kept getting bigger and stronger. They were afraid of his potential. Now he's been tied up on the marshy island of Hafna long enough to develop quite the grudge. The gods turned him into what will undoubtedly be a self-fulfilling prophecy. He'll get to be the fabled *Twilight of the Gods* at long last."

I knew this story. Gleipnir and Tyr had worked together to secure Fenrir until the end of time. I wasn't sure how a human, a treasure goddess, a valkyrie, and some forest fae who loved Sour Patch Kids and *Rick and Morty* were meant to unbind him.

Fauna knew me well enough by now to expect a litany of questions. I faced her as I asked, "And if we free him? What about when we're done with Anath? He's not going to wander willingly back into his special prison made of chains forged from cat spit and fish's breath or whatever."

"It was bird spit, not cat spit."

She was right. I'd had the main character in *A Night of Runes* collect the chain's six ingredients. The roots of a mountain, a bear's sensibility, the beard of a woman, the sound of a cat's step, a fish's breath, and a bird's spittle. I'd used each ingredient as a riddle that the character had to crack to understand its true meaning, since none of those things truly existed.

"How would we break a chain that he can't break?" I asked.

Ella plucked a thin knife from the lacy garter securing the weapon to her upper thigh. "It's useless against a god, but quite effective against magical items. It's one of my favorite treasures. I'd guess Fenrir would be glad just to have the chain off his neck."

"You have a god-killer!" I gasped, not bothering to hide my surprise. "Could you—"

Estrid cut me off. "God-killing is two-fold. If you want them to stay dead, it has to be by both some*one* and some*thing* that can kill gods. If a human has a god-killing bullet, they'll buy themselves time. A temporary death, at best. If a god has a standard steel sword, they might behead another god, but once again, they've only bought themselves time. Permanent death requires both the object and subject to be qualified."

"So…" I looked at Hnoss, the seductress, the goddess of precious treasure. Of course, she'd have a few things up her sleeve—or silky dress, rather. "Ella could kill him?"

Her sympathetic smile dripped with apology. "On paper? I guess so. In practicality? I'm…Well…Combat isn't my thing."

I looked between Estrid and Fauna. "And no one else has cut him free?"

"We'll make a deal," Ella said brightly, drawing the attention away from her comrades. She steered the conversation forward, presumably to soothe Estrid's worries about bringing her into such a dangerous situation.

"Fauna?" I asked. "Is this how we free Caliban? Are we sure…" I stopped myself, as I didn't know what I was asking. Was I sure he was worth the end of the world? Yes, I was. Was I sure he was worth the danger? Yes, I was. Were we sure Fenrir would work with us? Well, no, that part was a gamble, but it was one I was willing to take.

Fauna remained nonverbal, which did nothing to soothe my nerves.

I sucked in the misty air, trembling at the odd flavor it left on my tongue. It wasn't raining, but the dampness stuck my hair to my face and my clothes to my body until I shivered against the chill. A snap drew my attention sharply to the right. Ella and Estrid stopped mid-step. I wasn't sure what could possibly be brittle enough to snap in a climate so damp until I began to eye the branches dotting the marshlands and noticed the smooth, rounded ends intended for joints and sockets.

Fauna tightened her grip on my arm, which was anything but reassuring.

I wished they'd left me in Álfheimr.

"Maybe there's another way," I said quietly. "If you waste resources protecting me because I'm a fleshy, powerless human, then I'm to blame for Caliban staying with the Phoenicians. I could end our resistance effort before it gets off the ground. I could be the reason Azrames dies. I'm useless. I'm *worse* than useless. I'm a liability."

"Don't be a coward," Fauna hissed.

"Why not? This seems like a perfectly reasonable time to be cowardly."

Estrid waved for us to stop talking, which made me aware of how silent the marsh had grown. No longer could I hear the buzzing of gnats or cawing of crows, nothing that might lead us to believe anything else lived on the island. The only sound was the sharp, scraping ring as Estrid slowly unsheathed her sword. Beside her, Ella plucked the diamond shield from her back and lowered it in front of us. Ella may not have had experience with swordplay, nor Estrid the ability to wield both sword and shield simultaneously as the fabled shield-maidens, but together, they were an unstoppable pair.

Uneasiness leached into me as if the mud had been laced with physical dread. My imagination grappled with the nightmares that could be lurking in the mist, but between the undead armies of Norse mythology and the frost giants of Jötunheimr, I was confident that anything that had Ella and Estrid on high alert was not something I wanted to meet. Cold sweat joined the fog that beaded on my forehead, trickling down my face, barely missing the open mouth that struggled to pant in short, shallow breaths. I blinked rapidly through the thick, white cloud but saw nothing. Ella and Estrid remained at the ready.

And we waited.

And waited.

Estrid lowered her sword slightly, relaxing her posture. I continued to stare at the back of her head, comforted slightly at how she released her shoulders and how her partner's stance softened in response. Ella muttered something to her, but I couldn't make out her statement. Their words were lost as sound fell away. Time slowed as I turned to look over my shoulder. My eyes barely had time to widen; I didn't have time to scream.

Fur, teeth, snarling, fear, horror.

I could scarcely react as the wolf pounced.

Before breathing, before thinking, before two brain cells had a chance to rub together, I'd raised my free hand and shoved Fauna as hard as I could out of the lunging wolf's path. She hit the wet ground with a thwack the moment the creature connected with my chest. Sharp claws, bared teeth, black glistening eyes, and wet, gray fur covered me as I disappeared beneath the creature. I barely felt its paws on me before my head hit the ground, air escaping my lungs.

I heard a scream.

The ring of metal.

A snarl.

The attack was upon us before I understood what was happening.

Panic and adrenaline tasted like copper on the back of my tongue. I gasped for air as a hand flew to my shoulder. My fingers came back red and sticky with blood, seeing the evidence of a goring bite before the wave of pain hit me. I tried to move my arm but couldn't. I had to act. I had to move. I had to run.

I whipped my head up at the valkyrie's rallying cry to see Estrid swing her shield and knock the wolf from its advance. The wood connected with the broad side of the beast's body in time to send it flying. She cried out again to antagonize the wolf as it slid across the marshy soil. Rather than advance, it planted its feet and threw back its head in a howl.

My eyes widened in panic as I silently begged Ella and her diamond shield—whether for the practicality of its remarkable durability or the beauty of its shine—or Estrid with her power for war to do something.

Ella moved her shield to protect both her and Estrid, and I heard a scream once more.

Fauna.

I clutched my shoulder and scrambled onto my knees to see her muddied shape still on the ground, holding out her hands in opposite directions. She wasn't screaming in fear. She was crying out for Estrid to stop.

Estrid barely skidded to a halt in time for her to shift her gaze to the wolf.

Fauna said something to it, but I couldn't understand what.

The wolf's hackles remained up. It continued its low, unrelenting groan as she repeated herself more forcefully.

"Stand *down*," she commanded. It wasn't alone. She looked from the wolf who'd led the charge to the array of bared teeth, the low rumble of growls, the many glittering eyes of a bloodthirsty pack. She'd slid through the muck, and it dripped from her hands, arms, and hair with the slow ooze of tar. She didn't move a muscle as she stared at the alpha wolf.

I was in the park all over again. We'd been two women for all the world knew, helpless and alone in the dark, when nature itself had sprung into action to defend us. I pictured the overturned earth, the brand-new oak, the bloodcurdling screams, the damp, blood-soaked soil, and the eviscerated security guard, lost forever to the wrath of a forest deity.

My forest deity.

The wild pack demonstrated more self-preservation than the guard.

With an aggressive huff, the wolf shook off her command as if she'd spritzed it in the face with water. There were so many. An ink-black wolf. A forest-brown wolf. One with the gray and fawn coloring of a coyote.

"Stop!" she said to the pack through gritted teeth.

The wolves didn't move.

"Estrid," Fauna snapped, "put away your sword."

"But—"

"Put it away!"

I couldn't believe what I was seeing. With cold command, she ordered the valkyrie and wild beast alike. Her teeth were bared, making her lovely features as lupine as the animals that stalked us.

I didn't mean to make a noise, but one escaped my lips as a fresh wave of pain hit me.

"Estrid," Fauna directed, jerking her chin toward me, "wrap her up."

Estrid nodded and came to my side, fetching things from her bag—the fabled valkyrie deeming me worthy of her mercy on the battlefield. She eased my arm from the jacket and wrapped my shoulder with the grace and speed of someone who had centuries of practice, but I saw none of it. I couldn't take my eyes off Fauna.

"Now," Fauna said to the wolves as she got to her feet, "take us to Fenrir."

The largest of the wolves huffed again, almost like a sneeze.

"It wasn't a request," she growled, voice dripping with hostility.

My eyes left the exchange long enough to beg Estrid to explain. My forehead creased, brows knitting, mouth opened in shock and pain as I asked, "What's happening?"

I groaned against the pain as she popped my shoulder back into its socket.

"Do you really not know who she is?" Estrid asked, voice ripe with surprise. She kept her question low enough so as not to disrupt the standoff happening only paces away.

I could only shake my head.

"The wild is hers to command," Ella supplied. I awaited further explanation that never came.

The elfin nymph, delicate features obscured by dark smears of silt and grime, held the wolves at bay through sheer force of will alone. My heart dropped into my stomach as I watched the chaotic, licorice-eating smartass force the pack to bow at her feet. Ella had returned her diamond shield to where it belonged on her back. Estrid had fallen into line at Fauna's order. It was with awe and dismay and shock and confusion that I realized this friend, this companion, this guardian who'd stepped into my life from the shadows was someone I didn't know at all.

I winced in pain again as Estrid tightened my bandages, Fauna's words ringing through my memories from before we'd left the mortal realm.

You think they're going to send a nobody to watch the Prince's human? she'd said, laughing as she'd taken my hand to guide me into the unknown. *I'm no more of a nobody than you are. And you, Marlow-Merit-Maribelle, are not a nobody.*

Chapter Fourteen

THE WOLVES LED THE WAY WITH FAUNA AS THEIR MASTER, leashed with an invisible tether. We trailed behind as we trudged through the sickening slurps and loamy soil of the marsh. I didn't miss the polished bones scattered throughout our path, but I was no longer afraid. I did wonder what sort of prey was large enough to sustain a wolf pack, but then again, far stranger things had happened today than the ecosystem of a marsh lake.

After all, we were here to meet with a god-killer.

Estrid alone could famously fight man or fae.

Fauna could handle whatever nature threw our way.

Hafna's fog did not lift. Instead, we remained in the dense cloud, a gray-white world free from sun or sky or anything that could indicate the passage of time. Only the ache in my lungs, the burn of my thighs as my legs battled the ground with each and every step, and the carnation-red bloom through the bandages of my injured shoulder confirmed that we'd been walking for a long, long time.

The crumbling of ancient mountains, the crack of thunder, the rumble of earthquakes, the splintering of frozen lakes filled me as a single question pierced the fog.

"Who disturbs me?"

I wasn't sure what stopped first—my heart, or my breathing. The party around me froze. I caught the smallest flick of

Fauna's fingers as she released the pack. They scrambled free like mice before a cat.

Fauna took three silent steps backward until she was at my side. Slipping an arm behind me, she planted her hand on my lower back and urged me ahead of the group.

"What—"

"Tell him," she whispered.

Tell who? I wanted to demand. I saw nothing through the thick wall of white. The voice came from everywhere and nowhere. I knew in my core that it belonged to Fenrir.

The drugs had loosened my tongue as I spilled our motives to Ella, Estrid, and my ancestors. Telling the bringer of Ragnarök why I'd trudged through Hafna's bog to find him was another matter entirely.

"I…" I stammered, looking at Fauna with wide, pleading eyes. I shot a look over my shoulder at Ella and Estrid, but they gave me tight, urgent looks to hurry. I swallowed as I turned my face forward. Fauna gave me another short shove, and as if the hand forced the message from my diaphragm and out of my mouth, the words escaped me. "We need help killing a god," I said.

A low chuckle.

I tried again, sweat and fear and adrenaline spiking me like the bites of thousands of ants. I felt them on every part of me, pinching me, wounding me, filling me. I was worried my heart would catch in my throat and I'd choke on its flutter before I could say what needed to be said. "I'm Merit. And I'm…well, I suppose I'm positioning myself against a couple gods at the moment."

It was the least convincing sentence in the history of mortal languages. I was fucking up. I was dropping the ball. Gods and goddesses, I didn't know what to do, what to say, how to pull myself together to address someone—or some*thing*—so ancient, so worthy, so omnipotent. I wished Fauna would take over, that she'd speak over me as she so often did. But no. She left this to me.

122

The pause that followed contained an energetic charge, but not of disapproval. I could feel curiosity as it tingled through the mist.

"I'm…" I didn't know how to say what I was. It felt hollow on my lips. I'd only heard it said by others, but I knew the weight it carried. "I'm the Prince of Hell's human."

The low, deep voice growled, "Oh?"

I couldn't fully comprehend why the words mattered, but they elicited the desired reaction. Maybe everyone wanted to garner favor with a powerful realm. Perhaps they all saw Caliban's mention as a reason to hasten their claims or rush my allegiances, as had Silas and Fauna, in their own ways. Whatever it was, no one responded to the statement with neutrality.

"There's more," I swallowed. "The king of Heaven set out to have me bond with an angel. He intended to turn the war tide in their favor, against Hell. And one thing led to another and…I'm more or less responsible for the death of Astarte. Now her sister, Anath, has the Prince."

"So," said the voice, deep as the trenches at the bottom of the sea, "you've made enemies of gods from two realms, and you seek me because you'd like to make enemies of three?"

I looked at Fauna.

"The time has come," Fauna said to the beast beyond the mist. "Listen to her."

At my side, Ella nodded with hopeful encouragement for me to continue.

"I'm Nordic," I said uncertainly. "Partly. It's why I'm here. It's why Fauna—" I was making it worse. I had no idea what I was saying. I had no idea what to say to a god so powerful that he'd made Odin tremble to bring about the Twilight of the Gods, as they'd called it. "I have no qualms with the Nordes. To be honest, I don't even hate the Phoenician gods, or the god of Heaven. But Astarte and Anath kept a god—Dagon—captive for hundreds of years to serve their agenda."

A low snarl emanated from the dense, white void.

I pressed on. "The god of Heaven has attempted to use me as a pawn in his war, and the angels who serve him have no say in their lives. We're slaves to their whims and agendas. Now the one I love is in the Phoenician realm because he stood against the will of a powerful deity. I just don't believe gods should be able to make choices on behalf of others without their consent."

"That, human," said the voice, "is how I feel precisely."

"Will you help me?"

The dense cloud thrummed with tension while I waited for his answer.

"You'll cut me free?"

"I will," I said. I didn't know much of Ella's precious knife, but if she believed the treasure could cut the chain, then I trusted her judgment.

"And you have a plan, human? Or have you come to waste my time?"

I looked over my shoulder toward Fauna, but saw only mist. "I have something better than a plan. I have spite, fire, motive, and a powerful team."

"Why should I not take my freedom and run from those who might capture me once more?" he asked. "What would I get in return for aiding you?"

After a long pause, I landed on the only answer that made sense to me. A tiny smile tugged at the corner of my mouth as the word filled me. It tingled in my fingertips, dancing on the tip of my tongue as I realized that I did not want to make a deal. I didn't want to return Fenrir to this marshy purgatory. I didn't want to give him anything that he himself didn't want.

Smile still on my face, I offered a single word.

"Anarchy."

✦

Finding Fenrir was the hardest part. It had been arduous, terrifying, and had left me with a throbbing wound to the shoulder. As Geir had not joined our party, blood trickled freely from where I'd been gored by the wolf. My companions remained deathly still as I outlined the terms of our agreement while skirting the binding oaths of the immortal. I would set the wolf of Ragnarök free. What he did with his liberation was none of my business.

Ella exhaled slowly as she stepped into the cloud bank and was swallowed by its opaque walls. Seconds stretched into minutes without a sound. I wasn't sure how long I was supposed to wait before I asked Fauna or Estrid what we needed to do.

A small grunt, the ring of metal striking metal, and a sharp growl cut through the air. I blinked rapidly as my eyes adjusted, almost as if I'd been staring at static for far too long. The sun made a distant, muddied appearance. It grew clearer with every passing moment as the mist thinned, evaporating as it leached from the island and washed over the dark lake that surrounded us on all sides.

As the fog disappeared, I craned my neck, expecting to see a wolf the size of a mountain. The large shape before me was not that of an animal, but an enormous boulder. I heard metal against rock and caught the glint of something as the sun pierced through at long last.

I saw Ella. I saw a rock. I saw the silver-white gleam of the tether that had contained the god-killer. But I scanned the space in search of a giant who was nowhere to be seen.

Prancing toward me over the marsh was a dog wagging its tail.

Not a titan, as I knew one.

Not a monster.

Not even a wolf.

The long black and reddish coat of a large wild dog caught in the sunlight. Its sable, shepherd-like tail trailed behind it. It took a seat in front of me and looked up at me with wickedly deep, wise eyes. I looked away from it only long enough to see that, as the fog fully lifted, I was in the empty, marshy wilds with no other beast to be seen—only green clumps of grass, sitting water, clusters of gnats, and the white shapes of long-dead trees.

The beautiful dog looked at Fauna and huffed before turning his attention to me.

"Fenrir?" I barely breathed his name.

Without opening its mouth, it said, "Shall we get started?"

Chapter Fifteen

HEAT, DIRT, AND NIGHTLIFE WERE AN OVERPOWERING contrast to the island's marsh or Álfheimr's cool mountain air. This was the day that never ended. Going from a fantastical realm to a miserable island to a bustling human city was its own form of disorienting torture. My outfit—the same from my departure of my very human apartment only hours prior, now with fresh bog stains and evidence of dried blood—did not fit the ambience.

"Fenrir?" I whispered his name. The shaggy dog's nails clicked against the pavement ahead of me. He did not turn. "Shouldn't we be realm hopping? I have urgent business with the Phoenicians, and—"

Into my mind, he replied, "Who is so unwise that they would seek help, then disregard the aid that is offered?"

Gods, how I missed the days when I had been able to write this off as insanity.

I was no weather professional, but I was familiar enough with the Mediterranean region to know we were baking in eighty- to ninety-degree temperatures. The sidewalk slowly released the day's heat, radiating from the dusty cement and soaking my clothes with sweat as we walked. Still, I hadn't been able to get warm since Fauna had told me who we were going to visit.

"People are staring." I cast a glance at the goose bumps running from my elbow to my shoulder.

"Of course, they're staring!" Fauna flipped her hair over her shoulder as she kept pace beside me. She managed to possess an effortless sense of belonging everywhere she went, whether she was in the pits of Hell, the arts district of my hometown, the Nordic city, or the well-lit paths of metropolitan Greece. I'd only been to Athens once, and it had been with a client. We'd avoided the tourist traps in favor of the islands with his yacht. I'd eaten calamari and done my best to maintain the appearance of eye contact while I'd unfocused my gaze to look through his skull and at the horizon beyond. Maladaptive daydreaming during my client sessions had done wonders for my future as an author.

This adventure would be a bit more pedestrian than our bloodied, marshy trek through the bog to set Fenrir free.

We'd had the time to wash and change at Ella and Estrid's, so Fauna had returned to her normal sparkly self. Between Estrid's muscular frame and Ella's ample bosom, their clothes hadn't fit either of us. Regardless, Fauna had a knack for tying and cutting things. She'd smeared a sparkly paste into my wounds, then rewrapped them in clean bandages before knotting the white tunic at my midriff. My shoulder no longer hurt. I had a feeling that by the time I was able to shower and wash for the night, the gory evidence of the wolf attack would be little more than shallow pink memories.

She looked over her shoulder as she continued her purposeful walk under the metropolitan lights of Athens. Her exasperation was heavy as she responded to my exclamation with, "You're a famous author standing next to a movie star on a walk with a terrifying off-leash pet. This is your role. Be an immersion actor. Own it. Move forward."

I half expected Fenrir to look back at me, but he did not. He trotted a half step ahead of me as if he were a well-trained show dog, rather than a powerful horseman of the apocalypse. The blacks and browns of his glossy coat caught in the

128

amber glow each time we stepped from the shadow and into a new pool of lamplight. His nails tapped gently against the sidewalk as we made our way forward down the late-night streets of the Grecian capital.

Estrid and Ella had opted not to join us.

The conversation that had followed in the marsh had been far more stressful than Fauna and her devil-may-care attitude had ever led me to believe. Given the couple's willingness to join and Fauna's nonchalance, I'd been under the supposition that we were off to start a minor skirmish. They'd asked so few questions. They'd been so willing. They'd given me no further inclination as to the weight of my actions. It wasn't until Fenrir was freed and the deal was made that Fauna had uttered four chilling words.

"The Phoenicians have allies."

My hands dripped red with Astarte and Jessabelle's blood. Perhaps her treatment of Dagon might mean Astarte's death would not be openly mourned. Still, stepping into the Phoenician realm to take on their remaining goddess of war—Baal's only living partner after the slaughter on Bellfield soil—would surely not be taken lightly. Not only would we be taking the battle to them, but our arrival would be just cause for the allegiances they'd forged over thousands of years to answer their battle cry.

"They do," Fenrir had replied. "The enemy of my enemy is my friend."

"And…" I'd dared, "Every pantheon has a bone to pick with monotheism."

When I'd asked Fauna why she hadn't told me about the Phoenician's allies, she'd given me a familiar speech about the uselessness of knowledge. She'd asked quite pointedly, "Would it change what needs to be done? No? Then why tell you?"

Understanding that I was not simply causing an upset in the largely-ignored Canaanite pantheon, but that the act of interceding on behalf of Caliban and Azrames—and Silas, depending on our mood—would be declaring open war with anyone who'd ever forged an allegiance with the Phoenicians, made me acutely aware that we were not yet prepared for the task at hand. We had one more stop to make before we were ready to meet the Phoenicians.

I looked between the domed tops of the sand-colored buildings that shared the block with slick architecture and the small grassy park that preserved what remained of a pocked ruin. We were too far from the ocean for me to see it, but I could still smell the salt on the damp night air. Between the dust, the city smells, and the heat, I could barely detect Fauna's fresh scent. I narrowed my eyes at her.

"You're not a movie star."

She rolled her eyes and shoved her hands into her the pockets of her billowy pants. "Then they're staring at you because it's nearly midnight, you're an American idiot, and you're bothering them. What do you want from me?"

"How much further?" I wished I had GPS access, but my pockets were woefully empty. I grumbled at having lost yet another phone. If I was going to leave an expensive piece of electronic equipment behind every time I jumped realms, I'd need to start buying cheap burners or upgrade to an Apple watch.

She made a face. "I haven't been to Athens in two hundred years. Ask Fenrir. He seems to be leading the charge."

Fenrir looked over his shoulder at that to huff out an unimpressed breath of air.

I spoke for him. "Fenrir has been chained to a rock since before you were born."

"A little after I was born, actually."

"Great, you're old. That's really helpful, Fauna. All the more reason for him to be leading instead of you. I never follow senior citizens." My face bunched into a frown as I redirected my attention. "Fenrir, how do you know where we're going?"

He didn't look over his shoulder, nor did he open his

jaws as he used whatever mind-to-mind skill he'd used in the marsh. "My nose, of course."

I glanced around the street at the well-dressed humans who leaned against the walls to smoke, but they didn't balk like people who'd heard an animal speak. They simply looked horrified that a scary dog lacked a leash. We were probably violating numerous laws, but I certainly wasn't going to be the one to suggest to Fenrir step into a leash after a lifetime of shackles. I'd be happier to be written up and pay the fine than to ask the being so powerful that he'd threatened Odin's very existence to put on a collar.

We paused briefly at an intersection. Artificially planted skinny palms lined the streets. The alleys between ancient, crumbling stones had been filled in with clean concrete, glass, and steel. Chairs had been stacked upon tables for the night. Shutters were closed. Canvas awnings had withdrawn for the moonlight to filter through the amber glow of modern thirty-foot streetlights.

"It's a left here," Fauna said. A horn blared behind her as city life scuttled about in its loosely organized chaos. I didn't know the country and its emergency noises well enough to understand whether I was hearing a fire siren or ambulance. If I was lucky, one of them was coming to haul me away and spare me from whatever it was she had to say next.

"How do you know?"

She pointed at the sign.

"You read Greek?" I asked, genuinely surprised. In one of our first meetings, Fauna had spoken to me in numerous Scandinavian languages. I'd expected her knowledge to spread through everything with Germanic ties. The letters on the bright blue sign with white lettering above were Hellenic in origin.

"Of course, I read Greek," she scoffed. "You think I'm going to be alive forever and not pick up a thing or two?"

"I guess, but—"

"I even speak Klingon."

"You do not."

"*HIja'.*"

I blinked at her once again in the late-night intersection, seeing her red-and-white freckles, her curious bohemian clothes, and her coy smile as if she were the mud-covered nymph, teeth gritted, holding wolves, valkyries, and warriors at bay.

"Who *are* you?"

She smiled the same happy, toothy grin I'd seen between handfuls of sweets, the fae who'd punched all of the buttons in my car, the one who'd jumped into Azrames's arms, the one who'd held my hair and comforted me as I cried in the shower.

"Life's comfier when you can box people in, isn't it?"

We took a left and began the slow process of cresting a hill. My feet throbbed from the walk. I wanted to ask why we hadn't stepped into a space closer to our destination, but I'd learned from Azrames when he'd forced us to pop into Bellfield forty-five minutes from the hotel. We couldn't risk humans seeing us appear out of nowhere. Fauna had presumably picked the closest empty park for our transition between realms. Though I caught glimpses of the rocky outcropping of the hilltop acropolis between buildings, I had no idea whether we were headed to the ancient monuments or just in their general direction, and it didn't seem polite to question Fenrir's ability to lead.

Fauna's sugar addiction hadn't forced us to make any pit stops, nor had Fenrir so much as requested a drop of water since we began our journey. I'd hoped one of them would give me an excuse to gather my thoughts, but they were too mission focused to bother with mortal comforts. The precipitous cliffs loomed ahead with a sense of foreboding. I was already sweating through the heat of the Mediterranean night. The stress-induced dry mouth and wet palms weren't helping.

"Is there anything I should know before we get there?" I asked.

"I think you know most of it," Fauna said. "Your Pantheon books did better with the Greeks than with the Nordes. They make their history a lot more available, so it's harder to fuck up."

"And..." I swallowed, trying to summon saliva. It failed me as I looked between Fauna and Fenrir. "You have a good relationship with them?"

She made a sound. "No. I've met her...once? Maybe? Fenrir, have you met either of them?"

"I have not," he responded calmly. "I've been chained to a boulder."

"Am I still recruiting them to help me with my doxxer?" I ask, testing the edges of Fauna's temper.

The anger did not return. Her voice remained light as she said, "No. Now we're simply following Ella and Estrid's guidance on the next best step."

Lies, of course, but important ones. Our loophole around Fauna's promise to her fae informant was wrapped in my intoxicated slip of the tongue. Our plans to realm hop behind enemy lines hadn't been calls to action, but organic side quests born after my farcical spiel about needing a valkyrie and a treasure goddess to assassinate some whorephobic senator. I still didn't fully comprehend the limits of the fae and their oaths, but my lesson on immortals and their bonds had been earned through blood and tears. I would go on allowing Fauna to lead the dance of how much we could safely say to anyone else we happen to meet so that her word remained unbroken, even if that meant spinning verbal propaganda when no one appeared to be listening.

I controlled a tiny, shaky breath through my teeth as I said, "And, why do you—why do Ella and Estrid, I mean— think these two will help us?"

She snorted. "We have a few pretty convincing reasons on our side. The least of which is: Aphrodite hates Astarte. She has for thousands of years—mostly because of the popular international lore that Aphrodite was *based* on Astarte. Talk about cultural erasure on both ends."

I shook my head uselessly. "What does that have to do with the couple we're going to see?"

Fauna twisted her hair into a spiral and tucked the loop in on itself in a secure knot to get the heat off her neck. She shrugged. "I bring her up because the Greeks and the Phoenicians haven't been poised to be buddies, right? It helps our cause that there's already this seed of dissent between the two realms."

I understood this qualm. Though the Phoenician gods came from the cradle of civilization and were among the earliest known gods, their popularity had been usurped and conflated with their Greek and Roman counterparts. It was bound to wound the ego.

"The Hellenic pantheon is powerful enough to turn their noses up at pretty much everyone, and they're pretty happy with the way things are in the world," Fauna said. "Most of them have no incentive to meddle. They're alive and well in the public eye whether they remain in their realm or set up shop among mortals. They have literature, media, practitioners; you name it."

"I understand why Astarte opened some prestigious fertility clinic," I said. "She found a way to remain powerful and relevant when her temples were abandoned and worship ran dry. But why would any of the Greeks need to be topside?"

Fauna lifted a shoulder. "For shits and giggles. Eternity is long. Monotony is boring. Newness is one hell of a drug. But given their content status, if you want Grecian help, you're going to need someone in a Fenrir situation."

Fenrir glared over his shoulder this time. He narrowed his eyes at Fauna rather unmistakably before returning his large, dark gaze to the sidewalk. I followed his line of sight to see the Parthenon-style structure and its incredible pillars that bloomed into view at the end of the street. We'd almost reached the end of our journey.

Sticking up for Fenrir, I said, "I hardly think what happened to these two can be compared to what Odin did to Fenrir."

"Thank you, human," Fenrir replied, front-facing once more.

She chewed on her lip. "I guess that's fair. Regardless, these two have some…common goals with Fenrir."

I wasn't sure what the dreaded wolf of Ragnarök could share with two exceptionally prominent Greeks, but I doubted it was anything pleasant. I wished I had something to do with my hands. It felt childish to twist the fabric of my shirt, but I had so much nervous energy and nowhere to put it. It had been terrifying enough to make it through the marshes and find Fenrir. Each new step felt like a nail in Caliban and Azrames's coffin. "I get that we can't go into the Phoenician realm poised to fail, but I'm struggling to understand why you think this is a good idea."

Fenrir made a sound I could only describe as snorting. "You do understand. You know exactly why they'll help, just as you knew why I would help. I don't care who in the Nordic pantheon has hurt me or helped me. I'm here for the end. Nothing more."

My blood cooled ever so slightly as I thought of the word that had coursed through me when I'd known precisely what Fenrir had wanted. I had known at my core the only deal that would win him to my side.

Fenrir thirsted for rebellion like it was water in the desert.

City lights blinded me. I cast my gaze to the side, watching dots of red and yellow disappear as they dotted the hills with distant shimmers. I shook my head. "But it's different…"

"Is it?"

I trembled as I looked at Fauna for answers, but she wouldn't meet my eyes. The large, long-haired dog continued

135

its forward path. I wasn't too dumb to get what he was saying, but I was left stunned by his implication.

We kept the cliffs on our left as we swung wide toward what appeared to be an enormous estate. If I hadn't been told otherwise, I would have thought we were approaching an embassy, or some brand of well-guarded political estate. I cast another glance at the slowly disintegrating rock wall, knowing the lore that filled the buildings resting on its top.

No one had mentioned the lore that resided slightly off to its side.

I finally argued, "It's not alike at all. That's not what these two do! That's not what they're known for. Greek mythology doesn't have *end of the world* lore in the same way. The Greeks just have some loose prophecy that the gates will be thrown open to—"

"To their Underworld," finished Fenrir just as we reached the base of the enormous structure. My heart rate had steadily increased with every step that drew us closer to our destination—the largest private museum in Greece. Enormous flowering gardens, statues, and fountains lined the outdoors for several blocks in all directions. The inside boasted the most pristine collection of artifacts of the afterlife from around the world. "And who guards the Underworld?"

We mounted the steps and began the climb to enter the building. Fenrir slowed slightly until I led the pack as we closed the gap between ourselves and the after-hours museum. I knew the door would be locked but extended my fingers toward the vertical steel bar anyway. Before I had a chance to wrap my fingers around the cylinder, it swung outward, stopping me in my tracks.

I froze as a tall figure leaned against the door. Despite the floodlights illuminating the museum's exterior, nothing refracted in his dark eyes. I could see very little aside from the black hair, the square jaw, and the strong build of the man who towered before me. The shadow seemed to pool around him, as if caressing him with its concealing waves. I didn't have to wait for an introduction to know exactly who stood before me.

"We've been waiting for you," came the deep, smiling voice.

I suppressed a chill as I spoke his name.

"Hades."

Chapter Sixteen

S O, THIS IS THE BRIDE OF HELL?" CAME A FLOWERY, FEMININE voice.

I gawked at a room fit for godly opulence and the after-hours executive suite of someone who worked somewhere between Wall Street and a black-market antiquities dealership. I gripped the edges of the stone table—perhaps the only gray, ageless writing surface in the modern, high-stakes business office. The speaker wasn't quite the billionaire's trophy wife that the media had led me to expect from these environments. She looked like the most gorgeous attendee at Burning Man.

The breezy, captivating hippie was the only thing capable of tearing my eyes from the crooked smirk of the masculine figure before me. Her voice wafted musically through the tasteful, modern boardroom that would have been more fit for art stock market traders and their presentations than our unholy alliance.

I didn't think it could be possible for anyone to look so much like the paintings, the renderings, the sculptures that had filtered down over the centuries. I wasn't sure where along the lines pop culture had begun to depict her with pink hair but had assumed it was a rather cartoonish fiction to connect her with spring blossoms.

I was wrong.

I knew who she was the moment I saw her.

She grinned as she swept across the room in a loose, flowing dress. Her pale hair had been interlaced with a halo of pink lowlights that blended into a gentle gradient, starting with icy roots and ending with light, rose-colored tips. Her lips, her eyelids, and her cheeks were in complementary shades of rose and peach. Her fingernails had been painted pink to match and were manicured into somewhat threatening points.

She snatched up my hand in both of hers.

"Persephone." I offered a breathless smile. She squeezed my hand.

"I go by Poppy," she said, dazzling teeth flashing. Her eyes were an incredible mixture of blue and green. She didn't look Greek. She didn't even look human. She looked like...spring. "And you and I have something in common."

"Poppy, sorry," I corrected, bewildered. From what I knew of names, I wondered if Persephone was even her real name, or just the one she'd preferred when Homer and Hesiod had been busy transcribing their stories. "And, Hades?"

Hades smirked from across the table. While Poppy and Fauna could perhaps swap bohemian outfits, he was dressed like a high-end weapons dealer from a spy movie. I couldn't fathom two more opposite aesthetics in the same building, let alone the same room. Her dress in contrast with his slick black suit looked like they belonged to the sort of people who wouldn't speak to one another, let alone be a couple.

He propped his chin up on his elbows and said, "You can call me—"

"Don't be crude," Poppy cut in, presumably knowing where his joke was going. "The Prince of Hell and his bride? Come on, darling, how often do we get to meet a couple like us?"

"She's missing her better half," he said.

"She *is* the better half," Poppy said, positively twinkling. She released my hand and perched on the arm of Hades's chair. "He's going by Dorian. Dorian Castellanos, if anyone asks who's running our museum."

I rolled the name around in my head. "Dorian, as in... Gray?"

From across the table, Hades's smile grew. "Precisely. Corrupt the soul, keep the pretty face." He ran his hand down Poppy's back. She closed her eyes and leaned into the touch.

"Why a museum?" I asked. I awaited an elbow in the ribs from Fauna for not filtering my thoughts, but she leaned forward, as if interested in the question.

q"Big fan." She winked.

"Fauna is her Nordic companion. And this is Fenrir."

Poppy sobered instantly. She offered Fenrir a respectful nod. "It's an honor to have you, Fenrir. And on behalf of us both, we're deeply sorry for what you've endured."

I'd never considered the lore gods from other realms told one another, but Fenrir was something of a legend. He stayed silent as he had with Dorian, but closed his eyes and bowed his head slightly in acknowledgment.

"How were you freed?" Poppy asked.

Fenrir looked at Fauna but said nothing.

Dorian took control of the conversation a moment later. "I'll be honest. We weren't sure, but...we thought you might be coming."

Fauna cocked a brow. She folded her legs beneath her and made herself comfortable as she tucked herself into the chair. "Color me curious, *Dorian*."

"The worlds know when a goddess falls," he said. The embers of his amusement continued to smolder. "Astarte's body was still warm when they discovered it."

I swallowed as I gauged the room's temperature. I was responsible for something unforgiveable.

"Who found her? Was it one of yours?" Fauna asked.

Poppy's pink and blond waves moved gracefully around her shoulders as she shook her head. "No—a friend of a friend. They wiped forty-eight hours of security footage as soon as they arrived. Little bestselling author Merit Finnegan here was all over them. Can't have her reputation ruined by a gruesome crime scene, can we?"

"Didn't you hear?" Fauna asked. "Her reputation took the hit regardless. I'm not sure if the news was international, but our favorite writer was outed for her previous career."

"Tut, tut." Poppy's brows puckered. "Nearly every god and goddess from Rome to Greece had sacred and holy roles for divine sexual worship. Your reputation has *not* been ruined now that more of us know who you are. We simply see that you're a more complex character than otherwise assumed."

I was speechless. She and Fauna exchanged a quiet stand-off of polite, restrained looks before Poppy returned to her previous conversation.

"As for the footage...when we saw the Prince, well...I told Dorian it would only be a matter of time before we heard from you."

My fingertips went unconsciously to my throat as if to soothe the uncomfortable constriction as I asked, "Do they know who killed her?"

Dorian gave me a serious look. "Were any other god-killers present?"

I chewed my lip as I thought. "I don't know. Can angels kill gods?"

Gooseflesh pebbled my arms and legs as the room chilled. No one moved.

Dorian's tone remained the same, but his face was an unreadable mask as he asked, "An angel, or an archangel?"

I looked to Fauna for the answer. With a reluctant puff of air, she said, "Do you know Silas?"

Dorian's eyes darkened at the name, but Poppy lit from within. "That's *great* news for your Prince! It doesn't matter if there's no footage of Astarte's murder. If Silas was there, no one will blame Hell. As a matter of fact, they might assume Hell was only there in response to the angel's threatening presence."

I couldn't explain the hollow whistle of air that blew through the hole in my chest. I wanted to revel in the joy that Caliban wouldn't be blamed, but new thoughts smothered my joy. Was Silas an archangel, that the blame might be pinned solely on him? Where did that leave him? Did it matter?

Dorian squeezed Poppy's hip and said, "As it stands, we're glad you're finally here. We've been itching for a little chaos."

"Well"—I swallowed as I looked between the two of them—"you can take your chaos. Fenrir can have his anarchy. I just want Caliban back."

The couple exchanged looks.

Fauna perked up at my side. "It's her name for the Prince. It's good, right?"

"I must know," Dorian said. "How did you do it? I mean, gods and mortals have love stories for the ages, but when it comes to you and the Prince...The pantheons have watched his growing affections with a curious eye through your lifetimes. I suppose you don't remember how it started."

I did remember, though I couldn't explain why.

I felt the heat, the blood, my mortal body's pain from 900 BCE as if it were yesterday. I'd been stoned and left for dead nearly a thousand years before the clock had reset and begun at zero once more. He'd found me there, broken and dying, and I'd asked him to stay with me.

So he had.

"I don't know most of the cycles," I said, "but in this one, he didn't want to see me suffer. He checked in when he could, always trying to cheer me up and be a point of joy in a very dark childhood. I wish he could have done more. Fuck, I would have loved to have joined the missing person's posters and been swept into the fae realm."

Poppy clicked her tongue sadly. "There's not much free will in that, though, is there?"

"I didn't want free will," I said. "I was told I had it growing up, but is anything freely chosen when there's a knife

142

at your throat, daring to slit you from chin to collarbone if you choose wrong?"

To my surprise, it was Dorian who took offense. "Lore loves to play fast and loose with deities abducting their brides. A lot of villains are born from ignorance. I'm positive he did what he could to help you without crossing any boundaries until you were old enough to decide for yourself."

Fauna snorted, but quickly apologized given their shared alarm. "I'm sorry, I'm sorry, it's just...as soon as she was old enough to consent, she decided he was made up and she was insane. It wasn't an ideal outcome. So, enter Fauna, stage left."

I shot her a glare.

"What?" She leaned back in her chair. "You don't give me nearly enough credit for saving your life."

Dorian clapped his hands together. "Are we off to topple some kingdoms, or shall we spend the night wandering amongst my antiquities? Because I'd like to see a few heads roll."

Fauna cleared her throat loudly enough to stop everyone in the room.

I supplied: "For all intents and purposes, we are here because of the politician who doxxed me, and no other reason. Anything else that happens is purely coincidental."

Dorian positively glowed. "Well, isn't that delightful."

Poppy got to her feet. "That's enough of that. You're our guests, and we're all here in good faith. Now that we've exchanged the formalities of our preferred monikers, there's a life to be lived! We're not going anywhere tonight—for all intents and purposes." Poppy shot me an air-kiss, informing me with one throwaway gesture that she understood more from my two sentences of immortal beings and their semantics than I could ever hope to achieve. She waved for us to follow. "Come now, we can't very well spend the night in the boardroom. You'll stay at our place, of course. You look like you need a good washing."

It was anxiety-inducing enough to meet Hades and

Persephone in the flesh. I didn't need the reminder that changing into Estrid's clean tunic hadn't gotten rid of the sulfuric marshy stench or lingering wolf hairs.

I looked at Fenrir and his beautiful, glossy coat, and resisted the urge to pet him. Surely, it was improper to stroke a god's stunning fur. But that didn't make keeping my hands to myself any less challenging.

Dorian took his time getting to his feet, smoothing his jacket with idle hands. I shot Fauna an uncertain look, but she looped her arm through mine. Fenrir followed on Poppy's heels as she led us into the palatial museum atrium and toward the elevators. I didn't have time to absorb the floors upon floors of exhibits, the balconies, the statues, or the banners in the dim after-hours lighting as I kept up. Dorian flicked the lights off behind us and brought up the back of our small crew. I was surprised to see Poppy hit the arrow pointed down and frowned as we got into the elevator.

I opened my mouth to ask if we were going to Hades, but as if to preempt my question, Fauna pinched me.

I suppressed the urge to cry out in pain. Dorian caught the exchange but seemed to enjoy our tiny display. Moments later, the doors opened. I was instantly glad I'd said nothing, as the shiny doors parted not to the Underworld, but to a parking garage. Poppy led us to the only remaining vehicle in the otherwise empty subterranean room. I knew enough about cars to be pretty sure the black Aston Martin was the same make and model as the one driven by James Bond, which only deepened my preconceived notions that Dorian's earthbound profession was something more closely affiliated with the mafia than with museum work.

Fauna opened the door to the back seats for Fenrir and he leaped in first, crossing to the far side as if jumping into a vehicle were the most natural thing in the world. I crawled in next and wedged myself in the middle while Fauna slid in beside me. I kept my eyes on Dorian as he crossed to the passenger's side, and for a moment, I was confused about who was expected to drive. Then he opened the door for Poppy and ensured she slid in safely before he got in.

"Why don't we just jump to their home?" I whispered to Fauna.

"And leave a car this nice behind? Please."

She was right. I supposed even the Lord and Lady of the Underworld had appearances to keep up if they were masquerading as humans. The car purred to life and Dorian eased it toward a small security tower. He scanned a card and thick protective doors eased open to release us onto the streets of Athens.

Thirty minutes later, he slowed the vehicle as he turned into a driveway lined with tall, manicured cypress trees. A thick iron gate swung open as he approached, then eased shut the moment we passed its perimeter. I wasn't sure if this was a mortal mechanism or magical intervention, but the gate was the last thing on my mind as he pulled up to the cliffside villa of my fairy-tale dreams. I tried to pick my jaw up off the floor as we got out of the car and approached the door.

"Oh, you go ahead and get the others set up," Poppy said to Dorian. "Please see to it that Fenrir is given the most kingly treatment after all he's been through. In the meantime, I want to show Merit the infinity pool." She looped her arm around mine before I had time to protest. Despite her cheery disposition and insistence that we were kindred spirits, the look of alarm on Fauna's face at our separation put me on edge. I didn't miss the flare in her eyes as she sent me a silent warning—for what, I wasn't sure.

My heart continued to skip uncertainly as Poppy led me around the edge of the house to where beautiful gardens and olive trees fell into a smooth, sunken firepit lined with posh cream patio furniture. I wondered if they left the fire burning at all times, or if it had been turned on in anticipation of our arrival, which did nothing to assuage my worry. The fire didn't hold my attention long as she guided me past the landscaping to a glossy black surface that fell away into the sea.

"Wow," I murmured appreciatively. I'd been to luxury resorts around the world. I'd stayed at five-star hotels and taken calls at multimillion-dollar mansions. The limitless blue where the sky met the ocean never got old. It was a moonless night, dotted only with the few stars that weren't muted by the glow of Athens. "Owning a museum must pay pretty well?"

She giggled lightly beside me. The sound reminded me of new leaves rubbing together, of chirping birds, of bright, sunny days. "The museum is a pet project."

I knew it, I thought. I'd have to ask Fauna later if the Greek god of the Underworld really did run an arm of the mafia.

"I prefer it up here," Poppy said in low agreement to any unspoken question. "In the human realm, that is. Don't get me wrong, the Underworld has its luxuries. We're deities in our realm, but...we're subjugated gods." Her words dropped off as if catching on the wind that breezed over the cliff. I turned to look at her, but the pretty slope of her nose and apples of her cheeks were barely discernable against the dark sea. All the light remained at our backs as the fire danced quietly in its smooth cement cage.

"Subjugated?" I repeated the word uncertainly.

"I have a goddess for a mother—then again, I probably don't have to tell my story to the great Merit Finnegan. I'm a minor deity—a lot like your Norde companion, actually. A bit more famous." Her face scrunched in a genuine smile. "Dorian's a true god. They're brothers, you know," she said. There was a blue note to her final statement as her words met the ocean, lost along with her distant stare.

I fidgeted. "Zeus and Hades?"

I didn't miss the way she frowned. "We aren't using those names these days."

"I'm sorry." And I was.

She turned toward me. I monitored every movement as she closed the small space between us and ran her soft fingers

146

along my arms, urging me to look at her. Our bodies turned so the fire lit one side, and the ocean was at the other. Humans didn't touch each other like this. At least, none that I knew.

I was still tingling from the vaguely ominous motion that I knew was intended to be comforting as her soft voice said, "Gods can kill gods, you know. They're equals. You'd think they'd be treated as such, but that's never been the case."

I didn't know what to say, but I had a feeling that silence was fine.

"Dorian and Caliban have something in common."

My lips parted briefly at hearing the Prince's allotted name on her tongue.

Undeterred, she went on. "Caliban is patient—legendarily so. We've known about you for a long, long time, Merit. Well, we knew about the Prince's human. It being *you* was a surprise. So, he won't rush you, even if the realms wish he would—and they do, Merit, make no mistake. But Dorian's like that, too. True gods are excellent at outwaiting their enemies. Perhaps it's why lessers need to nudge things along. Not everyone has the patience for eternity."

I had no idea what to make of her warning. Each word made sense individually, but her message was lost on me. I wasn't sure if she wanted me to reply. For lack of anything better to say, I answered with, "I appreciate your willingness to help me get Caliban back."

Her laugh was a single short exhalation. There was a sadness to the sound, stolen quickly on the wind that carried over the Mediterranean Sea.

"Do you know what so many of us like about Hell?"

My hair tickled my shoulders as I shook my head. She'd changed topics so quickly that I was forced to assume everything was interconnected in a way I couldn't possibly comprehend. At this point it would be shorter for me to make a list of the few things I did know rather than to assume I understood anything about the other realms.

"There are no gods in Hell," she said. "There are courts,

sure. They have royal families—the King and the Prince, the infernal divine, the other courts, what have you—but it's nothing like the absolute supremacy of gods in other realms over their subjects. Hell's king dreamed of equality. Hell stands for the egalitarian rule we laud. I think it's part of why so many of us spend our time in the mortal realm. Here, Dorian and I aren't squished beneath another god's thumb. Few humans are—though I suppose there are exceptions even in the mortal realm. Your presidents, your prime ministers, your queens—it's just a ship and its sail. The sail can be collapsed at any time, and then you can steer with rudders and oars. It's not forced obedience. Hell is doing something other realms dream of, and at a steep price. Heaven is a formidable foe—a nearly unconquerable one."

She searched my face for a light but frowned when I failed to latch on to her words.

Poppy tightened her hold on my arms as she said, "We've been waiting for you to make this happen."

I had no idea what to do with her intense monologue. I shot a look toward the fire, hoping salvation would come from the house. I looked deeply into the greens and blues of Poppy's springtime eyes as they caught the flecks of hellfire. "Waiting for me?"

Before I could react, she pulled me into a hug. She smelled like fresh-cut grass, apricot blossoms, and the earth after it rained. Into my hair, she whispered, "Please, don't waste this life."

"Mar?" came Fauna's voice from somewhere behind the olive trees.

Oh, thank god.

"Out here, Fauna," I called back, doing my best to keep my tone light. I wasn't afraid of Poppy, but my heart hadn't settled its arrhythmic skipping since she'd led me to the cliffs. Nothing about our conversation set me at ease.

Poppy pulled out of the hug as footsteps began to scrape

from the far side of the firepit. She whispered, "She wants it, too."

I frowned. "What?"

Popped dipped her chin, voice low as she said, "For the first time in countless cycles, you have fae blood. This is the first time another realm has been able to step in like this and intervene. Your Norde wants it every bit as badly as I do. Ask her why she's helping you. Ask her why she *really* came into your life. It was sudden, wasn't it? Out of the blue? Ask yourself why a *nymph* would be charged with such a task. With Fauna... You're important, Marlow. You deserve to know who she really is."

My lashes fluttered rapidly at her hushed, conspiratorial words. A numbness tingled my fingers and toes as I struggled to grip on to Poppy's warning.

"Mar?" Fauna called again.

I was once again overcome with images of a security guard mutilated in the park and buried, never to be seen or heard from again. A vision of ferocious wolves bowing to her will flashed before me. A chill snaked down my spine as Fauna approached.

Poppy dropped her hands and I turned to see my Nordic companion lit by the yellows and whites of the bright, clean fire.

I gave Poppy one last confused look, but she only closed her eyes and offered a single nod before putting her hand on my lower back and urging me forward. She called out to Fauna, "Did Dorian show you to your rooms?"

Fauna bobbed her head, extending her hand toward me as I was given from the Greek Lady of the Underworld to a Nordic forest deity, like a human toddler being passed off from teacher to mother after kindergarten. Fauna looped her arm in mine and rested her head briefly on my shoulder before saying, "You're going to love our room! He said we could have two different ones, but I thought it would be more fun to have a sleepover."

149

"Of course you did." I'd intended for my tone to come out dry, but there was a cautious edge to it that I hoped she'd missed. I shot a look over my shoulder at Poppy, but her face was serene and encouraging once more. She followed closely behind as we entered the home of Hades and Persephone.

Chapter Seventeen

"Wow!" Fauna stepped out of the en suite bathroom with a towel wrapped around her hair. "I knew she'd have nice shit, but did you see some of these things? This face cream has real diamonds in it! I'm going to have to get some for my place." Fauna hooked a finger into the cream and scooped a generous helping onto her face. I was quite confident she didn't need any creams to maintain her ethereal youth. Perhaps it was just the joy of knowing one was glistening with diamonds.

Poppy's words had stuck a needle in my veins, mainlining dread as I looked at my friend. I tried to remain as casual as possible. If I was going to get real answers, it seemed unwise to let her know that any part of me feared her.

I took my first stab at the seeds of distrust Poppy had sowed. "You're a nymph, right?"

"*Skosgrå* is the Nordic equivalent of *nymph*," Fauna said. "You know this. But I'm fine being called a nymph."

"But"—I dug my heels in—"you *are* a skosgrå? You're not something else?"

"They're imperfect comparisons," she conceded, "but as we've established, it's the closest term for public understanding. Now, do you want some diamonds? You could use them. You look stressed."

"I wonder why," I grumbled. I extended my hand to receive the mother-of-pearl container with the small golden whale on top. I went through skin care products too quickly to commit to something as ostentatious as diamond cream.

Fauna passed it off to me and took her hair down from the towel, scrunching it until the remaining droplets were absorbed. She crawled across the bed to smell my still-wet hair. "I knew you'd pick that shampoo!"

I shoved her away. "You did not."

"I tried them all," she said.

"Well, that explains why your shower took forty-five minutes." I finished applying the diamond cream and secured the lid. I frowned down at it while Fauna busied herself with her hair. Finally, I looked up and asked, "Fauna, you said you have a place in the mortal realm, didn't you?"

She nodded brightly.

"Where is it?"

She smiled. "On the beach!"

Yes, she'd said so before. I hadn't thought much of the elusive nonanswer the first time, but the more time I spent around her, the less I felt I knew her. Cute curiosities took on a more sinister note as I studied her. Inside me there were two wolves, or however the parable went. One who loved Fauna, and another who wasn't sure if I could trust her enough to help me get Caliban back.

"And," I tried again, "you said you pay your rent in favors. What sort of tasks does he have you do?"

She shrugged. "This and that. He knows I'm unavailable right now. I'm on a very important mission with a human."

"Fauna," I said slowly. Her brows lowered as she met my gaze, evaluating the gravity in my tone. I swallowed, then said, "If I ask you something, will you be honest with me?"

She tossed the towel to the floor and flopped backward onto the bed. "That depends on whether or not what you ask is worth my time."

Again, it was the sort of answer I would have dismissed

as playful or spirited. Now, I wasn't so sure if her chaos was impish, or if it was a particularly clever mask. I weighed the wisdom of my question, but ultimately, I had no loyalty to Poppy or Dorian. I wasn't willing to risk sowing seeds of distrust over misinformation. And even if Fauna had joked on more than one occasion that she would have let me die, she'd spent centuries aligning herself with a patron saint of women. I trusted Azrames, Betty, and Fauna to the ends of the earth…didn't I?

"Poppy said something to me on the cliffs."

She rolled to her side to look at me, and then the corners of her mouth turned down. She adjusted her posture in response to my seriousness, tucking herself into a seated position as she waited for me to speak.

"She said that this is the first time I've had fae blood, and so it was the first time another realm could intervene. She implied…"

A chill snaked through me at the cool look Fauna gave me. "What did she imply?"

I felt the nervous sweat of someone about to give a public speech, a girl about to break up with her first partner, or a child prepared to confess a sin to their parent. I had questions, but I wasn't sure that I was ready for the consequences of the answers.

"Why did you really come for me? That night with Silas?"

"Oh." Fauna relaxed. "Is that all? You want to know why you get a pretty guardian in this cycle? She's right. You didn't have fae blood before. Maybe if *Dorian* here were more of a playboy, you would have been one-eighth Greek and a real nymph could have shown up at your door. Your escort through this madness could have been anyone, from any realm. Is that your question?"

It wasn't, but I didn't know how to reword my question.

I made another attempt. "That night, Silas said this wasn't your war—the one between Heaven and Hell. That I should be left to the two of them. And you said that he should leave

153

it up to you what you did or didn't want to get involved in. That...that you were doing it so that Heaven didn't turn the tide in the war. Right?"

She made a contemplative face before saying, "Ask what you're trying to ask."

"Fine." I gritted my teeth. "What is your stake in the game?"

"Spit it out," she challenged.

Every muscle in my body clenched on instinct. "I know you. You don't do anything out of altruism. I don't believe that you're here on pure allyship with Hell. I definitely don't believe you showed up on pure coincidence because I'm a long-lost citizen. If you're just in it for Azrames, you can tell me. But you came for me long before either of our demons went missing. Why do you want this?"

"There we go." She smiled. "How's it feel to grow a pair?"

I didn't take the bait.

She tilted her head, waves tumbling to the side. "Did you play with dominos as a kid, Mar?"

My brows puckered into a frown. I knew a rhetorical question when I heard one, so I remained silent.

Fauna sighed, saying, "When one topples, they all go. Maybe if you'd bound yourself to Silas, Heaven would have won the war. We'd have ten thousand more years of sameness across the realms. Nothing would happen. But maybe if a pretty Norde named Fauna intervened, Hell could stand its ground and live to fight another day. Or maybe..."

"Please just tell me."

"Maybe Poppy's right and I don't give a shit about Hell. I mean, don't get me wrong, I love Azrames, and he has a great apartment...but if Hell fell to ruins, I'd just have him come live with me in Álfheimr. Or I'd stash him at my apartment in the mortal realm or something. Maybe I don't care about Caliban, just like Fenrir doesn't care about Anath, just like Poppy and Dorian don't care about the Phoenicians. You're missing the forest for the trees, here, Marlow."

Anarchy.

"You want an uprising."

"There's a smart girl," she practically purred. "The gods have had their fun."

"Odin? Frigg? Thor?"

Her shoulders lifted. "You saw what they did to Fenrir. Maybe they haven't done anything to me personally, but that's beside the point. That's the kind of shit the big gods do in every realm—whatever the fuck they want. Those below them have no say. But Hell's model...now, that's aspirational. *Let the ruling classes tremble at a Communist revolution. The proletarians have nothing to lose but their chains. They have a world to win.*"

"Did you just quote Karl Marx to me?"

Her dazzling smile was vaguely threatening as she said, "Now you're seeing the bigger picture, baby. Maybe you're a pawn, Marlow Frejya Thorson. But you're one important fucking pawn. And does it matter what brought us together? We're together now, and I'm not going anywhere."

She extended her hand toward me and wiggled her fingers, urging me in closer.

I didn't accept her bid for affection. "What's your name?"

Her fingers stilled. "It's Fauna."

"Your true name," I emphasized.

She waved it away. "You have to know by now how rude that is. We keep our names to ourselves for own protection. Haven't I been trying to get you to stop sharing your name from the moment I met you?"

I looked at the hand. "How can I trust you when you won't even tell me who you are?"

Genuine confusion rearranged her features. "I'm sorry?"

"You're only my friend because of the role you think I can play in some war of the realms. How is there any honesty in that?"

She scoffed. Her hand dropped. "Because before, when we were connected by distant bloodlines, *that* was a true

155

bond? This thing between us was so much purer when you were merely a Norde?"

"Well—"

She arched a testing brow. "Is that why you're so close to your parents? Is that why you stand by them and their excellent decisions? Because blood is so important? You matter to me, Marlow. You matter to a lot of us. And I don't know if you know this, but that famous quote about blood has been bastardized."

"Which one?"

"*Blood is thicker than water.* People use it to say the exact opposite of its original intent."

I twisted the fabric of my tee in my fingers as I prompted, "Which is?"

"*The blood of the covenant is thicker than the water of the womb.*"

I tasted her message. The implication was uncomfortable and did nothing to put me at ease. My fidgeting continued as I said, "I matter to you because of what I symbolize."

She didn't deny it. "Yes. And that would have been reason enough for me to guard you with my life. I know you're something of an expert at lying to yourself, so I'm sure you'll convince yourself that our bond is meaningless. But don't lie to me and try to pretend we don't care about each other, because I won't believe you. Now stop fighting our friendship and come here, sunflower. Tonight, we sleep. Tomorrow, we take over the worlds."

Chapter Eighteen

MARCH 18, AGE 7

I RECEIVED MY FIRST PINK SLIP FOR DETENTION IN SECOND grade.

My English teacher accused me of lying about my book report, claiming there was no way a student in grade two could do a book report on the fantasy novel I'd chosen, as it was far beyond the class-approved reading level. I trembled with rage, with indignation, with fury at the world as the yellow school bus wove through the countryside until, at long last, it dumped me at the end of a quarter-mile driveway. It was raining, which I'd liked. If I was going to cry, the sky should, too.

I cried the moment my feet hit the soil. It was both loud and sudden enough that the bus driver called after me to see if I was all right, but I'd already begun running toward my house. She closed her doors and the ancient machine lurched to dispose of the remaining students while my sneakers sunk into damp gravel as I put one foot in front of the other, tears mingling with raindrops, plastering my hair to my cheeks.

I slowed only when the white fox stepped out into the middle of my driveway. The thick green foliage, enormous tree trunks, and gently swaying ferns felt magical when it rained. And there was nothing more magical than an arctic fox. I wasn't even halfway between the drop point and our trailer in the woods when it sat, prim and proper, folding its tail around itself. I sniffed, wiping my eyes as I approached the fox. I sat down on the ground next to it and let myself cry.

I hadn't lied.

I'd told the truth, and I'd been punished for it.

It wasn't the first time I'd be wounded for honesty, and it wouldn't be the last.

The fox rubbed up against me, batting at me to get me to play with it, but I didn't want to. I shook my head, chin trembling, lip quivering. It was all I could do to keep the hiccups inside as my eyes continued to water. A crack of thunder told me it was going to start raining again, but I didn't want to go in. I looked down at the pink slip of paper as tiny raindrops began to soak it.

The fox nipped the edge of my thrifted ski coat, too warm for the season, too outdated for the decade, and began to tug on the sleeve. I told it that I didn't want to play, that I didn't want to go inside, that I didn't want anything. I couldn't risk yet another adult yelling at me for something I hadn't done. But the fox was persistent, and one cold raindrop at a time, the weather won the fight. The animal continued to lunge back to tug at my coat, wagging its tail until a giggle broke through the tears. The fox took turns prancing ahead of me and venturing back to urge me forward until we got to the house. With a housecat-like final rub against my legs, it bounded into the forest, disappearing between the ferns as though it had never existed.

My mother was deeply unhappy that I was so wet when I got into the house. She opened her mouth to scold me, but a cry broke from my belly against my will. I was wailing before I could stop myself.

She dropped to a knee. "What happened, Marlow?"

Shaking from head to toe with my sobs, I handed her the pink slip of paper. She squinted through the rain droplets as she read it once, then twice, then a third time. She unzipped my backpack and dug for the book in question. She stared at the tattered cover for a long time, for she knew it well. The books about talking animals and adventurous children and tales of good and evil had belonged to her before she'd gifted them to me. "Your teacher said you were lying because you read this book?"

I focused on the rain pounding against the tin can of our trailer. I nodded, wishing the storm could wash me away, too.

She unbuttoned my coat and wiped away my tears. She took off my shoes and bundled me into a hug, shushing me. I felt seen and loved and understood as she said, "Marlow, you are so much smarter than anyone at that school. You read a big book. I saw you read it. I helped you sound out every big word in it. And no one will punish you for being smart. Okay?"

I cried in her arms until snot bubbles made it impossible to breathe. She tightened her embrace, and in turn, I clung to this life raft of kindness.

The sounds of yelling adults clattered over one another minutes later as Lisbeth Thorson, my mom, my book report hero, screamed into the phone. I watched her like she was a warrior in a coliseum, her words and hot temper acting as her sword as she fought for me. She didn't care that it was after hours. She called my teacher's home number from the phone book, and made it clear that if a teacher like her wasn't prepared for a student like me, then she'd be at the school tomorrow to have me moved up a grade.

And I was.

While I went to math, science, and geography with the other second graders, after lunch time, I was walked by a teacher's assistant to the fourth-grade room for English so that I could be challenged. When I was meant to advance into sixth grade, they transitioned me fully into grade eight.

In the years that followed, my mother's screams were rarely in my defense.

Still, I clutched that memory every time she hollered. I clung to how good it had felt when she'd held me even when she took the leather belt to beat the sins out of me. The cold waves of her mercurial emotions crested and broke, dipped and peaked, always unpredictable, often dangerous, always terrifying. It was confusing to look at the woman and tell myself she was my life raft, even when I knew it was she who was the storm.

But she knew I was smart, and told me she was proud of me every time I turned the last page on a newly finished book.

So, I read, and read, and read.

I had to thank her for three things: she made me a voracious reader, she was the reason I needed escape, and ultimately, if it weren't for our poverty and her attempts to enrich my childhood, I would never have developed an appreciation for long-form tales.

We owned a television, but it had a single dusty VHS player, and the only tapes were historical documentaries or nature programs. Instead, for entertainment, my mother had taught me to be very patient and very still from a young age as I sat on her bed and she read to me. I'd fall asleep on her stomach as a four-year-old listening to her read *To Kill a Mockingbird*, or *Where the Red Fern Grows*, and of course, every morning before school, we'd read out loud from the Bible.

By the time I was five, she dared to tackle *Lord of the Rings*. It was too big of a book for me to try by myself, but I loved to listen. I had an excellent imagination and could picture everything with vibrant saturation. I smelled every flower and tasted every fruit. I felt the wind on my face. I was one with the sea spray and ice and fire. I became the hero as I lost myself in worlds where villains could be conquered.

People at Sunday school said the Bible was boring, but I was confident they only thought that because they hadn't read it. It had more war, battle, romance, horror, blood, magic, miracles, ghosts, witches, angels, and demons than any of the regular books my mother and I read together. Plus, my vocabulary grew every day as we struggled sounding out words like *leviathan* and *nephilim*. Every new word would result in an explanation, an understanding, a story. Words were keys to endless doors, each door the book to a fantastic escape.

Maybe the lesson was that the source of my love and my pain were often two sides of the same coin. Maybe the lesson was that those who promised to protect me would be the ones who hurt me most. Maybe there was no lesson at all.

Chapter Nineteen

I'M BACK!" FAUNA CRIED AS SHE THREW OPEN THE FRONT DOOR to Poppy and Dorian's home. In her left hand, she clutched a cardboard tray with four coffees. Her right fist was pumped into the air like John Bender at the end of *Breakfast Club*.

"Did you go somewhere?" Dorian gave his newspaper a dramatic flick, not bothering to look up from the lip of its pages. The morning light bathed the paper, the table, and the man in gold as if the gods themselves had blessed his unimpressed sass.

Then again, I supposed at least one of them had.

"Where the hell were you?" I crossed my arms, grumbling, "Drag me to Greece and leave me to wake up to a 'see you at breakfast' note."

Fauna plopped the cheap corner-store caffeine on the table amidst the array of pour overs, French presses, and Turkish coffees. I could smell her contribution of burnt bean water from three chairs away.

"It's the strangest thing," Fauna said in a theatrically conspiratorial tone. "I was simply walking to get coffee when a fae approached me. How peculiar to see another one of our kind in corporeal form, am I right? Anyway, he had an urgent message for you, Merit. Apparently, the Phoenician gods have invited you to their realm for a banquet.

Her acting needed work. Still, my mouth formed a perfect, silent O.

I'd been furious that some stupid oath had delayed our progress. I'd been clawing at loopholes to find a way to get to Caliban. Now that the moment was upon us, I wasn't sure if I could play pretend. I knew I was meant to act shocked, but only dust came out when I searched for words.

Poppy and her acting swooped in to save the day. "Our sweet human friend has been invited to a Phoenician banquet? What ever for?" she said, face wrought with worry.

Beams of morning light sliced over the cliff, cutting through the purpling vines that arced over the glass doors to their seaside estate. Each golden light illuminated Hades and Persephone—Dorian and Poppy, I corrected myself—at the lavish breakfast table like the gods they were. Gods who were terrible stage performers.

Fauna spun a quick tale connecting my confessions from the previous night about Caliban and our love to Astarte and her death, before singing for the walls to hear that it was a great honor for them to host me after an *angel* had killed their goddess and the Prince of Hell and his bride-to-be had intervened to save the day.

"I don't love this," I said, not quite under my breath.

"Hush. Our plan is perfect and we've all done our song and dance flawlessly. Now, Merit, it's time to prepare for our arrival."

Dorian rolled his shoulders in a half-amused shrug. He was no longer in black-on-black, but the white linen shirt did nothing to dissuade me from thinking he was the ringleader of an underground crime organization. Perhaps I'd read too many mafia romances, or maybe it was just how one looked when they were the god of the Greek Underworld. "I'm going with the Norde on this one. This is the only idea that makes sense. You and Fauna will go meet them for the banquet alone. Anything else will be met with outright suspicion."

It was hard to picture dark Underworlds and impending doom while sitting at Poppy and Dorian's breakfast table, no matter how high the stakes or dire the ticking clock.

Their home was even more splendid in the light of day. Everything I'd found breathtaking the night before was covered in twisted, flowering vines that I didn't know enough about botany to name. Their wooden trunks looked like dead driftwood, but they wove through one another, draping into a lavender flower that hung delicately from the end of each branch. The wall of windows and their multimillion-dollar view put my floor-to-ceiling windows overlooking the river to shame. Poppy and Dorian looked out onto their lovely patio, their infinity pool, then the sparkling expanse of the sea as it glittered in the morning light. I could just barely catch the curve of the Grecian coast and the white and cream buildings that dotted its cliffs before the shapes were lost to the custard-colored rock and disappeared into obscurity.

The ache in my chest was akin to the one I'd felt in Álfheimr. Perhaps there would be another day, another breakfast, another sunrise, where I could return to truly enjoy something so marvelous when the world wasn't coming to an end.

The *click click clack* of Fenrir's steps against the flooring preceded his arrival. The fabled world-ending god of Ragnarök ignored the breakfast spread, the Grecians, Fauna, and me, as he plopped down in a beam of light in front of the glass doors. He stretched like a cat in the sun, and I wondered how long he'd lived in Hafna's mist without true, golden daylight. Perhaps if I'd spent centuries in fog, I'd do the same.

The Apocalypse Dog's arrival was a reminder that the world would always be coming to an end from this moment forward. I may never get another peaceful moment to simply soak up a good pastry and a beautiful view.

Fenrir looked ever the part of a happy housedog, if only for a moment. Even I looked different in the light of day. It seemed that I couldn't switch realms without being dressed by my host, which made me feel a bit like a doll as I was passed once more from one fabulous owner to the next. I preferred my own clothes best. Fauna's thin white T-shirt had put me on display. Estrid's tied tunic had been utilitarian, but I'd been comfortable. The upscale bohemian clothes Poppy provided were excellent for the Mediterranean coast, but not something I'd wear anywhere else.

Fauna loved flowy clothing, but I'd never seen her in a dress. She'd crinkled her nose as she'd slipped into the forest-green number that circled around her neck and draped loosely down her back, exposing her from her neck to the scandalous space just above her tailbone. It hung to her ankles. Had it not been for the braided leather belt that she'd wrapped three times, there would have been no evidence of a waist. I, on the other hand, felt like I was stepping into a rather immodest nightgown rather than a dress as I changed into the cotton attire. Poppy had left a white, spaghetti-strap, above-the-knee shift for me. She'd made a comment that had reminded me loosely of Ianna's reference as the demon had styled me from head to toe in the metropolis's most fashionable design. Instead of calling me a future princess, Poppy had said something a bit more ominous.

For the Bride of Hell.

Our conversation paused as a housekeeper popped into the kitchen to refill our coffees. She bustled about the table to remove empty plates. Fenrir had been served steak and chicken in a silver bowl with a side of distilled water. The woman seemed to know she was interrupting, given her rapid apologies in a language I didn't speak, but Poppy was quick to assuage her guilt.

They exchanged niceties back and forth before the room was ours once more.

I tilted my head curiously.

"Tagalog," Poppy said politely, answering my unspoken question. "Tala is a darling. She was already in Athens, and it's convenient for our line of work to keep staff with whom we can speak. She's fluent in Tagalog and Greek, but can't overhear our business exchanges if we switch to English. Should you dip your toes into questionable practices, love, I recommend learning a few new tongues. Multilingualism is a useful skill, dear. You should put it on your to-do list."

I pursed my lips to keep myself from speaking my mind. The gods had eternity to learn every language they stumbled across. If I had access to infinity, I'd spend it reading every text and learning every language. Perhaps, given enough years, the earthlings would see me as a goddess of wisdom simply because I'd been alive long enough to be well-read and silver-tongued.

"Mar's already something of a polyglot," Fauna said appreciatively, touching my hand with her own as she defended me. Given how often she enjoyed ragging on my intelligence, I appreciated the gesture. "It's not common in the Americas, you know that. She's gone above and beyond for her cycle. You speak what, Mar, three languages? Four?"

"I speak three. I read four," I answered while feeling distinctly uncomfortable.

"Mar, or Mer?" Poppy raised a finger as she chimed in with her question. "I don't care for your birth certificate, darling. What would you like Dorian and I to call you? When we speak to you, and about you in front of others, that is?"

"Mer...call me Merit," I said, swallowing. I'd picked the pen name on a whim, appreciating its significance of working for that which I'd achieved. I'd never considered its importance would boil down to breakfast with the gods. "May I ask an ignorant question?"

"Is there any other kind?" Dorian asked, smiling into his eggs.

Poppy made a lofty gesture, tossing her pink and blond hair over her shoulder. "It's only ignorance until the moment it's answered. Be our guest. What can we help you with?"

I tried to maintain eye contact but found it challenging. Looking out over the glaring expanse of sunlight on the sea was no better. I frowned into what remained of my breakfast as I said, "It's about names. I know they all matter to…all of you. All of us."

Poppy took a dainty sip from her mug while she waited for me to spit out my thought.

"Well." I swallowed, uncertain as to how I'd phrase the garbage churning through the disposal of my mind. "How do your…how does…umm…?"

"She's a writer." Fauna winked, mocking me. "Real wordsmith, this one."

I straightened my shoulders. "Power comes from worship, doesn't it? How does power get to you if you're always changing your name? The Hellenic pantheon is overflowing with followers. You're thriving. But if you live by aliases…" My words joined a slope of liquifying jam as it disappeared over a scone.

"Do you want to take this one, or should I?" Poppy asked, looking prettily at her partner.

"You glow, baby. I'll box." He grinned, chomping into whatever he'd shoveled onto his fork.

She kissed him on the cheek, then returned her too-intense eyes to me as she asked, "Who gave us the names Hades and Persephone? Was it him or me?"

My brows met in the center.

"They're human names by human men writing human accounts," she said. "Homer and Hesiod for the Grecians, Ovid for the Romans. Dorian and I know one another's true names, but that's rare. Most gods won't share what belongs to them and only them. Whatever they say—Poppy, Persephone—they're channeling my energy. It's little more than a funnel."

Whether tired of the topic or trying to save Poppy from human ignorance, Dorian dusted his fingers off, clapping them together as he said, "Back to the task at hand. While you're welcome to stay in Greece with Pops and me as long as you'd like, I see no use in wasting time. You said you have two war-ready Nordes?"

Fauna confirmed. "Estrid is a valkyrie—"

"I've never met one!" came Poppy's excited response. The morning light caught on her pale blond hair as it melted into rose-colored strands. Her skin was even more divine in the golden morning beams. I couldn't help but feel that her undertones looked utterly inhuman. If I'd met her on the street, she would have lived rent-free in my head as I pondered her curiously anomalous features on sleepless nights for the rest of my life.

Fauna's face tightened at the interruption before completing, "And Ella is one of the most alluring deities in our realm. She can procure anything, save for a god-killer, apparently. I don't doubt her ability to charm her way into Canaanite hearts and good graces. Fortunately, if we have both Fenrir and you, Dorian, on our side..."

Dorian leaned back in his chair, draping his elbow over the back as he observed the table. I'd recognized the ghosts of his ease in human men I'd seen before, but they had been imitations of him at best. True wealth, true power, true money relaxed at the far end of our breakfast table. The sun caught on his black hair, his strong jaw, the curves of his muscular shoulders, the glisten of buttons on his well-tailored shirt. The morning light over the sea caught on what remained of the curving glass of the French press, the meticulously arranged array of breakfast breads and sweets, the trays of fruits dotted with fresh-cut blossoms, and the meats, cheeses, and saltier bits that complemented the meal so well. He looked perfectly at ease amidst the evidence of his prosperity, his otherworldly wife, and his conversation of the dethroning of ancient powers.

"You'll arrive in the Phoenician realm under the guise of a bride seeking her betrothed," he restated. "Fauna will pass easily as your Nordic escort for obvious reasons. She's been spotted with you about the mortal realm, and with your blood, it won't raise brows. Fenrir might be received with curiosity, but I think you need to play the human card on that one. Dogs are wildly important to their humans."

It appeared that whatever message Fauna had received en route to the café had freed her from her oath, as everyone was comfortable plotting in the open. I was certain Fauna had known her contact was somewhere in Athens and her trip had been just for show, if only because each of the cheap, burnt corner-store coffees remained black. There wasn't a legitimate version of Fauna in any realm who wouldn't have put an undrinkable sludge of sugar into her cup before returning.

Fenrir made a huffing sound of displeasure, though it was probably Dorian's reference to humans and their pets, rather than Fauna and her erratic moves, that had made him puff. Dorian made an apologetic gesture, but pressed on.

"Your contacts, the goddess and the valkyrie, should arrive next."

I nodded along, agreeing. "Yes. Perhaps they received word that their Nordic friend was in the Phoenician realm, and they are simply there as a political envoy. Like—"

"Ambassadors," Poppy provided.

Dorian conceded, using Poppy's supplied word as he said, "I'm confident Phoenicians won't be thrilled with the development, but they also won't have their hackles up when two lower-level Nordic ambassadors show up in support of their brethren. It's nothing like the alarm bells of Loki's arrival. With these two...it's an excellent guise. You'll have to hold down the fort on your own for a day or two in order to make Poppy's and my appearance believable. We don't have eyes or ears on the inside, but I think with Fenrir on your side and the Prince within their walls, you can stay alive for forty-eight hours."

"Topside or their time?" Fauna asked.

"Hard to say," Poppy replied. "Hopefully we can dig up an antiquity in Dorian's pile of ancient pieces set to Phoenician time."

My thoughts fluttered to old-fashioned train stations and their twelve-hour clocks displaying the time zones of major cities around the world. I wondered what the clocks and calendars at a train station at the intersection of realms would look like. As interesting as the thought was, I hinged on hearing Caliban referenced from Dorian's mouth.

"The Prince," I repeated. A fairy-tale nightmare of a dragon's castle surrounded by moats of lava filled my mind. It pained me to picture him anywhere against his will. I knew he was powerful, but I didn't have a clue as to what those powers looked like.

Poppy looked between Fauna and I, concern still playing on her lovely features. "I just don't like the two of you showing up at their gates not knowing how they will receive you. You're expected, Merit, but as an honored guest? I'm not comfortable with your departure until we know whether you await fanfare, or the sharp end of a spear. You're too important to be mistreated." She looked at Fenrir and amended, "I'm sorry, I don't mean to imply that the three of you are differently weighted—but the fact remains, Fenrir, they don't know who you are. Fauna may be welcome, but she's still unexpected. I just…"

Dorian waved a hand, not to silence his partner, but as if to scatter the worries to the wind. "It's written in the stars, Pops. What will be, will be."

"I don't like leaving so much to fate," she grumbled. She and Fenrir exchanged glances for such a long time that I began to wonder if they were having the same sort of silent conversation that he and I had shared.

As if in answer to my question, my mind filled with his words. I could tell from the contemplative look on everyone's face that he was speaking to everyone in the room.

Fenrir's posture was both rigid and noble. His ears twitched slightly, head cocking like a curious dog. "Poppy's fears are not unwarranted. However, Merit and I left Hafna with certain understandings. The terms of our agreement will remain unfulfilled if I allow harm to befall her."

He didn't disclose what I'd promised him, though I suspected divulging the reason for our union would only strengthen Poppy and Dorian's allegiance, particularly given what Poppy and Fauna had shared. If they were hungry for the toppling of kingdoms, then helping a human get her Prince back was a small price to pay in the bigger picture. I tried to imagine the man in the linen shirt sipping espresso from a tiny cup on the Mediterranean cliffs tackling gods and blood and gore. I did my best to see Poppy, her happy smile, her pink hair, her white teeth, her effortless beauty in the throes of conflict. Perhaps Fauna—her chaos, her grins, her candy—was the biggest surprise of all. The fate of the world would boil down to unsuspecting freedom fighters who championed equality over comfort. Nothing about their lives was so terrible that they should trifle with the order of the world. They could continue with their forevers in their roles, amidst their homes and gifts and titles of the realms, and live an inarguably blessed life.

But what virtue was there in that when the cards were stacked against so many?

I selected a flaky piece of sugary baklava if only to have something to do with my hands. I bit down, speaking through the crumbs. "So, Fauna will spirit me into the Phoenician realm. We'll approach their gates and—"

"They aren't gates, my sweet," Poppy said, correcting me gently.

I looked up from the pastry.

She and Dorian exchanged looks. She sighed and continued, "The Phoenicians haven't received major mainstream worship for some time. At least, not outside of the negligible few devoted practitioners held by all deities. Not only have they been more or less forgotten, but they've been... uninvolved. There's a multitude of reasons Astarte and her compatriots were motivated to relocate to mortal lands. Things haven't been good in their realm for thousands of years."

I could feel the way my forehead wrinkled into something between worry and puzzlement. I didn't want to jump

171

to conclusions, but it sounded like she was implying the Phoenicians were in shambles.

"If not gates, then what?"

Poppy twisted her mouth to the side before saying, "Fauna will bring you to their outer bridge, if I'm not wrong."

Fauna nodded in confirmation.

"Have you been there? Either of you?" I looked between the divine women.

"Word gets around," Fauna supplied quietly.

Poppy continued, "You won't arrive to gardens or crops or centurions or fanfare. Dagon has been held hostage for centuries, and with him, agriculture. Astarte, her sister, and a favorite consort of Baal's have abandoned their realm. That left Baal and Melqart—his son and equal. Melqart, like"— she cleared her throat—"like *Dorian*, is a god of death and the Underworld. Father and son without any checks and balances, without their natural order, without prosperity or fertility or femineity left to reign over the ruins of their realm."

"Did they like Astarte?" I asked.

The others looked at me as if they didn't understand my question.

"I mean: Why would Anath bring Caliban and the others there in the first place? Why would she expect a warm welcome after she abandoned her realm to live in Bellfield? Unless the gods there didn't like Astarte, and maybe Anath was a prisoner, the same way Dagon was."

"Who cares if someone *likes* a top deity?" Fauna said.

Poppy corroborated her statement. "Liking someone has little to do with it. Name, honor, pride are at the wheel. The realm's image is more important than anyone's individual feelings. I'm sure that's why Anath knew she could return with prisoners no matter what."

I looked down into the dregs of my honey-sweet coffee, then looked between Fenrir and Fauna. Both eyed me curiously, but I had nothing to contribute. I was a mortal playing the game of gods. I returned my gaze to Poppy before asking, "When do we go?"

She shrugged. "How much coffee do you have left?"

Chapter Twenty

WIND AND RAZOR-SHARP SAND WHIPPED MY HAIR WITH MY words. I pitched my complaint above the howling, desolate landscape as I gritted my teeth. I could scarcely make out the square reddish buildings dotting the dry riverbed. "I hate it here."

I expected Fauna to tell me to give it a chance. She was usually chiding me over every passing thought. But she steeled her expression and straightened her posture. She didn't bother looking at the red sky overhead, the haze of dust in the air, or the lifeless expanse of toppled ruins and sand on either side before responding.

Instead, she nodded. "Me, too."

Maybe this was what came from being stripped of gods of life, crops, and fertility. Their realm had been robbed of rain, growth, and greenery. I looked to my left, then to my right. My eyes strained to see anything beyond the cracked expanse of dried clay but perceived only empty nothingness. Whatever trust issues I had were put aside as I reached for Fauna. There was no cowardice in comfort, and standing before the ominous, jagged outline of the Phoenician palace felt quite like looking up at cracked obsidian shards that had been rough-hewn into a palace.

I caught a glimpse of motion over my shoulder and

tugged her to look in my direction. A swirling brownish-reddish mountain stretched from ground to sky, closing in on us with terrifying speed.

"Is that—"

"It's a sandstorm." She coughed. "We need to get under shelter."

Fenrir planted his feet and sneezed, rejecting the sand that assaulted his nose. His coat, like our hair, was already caked with the dusty mark of the storm.

I didn't know enough of impending walls of dirt and their timelines, but the distant memory of a college astronomy class had me betting that the sun overhead was the red dwarf of a dying star. The enormous, dull light in the sky fought for my attention with the cloud of dust caking my lungs. A thin film had already begun to stick to Fauna's face and hair. I was relatively confident that if we didn't get moving soon into the shelter of the Phoenician palace, we'd suffocate before I was reunited with Caliban.

"Why is their realm like this?"

I knew the answer before I finished forming the question. We'd discussed it. Several major deities had been away for centuries. This realm had not been given the opportunity to symbiotically thrive. While the others glimmered with slices of modernity, this one remained decidedly archaic.

Fauna opened her mouth but covered it with the back of her hand before speaking her mind. I saw the question on her face. She wanted to know if I was ready. Dry wind ran its dusty fingers through her hair as she closed her eyes against the onslaught.

I answered her by leading us forward, tugging her along with the crook of my arm as we interlocked elbows. The gesture was for direction and comfort rather than affection. We couldn't risk separation in a sandstorm.

Fauna coughed into her hand, but each jagged inhalation only brought more dirt into her lungs. I learned from her mistake and swept my shirt up over my mouth to filter the dust.

Fenrir ran ahead of us and barked once to hasten us forward. I squinted as a cloud of dust assaulted us on a gust of hot wind, tugging us over a bridge that had been doubtlessly intended for a moat. Now it was little more than a dry trench, a sorrowful memory of what once had been.

We reached the far side of the bridge with no resistance. A wall encircled the chipped onyx palace, providing just enough relief from the wind for me to take in our surroundings. It looked like there had once been clay houses neighboring the palace, but there were no doors on their hinges, no closed shutters, no signs of life as we pushed forward. I'd underestimated the speed of the wind—the cloud of dust spilled over the far wall like a looming fog.

"Come on," Fauna urged, pushing us forward.

We hurried down the remaining stretch as we crossed the space between us and the palace.

A stranger called out in a language I couldn't discern from just beyond our line of sight. Unable to do anything more than advance, we went toward the voice.

"Stop!" came the woman's thickly accented voice once more. Through squinted eyes, I looked up at a figure clad for the horrors of the desert and its storms. Her hardened armor would protect her against the glass-like shards of sand. The cloth around her mouth would protect her lungs, and another veil could be tugged down at a moment's notice to protect her eyes. She clutched a long spear with both hands.

Fauna had no patience for the imposition. "You have the Prince of Hell," she said. "This is his betrothed. She's been invited to your banquet. Let us in."

The sand hit my exposed skin like a million tiny knives. My bare shoulders, arms, and thighs were assaulted by the gust of hot dust as the wind descended on the city. I struggled to imagine that the Phoenicians received a lot of visitors. My arrival was expected, or so I'd been told. It made the guard's reaction all the more worrying. There was no gentleness in her posture nor her voice as she ushered us into the palace.

It took a while for my eyes to adjust to the window-less gloom of the antechamber. The iridescent rainbows of dark oil slicks blinked over my vision as I struggled to discern light from shadow. I didn't realize how tightly I was gripping Fauna's arm until she made a small sound at my side. I looked in horror at the deep purple-red marks my fingers had made on her bicep as I'd struggled to adapt.

Fenrir shook his coat as if he'd been caught in the rain, and a cloud of his dust filled the hall.

The guard called to someone unseen, once more using a language I didn't recognize. I knew a smattering from my upbringing in the church, a little from my studies writing the Pantheon books, and a bit more from my helpless week on search engines and computers while separated from Caliban after escaping Astarte's fingertips. The Canaanites had spoken a number of languages during their prominent time in the human realm, from a medieval relative of the still-living Hebrew, to Moabite, Punic, and of course, Phoenician. I wasn't educated enough to say so much as *hello* in modern Hebrew on a good day. While most of the gods I'd encountered had spent eternity flitting between realms, I felt a stab of uncertainty that the Phoenicians would be as accommodating to my ignorance as the others had been.

A thick, bearded man only a few inches taller than Fauna or I approached. He was dressed for the temperature, not the elements. Unlike the guard at the door, his knee-length tunic was sleeveless. A belt provided a hook for his dagger and water flask, but he wore little by way of protection. I wondered if he had unseen abilities, or if the weather was simply too uncomfortable to expect sleeves and pants beyond the wall. I was glad for the dresses Poppy had gifted us as we followed the man down the hall.

"No," came the same guard's voice.

The man escorting us paused as we all turned to regard her. My shoulders tensed as I held my breath, terrified our plan had been uncovered before it had even begun.

"No dog," she said firmly.

My pulse quickened. "He has to come with us. He's my dog. I can't—"

"No dog," she repeated. She used the dull end of her spear as a cane to herd him closer. I widened my eyes in panic, but Fenrir shook his head once. He didn't have to use his gift to tell me not to press the issue. I attempted to reason with myself that there would be no room or shelter or shed they could put Fenrir in that would be more terrible than being tethered to a boulder in a marsh and left to die, but it did little to console me.

He was powerful enough to bring on the Twilight of the Gods. I was with Fauna, a deity in her own right. I needed to take a breath. I needed to unclench my fists. I needed to focus on the fact that Caliban was somewhere here, within the walls.

The pair exchanged a few more quick words before the woman took off in the opposite direction, continuing to use the blunt end of her spear to urge Fenrir down the hall.

I looked at Fauna, but I wasn't sure why. I didn't expect her to answer, to translate, or to explain. She simply shook her head once, just as Fenrir had done, as she laced her fingers between mine. I felt a thin grime of dust in the gaps between our fingers. I ran my tongue along my teeth, doing my best to summon saliva and rid my mouth of the grit. I didn't want to ask for water moments after arriving.

The man stopped at a seamless stone wall. He pressed his hand against it, and a door without hinges pushed back from the unbroken surface before swinging open.

Shit.

I didn't have to look at Fauna to understand we were entering a cage.

We followed the man through the door. I looked over my shoulder as it scraped shut behind us. I squeezed Fauna's hand and jerked my head for her to look. It took her less than a second for her crestfallen face to tell me all I needed to know. The elaborate seal on the wall informed me we were in serious trouble. She sucked in a tight breath of unsullied air but wouldn't meet my eyes as she blinked at the ground. Her gaze stayed trained on the sandaled heels of the man before us, paralyzed by whatever she'd seen.

I tried a few grounding exercises I'd been taught in therapy for whenever I felt a panic attack coming on. The therapist had instructed me to ground myself by asking questions about each of my five senses, and by the end, I would be calm. I heard the steady slapping of feet on the corridor floor. I smelled sweat and grime and the ancient scent of decaying structures. I tasted dirt. I felt stifling heat, the slick nervousness of Fauna's hand in mine, and the near-painful pounding of my heart. And I saw darkness. Nothing but claustrophobic darkness as the walls, ceiling, and floor pressed in on me.

The therapist was wrong. The exercise had made things much, much worse.

He took us into an enormous windowless bedroom and gestured for us to stop. He didn't bother speaking to us as he held up his hands for us to wait, then excused himself through another seamless door. His hand summoned an invisible rectangle, drawn forth by his magnetism. It swung open by his will, then scraped closed as he stepped through.

In the absence of his shoes on the ground, I heard only the drumlike thunder of my heartbeat and the threatening hum of dizziness in my ears. I tried to pull in air, but it became harder and harder to breathe.

"Why would they...? I don't understand." I buried my fingers in my tangled hair. "We were invited. We belong here! Why would they put us in a cage? Why...?"

Fauna ran to the wall the moment he departed. It contained the same angular seal I'd seen on the first door. She looked like a mime against an invisible wall as she clambered up and down the stone. "Shit, shit, shit."

She continued scrambling against the seamless door. I stared vacantly at our circumstances, assuming my nymph was looking for something magical, something unseen, something that only a deity could summon. She reached the ground and groaned. She slammed tight fists against the door before rising again, skimming her flattened palms against the door.

I extended a hand from behind her. "Fauna—"

"I'm not done," she bit through gritted teeth.

I stumbled on my words. She was rarely short with me. I stared after her while she continued to search the wall for a slip, a crack, *something*.

I watched for thirty seconds. One minute. Three minutes.

I flexed and unflexed my fingers at my sides, inhaling through my nose as I forced myself to look away. Focusing on Fauna's panic would only rile me into a state of unrest. We'd been invited. Surely this was just rude, terrifying precaution. I wished I had the wits to appreciate my surroundings. Gauzy curtains, a four-post bed, and gold, black, and stone that my limited exposure could only affiliate with Egyptian hiero-glyphics crowded the room. The far wall had a black gem tub that ran nearly the length of the room. The black settee was curved with luxurious gold legs and angles.

I stepped away from Fauna's still-searching shape toward the bath to see that it was already filled with water and rose petals. Apart from the rose water, the scents of lilies and lemongrass wafted through the room. I couldn't find the source of the lemongrass, but a few overflowing vases had a curious blue flower that reminded me of lily pads and the pond lotus. I wondered if that was the floral scent on the air.

There was nothing else to see.

"Fauna—"

Her command came out in a desperate snarl. "Let me look!"

"Fauna!"

She rested one hand on the wall and turned to me with fiery embers in her eyes. I almost gasped at the crimson glower of her anger. She heaved as she looked at me with the true fury of a god. "What!"

I shook my head in surprise, taking a half step back. I bumped into the hip-high bath before realizing I had nowhere to escape. "We can't get out," was all I said.

"I'm trying to fix that," she hissed through bared teeth.

"We'll be okay," I said in a soothing, placating voice. I wasn't sure why I believed it, but I did. Maybe it was the lack of malice in the guard's voice. Maybe it was the accommodations we'd been presented. Maybe it was the number of times I'd been locked in a room, a closet, or a basement as punishment. I'd been shut into a crumbling building in the forest as a child, and Caliban had come for me. He was here now. Somewhere within these walls, I knew he was here. I'd learned the resiliency of patience through my cages. And our cage was gilded.

"We're sealed in," she said, voice hitching with panic.

"Caliban is here. We're guests, not prisoners. I know it doesn't feel like it, but—"

"What do you call this, if not imprisonment?" Each of her words was more frantic than the one before.

"Have you never been locked in before?"

Her brows turned up in the middle. Her hand dropped from the wall. Her honey-brown eyes widened into their doe form as she said, "I'm a deity."

I nodded, face softening. "I know you are. And I know this is scary. But even though I'm human, maybe I'm the expert here."

She sucked in a sharp breath of air. "I couldn't jump when I was in the mortal realm by *choice,* Marlow. I didn't go into Bellfield because—"

"Because Azrames didn't want you to go into a trap. But he and I went in. I don't know if it was his first, but it certainly wasn't mine."

Her face collapsed, expression defeated. Her hands went limp at her sides.

"We'll be okay," I said.

She looked at me defiantly, lip quivering. "These seals

prevent us from being okay, Marlow. I can't leave. It isn't just jumping to prevent others from seeing us entering. We can't move. We're sitting ducks. We're animals. We're—"

"We're sunflowers," I said. I extended my hand. My heart lurched at the motion, realizing the position I was putting us in. I'd had my reasons to distrust her, but I didn't. She was chaotic, and frustrating, and bizarre, but I knew in my gut that I loved her. "Maybe there's no light right now," I said.

She looked like she was about to cry. She took a half step toward me before lifting her own hands to her arms to hug herself.

"So, I'll be your sun, and you'll be mine."

Her eyes were glassy with impending tears. I understood from her face, from her insistence, that her fear was not for herself. She hadn't crossed the room to me, and she'd known me for scarcely a blip on her life's radar. Her panic had come from understanding the fortress of the Phoenician palace.

I tried once more. "We'll be sunflowers."

Chapter Twenty-One

APRIL 2, AGE 11

FOUR MONTHS AFTER MY NIGHTMARISH ELEVENTH BIRTHDAY party, I was desperate to make the girls in my class like me. Instead, I faced my first experience with a tomb.

Even in my innocence, I was no stranger to tension. Our trailer in the woods was no castle on a cliff. My parents kept the yard clipped and clean. They took pride in what they owned. But we were not well-liked, nor were we disillusioned as to our status in the community.

"Are you sure you want to do this?" I could hear the frown in my mom's voice. She brushed my hair into a slick ponytail on top of my head. I winced as the teeth of the brush pressed firmly into my tender scalp. It was a bit embarrassing to still have my mother doing my hair in middle school. Other girls had learned how to do their hair, but I struggled to keep my arms high and twist the band tight enough to get the desired result. I flinched as the brush once more yanked a bit too hard. My mom clicked her tongue, saying, "It hurts to be beautiful."

"I'm ready to go," I said, getting down from the chair. I dipped for the duffle bag resting beside the bed.

My mom crossed her arms as she looked between me and the bag I'd packed.

"Yes," I assured her. "Chelsea's never invited me to one of

her parties before, but all the cool girls get to go. I've heard her mom is really funny. She plays pranks and reads scary stories."

"Is Kirby going to be there?"

I fidgeted. My mother wasn't fond of my only friend since Kirby's parents didn't go to church. My mom permitted the friendship if only because it had been the single shred of kindness in the wake of my traumatizing eleventh birthday. As it stood, Kirby was only allowed to come over to my house because the visits could happen under good Christian supervision.

"No. Kirby isn't cool, either. Maybe if I get into the group, we'll both get in."

She tapped her fingers rhythmically on her bicep as her frown deepened. She looked off into the corner of the room and stared into the empty nothingness for a long time. "What if we make a bargain?"

I looked over my shoulder to see the empty chair that had drawn her attention. The stitched bunny my mother had made sat upright, ears flopping to the side. It stared back at me while my lips turned down. I looked up at her.

Reluctance and hesitation scratched at me. She wasn't the sort to strike deals. This home was a dictatorship under God's mighty plan with my mother as his mouthpiece, not a democracy. I felt the slumber party slipping through my fingers as I scanned her face for signs that she was about to take one of my first exciting social experiences away from me. "What sort of bargain?"

"Call me," she said. "Tonight after dinner, give me a call. If you still want to stay over, I'll drop off your bag. If you don't call, I'll assume you want to be picked up, and I'll come get you."

I was certain I didn't hide the confusion from my expression. She wasn't trying to run my life from behind the curtain. She looked genuinely concerned.

"Why?" I asked.

She looked to the rabbit in the corner again for a while, and the room grew heavy with the weight of unspoken sorrow. I wasn't sure how much time passed before she said, "When I was in high school, I knew a girl who was really excited to go to a party. She was pretty unpopular. Weird parents, weird girl, didn't get asked out very often. They gave her a bottle and told her it was beer, but it wasn't. One of the boys had peed in the bottle, and they watched her drink it."

I watched my mom while she stared at the rabbit. She'd settled into her cold, numb trip down memory lane.

Somehow, I knew that she wasn't telling a story about some other girl.

"Okay," I said quietly, because there was nothing else I could do. I was certain that it wasn't my place to touch her or comfort her. I wasn't old enough to know how to help, but I understood this was a memory best left in disconnect. "I'll call."

My father grunted something or other as we walked past where he sat with the newspaper in the kitchen, and I muttered an equally insincere goodbye. It was a twenty-minute drive from our trailer outside of town to Chelsea's house on the edge of town. She was one of the only other classmates who lived on the outskirts of town, even if her neighborhood was nestled within city limits.

My mother's discomfort grew as we pulled up to Chelsea's house.

"It's so pretty." I grinned in admiration at the Victorian-style house with enormous, white wooden pillars. The mature tree in the front had a tire swing, just like in storybooks. It was a far cry from our single-wide mobile home. "It looks like one of those old houses from a rich person movie!"

"It is," my mom agreed, peering through the windshield at the three-story home.

"I'll call," I said again as I closed the car door. She waited in the driveway to ensure that Chelsea's mom was indeed home before she pulled away.

What ensued was everything I'd imagined and more. Tiny snacks were served on trays. Festive, kid-friendly cocktails came out of the kitchen while we played a scavenger game filled with riddles and questions. I got to explore Chelsea's home in a round of sardines, where all seven of the girls at the party set off to find the elected girl in hiding. If you found her, you needed to crawl into the space beside her and remain quiet as the second, then the third, then the fourth one discovered you. The last one to find the pack of sardines was the loser. She had a basement, three stories, and the sort of dusty A-frame attic filled with cobwebs and antiques that I hadn't thought truly existed.

I was the only person who'd never been to Chelsea's house before, so I, of course, was the last to find the canned sardines.

"Do I hide next?" I asked.

Chelsea exchanged looks with a few of the others. They nodded before she asked, "Do you want to see something cool?"

Yes, I did want to see something cool. Chelsea announced to her mother that we were headed to the woods behind the house, which I found fascinating. She didn't ask permission, merely disseminated information. Her mother waved a supportive goodbye as seven little girls marched out of the door, water bottles in hand. Chelsea carried flashlights, a hammer, and cheese sticks in her backpack.

"Where are we going?" I asked. I was no stranger to the woods, but something about this felt different. My trees were safe. The trails, bushes, plants, and mushrooms near my house were my friends. Besides, I was never truly alone when I wandered outside near my house. My vibrant imagination kept me company in the form of a delightfully pretty fox. I was relatively certain there were no foxes near Chelsea's house.

We rounded a corner at the end of her street and began to walk down a poorly maintained gravel road. Grass sprouted up from the center. A tree had fallen toward the road's entrance, and though its leaves had died and it had begun to rot, no one had pushed it out of the way. I wondered how long it had been since someone had driven down this road. It was a relatively warm day. While we weren't yet in the sweaty grips of summer, our collective uniforms were the jeans, T-shirts, basketball shorts, and backward hats of middle schoolers.

"You're going to love it," said McKenna. She was the first in our grade to get a boyfriend. I'd never been allowed to go to her house, as her parents' reputation as barflies did little to impress my deeply religious family. "There's a haunted house in the woods."

I couldn't keep the tingling excitement from my voice as I repeated, "We're going to see a haunted house?"

There was a magical part of me, the part that had sat on the bed and listened to my mother read stories of secret worlds in wardrobes and kind wizards and important quests, that itched at the possibility that there might be something fantastic hidden just beyond a neighborhood, something that could be discovered by an intrepid crowd of voyaging friends. Maybe Narnia awaited us. Or maybe I'd get to show the other girls that I had an arctic fox for a friend, and they'd think I was cool after all.

Chelsea nodded as she marched us forward. "I've shown most of them the house before! It's really freaky. It's abandoned."

"Is it safe?" I asked. I wasn't sure if it was a question with a real answer. Nothing haunted was ever truly safe. I hadn't been allowed to watch horror movies, but McKenna had told us the plot of a rated-R movie where a family had moved into a house with ghosts, and we'd listened in rapture around the lunchroom table.

"Sure!" Chelsea said without looking over her shoulder.

They all turned to look at me with poorly concealed antic-ipation as we rounded into view of the home. The weath-ered gray wood of a two-story home sat at the end of the driveway. It was old, but not in the fancy way that Chelsea's home had been old. There was something forlorn about the farmhouse and its thin, splintering pillars. The windows had been boarded up with planks that matched the ancient home around it. The thistles, tangled rose-briar, and wild grasses nearly covered the ground-floor windows.

"It's all planked up," I said.

Chelsea nodded. "The door at the back is open. We come here a lot."

"Have you been inside?" I asked.

They exchanged looks again. I thought I caught a giggle, but took it for excitement over our shared adventure.

"It's really cool inside," Chelsea promised.

"So you've been in? How many times?" I asked as we picked our way through the grass. Thorns and brambles tore at my legs, and I wished I'd worn long pants. I swatted at an itchy bug as I followed our leader.

"It's so cool," McKenna said, echoing Chelsea's assertion. "You'll love it."

We kept to the house's perimeter, and I saw what she meant. The back door had a single large board on hinges. It had been padlocked, presumably by whoever owned the house.

"Are we trespassing?" I asked. I knew the word from the signs my father had hung on all corners of our property. While this particular home lacked the large black-and-red posters, the padlock told me that someone had made painstaking efforts to keep visitors out.

"Of course," Chelsea said, "but no one's going to find out. No one comes out here."

"Then why do they need a lock?"

She shrugged, which I understood. These were the sorts of mysteries that would probably never have answers. I took a step away from the group of girls to peer at the windows on the second floor. They were too far from the ground to require the same boards and protections as the ground floor.

188

I was about to point out that there was a stained-glass picture of a rose when Chelsea called out.

"You're first, Marlow."

The buzz of enthusiasm vanished. Worry replaced anticipation as I looked at her. "You want me to go in first?"

"Yup," McKenna agreed. She looked to the others, and they all nodded along. "It's like...what's that word for when you're new to a club?"

"Initiation," Chelsea said, handing me a flashlight from the backpack.

"Right," McKenna confirmed. "Initiation. It's your first time here, so you lead the pack."

Something wasn't right. I fought the urge to take a step backward. I wrestled with the cowardly voice that told me to run.

This is what it's like to have more than one friend, I told myself. *It's just scary because it's new.*

I took the flashlight from Chelsea and leaned around them to see in through the wooden board that stood ajar, padlock open.

McKenna opened the board wider and the fear became a mist, filling my lungs and seeping out through my pores. I swatted at another bug that bit into my skin, but couldn't tear my eyes from the tiny door at the back of the house. While the board covered the entrance to the outside, a thin atrium ran to the original detailed wooden door that separated us from the haunted house. Though the frame remained intact, the bottom panels had been punched out, leaving only a black hole that led into the belly of the home.

"You...want me to go first?" I asked again, hands clammy as I adjusted my grip on the flashlight.

"Just crawl through the hole," Chelsea said. "We'll be right behind you."

Don't.

This time, the voice in my head didn't sound like it belonged to me at all. I whipped around to the trees, but no one was there. My fear had taken on sentience. I shoved it down as I looked at the others, all smiling and nodding.

"And you've been in there before?"

"It's so cool inside," McKenna repeated.

They aren't answering your question because they've never been inside.

I whipped over my shoulder once more, heart thundering in my ears. The adrenaline made me begin to shake. I couldn't explain why, but I felt the sudden urge to cry. I extended my flashlight to Chelsea as I attempted to hand it back to her. "I don't want to go inside," I said.

Chelsea made a face.

McKenna's eyes may have stuck near the back of her head for how aggressively she rolled them at me. "I told you she wasn't cool enough to go in," she said.

"You were right," Chelsea agreed, with the others muttering similar disappointments.

"No," I protested weakly. "I can…"

A man's voice in my head spoke again.

Marlow, please listen. Do not go in.

I swallowed down the fear lecturing me from the most insecure parts of my subconscious. I reminded myself that there was no such thing as ghosts. I was being a big baby. They said it was really cool inside, and they'd be right behind me.

The voice in my head begged me thrice to stop, but I stepped up to the door. I looked over my shoulder, wiping sweat from my brow. It wasn't sweat of heat, but the physical manifestation of nerves that I couldn't contain. The slumber party of girls looked on expectantly.

We'd had a wonderful day. They'd fed me snacks, we'd gone on a scavenger hunt, we'd played sardines, and now they were showing me a special secret. I was one of them. I wasn't going to ruin it by being a coward.

I hoped my swallow wasn't audible as I stepped over a thicket of sprawling weeds and planted a foot into the atrium. I looked at them again. "Are you coming?"

There was an odd, gluey quality to the way their gazes stuck to each other's.

"We can only go through the door one at a time," Chelsea said, eyes on McKenna.

I looked at the black hole that gaped like a screaming mouth crying for me to stay out of its insides. She was right. There was only room for one of us to fit at a time. I nodded, ignoring their grumbles about how long it was taking me to move forward. The second I stepped into the atrium, the temperature changed. There were no windows for sunlight to seep through. The chilly air made the hairs on my legs stand up.

"Go on," McKenna urged. "We can't go in until you've gotten through the door."

In hindsight, I knew exactly what they were doing, even in the moment. I felt it deep in my bones, ringing through my thoughts, aching in my gut, though I forced my instincts to be silent. The evidence had been splayed out like a neon sign telling me that they were six sneaky bitches, and I was a lonely fool who wanted friends.

I'd barely squeezed through the pitch-black hole punched into the door when the board slammed closed behind me.

In the second it took me to crawl back through the opening and sprint down the short span of the lightless atrium, they'd secured the padlock. I didn't have the space for logic. Even if I had known that a shut padlock meant they couldn't let me out even if they wanted, I only had one tool at my disposal, and it was my fear.

I didn't waste any time with polite inquires or teasing calls to the girls who had posed as friends.

Panic was the only thing I knew.

I dropped all pretense of friendliness as my fists began to pound against the large, flat plank that had locked me into a perfectly dark, cold prison. I used the butt of the flashlight and the heels of my hands to beat the plywood with every ounce of strength I possessed. I screamed for them to let me out, begging them to open the door.

Adrenaline and frenzy suffocated me as their fading giggles floated through the door. I was dimly aware of sharp, horrible pain in my hands. I was sure that if I looked at them, I would see blood and splinters in my chewed-up palms. I choked on my tears as I screamed again and again and again.

Marlow, you need to breathe.

I didn't need to breathe. I needed to tear my way out. I needed to escape.

Marlow, calm down or you're going to pass out.

I didn't need to calm down. I was going to die in here. It was dark, and it was haunted, and it was full of zombies and rabid animals and ghosts and horrible monsters that would gnaw the flesh from my bones and drink my blood and drag me into the basement where I'd never be seen or heard from again.

I rammed my entire body into the plank and cried out against the shooting pain as a numbing sensation shot up and down my arm.

You're going to hurt yourself. Stop and breathe.

"I don't need to stop," I yelled at the voice inside my head between choking, smothering sobs. Every breath was like trying to gasp in bubbles of air while deeply underwater. There was no light. There was no escape. There was only the darkness, and the monsters, and pure, unadulterated fear.

Marlow—

"No!" I sobbed. I cried out as the pain in my hands cut through my panic. I struggled with trembling fingers to turn on the flashlight only to see fresh, wet blood dripping onto the wooden floor. I was going to die in here. Everyone who knew where I was had left me for dead. I lifted the shaking puddle of light to two smears of blood where my fists had pounded against the door. I sank against the door, flashlight pointed into the mouth of hell so I could see when the horrid zombies came for me at long last while I cried, and cried, and cried.

"Breathe," the calm male voice said aloud.

I yelped, dropping the flashlight onto the atrium floor. I fumbled with the light as I grabbed for the torch amidst the debris. I wasn't alone in the house.

"Who's there?" I tried to call out, but wasn't sure that more than a few disjointed, raspy syllables came out through my panic.

A brief moment pulsed between the phantom and me, patient, as if not to rush me. "I'm here. We're going to take one deep breath. Inhale with me, and exhale. Are you ready?"

The light was all over the place. I couldn't keep it still enough to remain fixed on the hole. The trembling took over my arms as panic consumed me. I was dizzy, I was choking, and I was going to die.

I'd been certain things couldn't get worse, but I was wrong.

The unsteady light began to dim, its bright white fading to yellow, then to orange. "No, please no, please," I begged of the flashlight.

"They gave you one with dead batteries," said the voice. It wasn't afraid, or warning, or accusatory. It simply *was*. "Close your eyes. The flashlight is about to die. Everything will be dark in a moment."

"Please—"

"Close your eyes," he repeated.

And because I didn't know what else to do, I listened. I didn't want to see the monster before it ate me. I closed my eyes as I tucked my face into my knees and cried with earth-shaking force. I wasn't sure how much time passed before panic surged through me once more as my worst fears were realized. The monster had reached me. My life was over and I was about to be eaten. The pressure of hands on my shoulders verified that this truly was the end.

"One breath in, and one breath out. You are not alone."

I tried to ask him who he was, but I couldn't get the words out.

"In," he said, voice calm, and waited for a long time until

at long last, I complied. "And out," he said. "Good," he said, gentle, quiet pride in his soft voice. "We're going to do it again."

And we did. Inhale, and exhale.

"It's not safe down here," he said.

"What's down here?" I managed to ask now that I was calm enough to speak.

"It doesn't matter," he said. Still no alarm. No urgency. Every word was picked with soothing intentionality. "We're going to go upstairs. The windows aren't boarded. It will be light up there. You can sit and wait."

"Wait for what?"

"For your mother," came his calm reply.

I wasn't sure who he was or how he knew my mother, but some part of me understood the stranger holding my shoulders was right. My mom would be waiting for me to call. She would come looking for me. I wouldn't die in here. There was a way out.

"Keep your eyes closed," he said. "I'm going to get you upstairs, but you shouldn't see what we're about to walk through."

"What's down here?" I asked again, nausea piggybacking onto my fear as my stomach twisted. I knew the answer. I knew that ghouls tore their way through the soil and ate children. I knew that demons possessed women in white dresses and crawled across the ceiling like crabs. I knew that messages were written in blood by ghosts and that haunted houses had gateways to Hell.

"It doesn't matter," he repeated. I felt a thumb brush over my cheek as he wiped at my hot tears. His hand was so much colder than the warm summer day. Even despite the chilly, sunless air in the house, his fingers felt several degrees cooler. "Keep them closed. I'll carry you up. Are you ready?"

I didn't see any alternative. If I said no, I'd remain in the ink-dark atrium with the rusty nails and broken glass. Maybe the man speaking to me was a murderer, though he didn't sound like one. Even if I was about to be killed, it didn't seem worse to be killed by him upstairs than eaten in the atrium by the frothing, feral animals, or the dripping, decaying skin of the undead that would tear me limb from limb if I remained. I couldn't bring myself to verbalize my answer, but he seemed to sense my response. I tucked my face against a shoulder as arms slipped under my knees and behind my back. I left the useless flashlight on the floor as weightlessness overtook me.

True to my word, I didn't open my eyes.

I expected the squeaking of boards as the man carried me, but we ascended the stairs silently. I felt the light before I saw it.

"I can stay for a minute longer," he said, "but you won't be able to see me when you open your eyes. It isn't time for you to know my face. Not yet."

He set me down gently in a large room. A moth-eaten quilt remained on the ornate brass-posted bed. Family photos hung on the walls. A fur was mounted on the coatrack in the corner of the room. I looked about the room at the armoire, the chest, the desk, my eyes landing finally on a stained-glass window that overlooked the overgrown yard where a handful of my classmates had stood and laughed only minutes before.

"Are you real?"

"It hurts me that this happened to you," was all he said.

I knew my face was still puffy and stained with salt. I stared down at my hands and wasn't surprised to see they were swollen, red, and dripping with fresh blood. I sniffled as the dull throb from my wounds reached me. I looked in the direction of the voice, even if there was nothing to see.

"Why did they do this?" I asked. I didn't know why I would ask my imaginary friend, but even if my mind had made him up, he was a grown-up, and he seemed nice. Grown-ups were supposed to know things. Maybe he was the part of my mind that knew things.

"This isn't the first time people have been cruel, and it won't be the last. Like calls to like, Marlow, and it will draw them toward each other and push them from you. The ones who did this to you are painfully human. They have the same goals, the same aspirations, and will lead similar, mundane lives."

I didn't like the implication that it was human nature to do something like this. I was human, and I would never have done this. I didn't have to be an adult to know how dangerous it was to lock someone in a haunted house with monsters and glass and crazed, wild wolves. They had tried to kill me, even if they'd thought it was a funny joke.

"Thank you," I said to him.

"Your mother will come," the man said. "Make me a promise."

I looked in his direction with both fear and confusion.

"When you're taken down the stairs, close your eyes again."

"What's your name?" I asked, knowing that it would be useless to try to ask him what horrors remained downstairs. I no longer wanted to know. I would sit in the light of what was left of the day. I would look at the stained-glass rose. I would explore the time capsule of fur coats and old letters and abandoned trinkets.

"You don't need me yet," he said. "For a few more years, enjoy your time in the forest and playing with the fox in the woods."

"You know about the fox?"

I could almost hear the sad sound of a smile in his low, quiet exhale. "I do," he said. A moment later, invisible arms gathered me into a hug, and I was overcome with the fresh scent of the forest. "I won't let anything happen to you," he said.

And though I continued to try to speak to my imaginary friend, no further answers came.

I walked from room to room to see if he was hiding around the corner, but there was no one to be found. No evidence that anyone had been here but me. And if my imagination had helped me get upstairs, away from the darkness and into the light, then it had helped me in my time of need. I said a quiet prayer as I thanked my guardian angel for helping me escape the dark, scary basement, and I settled in, knowing it would be a while before I was found.

I read old letters in dense cursive writing marked with dates from before my great-grandma was born. I picked up a hand mirror and looked at my tearstained face. I picked through the mildewy old clothes as I looked for treasures, knowing I had nothing better to do. My stomach grumbled as dinnertime came and went. Though the upstairs had unboarded windows and natural light, I knew that I'd only have a couple more hours before these rooms and halls were as dark as the basement.

I wished the man would come back, but no matter how I tried to conjure him again, he wouldn't come. Maybe if my imagination was this good, I'd be able to share it one day. I could write stories about mean girls and a brave heroine. I could tell magical tales of the brave, secret friend who helped her when she felt alone. I could grow up and fix everything, writing the sorts of fantasy stories that my mom had read to me in my books. In my fairy tales, no one would be stuck in a house. And if they were, the enemies who'd trapped them would be dealt with.

I wondered if my story would have a lion eat them, or a bus hit them, or a sickness sweep over the school where they all threw up so much that their stomachs ended up outside of their bodies and on the floor.

Then I smiled as I thought of a better end to the story.

I'd make the popular girls unimportant. Everyone would realize that the uncool girl was interesting, and pretty, and fun. And the characters in the book like McKenna and Chelsea would not have friends, or happy lives, or like who they were, because they knew the heroine was the true best person in the world, and that they were wrong and remorseful for hurting her feelings and treating her like zombie food.

As the sun set, red and blue lights filtered through the grimy upstairs window and flooded the house. I ran to the window and looked at three police cars and my mom's small green car. Cracks and splinters erupted as boards were torn from their hinges. Shouts and exclamations filled the basement. There was the static and clicking of orders, of alarm, of policemen as someone cried my name. I turned over my shoulder at the sound of feet thundering up the stairs.

I was too alarmed to say anything as a man with a mustache found me. "I'm with the police," he said. "You're safe. We've got you. Your mom's outside."

Close your eyes.

And I did. I squeezed my eyes shut as the man scooped me up. I kept them tightly sealed as the creaks of wood and the popping of boards filled the air. I knew there were many people in the house, and that I didn't need to see any of them. I kept them shut so tightly that stars burst on the insides of my eyelids. I hadn't realized I was gripping the back of the policeman's uniform until he began to lower me outside of the house.

I opened my eyes to my parents. My mother's face was so much like the one looking back at me in the handheld mirror upstairs: puffy, red, and stained with tears. She crushed me in a hug that was only broken when a woman in uniform had her carry me to the back of an ambulance. They made my hands sting as they poured a burning liquid over them and bandaged them up. They told my mom I needed to go to a hospital, and my mom agreed.

The doctor would give me many shots. One for rabies, one for tetanus, and a few others I didn't understand. They'd look in my eyes with bright lights, in my ears, and listen to my chest. I wasn't a child, but I wasn't big enough to understand half of the words. I didn't know what an overdose was, but I knew about drugs, and I knew about death.

In the days following the slumber party, I stayed home from school. We heard about the abandoned house on the news, and about the little girl rescued from a well-known drug den. The mattresses on the ground floor of the house had the bodies of two missing teens.

My mom was furious, and rightfully so. Chelsea's mom was equally furious. Even McKenna's mom was in agreement. I was the victim, and the girls were in trouble. And while the principal and parents saw that I was worthy of justice, eleven-year-old girls saw things a little differently. I'd gotten them grounded for the rest of the year. They were kicked off the basketball team. I'd ruined their lives. And for that, I'd pay the price.

For the rest of the year, they played a game called *Marlow Is Invisible.*

They wouldn't speak to me when I tried to see if everything was all right between us. They pretended they couldn't hear me. They'd get up and move if I sat beside them. And I could only cry myself to sleep so many times before my parents decided that I needed to change schools. What had happened to me was bad in the best of lights. The ripples that echoed through my life following the haunted house showed the scars that wouldn't heal, no matter how many elders prayed over me, or how many Bible studies I attended.

It was a month before I was in the car with my mom on the way to another doctor's appointment in order to ensure I hadn't contracted anything bad from my time in the haunted house.

"Mom?" I asked.

She didn't look at me while she maneuvered her car into the hospital parking lot and began searching for a spot. She'd had to take the day off work to get me to my appointment, and the air between us was tight and strained. "Mmm?"

I swallowed and looked at the fading scabs on my hands as I asked, "Why did they make her drink pee? The girl at that party?"

My mom stiffened. She wordlessly finished her search and eased the car into a space. She put it into park and continued to stare out the windshield for a long time. She turned it off and we listened to the ticking of the engine as the summer day consumed the car, yet she remained motionless. At long last, she said, "Because she was different, Marlow. And people don't like things that are different."

Chapter Twenty-Two

T HE STAKES WERE HIGHER NOW, BUT SO WAS MY FAITH.
I'd once called out to a god who'd never acknowl-
edged my existence. Now I knew that when I cried into
the dark, someone was listening. Wherever he was in the
Canaanite palace, we were under one roof together.

I studied Fauna's irises, the browns and ambers reminding
me so much of crushed autumn leaves. Her head shook again,
white and copper hair mixing like the blur of a baby deer
running from its terror as tears spilled over her lids. The tears
continued as I crossed the distance and hugged her.

"I know you're scared. I'm scared, too."

Her broken tears confirmed my suspicions. Her terror
came from realizing she'd underestimated Azrames's circumstances. She'd spent her time watching cartoons and eating
gummy bears, unwilling to picture him in a Phoenician tomb.

Her forehead collapsed against my bare shoulder, and I
felt the heat and water of her tears before the first shudder of
her sob. Her hand slipped around me, sliding against my back
and pinning me against her as she cried.

"You love him," was all I said.

She tightened her hold against me. Hell had been in a war
against Heaven from the moment they'd met, but I wondered as
to Azrames's involvement in the fight. He'd been busy working

with Betty across her lives for hundreds, if not thousands, of years. Fauna knew he could handle himself against humans, parasites, witches, and nuisances. When a seal had been terraformed, he'd kept her safe by disappearing without her. For all I knew, it was the first time he'd taken on a god.

Knowing what I did now of Fauna's ideology, I wondered how much had rubbed off on him, and how much she blamed herself for putting him in danger. It was one thing to fight for what you believed in. It was another to watch someone else fall because of those beliefs.

"He doesn't drag me into his shit," Fauna said, sagging to the ground. She pulled me with her to the floor until our embrace melted into the uncomfortable fibers of the jute rug. "He handles the world, and can tolerate me on top of it. The first time I bring him into my life is with you, and…"

I pulled away just long enough to look her in the eye. "This is my fault?"

She laughed, dropping her arms. One hand clasped onto mine while the other wiped away her tears. "No, this is the casualty of insurrection. It knows no realms, only revolution."

"Fauna…"

She dropped the hand against her cheek and grabbed me with both. "I stand by what I said. Maybe we were brought together because I saw your link between Hell and the Nordes. Maybe you were our missing piece. But I'm not some unfeeling terrorist, Marlow. I care about you. I care about Azrames. I wouldn't…"

She didn't finish her sentence.

She wouldn't what? Wouldn't sacrifice me? Wouldn't let Azrames die for her mutiny against the gods?

"We're here now," I said. The rest seemed unimportant. We were in a windowless sarcophagus that smelled of flowers and citrus. There was nowhere for us to turn. Her tears lost their volume as she leaned back into the hug, silent, salty streams running down her face and onto the exposed skin of my shoulder.

Fauna and I had switched roles. My urgency and panic had subsided now that we'd arrived at our destination, meanwhile hers had just begun. Maybe I was naïve. Maybe my ability to compartmentalize Caliban into a fictionalized version had allowed me to think of him as unkillable. Or maybe I was right. Maybe I believed in Caliban now the way Fauna had spent hundreds of years believing in Azrames. Maybe I had swallowed the lines about gods and their oaths and extended it to trust that we were here for a banquet, and we were being held as a precaution, even if our hosts meant us no harm. At least, I was trying to.

A sound tore our attention from our sorrow a moment before any movement. The same rough noise of stone rubbing against itself resounded from the wall as the door reemerged from what had been a smooth surface only moments prior. Fauna barely had time to get to her feet as two women entered and the door closed behind itself. They were upon us in a moment, stripping us from Poppy's clothes, scrubbing us with sponges, water, cloths, and oils.

Fauna yelled at them in numerous languages. I couldn't fathom how many different ways I heard her demand answers to her questions. If she truly spoke Klingon, then I assumed dead languages were long-conquered as well. These women either chose not to answer or were somehow unable. It seemed unfathomable that Fauna had been unable to get through to them, which solidified my belief that even if they understood, they'd say nothing. At one point, a girl with pin-straight black hair that had been cropped at the shoulders looked up to meet her eye, but it had been between her shouts, rather than in response to any one of them. Fauna tried language after language, frustration escalating to hysterics at their unresponsiveness, but they did not look up again.

We were bathed, perfumed, dressed, and ignored.

The clean gown was shockingly like the one they'd stripped from my body. Perhaps Poppy had selected our apparel based on her knowledge of Phoenician customs. I was once more

203

in a white cotton shift that was more fitting as a nightgown than as proper attire. Fauna had been clad in a shade of gray that suited no one in the room. She frowned at it deeply as the attendants appeared to observe how it contrasted poorly against her skin, her hair, and her freckles. Fauna was a late summer or soft autumn at best, not the washed-out shades of winter they'd selected.

There was no explanation, apology, or alternative.

When the women abandoned us, we sank onto the bed despondently. It was too stuffy in the room for us to climb beneath the sheet. I searched absently for a light source, but discerned none. It was simply me, the tub, the bed, the pictures engraved in the wall, and Fauna. Maybe it would have been better if we'd been left in pitch-black.

I wasn't sure how much time passed before I spoke. "At least we're here together." I didn't want to bring up Fenrir. There was nothing we could do.

"I wish I was stuck in a tomb with someone more interesting."

I was tempted to laugh, but pain seeped from between my lips. "If there was ever a time to shelve your sarcasm and be nice to me, it would be now."

Fauna rolled onto her side. She draped an arm over my waist and pulled at me until I looked at her. Once again, I wished it were dark. I'd known so many versions of her, but seeing her worried and in pain made me bleed in new, acute ways.

"Tell me about Azrames," I said quietly.

She closed her eyes.

"You love him."

Her eyes remained closed for a long time. "Love looks a lot of ways."

I kept my voice gentle. "I know that."

Brows furrowed, she asked, "Do you?"

I wasn't sure what she meant by that, and my face reflected as much.

204

"We're trapped in a grave, Marlow. It's either the time to ignore all our problems and play blackjack, or to face the skeletons in our closet."

I rallied my optimism. "They didn't clothe us and bathe us to leave us alone in our room. They're coming back for us. I'm sure we'll be at the banquet any moment. Besides, I don't expect to find playing cards tucked away like it's a hotel room."

"No cards? Skeletons it is," she said on a breath. "You were right to set boundaries with your family. Your mother is awful to you. They shouldn't be in your life. And yet, I think it's uncomfortable for you to reconcile that two things can be true. That was Aloisa's point, right? Maybe your parents are terrible, and you don't need to be around them, but simultaneously, they love you."

I struggled against my pillow and the cloud of her hair to shake my head.

"You figured out I'm a card-carrying anarchist. Did you immediately turn on me?"

"It's not the same."

Her constellation of freckles scrunched as she said, "It's not. And it is. I was brought to you for less pure reasons and loved you instantly. What about Caliban? Do you think he loves you less because he didn't disclose everything to you at all times?"

"This isn't about—"

"Isn't it? He knew you wouldn't be receptive, and he wanted to be in your life. Was it selfish, or was it kind? Or can it be both?"

"Fauna! I'm trying to talk to you about Az. I know you're excellent at avoidance, but I'm not going to fall for it. Do you want to prove that you love me? That my fucked-up parents love me? That Caliban loves me? Good for you. But do you realize how evasive you are when it comes to discussing *your* feelings?"

"I'm—"

205

"Wild and free," I completed for her. "I'm not asking you to be anything else." I forced myself into a sitting position and up and pulled my knees to my chest. "Scrambling against the wall wasn't about your wildness or freedom. You're scared for him."

She tucked herself into a position that mirrored mine. Her face turned toward what remained of the rose petals floating in the dark water of the bath we'd soiled with the sand and dirt from the storm. My eyes followed hers, fixing on a single pink petal that bobbed uncertainly, as if it weren't sure if it would cling to the surface or succumb to the grit that pulled it under. At long last, she closed her eyes and let her head hang heavy. The waves of her clean hair spilled like silk and gems overturned from a precious safe as they tumbled over her shoulder and dangled toward the bed.

"Even the gods die," she said quietly without looking at me. "Humans pass, yes, but you return in your cycles. If a demon is slain, well...you know the word *smite*, don't you?"

I looked at the fabric I twisted absentmindedly between my fingers.

"And if gods die—if they're *truly* killed—there's no rebirth." I continued looking at the back of her head, the slump of her shoulders, the tight cuddle of her arms around her legs as she stared into the distance, saying, "If Azrames dies, I can't be the reason."

"Some gods come back," I said quietly.

She looked at me below heavy, hooded lids. There was only sorrow within her eyes. "Azrames isn't a god."

I stretched out a hand to touch her. It hovered uncertainly above her back for a long while as I contemplated my incentive. I wasn't sure if I wanted to alleviate my own discomfort by touching her, or if I wanted to take away her pain. I wasn't sure I'd answered my question by the time my fingers found their resting place on her back. I fell into a familiar pattern that I seldom found an opportunity to use. My mother had drawn idle shapes with her fingers on my back while I'd stayed quiet in long church services. She'd scratched my back if I'd stayed quiet for hours or more during Bible study with the adults. Sometimes she'd touch my back while she read from convoluted historical texts, adding incentive to my love for theology and literature.

Memories of the actions were painful. I wasn't comfortable with believing my mother truly loved me.

After all, there were things love was, and things it wasn't.

Still, I traced comforting patterns along Fauna's back, her shoulders, her hair, until she relaxed into the pillow once more. I joined her on the bed, continuing my hypnotic tracings until they lulled us both into a sleep beyond the tight constraints of time. I wasn't sure who fell asleep first, how much time passed in the windowless room. Whether by the passage of the dull red sun beyond, or through some magic of our inhabitance, the lights dimmed with our drowsiness.

✦

I may have slept for three hours or ten when a sound roused me.

I stirred from a dream of winter, and wind, and fractured lakes. I looked through the fuzz of lashes and sleep to see what had woken me. Fauna slept soundly beside me, statuesque save for the soft rise and fall of her breath. The room remained mostly dark with the magic that I could only assume tracked the sun, save for a small, dim light in the corner. I blinked against the noise and turned toward the door.

My breath evacuated my lungs at a sight whiter than snow, brighter than the moon, purer than diamonds.

It was impossible. I wasn't ready. My heart skidded, love and panic coursing through me in equal proportions as I moved against the silken sheets.

The icy sight moved from the doorway's arch to my bedside before I could register its presence beyond my cloud of useless, low-vibrational panic. I lost control of my arms and legs as I scrambled from my tangled place in the sheets to the side of the bed. I couldn't get off the mattress fast enough. My bare feet hadn't had the chance to hit the ground before hands were on me. A hand cradled my face while the other wrapped around the lowermost part of my back. He scooped me against him as he knelt by the bed.

"Love," came his whisper, meadow-soft, moss-scented, drenched in loss and longing and sorrow and passion. "Gods, I've missed you. I'll never let you go again."

I tried to choke out his name, but he shushed me.

"But Fauna—"

His voice was as low as the rustling of ferns in the depths of the forest. "I promise you: I'll get her to Azrames. I won't let her wake up alone. But you have to come with me now."

I hedged for the barest fraction of a second, broken between loyalties. He'd preempted my fear. He understood my reluctance. He knew why I wouldn't want to leave Fauna, and exactly how to soothe my guilt. He'd promised that Fauna would not wake up abandoned, and I trusted him.

I'd expected to rise to my feet, but Caliban scooped me against him. I wasn't wholly certain I wasn't dreaming. The scents of moss, cypress, and petrichor were almost too good to be true. I was too sleepy for the champagne-and-gin drunkenness of his presence as I closed my eyes, resting my head against his chest.

Maybe I was dreaming.

I'd been dreaming as a child when I'd wandered away from the church gathering into the woods and been swept up into strong arms and returned to my family. I'd been dreaming as a teenager when I'd cried myself to sleep. I'd been dreaming when cool hands had shoved their fingers down my throat when, at fifteen, I'd swallowed everything in the cabinet, then had held my hair as I'd watched tiny white pills join the greens and yellows and blues of whatever I'd eaten for dinner. I'd been dreaming as I'd rested against a broad chest when I'd sobbed on the shower floor in college, desperate to be normal, to stop hallucinating, to see him no longer.

I decided that if this was a dream, it was a good one.

Maybe I'd been too deeply asleep to fully rouse when he'd arrived. Maybe I'd been too exhausted, or taxed, or traumatized to accept his presence. Maybe none of it mattered, for as he tucked me into the forest perfume of his soft sheets and kissed my temple, I was tugged under by the comforting lull of sleep, off to dream about ferns and damp bark and misty trails and love that lasted.

Chapter Twenty-Three

A FTER AN ENDLESS STREAM OF NIGHTMARES, I GAVE MYSELF over to the serotonin of sweet, restful fantasies.

"Is this real?" I murmured sleepily.

"Everything about us is real," he replied, voice low. "Yes, Love. We're *guests* in the Phoenician realm. When I heard they were sending for you..." His sentence drifted into curses. "I did everything I could to keep you out of it, down to summoning that fucking angel just so you wouldn't end up here."

"I don't care if we're in Hell or the Norse pantheon or Timbuktu. We're together."

I released a small, satisfied noise as hands slipped over my hips and worked their way up my front. Fingers carved a path up my torso, between my breasts, and gently traced along my throat. I swallowed, and felt the fingers move with me as my throat bobbed. My sharp intake of air was met with another hand, this time creeping through my hair and balling into a fist at the back of my head.

"I'm never letting you go again." He forced my head back, exposing my neck to the thumb and forefinger that compressed gently on the life-giving arteries running up and down my throat.

My lips parted against the dizzy explosion of endorphins.

The gold and white stars on my inner lids danced pleasantly against the pitch-black of the night. I arched my back and felt him. He pressed himself into me, hugging me to every inch of him until I was tucked so tightly against him that I disappeared. I moaned into my freefall through euphoria.

I reached a hand backward for him. My fingers worked into the space between us, navigating behind my ass and down his hip where a thin piece of material separated me from the bliss of his cock. My fingertips grazed his length, and he released a low, deep sound, hugging me closer to him. The tuft of his breath on my cheek sent chills down my spine. His hand tightened around my neck.

"I've missed you so much," I said, my words a mixture of tears, longing, and total surrender.

"There is no agony in this realm or the next like being separated from you, Love."

With swift movements, he nudged me forward until I was on my stomach. He rolled with me, his entire weight crushing me, pushing me into the obsidian depths of his bed. I inhaled the scent of him on the sheets as he pressed down on me. He swept my hair to the side and ran his mouth along the exposed skin between my ear and my shoulder.

"You came for me," he said against my flesh between kisses. "I would never have asked this of you."

I basked in the glow of his praise for the briefest of moments. Then shock forced a question to the forefront as I pictured my friend clawing at the door to escape. "I didn't come alone. We left Fauna behind."

"She is safe. I've seen to it that she'll wake up beside Azrames. He has asylum until the trial, as long as I remain here as his ambassador. But for now, let me focus on you."

"Trial?" I choked on the word.

He shushed me, if only to savor moments of pleasure and peace before we were forced to return to reality.

My arms stretched out beneath the pillow in front of me until I made contact with the headboard. I arched in anticipation, spine curling, ass pressing against him until I could feel every generous inch that had hardened with want.

I tried to turn over to face him, but he slipped an arm along mine until our fingers intertwined. I squeezed my hand and he reciprocated, mouth still moving on my neck, free hand slipping between us and grazing the rapidly soaking space between my legs. His fingers worked gently, tantalizingly against the thin material that separated us. I wiggled my hips again if only to let him know that I was here, that I wanted him, that I wanted to fade into him until I struggled to separate where I ended and he began.

I almost cried out in protest when his hand left mine but understood it a second later.

He used both hands to shove the shift dress up over my hips and traced chilling kisses down my spine while I squirmed beneath him. His mouth worked over the dimples at my lower back, and then I felt his teeth on the edge of my panties before my head exploded in fire as his mouth moved against the thin fabric on my most sensitive place. My hips bucked off the bed to give him more access, desperate for him to slip the fabric to the side.

His fingers went to my hips to keep me from wriggling away. A sound between a gasp and a yelp escaped my lips when he tugged the fabric over my ass. I felt him sit up behind me long enough to shuffle the material down past my knees and slip it over my feet, tossed into the puddles of shadows. It gave me just enough time to look over my shoulder at the ice-white phantom crawling back to me.

He dragged his mouth from my knee up the back of my thigh. I blinked against the darkness of the windowless room, unable to distinguish up from down as black contrasted against black. I tried to turn over, but once again, he pinned me to the bed. I made a sound again as my movements were denied.

I sucked in a sharp breath as his tongue swept through the center of me. I bundled the sheets into my fist with one hand and gripped the sleek headboard with the other as my hips rolled against the sensation. His appreciative noise as he tasted me was music to my ears. Strong fingers gripped my cheeks as he forced me up for access to my clit. Between the saliva and my desire, the bed below us was already a pool of our love.

"I want you," I said through clenched teeth.

"You have me," came his reply. I felt the vibration of his words in my deepest parts. My hips rolled again, and he grabbed me with both hands, flipping me over in a motion so swift that my equilibrium didn't have time to stabilize before his hands were beneath my knees, tilting me up as he devoured me. I reached for him, running my fingers through his silken strands, their diamond light the only color in the onyx darkness.

He carried me up, up, up as his mouth moved relentlessly on me, alternating between sucking and the swirling pressure of his tongue. He released one knee from my leg and it landed on his shoulder as his fingers searched for my breast, massaging it until they claimed my nipple with acute, pinching need. I cried out as he twisted, but he knew me well enough to know I liked the pain. I felt his smile as his mouth and fingers moved in time with one another.

He knew my body better than I did.

Touching myself, using the vibrator in my bedside table, and watching saved clips from particularly spicy scenes usually ended with me giving up before I came. I struggled to let down my mental wall long enough to enjoy time and space when I was alone. I was easily distracted by things I needed to do, thoughts from the day, stresses, wishes, wants, needs. It all evaporated when I was with Caliban. He took control, and I could let go. I could feel the licks, the kisses, the suctions, the fingers, the vibrations, the bites. I left my head and entered my body, fully present. I wasn't my thoughts, my actions, my past. I wasn't my hang-ups or insecurities or memories. I was only flesh and blood and bundles of nerves, all his to command.

My body rolled again, and he released the grasp on my breast, dragging his palm slowly down the front of me as his fingers worked their way toward the throbbing need between my legs. He brought his fingers to my entrance and chuckled as I bucked against them, trying to push them in. I was so close. I knew that it would take the barest of pressures to push me over the edge.

He didn't bother easing me in. Two fingers slipped inside me like a chilled knife through melting butter, slicing into the center of me. I clenched around him as he pressed into the innermost part of me. I gasped for air against the pressure within me. I knew the sheets were a lake. I knew I ran down his hand and his arm like a fountain. I could feel the raw scrape of my throat before I heard myself, unable to stop the cry of pleasure.

He carried me to the top of the ladder, one rung, then another, then another.

I heaved breath after breath as his tongue and fingers worked against me. My hands balled tighter in his hair. My legs tensed, muscles flexing, toes curling as I approached climax. I gulped for air, closing in on the final rung, holding my breath as my abs tensed, my body stayed locked, and my world froze. He took me to the top of the ladder and threw me over the safety of its ledge.

I cried out as my body buckled. I reacted to every rung as I descended, body flexing in convulsions as I pulsed through the orgasm. He was relentless as he carried me back down the ladder, mouth continuing as I gushed into him. He didn't slow his movements until my body relaxed while I gasped for air. I flexed again as he slipped his fingers out of me, kissing up my stomach, my belly button, my sternum. He slipped what remained of my shift over my head and I had no fight left in me to resist him, though I wouldn't have wanted to even if I'd had the energy. My body kicked again with involuntary pleasure as he swept his hands over my body and cupped my face. He kissed me gently and I tasted myself on his tongue.

"I love you," I said.

"I've always loved you," came his reply.

✦

Dark walls. Gold accents. Lemongrass. Rose water. The dim light from an indiscernible source. A heavy arm. Moss, gin, mist. Steady breathing.

I moved shifted slightly and shivered as I pressed against the man behind me. He'd always run several degrees cooler than the world around us. Given the stuffy heat and windowless room, his refreshing chill was like water in the desert. I looked down to see I'd fallen asleep with my fingers interlaced with his. It took me a moment to truly accept that all of it had been real. The muscles in my softest parts clenched. A dull ache raked through me as I rolled toward him.

I nearly lost my breath at the sight of him.

Every time he was more beautiful, more unbelievable than the last. He stirred slightly as I adjusted my position. His eyes fluttered open to reveal the brilliant crystals beneath sleepy, hooded lids. His lips tugged up at the corners the moment he caught sight of me, and he tucked me in closer, pressing a kiss to the space between my brows.

"I am so, so grateful you're here," he said, "but gods above and below, I wish you hadn't come."

My face pinched between pain and confusion. I stayed quiet against the morning haze, allowing sleepiness to cover me like a blanket. "They sent a messenger to invite me to their banquet. I was expected."

He said, "A spider would gladly invite a fly to its web if it thought the prey might respond. I'm angry with myself for letting you worry. In hundreds of lifetimes, I never would have imagined you being trapped here, surrounded by our enemies. I wouldn't have let you put yourself in danger, but I—"

"Then we *are* in trouble?" My stomach twisted. I felt like a fool for being the face of positivity all the while Fauna had been calling a spade a spade. Just as quickly as the knots in my gut formed, they unraveled. I decided I didn't care if I was here among friends or if I'd marched directly to my own demise. I reminded him, "I came for you in the mortal realm, too."

His laugh was scarcely more than an exhale. "And it was the best moment of my life."

I tucked my head against his chest as I asked, "So why didn't you think I'd find you now?"

"I've dedicated lifetime after lifetime to finding you," he murmured.

"Maybe it's my turn."

He slipped his hand behind my head, holding me to him as he said, "I've spent my existence doing questionable things. The most reckless has been loving you, in all your forms. I'd still cut Astarte down where she stood once I knew she had a claim to you, but maybe I would have tied you to the bed first if I knew you were going to march with a chaos Norde into the Phoenician realm after me."

I giggled lightly. "Fauna and I—"

He shushed me. Lips brushing against my ears, he said, "Don't say anything you wouldn't want the walls to hear."

My breath snagged.

We wouldn't be able to talk. Not about plans. Not about anything that mattered.

I pulled my face away long enough to look up into his eyes so he could see the worry that knit itself between my brows.

"Can you tell me about the trial?"

His face fell. "I'm a Prince, and our hosts aren't looking to make an enemy of Hell. But they will demand justice for what happened to Astarte."

I pictured an ornate dagger engraved with *etimas di mori* in Caliban's hand as he opened Astarte's throat. I bit down on my lip to keep myself from saying anything incriminating when I remembered Poppy's words. The clinic's security camera footage had been scrubbed. They had no concrete evidence of Caliban's involvement, but two of their citizens were dead, and the one who remained knew angels and demons were involved.

"How did it end?" I asked. "How did Anath subdue you and—"

He gave me a warning look. It wasn't safe to speak. Not when the walls had ears.

"Azrames will stand trial," I said, careful not to say anything that wasn't public knowledge. "Why? What crime are they pinning on him?"

"It's complicated," Caliban rubbed his chin while he considered his response. "Hell and the Phoenicians are allies, primarily because we share an enemy. Azrames—a civilian with no royal title or godhood to speak of—was present while an enemy soldier succeeded in murdering a major goddess."

"And?" I practically laughed at the so-called crime. This was so much better than I'd feared. They weren't charging him with Jessabelle's execution, or accusing him of Astarte's murder. He was simply...there.

"And"—Caliban's expression was pained—"the law demands that a civilian intercede on behalf of their betters. His crime is living, as he would have been expected to die fighting for an allied goddess rather than walk away without a scratch while a major deity in their pantheon was killed by an angel."

I stared at him wordlessly. We both knew that wasn't what had happened. Caliban had been wielding the god-killer when he had taken the dagger to Astarte's throat. Az had sunk the pointed, bludgeoning end of his meteor hammer into Jessabelle's skull. Silas had only been in Bellfield because I'd called on him for help at Caliban's behest. He'd rescued me from certain death.

"What about Silas?" My question barely escaped from behind my clenched teeth.

Caliban's eyes softened. "The angel saved you, Love. More times in this cycle than I care to count."

"I can count," I said tersely. "Three. Three times."

He laughed and folded me into him once more. "You say *three* as if it isn't a magic number."

Perhaps the demons couldn't intercede on behalf of an angel, but I had a few Nordes up my sleeve.

"And Fenrir—"

His fingers tensed against me with near-bruising strength. I almost yelped as he pulled himself away from me to search my face. His strength and intensity reminded me, if only for a moment, that he was no mortal. His eyes scanned me for information, willing me into silence as he discerned all he could from my bewildered expression. I shut my mouth tightly against the power of names as I let my brows tilt up in both worry and apology. I hadn't even considered the power in the Norse god's name.

Voice tight, he asked, "You brought your…?"

"Dog," I supplied, voice rife with anxiety. "I had no one to watch him, and Fauna said it would be okay to bring my dog. When we were met at the gates, the guard said I couldn't have a pet in our room. I'm not sure where they're keeping him."

He dipped his chin in understanding, but his eyes remained tight with stress. It took a while for his face to relax before he said, "It makes sense that you wouldn't be able to find anyone to watch your dog on short notice. I understand how important he is to you. We'll get you reunited with your pet as soon as possible."

"Thank you," I said, still tense. I kicked myself for the thoughtless slip of tongue. I justified to myself that I'd spent years speaking to Caliban freely, considering him little more than an extension of my madness. It was a steep learning curve.

His thumbs moved against the muscles in my back, melting the knots that had risen to meet my stress. "I'll take care of everything," he said. It was the same message he'd repeated again and again, perhaps until I believed it.

I made an appreciative sound at the movement of his fingers, but couldn't stay silent. "You have no idea how far I'm willing to go for you."

His hands stilled for the barest of seconds as he soaked in the weight of my words. I felt him absorb their meaning before he resumed the motion. He was the Prince of Hell, but I was its bride. Perhaps Caliban, in his infinite grace, cunning, and wisdom, could keep the realms together, but I was born to tear them apart.

Chapter Twenty-Four

I STIRRED AT THE LIGHT RAPPING OF KNUCKLES AGAINST THE door, though the sound wasn't demanding enough to truly rouse me from my slumber. My eyes remained mostly closed, though I looked at the shape beside me through the bleary cover of hooded lashes.

I'd never woken up to Caliban's broad shoulders, the ripple of his muscular back as he lay on his stomach, his lightly mussed hair, the sheets tugged around him, just barely covering his still-nude form as he clung to sleep. He was awake by the second knock, tilting his head slightly as his attention went first to the door, then over to me.

I tasted forest on the air as he slipped his arm around me and pulled me in to brush his lips against my forehead. Caliban took his time unraveling his fingers from my hair, gaze raking over me until I heated from the intensity of his stare. My toes curled at the hungry look in his eye, particularly as he chose the view over whoever requested his attention at the door. I couldn't help but be horrified at the idea that I'd ever woken up next to anyone else. There had been average human men in my bed. I'd woken up to drool, to groggy grumbles, even to snoring before I'd shaken them awake and firmly requested that they sleep in their own beds. Maybe my loathing for Caliban's predecessors had been because I'd always known who belonged on the pillow beside my own.

I swallowed as I looked into the eyes chipped from the moon itself and managed a breathy question. "Are you going to get that?"

The corner of his mouth tugged up in a crooked smirk. "I suppose. If I don't, they'll just come in. Then you'd have to get up, and we can't have that."

I tugged the sheet around me and sat up in bed, eyes glued on him. I'd fallen asleep next to an unbelievably sexy figment of my imagination countless times. In twenty-six years, I'd never been allowed the pleasure of feeling his weight shift against the mattress, of the pull as sheets moved, of the confirmation that the fireworks he'd lavished over me in the middle of the night were no wet dream.

I wonder how many times I'd find a fresh explosion of dopamine in the same three words: *he was real.*

He stepped into pants I hadn't even realized were present, but opted to remain shirtless. I reasoned to myself that I would neither know nor care whether any clothes had existed, as he'd tucked me into bed in the same bleary, half-asleep state that he'd known for nearly three decades. I'd been conditioned to affiliate cypress, mist, and the cool press of his touch with slumber. Convenient for transporting me in the middle of the night in a palace, perhaps, but something I hoped to quickly deprogram from myself. I didn't want to miss a minute with him.

The moment he turned his back to me, I sucked on my teeth, horrified at the idea that someone so ethereal might be subjected to a human's morning breath. I raked fingers through my hair, wiped the corners of my eyes, and did a quick scan of the room for water.

He paused at the door, hand extended to allow the knocker entrance, but then looked over his shoulder. He gave me another smile before he abandoned his task and went to the washroom. I heard the sound of rainwater and smelled the flower-kissed scent of perfume before Caliban emerged from the room adjacent to his kingly suite. He returned to the bed and handed me a silver cup of cold water.

I looked at the offering skeptically, then back at him with an unspoken question in my eyes.

"I heard your heart," he said with a shrug. "Whatever you're nervous about, I promise I can handle it. But whoever's at the door can wait until you're comfortable."

"I'm fine," I said, accepting the glass of water. I wasn't sure if it was true, but not for the reasons he might suspect. The truth was, I didn't know how to be fine with a partner like this. I was used to kicking lovers out of my bed and rolling my eyes at worms. I knew how to hold out my palm and collect money from those so far below me that they had to extend generous offerings just to spend a few hours in my company. I knew how to swipe left on dating apps, how to politely reject attempted kisses at the end of dates, and how to ghost any gender who tried to schedule a second date when I was tired of them. The one exception had been Eva, and I'd bolted on the eve of Valentine's Day at the first hint that I was falling in love. I was comfortable with chaos, with indifference. Safety was terrifying.

I was fine with the upper hand. I had no idea how to make sense of a love that wasn't going anywhere.

Caliban sent me a wink that made my entire body blush before answering the door at long last. The Phoenician in the hall spoke a language I didn't recognize. It sounded as foreign and musical as the wind over the dunes beyond the palace. Despite Fauna's compliments at Poppy and Dorian's table, I wasn't a polyglot. Still, my strained ear for languages told me this was something that had been lost to the sands of time.

Caliban responded easily in the speaker's tongue. They exchanged a few more formal words before he shut the door behind him. At least, I knew it to be a door, despite its slab-like appearance and utter lack of hinges. He leaned against the vertical rectangle and put his hands in his pockets.

"So, Love, what name does Anath know you by?"

My lips parted in surprise at the question. It had taken me a while to get a handle on giving out my pseudonym whenever I encountered a nonhuman, but I thought I was getting the hang of it. I specifically remembered demanding a meeting with Astarte's clinic while throwing Merit Finnegan's weight around. I struggled to recall whether my cover had been blown before everything had gone to shreds.

"I used my pen name when meeting with Astarte. It's how I got the quick appointment and VIP treatment. I don't recall them having another name, but then again..." I chewed on my lip as I looked into my memory. "Caliban, what did you say that got you into the room that day?"

He arched a frosted brow.

I nodded to double down on my question. "I was all set to fuck a very handsome—" At the unimpressed look on his face, I changed the course of my sentence. "Astarte had arranged a meeting with a number of potential suitors. Whatever you said had you sent directly down to the room. You told Astarte who you were? You identified yourself as the Prince of Hell?"

"I did," he said easily.

Something about the answer was disquieting. It didn't hold enough gravity.

"You just said you were the demon prince and she let you down? For...breeding?" I felt like a cartoon, the way a horrible, cold lightbulb went off in my mind. "A cambion. That's what she said on the phone. Cambions are half-demon, half-human children. That's...that's what you said to her."

He rested his head against the door, eyes still on me. "Breeding kink not your thing?"

"You're not funny. And she had no follow-up questions? She isn't from your realm. She didn't know I was *your* human. I was just *some* human. Why would she want to facilitate that?"

Caliban considered the question. "It wasn't altruism. It

might surprise you how many pantheons have tried to tip the war in Hell's favor. Everyone wants Heaven to fall. You have...*qualities*...that would make you the perfect vessel to expedite the process."

"A winsome personality and huge tits?"

He chuckled. "Yes, precisely."

"I guess I understand the motive for other pantheons to give Hell a helping hand, at least a little. Hounds can't scrap for the role of top dog until the top dog's been eliminated," I said.

I watched him cross the room and was caught by something almost unsettling. His lips tugged up in another partial smile as he asked, "What's on your mind now, Love?"

I felt my hair on my shoulders before I realized I'd been wordlessly shaking my head. I blinked rapidly before saying, "I've never seen you out of the human space—"

"Mortal realm."

"The mortal realm, right, have I?" I wasn't asking a question, and he knew it. I'd seen him as an arctic fox, as an imaginary friend, as a guardian angel. I'd seen him in my college dorm, in my apartment, and at the seedy motel in Bellfield. My encounters with Caliban stretched across time and space, but they'd always been duller, somehow. I reached out to touch him, dragging my fingers along his jaw as I appreciated an almost imperceptible shimmer beneath his skin. Starlight pulsed where blood should be. "You're different here."

His smirk bloomed into a true smile. "And?"

"You're too beautiful," I said, throwing the sheets over my head. I was mortified that I was a disheveled human in a flesh suit before glowing interdimensional royalty. I hated that anyone had ever perceived me as I wiggled deeper into the bed. His fingers found my shape, but allowed me the privacy of the sheet cocoon. He rolled me closer to him in the bed.

"You're beautiful in every form," he said, "but you don't look like yourself here, either."

I poked a cautionary eye up beyond the sheets. "What do you mean?"

He smoothed unruly hair away from my face as he said, "I'm bonded to your soul, not to your body. Your essence shines through in the realms in a way it can't when we're on mortal soil. Have you seen yourself?"

After arriving with Fauna, I'd been scrubbed, dressed, and held until we'd fallen asleep in a dark, windowless room. I hadn't looked into a mirror in the Phoenician realm, or in Álfheimr. I had looked wickedly handsome in Azrames's bathroom, but I'd assumed that was mostly due to his wildly flattering lighting and expensive taste. I sagged as I thought of Azrames, instantly saddened as I remembered why we'd come in the first place. Caliban may not be a prisoner, but he was perhaps the only exception.

His mouth twisted in a layered frown.

He looked up to see if there was a mirror in the room. Not finding one, he tucked a knuckle beneath my chin. Before I could react to the gooseflesh sent down my spine at his touch, I was jolted into the out-of-body experience of looking at myself through the eyes of another. My lashes fluttered rapidly, and I saw my body blink in response. I gasped, watching as my lips parted, quickly intaking air. I saw a pale hand cup my chin, a strong forearm, my muddy hair, my green-gray eyes, my upturned nose, the fingers holding a sheet against my chest to cover my uncomfortably full breasts. I swallowed at the sight and watched my own throat bob.

"I'm looking at me...through your eyes," I said, watching my lips move.

"Mmm," he agreed, not bothering to elaborate.

I pushed past the initial shock to search for something unfamiliar, something new, something...soul-like. I tried to shake my head in denial, but he forced my chin toward the ceiling, and I watched myself tilt my face upward obediently. At first I thought he was trying to show me my throat, but as I watched myself swallow, as I watched my throat bob, my heartbeat in my jugular, my dips and curves and skin, I began to notice…something. It wasn't within, but a quality just beyond the limits of my body. There was an opalescent glow humming with an almost static quality, its border outlining my own perfectly. I tilted my head and watched the static crackle and react like subtle lightning. I lifted my hands, wiggling my fingers as I observed the electricity stringing between my fingertips I smiled with the realization and watched the light in my eyes ignite. I saw it there, too. A crystal spark, almost as if it had been broken off from his starlit features, shimmered behind my eyes. When I smiled again, he crushed his mouth to my parted lips.

His fingers left my chin as they wove into my hair. His tongue lifted mine, pulling me against him until I dropped the sheet. I gasped against the sudden change in energy, forced from his body back into my own as he pressed into me. The sheet was gone in a flash. The only barrier between my still-naked form and Caliban was his pants. Part of me was surprised that he was hungry, that he was interested, that he had room to want me as much as I wanted him despite our predicament, despite the morning, despite the interruptions and the Phoenicians and the realm around us. Then again, I reminded myself as his fingers drew cutting lines from my breast to my inner thigh, he was a demon.

This otherworldly, beautiful, perfect man was no man. He was the Prince of Hell.

I inhaled sharply as two cold fingers slipped inside the warm, ready place that had always been meant for him.

"Caliban—"

"Nothing you don't want," he murmured, index and middle finger curling slightly until they pressed against that perfect spot within me. My intake of breath was so quick it made me lightheaded. My back arched off against the bed as a moan I couldn't have held in even if I'd wanted to escaped my lips. My hips rolled against him without any conscious effort on my part. I grabbed on to him as if the morning was a forgone conclusion, and he took the unspoken nod of consent.

I didn't hear a zip, or a button, or a rustle of fabric. There was no noise or earthly indication that anything had changed, but in one moment, his fingers were inside me, and in the next, the still-wet hand was around my throat. I gasped as the blood flow to my most important parts was restricted, starlight dancing about the room.

He took the moment of inhalation as an invitation. He matched his perfect penetration with my breath, entering me as I coiled with air, with life, with shock. My neck curved until I was only supported by the crown of my head, my tailbone, and the tips of my toes. His arm was underneath the small of my back in an instant, pinning me against him as he thrust into me. I jolted upward, burying my face into the space between his neck and shoulders. My hips opened up as I wrapped my legs around him, pulling him in close.

I panted against him as he rammed his hips into mine. As my breath hitched, so did his intensity. His fingers bit into my ass as he cinched my hips against him, pinning me to him as he pounded into me, harder, harder, harder still without changing his pace. Higher, higher, higher I rose as my breaths became shallower and shallower. Each thrust was a musical swell, the crash of a wave, the summit of a mountain. Louder and stronger and further he carried me as he crushed me against him.

"Breathe," he commanded, but he said it through gritted teeth. I could feel the cool vindication of his sweat as he bit back his own pleasure.

I couldn't breathe. I didn't want to.

The moment I attempted to bury my teeth in his trap was his signal that I was close. His hand tightened against my throat, shoving me into the pillow. His arm straightened as I bucked against him, writhing against the relentless manacles of his fingers on the piece of me that fed my life, my breath, my blood, my brain. My fingers went to his hand, and he met my eyes for the barest of moments to confirm what he already knew.

I wasn't pulling him away.

I pressed his hand further against my jugular, daring him to choke me out as he pounded into me. My legs tightened, thighs flexing, back straining with its arch. Blood pounded in my veins, my head, ears ringing with the delicious, rising threat of looming unconsciousness. Water gushed out from the apex of my thighs as I used whatever remained of my strength to hold him against me. He took the hint well, teeth glinting in wicked delight as his eyes locked on mine.

He didn't look away, silver flames dancing with hunger as he held my gaze, pinning me down as he railed me until I saw the creation of the goddamn universe. I knew he felt it coming. From the sound he made as my most sensitive muscles tightened around him, to the way his eyes fluttered to a close, to the grit of his teeth, I reveled in the pleasure he took from my satisfaction.

I would pass out any second. I didn't care.

He leaned in close to my ear in my last conscious moments and, in a growl, demanded, "Who do you belong to?"

I didn't have the wherewithal to hesitate as I gasped, "You."

"Say it again," he said through clenched teeth, flexing his fingers once against my throat. The black vignette pressed in on my vision as the life around me died.

"I'm yours," I tried to say, the words a phantom on my lips as I felt the countdown from ten, to five, to three, to two, to one.

The flex of his jaw as I signed over my ownership sent me over the edge. My entire body buckled. My fingernails dug into his back as I clung to him for dear life, riding a wave of want, of stars, of moss, of power, of desire, and of pure fucking bliss.

Maybe it was because he understood my body, or because he was perfect, or because he was a literal goddamned demon, but Caliban rammed into me time and time again, riding the wave as I crested over and over until I was little more than a twitching shell of a person.

He relaxed his hold on my throat, brushing gentle kisses against my neck and tracing them to my temple. He ran his fingers through my hair, panting as he reined himself in, absorbing the residual shocks as I trembled, moments stretching like taffy between the clenches and lurches as my body relaxed. I was cum-drunk, too lost on sweat and sex and the sweet, perfect oxygen deprivation that could only be performed to this exquisite extreme by someone you trusted implicitly. By the time I'd fully melted back into the bed, a thought clicked.

One piece of information had been irrelevant when Caliban had been fictional. I hadn't wondered, or worried, or cared for years when I'd been certain beyond all shadow of a doubt that I was the best brand of satisfied and insane, even as it had ruined my life and destroyed my chance at happiness with other partners. I looked at him now, taking in the Milky Way pulse of stars beneath his skin, feeling the way he throbbed within me until the last possible second. He gripped the headboard as he spilled pure starlight onto my stomach.

I was struck with a realization. "You've never finished inside me."

His jaw flexed again as he tightened his hold on me. "My pull-out game is strong."

I searched my memories. It was hard to catalogue the times we'd made love, the times he'd fucked me over the sink, or railed me in the shower, or feasted on me beneath the sheets. They'd been masturbatory fantasies from the vivid imagination of a writer with a family history of hallucinatory mental illness. I'd hated and loved the encounters in equal proportion. I'd wanted him and resented him. I'd relished my encounters with him and wished he'd never return. The memories ended with something glistening and warm, as

229

if the Milky Way itself had dripped down my inner thighs, pooling in my belly button, adorning the bedsheets.

"Wait, that cambion thing...that's real? Is that why you...?" I reached for the still-warm silvery sheen decorating my stomach.

His weight relaxed onto mine, interfering with my detective work.

"Caliban, for the love of god—"

He lifted his head to shoot me an amused brow.

"For fuck's sake, can I not reference god anymore? Is that not Hell-approved? Listen, Satan-spawn." He laughed at that, but I pressed on. "That can't be it. Astarte let you into her fertility clinic because, what, if you finished inside me, we'd definitely create a—"

"Love, no," he cut me off. His fingers traced along my outer curves until he was ready to slip out of me. I hated the moment I relinquished my hold on him. I missed his fullness instantly. "I promise I'll explain it to you—"

"When I'm older?" I glared.

He rolled onto his back, enjoying his smirk. "I was going to say that I'll explain it to you when we don't have to get ready for a banquet with the Phoenician pantheon surrounded by listening walls, but I suppose you'll be older a few hours from now, so, sure. Yes. I'll tell you when you're older."

My post-orgasm glow was cut short as I gagged at the images of parties and crowds. "I can't believe I'm expected to be social."

"It's pre-trial tradition. The realm likes to eat, drink, and be merry before a beheading." He rolled onto his side and propped up his head with one arm. He snatched my wrist with the other, pressing my fingers against his lips as he asked, "Did you forget we were here with a job to do? Or would you like to make this our new home? Because, to be honest, I could think of a worse fate."

"Did you say a *beheading?*"

"Gallows humor." He smirked.

230

"Oh, sure, hanging is better." I rolled my eyes. "You can think of worse than being trapped in a windowless room while our friends are held captive? If Azrames and Silas are set to be executed—"

"I meant ravishing you with no further thoughts or obligations. But your thing, too, I guess."

My eyes narrowed. "You're a bad friend."

His wicked grin was fueled by my condemnation. "I'm a spectacular friend," he argued. "I've stayed here with a citizen of Hell I've only known by his reputation before I met him through you."

The sudden shame I felt at having bathed in love and sex and joy while my friend suffered was suffocating. I was already so bonded to the love of Fauna's complicated life.

Caliban nodded. "He would have deserved my regard long before what he did for you and me in Bellfield. But the angel—"

I winced. "Is Silas okay?"

Once again, Caliban's eyebrow arched perceptively. "You've developed an attachment to the angel, haven't you?"

"I just know him," I mumbled. It was true, and it wasn't. Perhaps there was a bond forged by survivor's guilt that had leashed me to Silas, but the angel had been present in my worst moments. He'd come through for me in a spectacular way time and time again. Without him, I would have died at Richard's hands. I wouldn't have ever truly understood Caliban's existence. I would have been eaten by a parasite. I would have died in the clinic. I owed him.

"It's more than that," Caliban said gently. "And that's okay. He was there for you in a way I couldn't be, and I'm not so stubborn that I can't be grateful. I'm indebted to him, literally and figuratively. He's the reason you're here, Love. I'd move mountains for you. And sometimes those mountains take a heavenly shape."

"Haven't you been relieved of your debt? He called in his favor to send you to Bellfield."

231

"I'm free from a formal debt, yes. But he did me another favor altogether by snaring me in a god-catcher. No one—angel or otherwise—would come for my head while I was in an unbroken seal."

"Do we think—" I lowered my voice as if whispering would make a difference. Then again, perhaps if spies were listening, this was something they should hear. "Could he be rebelling?"

"He certainly isn't in lock and step with his boss. But I'm not willing to gamble on him defecting from Heaven. His motives are murky. What matters is he showed up for you, and he's behind bars now because of you. Whatever loyalty you've forged seems to flow both ways."

I'd never forget the metaphorical chains I'd wrapped around Caliban when I'd banished him from intervening. There had been no way for me to comprehend the binding nature of my words when Caliban and I had struck a bargain that he couldn't do anything without my explicit consent. Had it not been for that promise, he could have been the one who'd intervened when a man had broken into my apartment with the intent to kill. Caliban could have been the one who'd reached through Richard's throat and forced him to choke on his own tongue from the inside out.

Instead, Silas had answered Caliban's elite bargain.

I was still gnawing on my thoughts when Caliban brushed a thumb over my forehead.

"This is your friend Fauna's handiwork, I'm guessing…" he murmured.

I looked down at my body, then around, confused. His comment had come out of nowhere. "I forget you haven't met her. And sex reminded you of Fauna because…?"

His eyes crinkled. "Not at all. I see what she's done to your eyes. It was very wise. We can't very well have you going insane just yet."

I straightened slightly in bed. "Excuse me?"

He made a compassionate face before saying, "Your tattoo

232

is lovely. It helps you see things rightly in the mortal realm. But when you're in other realms, you need to see things... wrongly."

He spared me the embarrassment of having to repeat the word.

"What is your Norse ambassador? Do you know?" Caliban asked.

I tensed at the question, looking over his shoulder at the door.

"I only caught a glimpse of red hair while abducting you in the night. The Phoenicians will know who and what she is moment they meet her. I might as well know, too."

I blew a tuft of hair away from my face as I considered the question. "She's a sugar-addled, Scandinavian chaos goblin," I murmured. After a moment of reflection, I said, "She once made a comment about me committing deicide. I thought she was being hyperbolic. But then, not too long ago, I saw her do something with...wolves." I struggled not to say more than was wise.

"Wolves?" he considered. "I wish there was a clear-cut answer in the Norse pantheon. But if she can command wild animals, your friend might be a forest deity."

"That sounds right. She's also claimed she's a skosgrå. But I don't know if they get deity status."

His mouth bunched to the side. "A skosgrå who can command wolves? Has she done anything else?"

I thought of the security guard's twisted, horrified expression the moment before he was swallowed by a tree at Fauna's behest. Given that I wasn't supposed to share secrets while the walls were listening, I could only ask, "What do you mean?"

His eyes unfocused, as if reading a text in the depths of his mind. "Is she the reason you brought your *dog* with on this excursion?"

I chose my words carefully. "She reminded me that time passes differently in every realm. We couldn't leave him home

233

without a dog sitter if we didn't know how long it would take me to get back."

He touched my cheek. "I suspect she won't tell you her true name. Few of us are open about such things. But you could do worse than a deity. It explains her ability to take corporeal form, and how she accomplished this," he said, brushing his thumb over the same spot.

I joined him in the mind-library, wracking my brain for references to Fenrir. There was no overlap with a forest deity that made sense. "My...dog...isn't a wolf to command. Those things can't be related."

"I'm sorry that this is happening to you," he said. "All of it. I'm sorry that I happened to you."

"I'd rather die with you than live without you," I said. "Now, are you going to keep touching my head or are you going to tell me what the hell you're talking about?"

He smirked, but something akin to guilt colored his words. "True forms would be overwhelming for you, and that's not your fault. You're human. Your Norse deity friend has done you a great service. While the two of you are in the mortal realm, she's bound in human form. When you're in other realms, you're perceiving those around you in relatively human forms as well. If I didn't already like the Nordes..." His words trailed off, leaving me to consider how much had happened both to and around me without my knowledge. "If she's meddling in your mind, I should, too."

"I'm not so sure—"

"Only good things," he said, pressing both thumbs to my temples. After a brief compression, he released his hold on me. "I suspect Azrames has already done as much for Fauna. After all, Hell's affiliation with the Canaanites is far older than that of the Nordes."

"With language? I thought Fauna spoke everything. Eternity is a long time, or something. She speaks Klingon."

"You did say she watches a lot of TV." Caliban's expression was as reassuring as the low vibration of his words.

234

"The Scandinavian timeline is a little different from that of the Cradle of Civilization. I don't expect the Nordes to have been around when Canaanite languages were thriving, but Hell certainly was. It's only fair that you also understand our hosts, Love. Forgive me for not allowing everyone to speak around you while you remain in unfortunate ignorance, but we simply don't have the time for you to loosen your tongue the human way. Now, you'll have that linguistic access, too."

I gaped at the implication, but Caliban's affection knew no bounds. He brushed another of many kisses that morning against my temple with cool ease as he slid out of bed.

"Wait, get back here. Let's make a cambion, or whatever Astarte said."

He chuckled as he pulled a shirt over his head. "You've always been too smart for your own good."

"Fauna would disagree."

"Fauna is teasing you because she knows precisely how intelligent you are," he said.

I was decidedly displeased as my toes sought the warm obsidian floor. The entire room glittered with the dark, oppressive gemstones of a tomb. I fished the thin dress off the floor that I'd been brushed and groomed and slipped into the night before.

"Want to lend me your power so I can look at myself in the mirror?" I asked, voice dry.

"You look better than anyone deserves," he promised.

I sucked my teeth and let my expression settle as I muttered, "My mother always said demons lied."

That amused him far more than it should have.

"Why are there no windows? Hell had tons of windows."

"The sand, I expect," he said. "The important rooms are also deeply embedded within the palace to protect those who matter. Attendants, servants, and animals will presumably occupy the outermost ring."

"Is that necessary? They're in their own realm! Why would—"

235

"Humans are in their own realm," he said, not bothering to let me finish my thought. "Are all humans safe from one another?"

"No, but—"

"Name a pantheon that's never been under siege within its own walls, mortals included."

I scanned my memory. I knew of the Nordic gods not only from my books, but from my experience with Fauna, Fenrir, and their history lessons. Greek mythology was taught in most schools, and along with it came the sieges and infighting of the gods and goddesses. Christianity had the division between Heaven and its fallen angels...

My eyebrows perked. "Hell!" I said, a bit too cheerfully.

He extended his hand for mine, and I took it.

"I wish you were right, Love. But Hell has many courts. My court—the one you belong to—is unified, sure. My father is recognized as Hell's King, but within our kingdom, we are legion, for we are many." He smiled at his joke, even if the reference triggered my gag reflex. "That said, what if the Infernal Divine changed their allegiances? Or the Solar Court? Or if the Draconian Court were to turn on us? Or if the—"

"Draconian Court..." I interrupted. "As in...dragons?"

The fingers of one hand remained intertwined with mine, but his free hand tapped twice against mine with an almost paternal, placating gesture. "Excellent word association," he said.

"Fuck you." I glared.

"There's the spirit." He smiled. "If you're up for another round..."

"With you? Always."

There was a hollowness to his answering chuckle that twisted something anxious within me.

"What?"

He flattened a hand against the wall and leaned into it for support. "*Always* is just such a funny word, given that

236

you've spent this entire life cycle sending me away, convinced I wasn't real. Yet, the word still fits. Time has its cracks, its regrets, its imperfections. But you and I? We're always."

He succeeded in taking my breath away for a full eight seconds.

On the ninth second, something very human within me wanted to ask if he'd found other outlets—other lovers, for the times I'd sent him away—but resisted the urge. My body count was higher than any serial killer's...albeit not for the same reasons. He'd never expressed jealousy. He'd only wanted to know I was happy.

I was not evolved enough to feel the same.

So, I opted for wisdom. I wouldn't ask questions if I couldn't handle the answers, even if the concept tortured me.

"Are you ready, Love?"

"For the banquet?" I asked. "Isn't it morning?"

He pushed away from the wall. "Banquets aren't a meal. They're an event."

The introvert in me shriveled up like a pill bug at the thought. "They expect us there all day?"

"We'll have much to discuss. A major goddess has been murdered, after all."

"Yeah, but she—"

He shook his head once, cutting me off. "Don't use mortal logic here, Love. You bound yourself to her in a fair agreement—albeit, not one I'd have allowed either of you to honor. You consented. You offered your name, your word, your blood. It is you and I who broke a fair bargain. It would be a mistake to superimpose whatever black-and-white morality tempts you. Astarte was not a villain."

"She held Dagon..."

He nodded appreciatively. "There we go. Let's hinge on that. God-on-god crime is a much better argument than anything enacted by you or me."

The muscles between my shoulder blades knotted.

"We'll get Azrames out. But to do that, we have to

leave this room. Now, I would never ask you to be anything you aren't, Love, but with deities, there is a level of respect required of all of us. We aren't talking to humans. Spirited responses that might be admirable banter from one human to another, even lower class to upper, would not be received the same between gods, entities, or fae. Even Zeus, Odin, Allah, and Elohim speak to one another with respect. Tell me that you understand I'm not in any way attempting to temper your spirit or control your expression."

I shuddered at the casual mention of the gods that humans had bled, conquered, and died for. He continued to watch me for a response.

Be reverent.

Azrames had muttered the command to me on no uncertain terms before I'd met Dagon. Az was my friend. We had been on human soil. We had been meeting someone who'd been under a thumb, trapped in a terraformed god-catcher. And yet, his message had remained.

"I understand," I said, and I did. Perhaps I didn't need to grasp the gravity. The nuances weren't important. What mattered was that I'd believed Azrames then, and I believed Caliban now. Speaking to gods was not about personality or pride. Even Fauna, chaotic fae of sugar and sass, had put wolves under her dominion as if they were hers to command. I didn't have to be a believer or a showman, but I did have to show respect.

"I'm ready."

Chapter Twenty-Five

I WASN'T SURE HOW I WAS SUPPOSED TO EAT, DRINK, AND BE merry under the ticking clock of a trial, but I didn't have a say in the matter.

"You're as beautiful as ever." Caliban pressed a kiss to my forehead.

My lips parted as I looked at him and truly heard his words. He'd said them to me so many times, for so many years. Sometimes I'd smirk at the message, proud of myself for whatever inner monologue had led me to a day with high self-esteem. Other times, he'd say it to me and I'd sit on the bed and cry. His comforting touches had usually made it much, much worse. I'd hated the broken part of me that couldn't be normal—the pieces that had conjured an ethereal man to whisper things I longed to hear. It had been something I'd tolerated, something I'd appreciated, and something I'd despised.

His heat-appropriate clothes were linen, not unlike the ones Dorian had worn on our breakfast together. The servants had displayed countless jewels and bangles from which we could choose, but he'd forgone any and all adornment. The gray he wore, contrasted against his pale skin and frosted hair, reminded me so much of the arctic fox that had shared my childhood. Recasting my memories to understand he'd been a reality rather than a fiction was a feat that couldn't be conquered in a day, but there were three things I knew to be sure. The first was that Caliban, the gods, Heaven, Hell, and every pantheon of lore were beautifully and terribly real. The second was that I had never—not for a moment—been alone. And the third was that we could lose the love we'd fought for lifetimes to realize if we didn't make it out of here alive.

He stretched out his hand, and I offered mine. I followed him with quiet trust as he pushed open the flat, polished door to our room and led us down the hall. I didn't know how long he'd been in the Phoenician realm in order to become familiar with its layout, and I'd failed to ask. He didn't seem to be worried about the turns, the corners, the forks, or the rather intimidating sigils and seals on the walls as he navigated.

I took my cue to remain silent as we walked. The walls had ears, after all.

We took a flight of stairs before I dared a question. "Will Fauna be at the banquet?"

It seemed safe enough. She was my escort, after all. Besides, whether or not I was able to share the information with Caliban, a plan was in the works that required the comings and goings of Nordic ambassadors. If Fauna couldn't join us for whatever event we were about to encounter, then I wasn't sure how I was supposed to explain away the arrival of Ella and Estrid.

"Of course," he said lightly. I assumed the cadence of his words was intended for whatever carried his message on the wind than for me.

Thirty seconds later, I realized the question had been useless.

Caliban gave my hand a quick squeeze as we pushed into a banquet hall quite literally fit for gods. The ceiling was two—three—five stories high. The pillars were perfect, polished stone carvings of giants holding up the ceiling. Water features, sculptures, and overflowing vases of colorful, unfamiliar flowers spilled onto the floor in artfully curated

240

displays of beauty and life. I was overwhelmed by the sound of music, the babble of water, the twirl of majestic fabric, the patter of feet as entertainers swirled and danced, the smell of rich food, and the wine-fueled laughter. It felt like I'd stepped out of the dark, windowless palace and into a sparkling dome of life, excess, and opulence.

A woman in an indescribably beautiful patterned gown that flowed like flames off a bonfire danced up to me. She pushed a bouquet of pronged white flowers into my free hand and danced away before I could thank her. She rejoined women more beautiful than the sun, each shimmering with the inner light of fire sprites.

My escort turned the moment I entered the room. She'd been positioned just to the end of a table, with not one, but two chairs at the table head. Lord and lady, awaiting their seats at the far end of the banquet hall.

"Merit!" Fauna said enthusiastically as she pushed back from the table. Her chair creaked against the floor as she got to her feet with true enthusiasm, throwing her arms around me. She crushed me to her, thin arms possessing more strength than I realized as she held me as if I was water in the desert.

I was surprised at how emotional the fjord-like smell of forest and ocean made me as I breathed her in. We'd been separated for less than twelve hours, but coming together again felt like two halves reuniting to make a whole. I didn't want to be separated from her. I needed her discord, her energy, her irreverence, her joy in every moment of my life. She'd become my family in a way I couldn't articulate. And though I was excited to hold her again, I hadn't missed the two other blond heads that had turned at our approach.

Fauna didn't miss a beat, playing her role expertly. She pulled away to hold me at arms' length as she said, "Merit, please meet some distant relatives from our court! Ella and Estrid are from Álfheimr, my homeland!"

Both were already on their feet. Estrid offered a bow, but Ella pulled me into a hug, squishing me into her warmth in a genuine embrace. She looked over her shoulder at Estrid before releasing me, then at the others.

Fauna was quick to draw attention away from their tender moment, giving them whatever privacy they needed. She cleared her throat with intentionality. "And you must be the Prince?"

I lost my breath as I turned to catch his bemused, regal expression. He didn't look like a prince as he stood in the palatial banquet hall amidst dancers and flowers and fountains. He didn't just blend in. He looked like a god.

Something changed as I looked between the two of them. His expression remained joyous, but a cold fire danced in his eyes. His face remained tight when he extended his hand for a very human shake.

"Call me Caliban," he said.

A tiny gasp escaped Fauna's lips as she reached out a delicate hand to be engulfed in his.

I wasn't sure what surprised me more: the normalcy of the gesture, or the way Fauna's entire body blushed. Her smattering of freckles disappeared as her skin tone shifted to a matching heated shade of copper. I couldn't tell if I was surprised that she was capable of the respect, or inarticulately jealous. I made no attempt to conceal the lift of my brows.

"I had planned to tell you that I owe you," Caliban said to Fauna.

"You owe me nothing," she muttered, her crimson flush mixing with the music and performative swell of the banquet that overpowered her words.

His verb tense struck me as odd. He had planned to tell her he owed her, as if something had changed his mind. But if the walls had ears even when we were alone, then I certainly couldn't ask them at the banquet. Instead, I deflected. "Do you two need a moment?"

Caliban flashed a grin. "I suspect your escort knows precisely how hard you are to keep alive. If you appreciated it as much as either her or I, you'd understand my gratitude."

He slipped his hand around my waist and pressed another kiss into my hair with his final word.

"You'd be surprised at her capacity for ingratitude," Fauna said, plopping into her chair. She'd already shaken off her discomfort and returned to her typical irreverent self.

I took the seat beside her, sandwiched between my Nordic guardian and the Prince of Hell. He didn't release my hand, nor would I have allowed it as I leaned away from him and over the corner of the table toward Fauna. I whispered, "Estrid and Ella?"

"Yes," she said breezily. "I'd left word that I was headed with my human to see the Canaanites, and it's one of the realms they've never visited!"

I gulped. The wheels were fully in motion. If the valkyrie and the goddess of treasure were here today, would Poppy and Dorian truly arrive tomorrow? Ella and Estrid's arrival appeared to be tolerated at best. I couldn't fathom an excuse that would allow for a sudden Hellenic presence.

Ella propped an elbow on the table and grinned at me. "We haven't visited the Aztec pantheon, either. Shall we put it on our to-do list, Miss Mythology? Fauna tells us you're writing about South America next. So, what do you recommend? The Candomblé Ketu? Or maybe the Mayans, though I suppose the southern peninsula of North America and the Global South are different concepts for humans... Let me think on this..."

I knew that I'd need to be quicker on my feet if we were to keep up any such ruse, but curiosity got the best of me. "You've been to the African realms?"

Estrid scoffed behind him. "The Orisha are among the oldest deities. You can't come, Merit, as theirs is a closed pantheon. I suspect you'll get over it, given how many realms you've already managed to irritate in your short human life. But yes, it was one of the most important for us to visit. What's your human equivalent? Consider them prime destinations like Paris, or New York. We want to go to..."

I shrugged. "Mexico and Brazil?"

She smirked at my unwillingness to play along in her game of comparisons. Caliban had told me not to be spirited with the gods, and I would force my sarcastic nature to oblige. When it came to the Álfheimr lovers, however, not only did they happily tolerate Fauna, but I'd already been high in their living room. I was pretty sure they could handle whatever level of human embarrassment I could dish out.

Fauna took over the conversation, presumably before I could say anything I'd regret.

"Caliban," she said, blushing once more as she spoke the name I'd given him. "Merit tells me she's been an idiot this entire cycle. Tell me, has she always been this stupid?"

He released my hand, and for the briefest of moments, I felt the chill of abandonment. But then he leaned toward her as he slipped his arm around me to claim me further. "I suspect you know that not only is she brilliant now, but that she's always been brilliant. And I don't care how high ranking you are amongst the Nordes. You will not insult her again."

How high ranking could a skosgrå be? His words reverberated as if he'd issued a challenge. The tension was remarkably uncomfortable.

Huge parties were an introvert's worst nightmare even when everything went spectacularly. This one had so many uncertainties, I couldn't handle the two most important people in my life fighting, even if I didn't understand their bizarre tension.

Caliban's shoulders relaxed. "If I were a betting man—and when I bet, I rarely lose—I'd suspect your flippancy is precisely why you two made the perfect pair."

Fauna turned yet another shade of red. I wasn't sure if she felt flattered or scolded.

"Fauna," I blurted, "for the love of god, what's wrong with you? I've literally seen you be cheeky to—" I bit my tongue before mentioning Greek gods. Instead, I cleared my throat and said, "*Everyone.* You weren't particularly respectful in Hell, either."

She released a nervous breath as she said, "I'm just trying to make conversation."

I straightened as I grabbed her arm. I felt a genuine surge of perplexing worry. My eyes flared with the unspoken question.

She took her free hand and gave mine a squeeze, but didn't get the chance to elaborate.

"Guests!" came a booming voice from the far side of the room.

Amidst the dancing, the milling guests of fae, lesser deities, and citizens beyond the Phoenician veil, I hadn't noticed a terribly familiar face. The attendants stilled. Everyone quieted, either taking their seats or assuming reverent postures amidst the pillars as they dipped their heads in respect. A bearded man and a slick, handsome, youthful male at his side drew the crowd's attention.

"Today I'd like to raise a glass to our most welcome guests: Hell's Prince and his mortal companion."

I would have recognized that face in a sea of ten thousand. The Phoenician god of prosperity looked directly at me as he raised a goblet from the far end of the table. Caliban slipped his hands supportively onto my back once more to let me know he was there for me. I quickly scooped up my goblet and lifted it as I looked into the ancient face, the long black beard, the glistening-scaled robe, and the eyes of Dagon.

Three generations of gods looked upon us.

"My absence was involuntary," Dagon went on, "though others in our kingdom chose to live among the mortals." He looked beside him, just around the corner of the table, and my blood chilled. I must have reacted, for Caliban's fingers tightened around my waist to keep me still as I saw Anath watching. I swallowed and forced my gaze back to Dagon, but refused to let her leave my periphery.

Dagon continued, "It is my honor to laud my son, Baal,

245

who has ruled the Canaanites in both the mortal and eternal realms."

His son, Baal—Lord Baal, as I knew him from mythos—was at his side. The god was nothing like I expected him to be. Perhaps the aged pottery, dusty tomes, and aged texts had been wrong. Perhaps Fauna's gift to shield me from true forms had done me a service. The man who stepped forward didn't have the long, full beard of his father. His tanned skin had a similarly golden quality, his hair an ink-dark that matched the members of his court, but his face was clean-shaven, belying his eternal youth. The human in me wanted to guess him to be in his late twenties, though I knew the number was foolish. And while I was certain these were not appropriate thoughts to have of a god, he was breathtakingly beautiful. He caught me staring and nearly caused me to drop my wine when he responded with a wink.

The man—god, I corrected myself—beside him could have been his youthful twin. An informed guess pegged him as Baal's son, Melqart, guardian of Canaan's dead and the Phoenician Underworld. The pair had presumably ruled their realm as father and son while Dagon and the pantheon's major goddesses remained in the mortal realm.

I was on the edge of a headache. The mere thought of spending eternity with my family made me want to throw up.

Caliban leaned over to whisper, "Baal holds the first elite chair in the Ars Goetia of Hell's Infernal Court. He rules two hundred and fifty demonic legions. Dagon may be his father and Melqart his son, but Baal is the Lord of the realm."

Dagon was to ancient, unapproachable otherliness as Melqart was to the Herculean, himbo typecast. I was certain the thought alone would get me flogged, but sandwiched between the two, Baal was clearly most worthy of his rank. Their most high god was older than time, but he looked my age. More than that: he looked my type.

I hated myself for the involuntary way my body responded to his presence.

246

The gods on Baal's sides melted into the background as I focused on the beautiful man in the center. Returning Caliban's hushed tone, I asked, "Wait, a Phoenician god holds titles in Hell? Can deities do that in multiple pantheons without defecting?"

"The Infernal Divine is a court of appropriated deities—*demonized*, in a literal sense of the word—where other gods were captured and used as djinn. Solomon did to Baal what Astarte did to Dagon."

Solomon, as in the wise king in the Bible? I had a trillion more questions, and no time to ask them.

I rapidly tried to process the information, then suspected the bits of my knowledge would be useless to me. As far as I knew, Hell was a kingdom for adversaries. Perhaps those in a war against Heaven would band together with adversaries from any pantheon. I was already anxious over making a good impression on any member of Hell's multitudes. The idea of winning Hell's citizens to my side felt like the natural impulse of wanting future in-laws to like you. Instead, having recently been a catalyst for the murder of Baal's consort, I wasn't sure if his affiliation with Hell would work against us, or in our favor.

Baal raised his cup and looked directly at Caliban. "Tell us, Prince of Hell, how should my court address you this night?"

"Lord Baal," came the chillingly authoritative response at my side. "These days I'm going by Caliban. The name was gifted to me by my bride."

My throat tightened. The room whirred dizzyingly. The name I'd gifted my imaginary friend as a teenager was being spoken amidst realms, to deities, to pantheons, to the courts of Hell, with me as his bride. It was a marriage proposal I'd never been extended and hadn't formally accepted.

No one appeared surprised at his proclamation.

Perhaps changing names was a ready and common occurrence amidst realms. If I understood anything, then

247

I supposed Baal wasn't the true name of the Phoenician King—and that more than likely, his true name would be one I'd never be worthy to learn. I wondered if it was more common to change names in realms that had more exposure, then winced at the implication. Heaven and Hell remained in the mouths of humans across the globe, for better or for worse. I suspected Baal would not appreciate my disrespect for the kingdoms that mortals had long neglected.

"Thank you," Baal said, directing his gaze to me. The court's attention bore down on me. "And you have my gratitude for your role in my father's liberation."

I attempted to keep my hand from quivering as I held the goblet steady.

Be reverent.

Azrames's words, amplified by Caliban, echoed through me. It wasn't my place to speak. I dipped my head in respect while lofting my glass. I was positive I didn't imagine the collective relief as those on either side of me relaxed at my deferential reaction. I didn't blame them. I didn't have any sort of record of doing the right thing when faced with the preternatural. I thought briefly of the witches I'd called in my desperation to make sense of the sigil scrawled on my door, and wondered what they'd do in my situation. I was confident that they'd know better than to be, as Fauna so lovingly said, an idiot.

I certainly wasn't inherently worthy of the experience. I hadn't earned it. And the part of me that had been certain Caliban was a fictional manifestation of my broken pieces vying for positive self-talk would have told me that yes, I had worked for this. They would have told me that I'd studied, I'd worked, I'd learned the languages. I'd done the homework, I'd written the books, and I'd spent the time in the trenches for this. Still, as I stood here now, I felt certain I hadn't trained for it. Yet I'd be damned to somewhere worse than Hell if I didn't step up and live up to whoever or whatever Fauna and Caliban needed me to be.

Baal took a step away from his father and began to round the table.

Anath escaped from my periphery as I tracked him. He passed pillars, fountains, and reverently poised dancers. He paused just before he reached Estrid, but his eyes were trained on me. Baal stopped me in my tracks with his movie-star smile. Caliban's hand remained unmoving on my back. Perhaps he didn't want to startle me with any movement, as we both understood the importance of whatever transaction was occurring.

"Merit." My Nordic escorts parted as he approached. I was frozen beneath the glimmer of his obsidian eyes.

I tried to remember his powers. He was Canaan's most powerful storm deity. Syrian tablets had called him the god of life—both in opposition to death, and in new birth of man, livestock, and crops. There was something else...maybe it was leaving human women blank-brained and tongue-tied.

"Lord Baal," I said, careful to use his title. I'd intended for my words to come out with some sort of authority, but my voice did not carry. I wanted to say something eloquent, something important, but all that came from my mouth was "It's an honor to be invited into your home."

He laughed. The sound was unusual. Neither the light ring of joyful laughter, nor the coarse scratch of grandfatherly joy. There was a burning-coal sentiment to his amusement, as if chipped embers broke and sparked against another as he faced me. "Our realm receives visitors so infrequently," he said. "And now five are present? And thanks to your party, my father has returned, and he is whole. The honor is mine."

Baal closed the space between us. He was inches from me, staring into my very soul as I hummed beneath the electric scent of thunder and lightning. Estrid moved in my periphery, taking the subtlest of steps away from her chair. She'd positioned herself to attack. Caliban dropped his hand from my back, and I wished he hadn't.

I opened my mouth to apologize for Astarte's death, then snapped it shut once more.

Be reverent.

Fuck. Azrames had no idea how much of an impact he'd left with his words, but they may just have saved my life on the lakeside shores of Bellfield, and the cover of those around me. I lowered my eyes. Now was not the time to show bravery or entrepreneurial spirit. Perhaps those qualities would be lauded if I were an interesting recruit in a boardroom or a playmate in a friend group. But I was in an unknown realm amidst deities. It wasn't cowardice that kept my mouth shut as I waited for him to address me.

"Merit," he said.

I kept my chin high, trapped like a fly in honey under his gaze.

"I hadn't expected that the catalyst for the Nordes to visit the Canaanite realm would be a human, but I also hadn't expended Astarte to hold my father hostage in the mortal realm. Things tend to go awry at the end of a tale, don't you think? Life has one final surprise for us yet, it seems. I owe you gratitude, both for what you've done, and for what's to come," he said, tilting his glass.

I had no idea what he was talking about, but that had become my everyday norm since stumbling into the worlds beyond the mortal veil.

"You owe her more than gratitude," Caliban said carefully at my side.

Baal tilted his head slightly. "Caliban, is it?"

Caliban lifted his chin.

"It's curious, don't you think? I've met you in Hell, but never your human. Where have you been keeping her?"

It was with the unbothered energy of someone with nothing to lose that Caliban inspected his fingernails for invisible dust before returning his attention to Baal. "Merit has been to the mortal realms, Hell, Álfheimr, and is now here amidst Phoenicians. Aside from here and Hell, where have you been?"

It took all my power not to flinch.

Baal and Caliban remained locked in a stalemate for a long moment before his face cracked into a smile. "Your bride is well traveled," he said at last.

"And well accomplished," Caliban agreed. "Unless, of course, you'd prefer that your deity of crops and agriculture had remained in the human realms. It seems from the floral arrangements in your banquet hall that you're already benefitting from his return. I'm sure you're anxious for your first harvest in two hundred and...what was it? Forty?"

"Two hundred and fifty-two years."

"That's right. First harvest in your realm in two hundred and fifty-two years. She really is something to be grateful for, isn't she?"

Was Caliban...angry? I didn't understand what Baal had said or done that had set him off. Maybe I needed to elbow him and pass along Azrames's two-word advice.

I understood why he'd released me. He'd positioned himself fully against the highest god of their pantheon, a Lord in his own right amidst Hell's Infernal Court, ready to square off against Baal should the occasion call for it. I didn't know much of Caliban's powers. He could take the form of an arctic fox, though I didn't think that gift would serve us now. He could come and go throughout the veil—but then again, so could Azrames. He'd beheaded Astarte, but that had been with the god-killer. He'd allowed me to see myself through his eyes, but that had seemed so minor.

As they stood toe to toe in the banquet hall, I had a feeling that Baal would not hesitate if Caliban had little more than parlor tricks and a monarch for a father. I hadn't considered that his royal title might come with certain...assets.

Baal relaxed. "She certainly is," he agreed at long last. "Astarte gambled while playing with the rules of gods amidst the humans. We know a thing or two about leaving our power in the hands of mortals, don't we? Sometimes we have to take apocalyptic matters into our own hands," he said, looking at Fauna.

She plastered on a pretty smile as she said, "*Apocalypse* implies the end of the world, my Lord. I'd like to believe that Heaven's defeat would be the world's beginning. And when it comes to matters of eternity, I've learned not to leave things to the humans."

"Wise," Baal agreed. "And what has Hell learned?" he asked, looking at Caliban.

"I don't speak for Hell, or for humans," he said. "I'm here with my bride, and she has more than proven herself in this pantheon."

He lifted his goblet to his lips, smiling at some private joke as he made a show of inhaling his wine. I tried to remind myself that Caliban had mentioned Fauna's gift—the ability to contain my mind so I might see gods in their mortal form. I struggled to grip the information as I watched Lord Baal drink from his goblet. Between his square jaw, broad shoulders, and the glint in his eyes, I was reminded of how the most beautiful things in nature were often the most deadly.

Baal pulsed with whatever magnetism had compelled humans to worship him for centuries. The throb within me mingled between attraction and admiration. Despite my fear, my angst, my desire to grab Fauna's arm or back into Caliban's chest, a primal pull called to me. I loved it and hated it in equal proportions. I wanted to scramble from the table and drop to my knees in devotion, to claw out his eyes, and to take him in my mouth.

Fucking gods.

Resentment nestled its way between the emotions, burrowing somewhere amidst want and fear, crawling up to the surface above respect and compulsion. It broke free from the soil of my innermost being and planted its claws on the surface, staring Baal down. I nursed resentment at some joke, some insider knowledge, some exchange that I was either too human or too simple to understand. Resentment at the feelings, the confusion, the swirl of deeply mortal motives and needs and fears thundered over any other emotion until it was all that remained. He greeted the umbrage with a gleam in his eye.

Baal's smile widened. "I see," he said at long last. "Perhaps you have indeed found one worthy of you, Prince." This time, when he winked, it shot lightning through my core. He turned and strutted back to the head of the table. He drained his goblet before setting it down. "Anath reigned for two thousand years as a favorite along the Dead Sea. She thrived in the mortal realm, in the eternal realm, and served as a helpmate to a fellow deity amidst the humans for the last several centuries. In Astarte's absence, I would like to announce my sister Anath as not only my helpmate and deity of Astarte's war, but also as a bringer of peace in the form of victory. May she step into her predecessor's stead for a greater and more prosperous Canaan."

Baal spoke of her as if he respected her. Did they not blame her for her role in holding Dagon against his will? Had she been a victim of the god-catcher, too? I supposed it didn't matter. Their reputation and legacy were more important than personal feelings. They'd need to be a unified front regardless of how they felt if they hoped to thrive in Astarte's absence.

The table raised their glasses in celebration and acknowledgment.

"Anath?" Baal prompted.

Dagon and Melqart's appraising stares were stifling as they awaited the goddess.

"To victory," she said to the table. "Fear not. Astarte's blood courses through my veins, and her spirit will live on through me. May I bring peace when the world needs it, and war when she deserves it."

"Here, here!" cried Baal.

My stomach churned.

His people raised their glasses in response. The world relaxed for a while as everyone settled into their chairs, accepted their meals, and dug into their dishes. Meats, spices, vegetables, sweets, rice, fruits, and foods beyond my capacity for imagination were served time and time again by an endless supply of attendants, each more beautiful than the last.

"It's an offense to reject their food," Caliban said once the high Lord of the pantheon had left earshot.

"What was he talking about? What was so amusing?" I pushed the food around on my plate.

Caliban's anger hadn't fully subsided, but it wasn't directed at me. He remained bristled toward Baal as he said, "We are surrounded by the most tenuous of allies that could become our foes in an instant. Now is not the time to discuss an ancient deity's obscure references. Eat."

"I can't," I replied.

He placed a hand on my back, and a starved growl rumbled in return. I blinked at him in surprise, unsure if I was irritated that my human body was so easy to manipulate, or grateful that he'd spared me from committing an offense.

We were already here for murder, and the jury wasn't exactly comprised of our peers.

I wouldn't win any favors by dishonoring their customs.

My cup was never empty. Conversation did not idle. Entertainment resumed as dancers and musicians put on a show for the royal event. Estrid remained tense, which I assumed was her resting state. Ella appeared to be genuinely enjoying herself, though perhaps it was because she had no personal stake in the whereabouts of a demon and an angel. Ella was brilliant, making friends and bringing smiles with everyone around her. Estrid loved to stand back and watch her partner shine. Fauna laughed and cracked far too many inappropriate jokes, which bothered me. I'd gone mad with worry when Caliban was separated from me. She'd finally displayed a reasonable emotion when the doors had locked behind us in our room, and now she was carefree once more.

Caliban sensed my irritation and stroked along my spine to calm me. I wondered if his touch was soothing because I

254

loved him, or if he was controlling my cortisol with the same power that had emptied my stomach or enabled me to understand the Phoenician language.

Anath rose and waited for the last murmurs of conversation to die before she smiled at the crowd. "And what could go better with our meal than a dish best served cold," she said. "This banquet is about more than celebration as Dagon and I return to the realm. We come together for more than the guests who've graced our home. Though we lived peaceably among the humans for over two hundred years, it was the crimes of kingdoms that fell Astarte and Jessabelle on mortal soil. For dessert, please savor the divine justice of our newest citizens."

My heart plummeted as the words left her lips.

As the great doors to the banquet hall slid open, Fauna's sharp intake of air was the only sound louder than my heart's thundering. The room spun as two shapes stepped into the banquet hall. Flanked by armed guards, Azrames wore a single thin manacle. It served no purpose to my human eyes, which led me to believe its sole use must have been the inhibition of magic. I scanned him as quickly as I could for signs of injury, but he didn't meet my gaze as his eyes remained fixed beside me on Fauna.

My ears rang. My heart skipped uncomfortably. My eyes watered as I refused to blink, staring at my friend as I drowned in guilt. He was here because of me.

"Don't worry," he mouthed to Fauna. The corner of his storm-cloud lips tugged up in an unconvincing smile.

Nausea took hold of me at the sight of the almost imperceptibly glowing figure in the middle of the hall.

Bruises in various shades from red, to purple, to the sickly yellow-green of older wounds decorated his face. His wrists and ankles were bound so that he could do little more than take shuffling steps. Fresh droplets of glittering blood beaded from the cut on his lip as if he'd been subdued in the moments before entering. My stomach churned against his limping steps and the sneer of the guards around him, but I could stare at one thing only.

Tightly wrapped in binding circlets of obsidian rope were the enormous, white-feathered wings of an angel.

My mouth dried as Silas looked across the room and directly into my core.

Chapter Twenty-Six

I SCANNED THE FACES AT THE ROYAL END OF THE TABLE, DESPER-
ate for any clue. The banquet's attendants hummed with
subdued thrill. Anath vibrated with satisfaction. Baal leaned
back into his chair in amusement. Dagon and Melqart appeared
not to care in the slightest, as if simple court proceedings
were far beneath them. I didn't dare turn my head to see the
faces of Caliban or Fauna.

"Azrames of Hell," Anath said to the room, voice
booming with authority, "you've been accused of Astarte's
deicide through inaction. Her handmaiden, Jessabelle, befell
a similar fate. You, Azrames of Hell, were present when the
high goddess of your allied pantheon required assistance in
the face of our shared Heavenly foe, and yet you stand before
us, unscathed. How do you plead?"

"I fought, Lord Baal," Azrames answered honestly.

He'd fought, all right. I may have been drugged out of
my mind, but I had still seen him swing the meteor hammer.
His great crime in Phoenician eyes was that he, a lowly civilian, hadn't done enough to protect their goddess. I was fairly
certain we wouldn't be having this conversation if the security
footage hadn't been wiped.

I shot Caliban a panicked look. His face was unreadable
as he watched his fellow demon.

Fauna's fingers slipped around my arm. Her nails bit into my flesh.

Azrames broke eye contact with Fauna, straightening his shoulders as the goddess addressed him.

"Your Prince has remained in our courts as your advocate and has brokered an agreement. It was determined that the Canaanites will recognize our allyship with Hell. While justice must be served, we've reached an arrangement. Your Prince has requested that your life be spared in recognition of the efforts made to defend Astarte against her heavenly foe, despite your failure to do so. As your punishment, Azrames of Hell, you have been given a choice by the rule of three. You may serve as a ward of our realm for three centuries, choose three of Hell's citizens to be sacrificed in your stead, or kneel before the court and receive three thousand lashes."

Fauna's nails bit into me so hard I was certain she'd broken skin. I was grateful for the pain as it anchored me. I shot my gaze from Anath back to Azrames as we waited for him to speak.

Anath's tone was begrudging as she added, "Our brokered deal for ongoing allyship with Hell grants Azrames the Prisoner's Reprieve, as is customary to his realm before a sentencing. Azrames, you will be allowed to partake in our festivities, and are granted the rights of a conjugal night spent with a mate before your sentence is carried out."

My head spun. He was supposed to drink wine and fuck with this axe over his head? None of it made sense, and no one around me was helping piece the puzzle together.

I knew intrinsically that he would never let three innocents die for him, though I wished he were a little more wicked, a little more selfish. I was pretty sure I would kill at least twelve humans in my stead, most of whom were my clients, some of whom were girls I'd gone to school with. I was certain Fauna wanted the same, as she was doubtlessly thinking exactly what I was. Three hundred years in subservience to the Canaanite realm may be a mere dot in the face of eternity, but even

258

my twenty-six years had felt unbearably long. How could he possibly live in bondage for lifetimes?

I couldn't begin to fathom the carnage and gore of three thousand lashes.

I'd once dated a man who'd commented on his country's brutal corporeal punishment by saying, "Caning is the worst fate imaginable. If you're going to break the law, do something that earns you death." It had horrified me at the time, but this amplified that punishment to an unfathomable degree.

A few dozen strikes would kill a human. Between the blood loss and the chunks of ripped flesh, there would be no way to survive one hundred, unless they were carried out over the course of weeks and months. Azrames was a demon, and surely he would find a way to survive. But three thousand? The essence that stitched his being would surely shatter after the first thousand. He'd undoubtedly lose his mind after the second. The man who went into such a sentence would not be the one who came out.

I struggled to calculate what the number meant. Even if the one executing the punishment had the stamina to wind up and crack the whip every thirty seconds—an impossible task—it had to be more than twenty-five unbroken hours of unspeakable brutalization. It would surely go on for days, if not weeks.

My imagination filled with the image of Azrames's slate-gray, shirtless form lying in a pool of black blood. His iron face would turn to shades of bloodless ash. Irretrievable pieces of him would cling to the whip. He'd be little more than pulp by the time they finished.

He relaxed as if the options were far kinder than he'd expected. He dipped his head to acknowledge the ruling, then righted himself as he said, "I'll take the lashes."

"No," came Fauna's horror from beside me. She lurched as if to lunge around the table, but Ella intercepted her. The court shuffled with curiosity as they watched the Nordes react to the decision.

"It's okay," Azrames mouthed, speaking to Fauna once more. He kept his half smile, but the twinkle in his eye was absent, leaving only coal-black irises staring back at us. My heart cracked as the entire banquet hall watched him attempt to soothe her fears while saddled with the weight of indescribable torture.

"Do something," I pleaded with Caliban under my breath.

"I have," he whispered back.

It wasn't enough. This wasn't justice. I was the reason Astarte and Jessabelle were dead. I was the reason Azrames and Silas had been in Bellfield in the first place. I was the only one deserving of punishment at this table.

I looked to the Phoenician gods once more, but they remained unfazed.

"Excellent," Anath said with a flick of her wrist. "Your magic will remain limited until you've departed our kingdom. Rejoin your party and celebrate among us until your reckoning. But Hell needn't have all the fun. Silas of Heaven," she said, turning her attention to the battered angel. "Your life will be forfeit—"

"He didn't do anything!" The outburst clawed its way from my belly to my throat. I couldn't stop the words, though I may as well have, as my cry went utterly ignored. Silas's crime was the unforgivable act of helping me.

"—a sentence to be carried out on the third and final day of our banquet."

Baal joined her on her feet. "In our magnanimity, we'll grant a parting wish, angel. How would you prefer to die?"

Silas looked at me again and my blood turned cold. He was trying to tell me something. I saw the unspoken message in his eyes, even if I couldn't understand his meaning.

"Caliban—"

He shot me a look, but it was not silencing. It seemed several immortal beings in the room were trying to tell me something that I couldn't begin to understand. There had to be a way. One could talk to God through silent prayer, right?

I had no idea if demons or angels could hear mortal thoughts. Part of me was horrified at the idea, but I rolled the dice.

Silas, I cried out silently.

He did not react to my plea, but Caliban slipped his arm around my waist and dug his fingers into my hips with commanding force. Perhaps they were both telling me to shut the fuck up.

Silas rolled his shoulders and lifted his chin while he accepted his sentence. He leveled his gaze at the goddess as he answered. "By combat."

A slight murmur rippled through the gathering.

"What if he wins?" I asked under my breath. Clearly, I was not as quiet as I'd thought.

From across the banquet hall, Anath answered. "He will not."

"My," Baal said, teeth glinting in true amusement, "it is a party indeed. My subjects, my peers." He smiled at the people scattered throughout the room, then at the gods, fae, and deities around him. "And my most welcome guests. Please rejoin us for another day of merriment tomorrow as we celebrate Dagon and Anath's return to our kingdom."

The armed guards flanked Silas as they began to push him from the room, but allowed Azrames to stay back with only two centurions. The moment the sea of armored men parted, Fauna broke free from our hold and threw her arms around his neck.

"Go with Fauna," Caliban whispered.

I looked up at him with questioning eyes.

"No one will question me coming to fetch you later. Go." He gave me a squeeze. And while I loathed to part with him, I had to remember that we'd come for more reasons than one. I was not just a girl who needed to be with the one who held her soul. I was a human who'd infiltrated kingdoms and the domino with which we'd topple chaos. He understood the pain in my eyes, and didn't move from where he stood. It would have to be me who left him.

"Shall we?" I asked as I turned to Estrid and Ella. I forced a brightness into my voice and a smile on my face that no part of me felt. They gave Caliban a small, respectful bow as they left. I shot a final, desperate glance at Caliban before leaving with my Nordic party as we followed Fauna and Azrames from the banquet hall.

✦

I spun on my heels, the bobbing effect of the sign on my vision keeping me nauseated and reeling.

We hadn't returned to the room Fauna and I had shared, but were in a small wing of clustered suites. I paced by the adjoining doors and alternated between flexing and stretching my hands as I panicked. "What are we supposed to do?"

Azrames swept me up mid-stride with a grin. "You're supposed to say hi to me."

"How can you be so calm!" I was in hysterics. Azrames was meant to be enjoying a Prisoner's Reprieve on the eve of the end of the world, and he was acting like it was any normal Tuesday.

"Let her go," Fauna said tersely. "She doesn't deserve the love."

Azrames set me down and ruffled my hair. "Being mean to you is the truest sign she loves you, Mer-bear. It is Merit, here, right?"

I struggled to remember if any name aside from Merit Finnegan had bubbled to the surface in Bellfield, but I didn't possess the presence of mind to truly address it. I took a partial step away from Azrames to let him see my desperation.

"I won't let this happen," I swore.

There was pity in my eyes as he looked at me. The sentiment rippled through the room, shared by all but Fauna. "You have a lot of heart," he said. "You hold no blame for what's to come."

Fauna bared her teeth at me. "We spent a week together in your fucking apartment, and not *once* did you explain that

262

this all happened because you signed your life and blood freely to Astarte."

"Six days," I said under my breath.

"What?" She bit off the word.

I echoed the callous words back to her that she'd said on my couch in the height of my panic. "It wasn't a week. It was six days."

"What's done is done," Ella said, voice a gentle lull behind us.

"Bullshit, it is," Fauna snapped. She pointed a finger at me. "You went into a terraformed god-trap without me. You took on deities without me. You came back to me without *them*. And after trying to sleep with me, you gave me a woefully incomplete recount of events, Merit Fucking Finnegan."

Azrames draped an arm loosely over my shoulders, but everyone in the room understood the gesture. He didn't blame me, even if he had every right to. "You tried to sleep with her? And you failed? Damn, Fauna."

I shook free from the weight of his arm and stepped away from him. It caused me too much pain to look at him, particularly given his attempts at friendly levity. I didn't want to see the kindness in his dark eyes, his smooth skin, his hard jaw. I couldn't handle the easy, youthful face, the confident posture, the pretty lies of reassurance stitched together in grayscale.

"We need a plan. We need—"

Four hands flew up to silence me. I knew it wasn't just the armed guards posted outside the door to ensure Azrames stayed put. The walls had ears. My entire face scrunched, tendons flexing, muscles clenching as I fought the urge to scream. They watched my silent tantrum as I worked through my helplessness—immortals observing a human who barely had the wherewithal to keep herself alive, let alone survive the realms.

"My dog," I said suddenly. I looked meaningfully at Fauna. "I can't be expected to survive another night without my dog. You know how humans lose their minds when they're separated from their animals."

Azrames's brows met in the middle. His confusion was starkly contrasted against the wide eyes and rigid spines of Ella and Estrid.

It took far too long for Fauna to allow calm cooperation to replace the blame and rage painted over her freckles. Through clenched teeth, she looked at Azrames. "Merit needs her dog back. Does this gift for language flow in two directions?"

Caliban had been right. Whatever present he'd bestowed upon me had been extended to her as well. Azrames nodded slowly.

"Great," she said testily. She reached the door, and I watched a transformation happen. She shook the fury and betrayal from her features. A metamorphosis of butterfly proportions swept over her as she pushed open the door and called into the hall with a high, sweet, smiling voice. "Excuse me? We're in need of attention."

Two attendants appeared as if stepping from the sparkling walls themselves. Hewn from shadow and glistening stone, two enormous beings of any gender or no gender at all looked down at Fauna. She exemplified Ella, sugar-sweet and desirable with each dripping word.

"As her ancestor and appointed guardian in the realm of her bloodline, I've been made responsible for the Prince's human. As her escort, it's my obligation to ensure she's as comfortable as possible. She's been separated from her dog for a day now. I'm not sure what you know of humans and their dogs…" She paused, waiting for some form of acknowledgment from the servants, but none came. Fauna nodded along knowingly. "The last few centuries have become a circus in the mortal realm! The way they treat their pets, no god could guess the ruling species." She flashed a disarming smile, and I saw it land.

Maybe these Phoenicians hadn't been on mortal soil in

hundreds of years, but they weren't so detached from the realm that they couldn't appreciate human slander. One returned her smile.

"She's throwing quite the fit," Fauna continued. "I know the Phoenicians remain firmly allied with Hell. The Nordes wish the same for both the Phoenician realm and our allegiance with Hell. Please do three realms a favor and indulge this spoiled human. It should remain at her side throughout the rest of her visit to your beautiful kingdom. Will you see to it that her animal is brought to us before we have war over something as foolish as a girl and her pet?"

She was unbelievable.

The attendants exchanged a few muted mutters before returning to the stone from whence they had come. The moment Fauna closed the door behind her, the godly charm evaporated. She glared at me and stormed to the bed.

The Nordic pair chatted quietly amongst themselves in ancient Norse, presumably intelligent enough to remain far more cryptic in a foreign kingdom than I could ever hope to be. Azrames followed Fauna to the bed, scooping her tiny form against him. She looked like a kitten as she curled against his chest and began to cry. No one dared disrupt their moments together.

Ella and Estrid disappeared behind doors in our collection of suites. Given the day's tragic news, Fauna and Azrames deserved to remain undisturbed. Neither of them looked up from where they comforted one another while I went to the far door and gave it a tug. I was relieved to find that the next room was empty.

I closed the door and began the waiting game.

I hated that Caliban had sent me away from him, though I suspected he had his reasons. Maybe it strengthened the case for the arrival of Nordic ambassadors if I demonstrated their importance to me. I hoped it wasn't to give Fauna and I time together, as it was evident that she blamed me for the tragedy looming over Azrames. Perhaps he knew Fauna would have a better chance at brokering Fenrir's release without raising suspicion. She had been incredibly charming—alarmingly so.

My mind took me to the Mediterranean cliffs as Poppy had clutched me and demanded that I ask Fauna about her true intentions. I had no idea how much the nymph was capable of hiding, or if I was another victim of her subterfuge.

I was too stressed to choose the bed, but sank onto the floor, back upright I rested my head against the wall behind me. It was a nightmare. I'd awaken to see the leaves of the trees rustle over the river in the warehouse district. I'd avoid the internet, terrified of the flood of texts regarding Geoff Christiansen and what his doxxing had done to my career. I wouldn't check social media or read the news. I'd look at my phone to have memes and dry jokes from Nia and Kirby, knowing they'd be trying their best to salvage my mood while I was on the lam. I'd check my email and see that deadlines were still looming, if I still had a job in the wake of the news. There would be no gods, or kingdoms, or fae. There would be no travel between realms.

I'd been raised to believe in Heaven and Hell.

Christianity spoke of the prophet Elijah being so righteous that he was taken to Heaven on a chariot of fire long before his mortal days had finished. I'd told my mother that it sounded like he'd been abducted by aliens, and she'd very calmly told me that all alien lore was a misunderstanding of humans trying to interpret the signs of angels and demons. Accepting the reality of Caliban and Silas meant that my mother could be right about the *what* and *where,* even if she'd missed the mark on the numerous other questions that made sense of our world.

We'd visited a public museum once on a rare family vacation, and my mom had pointed to a statue from central Africa.

"Demons are clever," she'd said. "They've taken shapes and names throughout history to trick people into believing they're gods."

"So the Egyptian gods…?"

"Demons," she confirmed.

I'd thought of the art on Grandma Dagny's wall. I'd leafed through as many books on Norse mythology as I had of the fjords, of pictures of smiling women in wool bunads as I had of the homeland she'd ached for, even if she'd never been allowed to understand the call that pulsed through her blood. "Odin? Thor?"

My mother had nodded along with my train of thought while guiding me amidst the exhibits. All demons, of course. My father had trailed somewhere behind, tightly glued to his pamphlet. He was a smart man—just not one who was interested in a life with my mother or me.

"What's smarter, Marlow? To assume everyone around the world is a gullible idiot making up fairy tales? Or to think perhaps there's something very real going on—something sneaky, something tricky—that cultures and languages and people around the globe respond to?"

"So, they're real?" I'd asked. We'd stood between a plate and a fertility vase as everyone milled around me. "Thor is real? This goddess"—I gestured to the vase—"she's real?"

"God made the world," my mother had said confidently. "And *He* did not make idiots. He made angels who were beautiful and brilliant and powerful. When they fell, why wouldn't they want to be recognized for their power? Of course the resulting demons were intelligent. He made brilliant entities. It's no surprise something so resourceful would try to make themselves equal to God. Try and succeed, in many cultures, to call themselves false gods."

I'd lifted my fingers, but stopped just shy of touching the exhibit. I'd looked at it breathlessly. "All gods are demons?"

"Except our God," she'd agreed.

"Except our God," I'd repeated.

I wasn't sure whether to laugh or cry when I thought of her now. My mother, the powerful psychic with fae blood coursing through her veins, stood on the precipice of understanding. She saw it all. She perceived so much, she understood so much, and then zoomed right past the truth. The gods were real. Demons were real. It was all real. But she'd needed to filter it through her lens of comprehension.

Aloisa had applauded my mother for her feats.

I thought of my remedial knowledge of the Japanese pantheon and their loose use of the word *demon*. It didn't denote malevolence or goodness. It was simply a word to dictate a spiritual *other*. There were good demons, and bad demons, in their mythology.

Words were just words, after all.

It was something Fauna said to me time and time again. They were sounds—consonants and vowels—we spat out to form meaning around our understanding. Whatever we said, as long as we conveyed our message, it was fine.

Like true names, there was a core meaning to each word. Most of us are neither worthy nor able of comprehending their importance.

I suspected Aloisa thought my mother's solution was far more honorable than my atheistic denial of anything and everything beyond the realm of flesh and blood. Maybe my mother had prepared me for belief. Perhaps she'd prepped me to see things outside of how they'd been painted. Even in my most zealous evangelical state, I'd believed in angels and demons in a tangible, powerful way. But this…

"Mar?"

I opened my eyes and saw Fauna standing in the doorway to my room. The slabs of stone were so silent when they opened and closed. They swung shut noiselessly, and we were in a dimly illuminated space once more. I remained on the floor as I looked up at her. She took a few steps into the room and slid next to me.

"Mer, I mean," she corrected quietly.

Three words, but they each dripped with pain. I softened as I shifted to look at her. I hadn't spent a lot of time attempting to empathize with what Fauna might be going through. Her horror at Azrames's sentence...

"Your dog will be here tonight," she said. She fiddled with her fingers, watching them carefully as each movement betrayed nerves and stress. "And then you'll both go back with Caliban."

My mouth turned to cotton as I watched her. Dread filled the small room.

"I need to ask you a favor." She looked up at me with wide eyes at last.

There it was. The reason for my dread. The excellent command of emotion. The pieces of her that would tug at my heartstrings. I looked into her larger-than-life doe eyes and did my best to remain impassive.

"Caliban can end this," she said quietly.

I shook my head. Even if I was dreaming, I knew the rules of this nightmare. "Fauna, the walls—"

She bridged the short gap between us, wrapping her hand around mine. "He'd do it for you."

I swallowed against my instinctive protest. I hated myself as I said, "Azrames won't die."

The silver spikes of true tears lined her eyes as she laughed a sharp, humorless laugh. She blinked against the bubbling water, but a single stream ran down her cheek. She shook her head. "*Caliban* won't die," she emphasized, "but we're going to pluck out his eyeballs, and tear off his fingernails, and break his bones, for weeks, and weeks, and weeks. But he'll survive."

I looked away. I'd known my words had been thoughtless before I'd said them, but now I hated myself.

"I'm sorry. I care about Az. I..."

"He'll do it for you," she repeated. "Caliban can end this."

I looked back at her. "It might mean—"

She touched her ears, reminding me that the walls were listening. I bit my lip and drew a stilling breath before using one of the few lessons I'd learned in Sunday school.

It was a horrid, albeit useful, appropriation of language.

We were taught American Sign Language for all our favorite worship songs and Bible verses, not just at our church, but as an often-problematic trend in evangelical congregations across the country. Even at the time, it had been a curious choice. The teachers hadn't known why, save for the power of actions and body movement. One Sunday school teacher had suggested that they were always looking to recruit new members for the interpretation team, as many took turns rotating through sermons and messages throughout the week. My knowledge consisted of major religious language, the alphabet, and a few fun animals and curse words.

A dark part of me chuckled thinking of the worship leader who'd been so intent on teaching us the ASL to "Our God Is an Awesome God" as I turned to Fauna.

It was a slow process picking my way through the alphabet at every word I didn't know, but I gambled and told her, "It might mean war."

Caliban had said that the other gods had incentive to see Heaven fall. It was why Astarte had been willing to let Caliban into her clinic. Perhaps it was why her death hadn't been met with an instant battle cry from their pantheon. The good of the many outweighed the good of one deity, as long as they got some form of justice.

But I didn't care about their justice, their motives, or their rivalries.

After a long pause, she lifted both hands and made a few signs that were utterly foreign to me. I responded by holding my pinky to the middle of my chest for *I*. I used my forefinger and middle finger, pinching them to meet my thumb in a rapid motion as I said *no*. I used my index finger near my forehead, flicking and bending it to communicate understanding.

She made an amused face, then loosened her shoulders as she held my eyes. Fauna took her time as she picked each and every word with one hand, spelling them out. After each letter, she'd wait to see me mouth it to know I was up to speed.

T-H-E-N

I nodded along encouragingly. I knew these letters.

S-T-A-R-T

My blood pressure kicked up as I watched the intensity in her face.

W-A-R.

That was it. She knew exactly what she was asking of me.

She sat still as she watched me, examining every twitch, every shift, any micro expression that might convey what I was feeling. My eyes flicked over her shoulder to the closed door. Beyond it, I knew Azrames sat on a bed, ready to take three thousand lashes because he'd come to my aid. He'd been roped into this because she was tied to me, and he loved her. He was my friend, yes, but we would have never crossed paths had it not been for her.

I watched her honey-brown eyes burn with questions. Inhuman white dots mixed with the copper freckles that decorated her nose and cheeks as her face wrinkled with intensity. Her eyebrows leveled with panic and seriousness as she waited, and waited, and waited.

I thought of the King of Hell as he'd risked it all to stand against Heaven. I thought of the story of the Aesir and Vanir, and how Odin had chained Fenrir to a rock in fear of his power. I thought of Hades's subjugation in the Underworld. I thought of freedom fighters and abolitionists throughout human history. Ella, Estrid, Fenrir, Poppy, and Dorian were a new set of names in a long line of revolutions. Poppy's warning floated through my memory.

Ask her why she's helping you. Ask her why she really came into your life.

I held her gaze as I signed five letters.

C-H-A-O-S.

Fauna closed her eyes slowly. If I didn't know better, I would have sworn it was to keep herself from bursting into tears. She sniffed before pulling me into a hug. We didn't have long to revel in whatever came of our embrace before scuffling drew our attention. Despite the thick stone walls, the sounds of arrival and the call of our names cut through the door.

She pulled me to my feet as we pushed our way into the main room.

Fenrir sat politely in the middle of the room with his tail around his feet.

"She may keep her dog," the attendant said stiffly, as if the words had been practiced, "as long as it remains well-behaved."

I spoke over Fauna, answering, "He's extremely intelligent. He won't be a problem."

The surprise in their eyes confused me for a moment before I realized they were speaking what should have been a dead language to my human ears. Oh well. I was the Prince's human. For all they knew, demon royalty had selected me because I was a talented linguist. Let them speculate.

The closed the door behind them as Fenrir looked at me.

"You're intelligent yourself, Marlow."

My eyes widened in fear at the use of my true name. I gaped at the enormous canine in the room. A god-killer so powerful Odin himself had strapped him to a rock for eternity. Fenrir, the beautiful, shaggy horseman of the apocalypse.

Fauna gave me a final squeeze as she parted for her night with Azrames. Fenrir and I carried on alone, escorted down inky marble halls by servants.

"They can't hear me," Fenrir said into my mind. "I choose who can and cannot perceive my words. As such, I allow some to perceive me as the domesticated pet you claim, while few know me by my true name. Speak to me in your mind, and only I will hear."

I didn't bother to question him. I held his eyes and kept my mouth shut as I thought, "What do you know of our situation?"

"Tell me."

And so I did. I told him of Bellfield. I told him of my bond with the Prince. I told him of the punishments for both Azrames and Silas. I told him what our Phoenician hosts believed. I told him of Fauna's plea.

"There is much you do not know, human, and it is not for me to fill in those gaps. I honor your spirit, and I honor our deal. As you rightly identified, I have a taste for anarchy. My teeth are yours, as I am your weapon as we bring the world to its knees." The words rang through my thoughts as his lips pulled back from his teeth in a smile.

"Let's give them hell," I said, returning the smile.

"We'll give them more than Hell," he said. "We'll give them what Hell stood for."

Chapter Twenty-Seven

I HATED HOW CHASTELY WE LAY IN THE BED THAT NIGHT. Caliban and I changed into sleeping clothes, but remained dressed. Wearing clothes to bed was for pilgrims, not two desperately drooling, sexually compatible beings madly in love. He draped an arm over me, lulling me into the false sense of security I'd developed when I'd believed I was safely alone with my dreams. I hated the windowless rooms of glittering black stone that made it impossible to tell whether it was day or night in this well-protected tomb. I hated opening my eyes the next morning knowing that it was the second of three days before Azrames and Silas faced the consequences of meeting me.

Rage was actionable. Sorrow could be healing. Hate was not a useful emotion.

"Love," he whispered, running his fingers up and down my back in slow, gentle, unpredictable patterns. I hadn't slept much, but I allowed myself to relax into the soothing touch as my mind followed the circles and swirls of his fingertips. "Are you ready for a second day of banquets?"

"I hate events," I said quietly to the wall. I kept my back to him in hopes that he would continue softly tracing beautiful patterns from my scalp to my tailbone and everywhere in between.

"I know you do," he confirmed. "Extroversion has never been a quality of yours. Let me fill your cup when it's empty."

I rolled toward him and was relieved when his fingers continued to soothe me. It took the barest of moments to recall that he'd been present throughout my childhood. He knew the only calming memories I had with my mother were silent ones that looked exactly like this. She'd touch my back while the staticky television transitioned from soap opera to news. I'd lay my head in her lap and listen to the world events for thirty minutes, and then we'd have dinner as a family. They had been some of the few moments no one was fighting. There had been no talk of shame, or religion, or failure. There had been simply the calming shapes of her nails between my shoulder blades.

The sensation was different entirely when attached to the hands of someone who loved me unconditionally. I looked into silver eyes that didn't look away as I thought of how unflinchingly he'd seen all my pieces, good and bad. He'd taken the shape of a fox just to make me smile when I was nothing to him. He'd been there for me as my only companion. He'd listened to my woes as my imaginary friend while I'd raged as a wrathful teenager, as someone trying to win favor with her church, her mother, her pastor. He'd held me through the fun and the guilt alike as I'd tried to figure out who I was in college. He'd celebrated my nights when I'd transitioned into sex work, and had helped my career as a writer so I could truly live deliciously. He'd endured every part of me and loved me unconditionally.

"All day today?" I confirmed quietly, knowing the answer.

"And tomorrow," he agreed.

"Does that mean—"

"No gore today," he finished my thought.

In the absence of trials and sentences, Azrames might even be present on the second day of the banquet. They'd made it clear that he was to celebrate his final days of freedom like a death row inmate granted lobster and wine for a last meal. Silas would certainly not be extended the same generosity. I wondered if Caliban had already checked on Fenrir, then felt anxious. Fenrir was a powerful god. I had no idea what he needed or didn't need, only that he was not being treated as such.

"I'm fine," came a deep, soothing voice from beyond my line of sight.

I looked to the settee where I'd hoped he'd lie but he'd opted for the chill of the sparkling stone floor. I couldn't see Fenrir from his position past the foot of our bed, and I wondered if it had been strategic on his part. He didn't need to be exposed to whatever it was the Prince of Hell and his bride did in the quiet hours of night.

I spoke to him in the silence of my mind, saying, "Do you need to go outside, or—"

"I'm a god, mortal," he said curtly. "The sooner you stop human-washing the deities around you, the more cunning you'll become. Your friends, your allies, even the one who holds you—they love you, they care for you, but you would be wise to remember that they are not people. The one you call Fauna is no human. Your Prince is no human. Their definitions of love and morality will not reflect yours."

I hedged uncomfortably as I tried to peek unsuccessfully over the lip of the bed. Caliban's fingers continued to move, whether he understood an unspoken conversation was happening or not. I had one more question for Fenrir.

"Is there anything you need from me?"

I could have sworn I felt a laugh. "I've never needed anything from anyone. You made me a promise. Whether we enact it today or ten years from now, I know I'm here for one reason alone."

I remembered.

I released the silent tether we had on one another as I looked at Caliban. He was watching me speculatively, but not intrusively. Whatever had happened in the banquet hall, I could tell he had not been privy to our conversation. It did, however, bring me to a question.

"Can you hear my thoughts?" I asked quietly.

He looked at me for a long time. He asked, "Have you heard mine?"

I frowned. "No, of course not."

He matched my expression. "You could, you know. And yes, I can...sometimes. And you could hear mine if you chose to. Generally, it's only when we're speaking to one another."

"Is this the part where you tell me I have a mutant super-power and can read minds?"

His face twitched as be battled a chuckle. "No. With me, it's quite specific to someone calling on me. As for you, I'm relatively certain it's not your gift, either—that's not to say there won't be any in the realms who can't tap into your mind, so it would be wise to stay as blank as possible when around new deities. But let's focus on the now. You and I have a bond. Call out loudly in your mind, and I'll be the one who answers. Do you want to try?"

My smile faded. "Aren't we a little...busy?"

He shrugged. "It's a three-day banquet. Time is arbitrary when you live forever."

"I don't," I whispered.

"You do," he countered. "Your cycles just look a bit differ-ent than mine. You've done it before, Love. Give it a shot."

"I've read your mind before?"

He made a patient sound, then said, "You didn't always fight your clairsentience. In the 1700s, you were a part of a practicing coven and developed it with quite the intentional-ity. Think of it like working toward turning up the volume of a speaker. This time, thanks to your fae blood, your speaker is stuck on loud."

A green-haired witched on a frantic Zoom call had said something similar. She'd told me to picture a dial and crank up the volume.

I frowned and thought his name while he watched me. I thought song lyrics. I thought a snappy quote from a favor-ite motive of mine. I told him he was incredibly sexy, that I loved how he felt, that he did indescribable things with his tongue.

"Love." He broke my reverie.

I heated. "Did you hear the tongue thing?"

He flashed a wicked grin. "Alas, I did not. But believe me, I wish I had."

My cheeks cooked under his smile. It was so much harder to look at this beautiful, perfect, devilishly sexy man now that I knew he was real.

"Let me go first. Have you tried meditation before?"

My thoughts returned to Xuân's instructions. She'd been the breakthrough I'd needed to see the sigil painted so clearly on my door. I frowned at him. "Yes. Poorly."

"Poorly is all I need," he said appreciatively. "Calm your mind and think of a cave."

My quizzical look was enough to prompt explanation.

"It's a tool, and an effective one at that. Close your eyes," he whispered. He pressed a kiss into my eyelid the moment I complied, and my body melted beneath his touch. "Don't speak, just listen. Picture yourself in a dark cave. You're looking into the blackened end, and your ears are straining. All around you is nothing but wall. You listen, and suddenly you hear..."

I listened in the dark cave.

"I love you."

It took me a moment to realize I hadn't heard it with my ears. My eyes shot open. I jolted against the bed and might have toppled out of his grasp if he hadn't been clutching me. He kept his eyes shut while struggling not to laugh.

"Get back in the cave."

I giggled for both of us. I exhaled slowly, grounding myself as I pushed past the rush of nerves and anxious laughter. I let the visual of a dark, stony room fill my mind. Thanks to a family vacation to a national park when I was younger, I was able to pluck choice memories and decorate the image, to paint it over my closed eyelids. Stalagmites lifted from the damp cave floor, frozen in their reach toward their icicle-like counterparts. A distant dripping came from somewhere in the shadows. I could feel the darkened chill of a room that had never known the sun.

Something moved within the darkness.

Had I been in a physical cave, I would have felt afraid. But I knew I was in Caliban's arms, safe in his instruction. I stared as the shape shifted from nearly indiscernible shades of black and gray to something lighter, something more defined. I kept my eyes screwed on the shape as it grew brighter and closer, like a small star rising from the bottom of the sea. I nearly lost my breath when I realized what I was seeing.

"It's you," I said through an inhale.

The white fox padded up to me carefully. He sat upright, wrapping his luxurious tail around his paws as he did. He tilted his head to the side and looked at me with piercing silver eyes. "Don't say it with your mouth," the fox said into my mind.

Fenrir had communicated this way, which set me to remembering what Caliban had said only moments prior about some deities and their gift of hearing thoughts. I hoped I hadn't thought anything I'd regret while around the Nordic god.

"It's like praying," I said silently.

The fox dipped the coal-black point of its elegant snout. "Praying to Elohim was a soliloquy. You speak, yes. It's seldom he answers those who cry out to him. I wonder how many would remain Christian if they knew that sometimes when you went to a god in prayer, the deity replies."

I was quick to parrot a lesson that had been drilled into me for years. "It would be a trick. A dem—"

My thoughts chilled.

Caliban's fox eyes narrowed in good humor. "*Demon* isn't a dirty word, Love. I know where the premise comes from, and for what it's worth, Lisbeth wasn't wholly wrong."

I knew it wasn't time for me to speak, so I watched the metallic flames of his vibrant eyes.

"Your mother is more open-minded than many."

It was a battle to not roll my eyes.

"She is," he insisted. "Many Christians don't even believe in their own god. The others would end at this belief, without accepting angels or demons. At least your mother acknowledges what she calls pagan deities, even if to her, there are only two categories: things of Heaven, and things of Hell. Every pantheon in the world overflows with demons in masks, as far as she's concerned. I'd say that's more open than refusing to believe at all. Now, I know you'd love to spend more time talking about how your mother wasn't the monster you think she is, but there are some things you should know. The first is that you're doing great, but I don't know if we can rely on your ability to access the meditation plane if you're in a high-stress environment, or if time is of the essence. However, should you need to call, there's a reason it's effective to look into the mouth of a cave."

"Why?" I asked breathlessly.

"You're accepting that you're looking into the unknown— that anything could be there. It creates a portal of sorts. You could speak to Fauna this way, though you might not want to. She, unlike me, may not feel compelled to answer your call, but you can still call into the dark nonetheless."

"From anywhere?"

"From anywhere." He nodded, triangular ears tilting with interest. "From the same room, from across the seas, from other realms. She's a deity, and worthy of more caution than you give her."

"But..."

"I don't want you to get hurt, Love."

I balked at his words. He hardly knew her. He had no idea—

"I can hear your rejections and justifications. You're filtering her through a very binary understanding. You'd be much better off if you took a piece of advice. Mortals have learned to think of good and bad in terms of black and white. Perhaps it's best you consider that for those of us beyond your veil, good and bad are matters of orange and green."

✦

I ran a hand over the silvery bangles that decorated my dress like a chandelier. When the attendant had arrived to dress me for the second day of the banquet, I'd made a face at the gown, expecting it to be rough, metallic, and uncomfortable. To my pleasant surprise, the diamonds were not firm gems, but moved and flattened under my fingers as if I were running them over water.

I was to remain barefoot today, apparently.

She'd slipped on a matching jeweled cuff that ran from my ankle to my toe, offering the illusion of a sandal without the support of a shoe. I supposed it was a demonstration of the cleanliness and luxury of their palace. The floors were made of glittering, black polished stone. The smooth obsidian was warm enough to keep my toes from chilling but cool enough to keep me from being uncomfortable. I didn't have to look at myself through Caliban's eyes. I knew I looked like a meteor shower.

I spun, creating a celestial event of swishing and starlight.

Caliban flashed brilliant white teeth. "Do you think they could get me one to match if I asked now? You're having far too much fun to keep it to yourself."

I looped my hands through the crook of Caliban's bent elbow. He opened the door for Fenrir first, offering a silent, reverent bow for the Norse god. Caliban was the one who knew how to navigate the halls, but his show of respect reminded me how much I'd been taking the powerful beings around me for granted. Fenrir exited the room, after which Caliban took the lead.

I knew better than to say anything about Fenrir's involvement, so I returned to the visual of Hell's silver Prince in a gown of starlight.

"I'm sure you'd look marvelous in a dress," I said, "but

281

this one is cut for curves." I chewed on my lip a bit uncertainly before asking, "Is anything supposed to happen on the second day of the banquet?"

"No. Sentencing will be carried out on the third day. Today, try to enjoy yourself. I know demons and deities, of which Azrames is no exception. He won't want today to be sullied with tomorrow's woes. Live in the present for him and for all of us."

It was an impossible ask, and he knew it. It had to be why he was warning me in the hall long before we entered. He'd known me for twenty-six years, and was aware of exactly how I'd internalize things.

"He's right," came a deep, ancient voice in my head. I didn't look over my shoulder while Fenrir spoke to me alone. "And you have a role to play. They expect you here as the Prince's bride, and nothing else. The Nordes are extended tentative grace as escorts of your lineage. Do not ruin it with your morality."

"Fauna wants me to start a war." I spoke to Fenrir with my mind. "I'm supposed to relax and party, but it's all a façade. She's urging me to push Caliban into battle. Why does she want this so badly? And why is no one speaking their truth?"

"Some of us were born for a purpose you can't fathom, human."

"Why is everyone on my case for being human?" I grumbled. I hadn't fully intended to say it to him, but I also hadn't ensured that he'd broken his connection. I was mildly horrified when Fenrir responded.

"Because you're a mortal playing the game of gods."

I felt the absence as Fenrir left my thoughts like a breeze through the room.

As with the day before, we seemed to be the last to the party. Entertainment was in full swing. Goblets clinked, laughter swelled, drinks flowed freely. Banners and dancers and music laced through the air. Once again, Caliban had been given the seat of honor on the far end of the table.

Directly beside it was an empty chair for his betrothed. And beside that...

Black horns peeked through permanently disheveled hair. A gray arm draped around the back of Fauna's chair. Azrames appeared to be in the middle of eating a turkey leg larger than his fist when he caught our eye. He smiled easily, waving me over as Fauna turned to see who'd drawn his attention. He looked so relaxed. His wicked smile made it hard to believe he was on the eve of unspeakable torment.

Azrames got to his feet. Two armed guards flanked him at the sudden movement, but he paid them no mind as he squeezed me so hard my back nearly popped.

"Mer-bear." He smiled. I'd never been so happy to lose myself in a hug as I was in his strong, incense-laced arms. He released me and dipped his head in a small bow. "Your Highness."

The Phoenician guards kept their hands on the hilts of their weapons until Caliban waved them down.

Extending his hand to Azrames, he said, "We've fought together, are citizens in a foreign realm together, and have nearly died for the same woman. We're friends. I'm going to need you to stop using my formal title."

Azrames clasped the outstretched palm. They shook once as if sealing a bargain. When we sat, it was Azrames who was beside me rather than Fauna. I tried to catch her eye but was unable to snag her gaze.

Ella and Estrid raised their glasses appreciatively, fingers interlacing. I couldn't quite hear them from where I sat, but they seemed to be having a great time. Fenrir was offered water and fine cuts of meat in elaborately decorated bowls. Wine flowed, music filled the air, the scents of flowers, perfume, and decadent food mingled, and the dancers seemed to be wearing less and less clothing as they moved sensually through the hall, never growing tired. The Canaanite gods were dressed in shades of gold, red, and black. The laughter and merriment at the far end of the table was that of friends and family who'd spent far too long apart.

I hadn't thought it would be possible. I was so certain the anxiety, the guilt, the armed guards, the enemy territory, the ticking clock of the trial would restrain me, would shove me into my chair and force me to look into the dark face of the evening.

But I was wrong.

The wine certainly didn't hurt.

Maybe it was because I'd never gotten to see Caliban so happy. I loved watching him swap stories with Azrames. I loved listening to him laugh. I loved eating with him, and how he squeezed my knee beneath the table, and the small wink he'd shoot me when someone else was speaking to let me know that his attention was still wholly on me.

The meals continued, the hours stretched on, and the food, the drinks, the music, the dancing changed time and time again. With no windows to betray the hour, I had no way to mark the passage of time. The drunker we got, the more we joined the entertainers in spinning, swirling glee. I hardly put up a fight when tugged onto the dance floor, too drunk on wine and high on love to resist Caliban as he twirled me into his arms. I shouldn't have been surprised that he could dance, but even in the midst of song, his movements were strong, solid, and utterly commanding. His eyes hardened as if he had only one thing on his mind. His shoulders remained straight as he threw me out, yanking me back in with a hand. When he dipped me, it was not the way I'd seen it done in movies, where a couple would press together during a sensual tango, hand on back, hair dipping to the floor.

My eyes flew open in alarm as his grip found my neck. My hands flew to his wrist in panicked instinct, and I understood why a moment later. I provided the counterbalance on threat of death as he lowered me to the floor, fingers flexing around the blood that pulsed through my throat. I swallowed as the world spun. I kept my grip tight as he stepped in front of my prone form in the last second of my dip, planting his feet before he pulled me up from the brink of asphyxiation. A moment later, I was on my feet once more. He slackened his grip ever so slightly, but kept his hand on my throat as he pressed his forehead to mine.

I wondered if the entire court could tell how lost I was. I was soaked, and drunk, and deeply in love. I trusted him, but not because he was safe, for he was anything but. No, I trusted him because as I was licked by the flames of danger, I knew exactly who held me.

I didn't remember being handed off to Azrames for a far more lighthearted dance, though as his horns caught in the firelight, my alcohol-addled mind remembered a comment Fauna had once made about borrowing him...

I tried to shake the visual from my head, but from Azrames's laugh, I was suddenly worried I'd voiced my filthy thoughts. In the next shameful moment, I caught another glance of the watchful guards who kept their eyes on every step of our dance. This was all happening because of me.

"I'm so sorry." It was all I could say.

"Just have fun, Mer," he urged. "Do it for me. Don't let my last day as a free man be a sad one."

I was in Fauna's arms before I could process the gravity of his comment.

"I'm still mad at you," she said, but the sting was no longer in her words. "But lucky for you, this is one hell of a party. And you shouldn't be the only one who gets to play."

It felt right to be with her again. And maybe it was because I was drunk, but I babbled about how much I loved her, how sorry I was for putting Azrames in harm's way, how beautiful she was, and how heartbroken I'd be if she ever tried to leave me.

Fauna grinned. "Let's get you drunk on sacred wine more often! I would have been offended if I was the only one you hadn't tried to fuck tonight."

I was pretty sure I hadn't tried to sleep with either her or Az, but then again, Caliban had abandoned me as little more than a slippery mess on the dance floor. I could hardly be held responsible for who spun the puddle next. Fauna's stamina was eternal. Her hair stayed perfect, her skin soft, her smile endless. Mine was fueled by booze, but eventually I felt the sweat and burn and exhaustion of a day of partying. I wasn't in college anymore. My body could only take so much.

"I've learned my lesson," Fauna giggled.

"About what?" I panted.

"Have you heard of the dancing plague of 1518? Over a dozen deaths. It took some of us a while to feel out human limits before we quit murdering people."

"Fauna!" I slurred her name in a drunken rebuke, too tipsy to do anything more.

"It was an accident!"

She looped her arm around my waist and helped me off the dance floor, returning me to my chair. I was loosely aware that I'd probably be humiliated the next day that I had been the only sloppy human cuddling up to a Prince in the company of gods, but for now, I didn't care.

Day became night as we partied away. We were one step away from me commenting that the only one missing from our day of debauchery was Bacchus when a sound cut through my drink-addled haze. It was a creak, followed by a murmur, then a gasp.

I'd been on the verge of falling into a well-deserved nap against Caliban's chest when I opened my eyes to see everyone whipping around. The dancing stopped. I looked to the far end of the table to see that Dagon, Anath, Melqart, and Baal had stirred. I turned in my seat and immediately understood why. Two stunning figures strode into the hall in banquet-ready attire. One was dressed in a flowing spring gown with a flower in her hair. The other's linen shirt was unbuttoned ever so slightly, hair slicked back, wicked grin on his face.

"What the hell?" Anath demanded, teeth clenched, face reddening with indignation.

"I think," Dorian responded, "you mean: What the Hades?"

Chapter Twenty-Eight

"W HY IS IT," DORIAN SAID CONFIDENTLY TO THE HUSHED, crowded room, "that my party invites always seem to get lost in the mail?"

We were all on our feet, though I wasn't sure if it was out of respect, or in preparation for a fight. Tension flooded the room, sobering the joy I'd felt only moments prior. It didn't matter that I'd known Poppy and Dorian were coming—I was as afraid for them as I was for all of us. The only thing on my mind was what it might mean for all of us now that they'd arrived.

"Hades," Anath said slowly. She bared her teeth at Melqart, as if waiting for him to say something. I couldn't fathom what she expected Baal's son to say, aside from, *Hey, Hades, only one god of the Underworld permitted per party.*

"Please," he said, "I'm going by Dorian. And you'll refer to my partner as Poppy."

"Dorian," Anath began again. She took the name change in stride, which I supposed years of living in the human realm had allowed. Astarte had taken on a new moniker. I'd never learned Jessabelle's Phoenician name. While Anath had intended to remain unseen in my presence, there was a very real possibility that she'd walked among the humans as Vivian, Ruby, or Caroline. She looked at both Poppy and Dorian before saying, "You'll see that no Greco-Roman peers are in attendance. You were not intentionally excluded."

I found the response profoundly curious. I'd expected the Canaanite gods to greet him with anger or defensiveness. I looked at Fauna, but she caught my questioning eyes only long enough to shake her head.

"Exclusion is a grave insult among gods and fae alike," came Fenrir's voice within my head alone in answer to my unspoken question. The powerful son of Loki, the wolf of Ragnarök, the god so terrifying that Odin himself had locked him up in fear, was explaining godly politics to the stupid human. "Dorian is right to call on it as his cause to arrive, and Anath is right to point out no disrespect has been committed."

Fenrir looked away from me, and I took my cue to train my eyes on the exchange. Questions could wait.

"Melqart," Dorian greeted his peer with a smile. "It's been ages since I've had the chance to talk shop with a fellow guardian of the Underworld. What do you say? Care to share a few glasses of wine with a neighboring protector of the dead?"

The room was quiet enough to hear a pin drop.

"Of course," Melqart boomed. I realized this was the first time he'd spoken loud enough for the banquet hall to hear since my arrival. I'd mistaken his initial silence for meekness. I saw him now, chest puffed, shoulders straight, as a youthful, Herculean figure—muscles and bravado—contrasted against his father. "You are most welcome in our realm."

"Dorian," Caliban said easily at my side. Our places at the table had us at a disadvantage. He was positioned in such a way where I couldn't make out anything about his expression. "It's been too long."

"Well, we both have Underworlds to run," Dorian said, moving his fingers from his forehead as if tipping an imaginary hat. "But a little birdy told me that four realms were present. The Canaanites, the Nordes, Hell, even Heaven, though I don't see any angelic feathers here to ruffle at the moment."

288

"And the humans," I offered in a strained attempt at humor. Maybe I wasn't entirely sober, or else I would have surely kept my mouth shut.

Dorian chuckled lightly. "And the humans," he repeated. "Which makes five. That isn't a very magical number. Six, however…"

"We're honored by your presence," Anath replied, choosing her words carefully.

"Great!" Dorian clapped his hands together enthusiastically while approaching the table. He grabbed the chair nearest to Caliban and pulled it out for his wife. She smiled prettily at him as if nothing in the world could bother her. "It's been ages since Poppy and I have gotten out. But, now that we're here, what's the occasion?"

Baal narrowed his eyes from the far end of the banquet hall. He didn't need to raise his voice for it to carry. "That wasn't included in your little birdy's message?"

"Oh." Poppy rolled her eyes at Baal. I was shocked at the hardness in her tone. "Don't be a sourpuss. You know how the realms talk. Now, will someone be putting food on my plate, or do I need to serve myself?"

I gaped at her boldness, but watched the corner of Dorian's mouth twitch upward. She was a vision in pink and spring beauty—the firstborn daughter of Demeter, and a goddess of fertility, whether humans, plants, or animals. The sparkling obsidian pillars made her pale hair with pink-dipped ends stand out like an orchid in the midst of winter. I'd read that her abilities enabled her to give life to the dead, communicate with spirits, and bring a peaceful afterlife to those who deserved it. She'd seemed like such a benign figure in my mythological research.

Hades, like Zeus, was the son of Cronus. He was one of five in the first generation of powerful deities in the Grecian pantheon. Keeper of souls, conjurer of invisibility, master of Cerberus, and often believed to have control over the earth's riches. He was not one to be underestimated.

I cocked a brow as I looked at them and marveled at how I'd ever found Persephone's character mild, quiet, and congenial. Her femineity was no weakness. She dripped honey, which lured one in for the sting. Of course, they wouldn't be fated mates if they weren't well matched in every way.

Melqart flicked two fingers at an attendant. She moved quickly from her place amongst the others, the silken scarves of her banquet attire billowing behind her as she rushed to serve them. Her hands shook as she dished food onto their plates. Poppy touched her arm gently, which nearly caused the attendant to jump out of her skin. They held eyes for a moment until I saw the attendant visibly relax.

The woman's immediate fears may have been assuaged, but mine certainly weren't.

Anxiety weighed me down like lead. My heart skidded uncertainly, confident that the jig would be up any moment, that we'd be found out, though I wasn't sure exactly what we were hiding. I had participated in the gathering of forces, ready to rescue my friends and my beloved, though it seemed I'd wildly misjudged the tenor of our travel. Fauna had readied me like we were going into battle, yet Caliban reacted to the presence of Nordes and Hellenic gods as if he knew more about the plan than I did.

It wouldn't be the first time I was left in the dark.

It might surprise you how many pantheons have tried to tip the war in Hell's favor. Everyone wants Heaven to fall.

I trained my eyes on Poppy and Dorian. His expression remained relaxed and amused. Poppy's face stayed utterly serene. But there was something in the way she touched his back as he slid into the seat next to her. There was a comfort to it—a reassurance.

My lips parted as I looked at Dorian, ever the picture of power and cool indifference, and I understood what Poppy was doing.

The support was there in the face of rejection.

We're subjugated gods, Poppy had said.

I saw it in every comforting stroke as she sustained him. His nonchalance was a beautiful show. I was on the Mediterranean cliffs once more, listening to her plea for change. They were Poppy and Dorian—Hades and Persephone. She held his jagged heart in her hands. Much like Fenrir, he'd been mistreated, overlooked, and underestimated by gods who were his peers in every way for thousands of years.

They're equals. You think they'd be treated as such.

Melqart spoke this time. His tone was matter-of-fact as he met Dorian's eyes, two champions of the dead discussing an immortal soul about to depart. "The banquet is on behalf of a trial. You've arrived in time for sentencing to be carried out. The citizens of Heaven and Hell, as I'm sure you are aware, were tried for crimes against our pantheon. The demon has opted for three thousand lashes, and the angel has selected death by combat. Tomorrow should be marvelous indeed. I'm pleased you could join us for the show."

The words were horrifying, but the tone was inclusive.

I was equal parts relieved to hear Melqart smooth things over, and filled with dread as I remembered why we were here.

There was true regret on Dorian's face as he said, "You know, I would love to. I'm a huge fan of torture." He stopped to grab an artistically carved pitcher and poured wine into two clean goblets. First, he filled Poppy's, then his own. "But you see, the lady isn't a fan of my proclivities. And hey, we can't force our partners to love our hobbies, am I right? We've woven something of a nonviolence clause in our vows. So, if you could hold off on the bloodshed until after we've departed, I'd consider it a personal favor."

I could have cried at the surge of relief.

Dorian didn't know Azrames, but he'd put his neck on the line to buy more time for our cause, though our motives may have been different. I was there to be reunited with my love, and to spare a demon and an angel from suffering on my behalf. Fauna cared deeply for Azrames, but as I looked at the

291

Nordes and Greeks, I was certain she would have marched into the Phoenician realm even if her beloved had remained safely in Hell. They'd all come for some grander purpose. One that was inscrutable to me, aside from Fauna's command.

Then start a war.

Azramess's shoulders slumped forward slightly at my side. I hadn't realized he'd remained tense from the moment the newcomers had entered. Of course, he had no idea why they'd come or what their presence could mean. I didn't miss the way Fauna's fingers tightened around his bicep.

"Fine," Anath said, the semblance of patience evaporating on her lips. "Poppy doesn't like blood, you say? We can oblige." She turned to the banquet hall and lifted her hands with renewed vigor as she said, "Good friends, gods, and citizens! Tomorrow, on the final day of our banquet, we will see Heaven's ambassador face our divine wrath in combat to the death."

Poppy lifted a finger in protest, but Anath cut her off before she could speak.

"Don't worry, goddess of spring and the Underworld. You are our guest, and we'll honor your wishes. There will be no bloodshed. The estries will ensure there's no blood at all."

The word scratched the back of my brain ever so slightly. It was familiar. It was...My thoughts were cut short as Caliban rotated to look directly at me, apology in his eyes.

My brows furrowed with confusion.

A screech tore through the halls. It echoed off the walls, bouncing between pillars, penetrating me to my core. Wherever it resided in the palace, the intelligent harbinger of doom was listening.

I understood Caliban's expression and my blood chilled. He was remorseful because he knew I cared for Silas. And whatever this announcement was...that was when the memory hit me. It was an old bit of folklore from the cradle of civilization that coincided with the timeframe around the Canaanite reign.

It was a succubus, a vampire, a demon. It was a creature of beauty, darkness, cruelty, and bloodlust. It was an alluring monster who sucked you dry and left nothing behind.

It was death personified.

It was the estries.

Chapter Twenty-Nine

A N ESTRIES?" I REELED. I'D WAITED UNTIL WE'D GOTTEN back to the room, but I couldn't keep it in any longer.

"Love—"

"Do not speak," came Fenrir's silencing command.

I looked between the Prince and Ragnarök's wolf helplessly.

From the way Caliban turned to regard Fenrir, I knew they were speaking. After a long pause, he grabbed my hand.

"Come with me," Caliban said.

Fenrir padded off to the settee and made himself comfortable while Caliban led me into the washroom. The enormous, black, glassy bath appeared to have no edge. It tumbled off into infinite darkness, disappearing into the onyx on all sides. It was more like a small pool than any tub I'd ever seen.

I was so distracted looking at the bath and admiring how different it was from the comparatively small tub that had been in my and Fauna's room that I hadn't noticed Caliban's hand. He reached for the strap of my dress. I went to brush him off, but wavered slightly as I lost my footing. The shocking turn of events at the day's end had replaced the hum of alcohol with adrenaline. Now that it was wearing off, I became acutely aware of just how much I'd consumed.

"Are you trying to get me into the bath? Right now? It's an estries, Caliban! A fucking—"

He snatched the wrist of my hand, which had been pointing in animated fury. "Are you going to be quiet on your own, or do I need to make you?"

I didn't take the bait. I shoved against him with my free hand while yanking my restrained hand away. I succeeded only in dipping half of my body close to him while the other half jolted away. In doing so, I lost all ground. He wrapped his free arm around my back and pinned me to him.

"Try again," he dared.

I snarled. "Let me go."

He crushed me against him. His expression remained indifferent as he said, "You're drunk, Love. When you misspeak, you won't be the only one who suffers the consequences."

"*When?*" I glared against the insult. I struggled to free myself from the hold, but his arms were like quicksand. Every wiggle further constricted me in his powerful grasp. I grunted helplessly as a new panic began to rise. "Let go!"

"Stop," came his single firm command.

I rammed my bare foot into his instep, but it did nothing. I felt his chest swell with his impatient intake of air. "I'm trying to help...*everyone*. We aren't in the mortal realm. If things go poorly, they don't go poorly for just one human lifetime."

I went rigid. My jaw fell open at the implication.

He seemed to take it as compliance, for he loosened his grip.

"Because," I said in horror, taking a step away, "if it were just my human life at risk, that would be fine? If only I die, it's no problem, right? If I were the one facing an estries, who gives a fuck?" The tendons in his hands flexed in a controlled anger while I backed away. My temper burned hotter as I created more space, backing closer and closer to the door. "That's it, isn't it? That my life is so temporary that it doesn't matter. You just press restart if you lose me. You don't give a shit if I survive. I'm just—what do you keep saying?—a cycle. I'm just another meat suit in a sequence of Marlows, trapped in a loop of new, shiny versions of myself and fresh starts all the damn time. I'm the reason Astarte's dead. Maybe I should volunteer myself in Silas's place. Perhaps if they need blood spilled—"

I didn't even see him move.

His anger was silver fire. One hand was over my mouth, the other cupping the back of my head as he slammed me into the wall behind me. He pressed into me until the air was forced from my lungs. I squirmed in rage, in fury, in panic, in a flash of pure terror as I fought uselessly against his hold over me.

"Fight me again," he said through clenched teeth. "I put out a tier-five favor to save *this* mortal form of yours. I gambled with my life, my realm, our victory in the war just so you wouldn't suffer. I—"

I threw an elbow in an attempt to scramble away. I couldn't breathe. Each shallow pant bounced uselessly against his palm and shoved my own hot air back into my mouth. Tears lined my eyes as I buckled against the need to sob.

His lip pulled back in a half snarl as he looked at me. "I'm not asking; I'm telling. I'm going to take my hand away, and you're going to be silent."

He was a demon. He was a fucking demon. He was no angel, no imaginary friend, or fairy guardian. He wasn't a benevolent god. He was—

"Then you're going to get in the goddamn bath and meet me in the cave."

I choked on the words. He lowered his hand just for me to spit out, "What?"

He raised a single finger like a scolding father.

"Fuck—" The second word didn't have a chance to escape. He held me as I trembled with rage. He absorbed the punches I couldn't throw. He crushed me against him, hand over my mouth as I struggled through my haze of wine and anger.

Frustrated, helpless tears lined my eyes when it became clear I couldn't break free. I couldn't say my piece. I couldn't scream at him or run away or do anything except look up into the icy fire of his patient, powerful eyes.

I slumped against my powerlessness. My arms slackened. My lids fluttered shut. Caliban lowered his hand and wrapped me in a hug. I was still angry, but not at him. I was angry at my confusion, at my helplessness, at my inability to understand the game of gods and their cavalier attitude toward life and the way they moved about with so much confidence while I was falling apart. I'd wanted to throw fists at the sky, but he'd outlasted my will to scream. When I looked up again, his long-suffering expression was tinged with love, compassion, and the barest edge of amusement.

I looked between him and the overflowing water at the infinity edges of the tub. I flickered to the words he'd said before my failed attempt to curse at him. The cave? He wanted me to…meditate with him? He was slow to step away. He ensured my breathing had steadied, that my feet were firm beneath me, and that I was no longer a flight risk before he released me. He raised an impatient brow.

"Turn around." I glared, too bitter to undress in front of him.

His lips twitched in amused surprise. "To be clear, I am also getting in the bath."

"Fine."

"So, I'll be naked with you in less than thirty seconds."

"I get it," I bit, "but right now, I'm mad at you."

His broad shoulders softened slightly. His face relaxed in ongoing amusement as he turned away. "Fair enough."

I grumbled unintelligibly as I slipped the straps off my shoulders and let the dress pool at my feet. I looked down at my body, then planted my hands on my hips defiantly. I had no bodily shame. This body wasn't just a temple, as they were free to access and open to all. It was a Michelin restaurant, an elite resort, a millionaire's yacht. Better still—even

A-list celebrities could bully their way into coveted places with enough clout. There would be no bullying, no bluffing, no clout when I had full autonomy. I could always say no.

Not even the Prince of Hell could see me if I didn't want him to.

I continued my muttering as I dipped my toes into the bath. I didn't miss the subtle shake of his shoulders as he chuckled at my anger.

The tub was far deeper than I anticipated. I nearly tripped as I stepped down, gasping when it came nearly to my breasts. Though the water had looked black from the outside, I could see through the crystalline ripples that it was simply the color of the stone. My pale shape cut through the shadows, offering little coverage.

"Great," I muttered.

"What was that?" he asked.

I didn't answer him as I felt around. My toe bumped a submerged ledge, which was precisely what I'd hoped. A tub this deep needed an option to avoid drowning. I slid onto the onyx seat. I eyed the inverted triangle of his shape, his white shock of hair breaking up the darkness of the room. I narrowed my eyes at him.

"Strip for me, Prince," I said, conjuring as much venom as I could.

His exhale was an amused huff of air. "See? Hellfire runs through your veins."

A moment later, he reached a single hand over his head and gripped a handful of his shirt. It was off in a flash, revealing the iridescent shimmer beneath his skin, his muscles, his broad, perfect...

Fuck. Was I really such a sucker that my anger dissipated at the sight of him? It seemed impossible. My eyes widened, cheeks flushing as he turned around and caught me staring. The blush spread to my body as confusion pulsed through me. The resentment I'd felt only moments prior was muddled in the water. There was no trace of the anger or power I'd seen flash through him as he'd advanced on me. He gave me a very intentional up-down from where I sat in the glass-clear water.

"Close your eyes," he said, mocking me with deadpan delivery.

Rage flared through me again, but the emotion was different this time. I turned my face away without closing my eyes, simultaneously obliging while keeping my feet planted firmly in disobedience.

I should have heard several sloshing steps. I'd anticipated the slow breaststroke of advance as he crossed from one side of the large, flat tub to the other. Instead, in a moment he was on dry land in the washroom, and in the next, he was beside me. It took my breath away as he slid a hand onto my thigh, rotating me so we were facing one another.

"Why?" I stumbled over the question. I cleared my throat and repeated myself, shocked and angry at the effect the god-like, perfect man before me had on my mental capacity. I rallied for some of the residual anger, but my body had a different reaction to remembering the flash of force and power as he'd shoved his hand over my mouth, protecting my head from the impact. I fought to get my words out. "Why the bath?"

"Water is an effective conduit," he said as if it were the most obvious thing in the world.

My brows met in an upturned question.

His evaluating look added to my confusion. "Did you never wonder why I was always pulling you into the shower?"

My mouth dried. "Because it's sexy as fuck?"

"That it is," he agreed, fingers kneading my thigh. "But we weren't in Hell then, and we aren't in Hell now. Power flows through water more easily even when you're outside of your own realm."

"And now?" I asked breathlessly.

"Now," he said, thumb still grazing my thigh beneath the water, "you're drunk, and we're leaching the effects of the alcohol."

His words stunned me. I was horrified at their implication as I thought once more of the lowest point in my life, when a figment of my imagination—evidence of the very insanity I was attempting to escape—had pulled me under the running water and held me against his chest as he'd forced me to throw up pills over and over again. There had been so many times...

"You make me feel stupid," I said quietly.

He was horrified at the words. His face crinkled, lips parted in wordless regret.

I shook my head, the ends of my hair dangling in the water and clouding around me as I moved. My gaze dropped to the ripples. "I'm twenty-six and I have to recast every major event in my life. Every trauma, every victory, every psychotic break where you were far too real..." I looked up at him, unable to keep the sorrow from my eyes as I mourned my past. "I'm educated," I said. "Not just academically, but in global theology. While in the church, I had a robust faith and active spiritual life. I'm socially intelligent—which is a goddamn priceless quality in sex work. But now...with everything..."

I saw his concern transition to understanding.

"Shh." He attempted to calm me. He removed his hand from my thigh. His palm broke the water and cupped my cheek.

I looked at the naked place his hand had abandoned. "Were you even touching me to touch me? Or is it just... to...what? Access an ability? Sober me up?"

His lips flattened into a line. "You can't be held accountable for the things you say when drunk, and you had every right to drink until you couldn't stand. Things changed quickly, and I'm just giving you the same footing that everyone else in the palace has. It's unfair for you to be at any disadvantage. And I'm not the only one who needs you to be at your sharpest right now, Love."

He looked at me expectantly.

I frowned. I crossed my arms, tucking them against my chest to cover myself. I was still angry, but it was the sort of rage born of pride and principle, even if the emotional tide had passed. I saw the wisdom in his reasoning, but that didn't make it any easier for me. I didn't know how to move forward, but there were things that needed to be discussed.

"So...cave?"

He motioned for me to lean forward so he could tuck his arm behind me. He patted his free hand against his chest, encouraging me to relax against him. I rested my face on the cool skin that felt so nice in contrast to the warm water. I closed my eyes and let everything go dark.

"You're lucky I have a vibrant imagination."

"Tell it to the cave," he murmured into my hair.

So, I did. I looked around to see the textured columns, the stones frozen in drips like water, the wet, rocky walls, and the dark belly into nothingness as I waited for a fox. It was not an animal who appeared from the darkness this time. Caliban strode out from the depths, hands in pockets. He smiled affectionately and outstretched a hand toward me.

"Are you taking me deeper into the cave?" I asked it in my mind this time.

"I'm not taking us anywhere," he said. "Turn around and lead us out of the cave."

I wasn't sure if he was serious. His expectant face wiped away my doubt as I cautiously rotated, expecting to see more cave. Instead, I saw the world. We broke from the mouth of the cave onto the deep red sand of an empty, silent desert. The Milky Way soaked the sky overhead in a concentrated display of brilliance. In the midst of the sand stood a short flight of stairs and a door. No walls. No building. Nothing more.

"Where are we?" I asked, shock rippling through me.

"You tell me," he responded.

I looked at his fingers interwoven with mine, then up at him. He was admiring the scenery with equal appreciation.

"You've never been here?"

"We're in your head," he said. "This is your place."

"But the cave—"

He cut me off. "The cave is a tool, not a location. It allows you to look into nothing and allow something to appear. The cave is not your mind. This"—he gestured to the stars, the blowing, drifting sand, the dunes, and stairs leading to Hell knows where—"is you."

I led us cautiously forward as we approached the out-of-place wooden door. A set of stairs without rails, without buildings, without suspension or rhyme or reason. It was old. It was neither ominous, nor inviting. It simply *was*. Through the cracks at its edges, I didn't miss the bright glow of whatever waited on the other side.

"It looks how I imagined the light at the end of the tunnel," I said quietly.

"Maybe it is."

I looked back at him in surprise. "That could be where you go where you die?"

He twisted his mouth in consideration. "I doubt it, but it could be. It goes someplace else, that's for sure."

"Where?"

I knew before meeting his eyes that he didn't have the answer. Embarrassment was a predominant emotion when I realized how patient he had to be with me, followed by a resurgence of frustration that he'd experienced this like the tides. I was an ebb and flow of comprehension and idiocy through my lifetimes. It was humiliating to think I had to start each cycle as an ignorant blob, and infuriating that he'd had to develop monastic patience to endure my cycles.

"Why are we here?" I asked, agitation coloring my words. "Not here in the desert with the cave and door and night. Why am I naked in the water with you out in the real world—or, is their realm even the real world? God, just, help me understand what's going on."

"We need to be able to talk. It's a gift many deities have.

You're at a disadvantage, but you don't have to be. Especially with your fae blood, your access to your clairabilities is kissing the surface, eager to break through. You resist them. But we might need to talk again, out there. Agree to a signal with me? Something subtle, should we need to meet in the cave while we're out?"

"Any ideas?"

He smirked. "Bite your lip and hold my eyes for three seconds."

"Caliban." I blushed.

He ran a thumb over my heated cheeks. "This is precisely why. You can't do it naturally. You're fine when you're acting. You'd mask excellently if I were a client. You play the role of confident seductress like a star. But you wouldn't be able to do something so out-of-character with me unless you were slipping into a role. And that role will be to signal me."

"But I'd look like—"

"A demoness?" He chuckled. "With a demon. It's perfect, Love. They'll expect nothing less from someone who's gotten into bed with Hell."

My fidgeting only seemed to amuse him.

He dropped the topic of sultry roleplay and tugged me to a slope. We sat on the sand, and he looked at me seriously. "Did you know the Grecians were coming?"

My lips parted. I didn't even have the time to inhale in surprise.

"So, that's a yes. Is there anything else I should know?"

I fidgeted. "I suppose you've guessed Ella, Estrid, Fenrir, Dorian, and Poppy aren't here for the party."

"Are you asking me if I think we've collected god-killers on a whim? No, I have more of an eye for strategy than that. So do the Phoenicians. They're no fools. The Nordes were not well received, though the allowance was reluctantly made. Right now, our only truly hidden asset is Fenrir."

My entire face crumpled in a frown. "You said they'd know who Fauna was the moment they met her, right? Fenrir told me that he can control who he speaks to and who hears him. Is that how he's remained hidden?"

He gnawed on his lip for a moment. "Fauna isn't trying to be anything she's not, except with you, I suppose."

"Who is she trying to be with me?"

"She's a deity. An important one. She's bent over backward to put you at ease with her humanness. There isn't a god alive who can't spot another deity in full force. Fenrir, on the other hand, hasn't been seen since the earliest age of man. There's no reason to believe that a mortal would show up with the veritable horseman of the apocalypse, and every reason to believe you're a mortal traveling with her pet."

I smirked. "I called him an apocalypse dog once."

I didn't think it was possible for him to pale, yet somehow, he managed. "You didn't."

"Not to his face."

"Thank fuck, Love. I know accepting the realms is new to you, but you've built a lucrative career being informed on what humans have spent centuries calling mythology. I'm going to need you to abandon mortal concepts and swallow reality whole. Do you know the saying, 'You can't write about a concept while looking down your nose at it'?"

A librarian had said the same thing to me not too long ago. She'd watched me page through books on sigils and gods and mythology for days before bluntly stating that I'd never have a breakthrough unless I opened my mind.

"It's an old expression in journalistic integrity. I thought it might connect with your writer brain. I digress. The point is, a reporter is incapable of being unbiased if they already think something is false, or silly, or wrong. Apply that to anything. You can't write a good Barbie comic if you think dolls are dumb. You can't capture an excellent folktale if you think the society is backwater. And you can't walk with gods and fae and angels and demons if you continue to force everything through human limitations."

I wrinkled my nose. "I feel like you're educating me.

You're not my dad. Honestly, I'm not even sure that you're older than me. How old am I? Two-thousand-some years?"

"Older." He smiled softly. "But you and I have been bound for just over two millennia. Still, those are thousands of human years. Did you insist you knew more about Colombia than the locals when you arrived?"

I groaned. "I forget that you've been goddamn everywhere with me."

"Good luck shaking me." He flashed me a smile wide enough to reveal the sharper edges of his teeth.

"Fine. What do I do?"

"Well," he said carefully, "tomorrow is going to be a rough day."

"Silas took the fall for you," I said. It wasn't an accusation. It was simply fact. "Azrames has been charged as an accomplice because of you. Because of *us*."

"They lost a battle so we might win the war."

"It's not Silas's battle!"

"It's everyone's battle," he said, eyes hard. "Azrames knew the risk. Silas gave you his poppet knowing your affiliations with Hell. Everyone in Bellfield knew things could end badly. I haven't abandoned them. I can't control everything, Love. We may be allied, but this is not my realm, and these are not my people. I've used every drop of my negotiating power to spare Azrames, at the very least. I know these sentences seem barbaric, but you must consider how the gods like to carry out their punishment. The King of Heaven cast my father out forever for requesting equality. Prometheus was chained to a boulder to have his liver eaten out every day for giving humans fire. Fenrir...well, Fenrir's crime was existing."

He had a unique quality of explaining things to me without sounding condescending in the least. He was Fauna's opposite in many ways. The comparative reminders did soothe me, if only slightly.

"Thanks to Poppy and Dorian, Azrames is safe for another

305

day," I said, pained at the thought. "But he can't go through with the sentence. He can't—"

"He was supposed to meet his death, Love. I don't have authority in this realm."

"But aren't you their peer?"

He shook his head. "You know the saying 'separate but equal'? Baal, Dagon, Anath, Melqart, Dorian, and my father are separate but equal in title. I'm a guest and political ambassador. They will treat me with respect as a figurehead of Hell. They outrank me, Love. I may not be less powerful, but I do understand the pecking order."

"You've already killed a goddess."

"There's no evidence to support it, as you're the only living witness."

I winced at the flood of gore and blood that savaged my mind. Whippings and cruelties and combat and battles to the death broke the reverie of my beautiful meditative sanctuary. "But Silas…"

"Silas will fight an estries." I made a sound in protest, but Caliban stopped me. "He will. There is no stopping him from entering the ring, or the events surrounding it."

"The estries…the vampires…they're immortal," I said, filled with defeat.

"So are angels," he countered. "He's on more even ground than you think. I believe the Canaanites will unbind his wings. It would be unfair for her to fly and him to die on his feet. They'll probably allow him a weapon as well. His powers, however, will remain constrained."

I was aghast. "We're just going to see if he wins and leave his life to fate?"

"Yes."

"I can't."

Caliban's look was tense, but not unkind.

"He's not a citizen of Hell. Fuck, I know angels are your sworn enemy. But Richard would have killed me if Silas hadn't slain him."

"That favor was called in."

I lifted a hand to carry on. "Silas returned when I was caught in Richard's basement with a parasite. I would have starved to death in the soundproof basement of a serial killer without him. He didn't just fly into harm's way to get me out of Bellfield. He went *back* to help you and Azrames. And now he's taking the fall for Astarte's death."

"Love—" His brows pinched, eyes pleading, lips pulled back in an expression I'd never seen before—something between anger and pain. Was it helplessness? Frustration over my stubbornness? He couldn't be jealous that I was arguing for the life of an angel, could he?

Fire bubbled in my veins. "I should hate Heaven and its angels as much as any citizen of Hell. But I don't hate him. And I won't let him die tomorrow. Not for me. Not for this."

I stared into Caliban's diamond-chipped eyes, struggling to read his indiscernible emotion. He wasn't happy. He wasn't angry, either. I didn't need him to understand the underlying feelings motivating my position. Only that I was standing my ground, no matter what.

I thought of the metallic glint of Azrames's cuff. Of course, they wouldn't want Silas to access whatever Heavenly power might aid him in his final hour.

"Could he win?" I asked.

I couldn't quite distinguish the expression on Caliban's face, but I thought I saw a flash of jealousy. His eyes narrowed almost imperceptibly.

"How it ends is entirely contingent on what you ask of me. I can save the angel. I do owe Silas more than I care to admit. But intervening will cost Hell greatly. Letting him die, on the other hand, will mean the favors go away. The debts he holds will vanish."

"No," I said, quiet but firm. "He cashed in his formal favor to you. His debts are mine. He showed up when I was trapped in a serial killer's basement with a parasite. He came to the clinic when I called out for him just as everything went to shit."

"I know," he said. "I don't want him to have that hold over you."

"It's my call whether or not to feel responsible for him, and I do. You can't take that from me."

The look was more prominent this time. He set his jaw as he said, "If you want me to start a war, I need you to be fully aware of what you're asking."

"He can't die."

"Love—"

"I won't let it happen. You think he stands a chance in the battle? Fine. We'll let him fight. But if things start to turn..."

Caliban's pause stretched the width of the Grand Canyon. "If you're asking me to start a war, I need to know it isn't over...I'll do anything for you. I'll be anyone you need me to be. I'll burn the world to the ground for *you*. But for Silas?"

I chewed on my lip. "This isn't about the Phoenicians," I said finally. "It isn't about how we fucked over Astarte or the repercussions of some contract. I want to save you, and Azrames, and Silas. I don't care about tradition. I don't care that this is the way things have been done for eternity. The fissure between the Vanir and Aesir is why Ella and Estrid agreed to fight. Fenrir is here because of what Odin did. Poppy and Dorian are here because of centuries of slights from Olympus. None of it has anything to do with Heaven, or Hell, or the Canaanites."

He remained expressionless as he held my gaze. "And yet..."

"And yet," I pressed, "it's all interconnected. I might not be part of their grand godly movement, but something's happening that's bigger than all of us. And personally speaking? I don't care about the bigger picture. What matters to me is that I can get my friends out. I came for you, Caliban, but I'm not going to let Azrames be whipped until he's little more than pulp. He's my friend. I'm not going to sit by and watch Silas be drained by a horror movie monster. I'll stop it."

He was quiet. "There will be repercussions if you intervene."

"I know."

Caliban stared off at the galaxy.

The hush of the desert night rushed around us. There was no wind in my meditative space. The silence had an airy, cleansing quality. Desert was utterly still. There were no biting bugs. There was only the glow of the peculiar door, and the lingering question as I waited for Caliban to react. At one point, I inhaled, and kept it in. I wasn't sure if I'd breathe again until I knew how tomorrow might look.

When he looked at me, it was with an expression I'd never seen before. With cold gravity, at long last, he answered.

"So, we start a war."

Chapter Thirty

FAUNA BALLED A FISTFUL OF FABRIC FROM MY DRESS INTO HER hand, clutching me nervously. The gesture was just out of view from those around us so no one else could perceive her anxiety. I leaned into her until our shoulders touched, shielding her display from curious eyes. They wouldn't expect her to have any emotional response to an angel. Even I was somewhat surprised. Her emotions ran so hot and cold, I hadn't been sure how she'd feel.

Caliban led me beneath the low lighting to the stadium's centermost seats—seats of honor I supposed. He was kingly in every regard and treated as such. I was extended courtesies for being on his arm and little else. It was for that diplomatic courtesy alone that I'd been allowed the human indulgence of bringing my dog.

I didn't love that everyone insisted on dressing me in white wherever I went, but it evaporated from my mind. Music was playing, as it had been the last two days of the banquet. There was a vibrant buzz about the crowd as everyone celebrated the final day of festivities. I was reminded of the time my father had taken me to see the rodeo when I was young. It was one of the few days he'd been left alone to entertain me, and we'd ended up in a tin barn with a dirt floor and a number of horses, clowns, and cowboys.

The Phoenicians didn't need the enormity of a Roman coliseum for human rulers. This arena was where gods quenched their bloodlust. It was dark, and despite the dim lighting, there was a wealth about the space. I expected a dusty theater spotlight to pop into the center at any moment.

I kept my face set with neutrality as attendants served wine. Poppy and Dorian were in the row just above us, her draping finery and his dark linens making me wonder if they'd brought their own attire. She'd offered me a polite wave, Dorian a kindly nod as we sat. I would have thought nothing of it, had I not remembered our conversation of ranking. Dorian, Zeus's equal by blood, Baal's equivalent in rank, was higher in the pecking order than a prince.

They'd been offered equal ranking with Baal and Anath. Baal's finery was also airy in a way that denoted his status. It was only someone protected and royal who needn't fear power or armies or weapons. Breezy garb was a luxury of those without enemies. At his side was the iridescent shimmer of Anath's raven-black dress. Her night-dark hair had been swept dramatically to one side, the blue, purple, and silver smattering of galaxies decorating her eyelids like incandescent war paint.

Our eyes met for the briefest of moments. If she hated me, I couldn't tell. Perhaps I was too insignificant for her to bother with a feeling like hate. I couldn't answer the question, myself. I supposed she was doing precisely what I was. She stood firm in wanting justice for Astarte. I was fighting for my friends, too.

Even if I could empathize with her position, I sure as fuck didn't like her.

Fauna was escorted in by a Canaanite attendant, Ella and Estrid trailing behind her. The servant ushered Fauna to the seat beside me. While she grinned with the excitement of someone about to see the midnight release of a favorite film, I knew her well enough to see that, though the skin around

311

them crinkled, her eyes remained joyless. The moment she took a seat beside me, my suspicions were confirmed.

Fenrir sat primly between us, sable fur glossy in the dim lighting. He remained stoic and alert as he watched the world mill about.

Pork and cakes and wine didn't need tables to be served. Attendants bustled about for our elaborate dinner theater. I looked down at the perfectly crisped skin of my dish, but felt anything I ate might come up at any moment. I knew what awaited us. And from Fauna's nervous fist, so did she.

I kept my tone easy as I leaned over to Ella and Estrid. "I'm so glad I was able to make more friends from the Nordic realm! I hope to be able to visit your home on our next ambassador trip. Do you have excitement like this?"

Estrid attempted to play the role, but faltered.

I saw my mistake. Battle was not for actors and jokers, and she knew it. A valkyrie would find nothing amusing about the execution of an angel. She stumbled through a word or two before Ella took over.

"Oh, I keep things dull." She winked. "All's fair in love and war, right? She may be born for bloodshed, but I know a thing or two about lust, and we both know how much more sway it has over the heart."

"I'd hardly call that dull," I countered. And I recognized the voice speaking. Perhaps I wouldn't have noticed the shift had it not been for the way I caught Fauna's subtle glance. Maribelle was speaking. Maribelle, who could navigate horrid social situations, who could do what needed to be done to close the deal. Maribelle was at the stadium today, and it was her who would get me through this.

"Wine, my lady?" asked an attendant. I had been almost certain I'd been holding a glass. I wasn't sure where it had gone, but nodded and accepted another. Beside me, I noticed Caliban throw back the first glass before returning to his normal chalice. I wasn't sure how much more it took to get a god drunk, but he extended both glasses to the attendant.

312

"I'd appreciate it if you kept them coming," he said.

I felt something strange as he nodded at the helper and took another swig.

Caliban was in pain. Once more, his hands were tied. He'd chosen time and time again to insert himself in realms where his reach was limited. He'd struggled through the mortal realm as he'd watched me destroy myself and push him away, yet he'd refused to leave. Even if Azrames took three thousand lashes, I understood that he intended to be present. Every crack, every cry, would be his guilt to bear. Silas was another in a long line of responsibilities he'd shoulder.

I inhaled the rich spice of the red wine. The chalices were a dramatic gold. Maribelle was fine with red wine. She'd drink anything. She'd wear Louis Vuitton, laugh at the unfunny jokes of tech bros, and keep her pretty face neutral and alluring. Marlow, however, wanted to put ice cubes in her white wine and put on her pajamas. She wanted to be alone in her bed, using her laptop as a television. She wanted these horrors to be in her imagination, just as Caliban had been.

But I was far past that now. I could be neither, or I could be both.

"Have you been to an event like this?" came the spring-like tinkle of bells from above me. I turned around to see Poppy's kind smile. She was making conversation, and she wasn't. I knew a distraction when I saw one.

"It's my first," I said miserably.

She nodded, slipping her fingers into Dorian's as she did so. He broke whatever conversation he'd been having with Baal to regard his partner, looking down at her delicate hand and giving it a squeeze. He returned to his chatter, but I knew he'd left more than half of his attention with her.

"I've attended a few," she said. "Dorian wasn't exaggerating. I don't care for blood. We all make our concessions in partnership."

"What concession did you make?" I asked.

313

She chuckled and looked at me knowingly.

Ah, yes. Persephone famously abandoned the spring, the sun, the flowers, the sky. She'd left her mother, the Olympians, and the world around her for her life with Hades. That was a promise made long before they'd become Poppy and Dorian. I wondered what their true names were before legend had dubbed them Hades and Persephone. I wondered if they spoke them to each other in the quiet of their home, in the secrecy of their realm. Or perhaps they gave themselves a fresh start by choosing rebirth with each new name.

I'd given Caliban several names, so I'd been told.

But for me, he'd offered only one. No matter what my birth certificate said, what language I spoke, or what my friends and family had called me throughout the ages, I remained unchanged.

I scanned the crowed, curious if I'd be able to piece together bits of lore from the various beings scattered about. I thought I'd spotted a djinn until the dark hair attached to the horns turned and I caught the unmistakable profile of a perfectly gray nose. I hadn't expected Azrames to be invited to the gruesome festivities. Given the armed escort surrounding him on the lowest level, I suspected that he was there to watch as warning, not as a guest.

"Honored guests," boomed a voice from overhead. I turned to see Baal, smile glistening, hands open as he gestured to the arena. While Baal was charm and candor, the son beside him grinned with muscles and pride. I was liking Baal more and more every moment I had to be around his family members. He continued, "We haven't reveled in such pleasure in centuries. Not only have we been granted the return of my father and a most esteemed goddess of our realm, but the chance to host this ambassador mission with our friends and allies."

A smattering of toasts, cheers, and revelry came from those in the stands. The Nordes, the Grecians, Caliban, and I gave our politest smiles, but contributed to none of the jolly

314

noise. Only the esteemed members of the Phoenician realm, major and minor gods and goddesses, prominent entities, and powerful beings celebrated the accomplishment. The crowd was unnervingly intimate. It was a sacred event, meant only for those worthy of its attendance.

"And it is with these friends that I offer retribution for our beloved goddess's death: the gift of justice against our shared enemy."

The audience erupted into earsplitting cheers. I swallowed as Fauna's fist twisted the fabric of my dress. She channeled her energy well, keeping her face as happy and unbothered as I'd ever seen. I didn't dare look at Estrid, but I suspected everyone in the audience would be understanding of any expression worn by a valkyrie.

I stifled a gasp as a true spotlight appeared, whether through torchlight or magic. I'd been certain such a thing would be impossible among gods. It was too much like an unholy circus. To my horror, the music did not stop. The band adjusted their song, interlacing the minor chords of their plucked strings with anxiety-inducing percussion.

The orchestra was going to score the battle.

I heard the grunt before I saw the angel. He stopped upright, refusing to stumble. He was battered and bruised, but kept his shoulders back and chin high. He clutched an unimpressive sword, but they'd offered him no shield. He raised his forearm in a defensive position to act as its counterpart. A glittering cloud of dust, interlaced with whatever bits of mica and pyrite might set a pantheon's arena to starlight, sparkled in the beam of light. I lost my breath as Caliban failed to suppress his words beside me. I could just distinguish the low sound of his disbelief amidst the crowd.

"They didn't unbind his wings."

We weren't the only ones who were horrified. Estrid's controlled grunt of protest interjected into the stadium's murmur. She and the Nordes had no allegiance with the angels, but she knew a warrior who'd been unfairly disadvantaged when she saw one.

"And now"—wicked amusement colored Baal's declaration—"our champion!"

Silas was no deity, nor should a god sully themselves by facing him. Instead, he was to face a soldier in their pantheon. She was the night owl, preying on the blood of anyone who worshipped rival pantheons. He was the falcon, the unclean bird of the Old Testament lore, tangling with monsters.

A second beam of light cut through the arena. The estries stepped a single foot dramatically into the pooling floodlight, then another. The light took its time crawling up her frame, exposing her boots, her leather pants, the hardened leather of her top, the sharp, glittering sword in one hand, the hair slicked into a long, dark, high ponytail that dripped down her back in a single braid, and the enormous expanse of bat-like wings that flared at her back.

Caliban and Estrid weren't the only ones making noises of disapproval.

If this was to be their only blood fuel in centuries, the people wanted a good fight. Perhaps their disappointment was only in knowing their banquet would end early today as the estries expunged Silas from the realms before they'd finished their third glass of wine.

The estries turned toward the people and smiled, the unmistakable gleam of vampiric fangs visible even from where I sat in the audience. She was every bit as beautiful as I'd imagined a succubus might be. I didn't remember enough of her lore to know if she was meant to be so unfathomably beautiful, or if this was an extension of Fauna's gift to see *wrongly.*

The estries lifted her hands to incite the crowd, and they responded to her hunger for attention. The band swelled with dramatic enthusiasm, giving their deadly heroine a theme song. I slipped my hand toward where Fauna's had gone bloodless and white from tension on the now-wrinkled part of my skirt. She took my hand without looking at it and offered no mercy as she squeezed my bones until my knuckles cracked. Fortunately for us both, I savored the pain. It was a grounding exercise, reminding me that I was here, the problem was now, and everything was real.

To my surprise, it wasn't Baal's voice that carried on facilitating the battle. The goddess of war stepped up to bellow through the crowd. "Are you ready?"

The audience responded with feral enthusiasm. The clink of metal on stone echoed as some lost their wine goblets. Screams from men and women tore through with the joy, the vengeance, the need of centuries of neglect, for justice over Astarte's death. Their cries told me they believed they were owed this sacrifice. Seeing Heaven's accountability was their birthright.

The orchestra remained low, building anticipation with each minor chord of a string instrument, each reverberation of a bass drum.

The estries smiled a brilliant, terrible smile. She had strolled off the set of a vampire novel, her model-esque beauty meant to lure, to disarm, to stun. Yet she was an agent of death, and she needed us all to know that she would deliver. She brandished her fangs, grinning at Silas as her wings flared behind her.

"His wings!" Estrid shouted out. I'd heard the same frustrated anguish in football fans at bad calls, at coaches when their players had been benched, and now as a valkyrie watched an angel cut off at the ankles. This was not a fair fight.

If Silas was afraid, he didn't show it.

I'd been too anxious to truly regard him after catching the purple of his bruises and the ropes that restrained the two gilded, feathered appendages that might have leveled their playing ground.

His expression should have reassured me, but instead, it cracked my heart.

Silas's face was neutral. His jaw was set. His sword was raised. Everything about him said he was ready to fight to the death, because that's exactly what this was. He tensed in preparation for his last fight. There was a finality about his aura that chilled me.

"On my count!" came Anath's proud, happy battle cry.

The warriors fixed their footing. The drumming increased. The crowd began to pace their cheers with the thrumming percussion.

"Three!"

My sight flitted, hornet-like in its stabbing lurches as I looked between Silas and the estries, his jaw ticking, her grin glistening. The drum beat quicker and quicker, its roll swelling, nearly about to break.

"Two!"

Two of my knuckles popped as Fauna tightened her grip on my hand so hard that my fingers ceased to belong to me. My lungs burned as I refused to inhale or exhale. The crowd could barely keep up with the frantic percussion as the beats became so fast that they were scarcely indistinguishable.

"One!"

Half the audience went wild at the musical feat of the hummingbird thrum of constant drumming. The other half of the audience froze. We watched in collective, breathless anticipation. Tension rippled through the multitudes, from the excited onlookers to the horrified ambassadors, as we strained to watch the two on the ground.

"Fight!"

Chapter Thirty-One

I T HAPPENED SO QUICKLY THAT I MISSED THE FIRST LUNGE
entirely.

The estries launched herself at Silas, sword-first. She dove
as if he was a pool, ready to breaststroke her way through
his torso, bathing in his blood as his abdomen gave way. Her
wings tucked to her side as she plunged, which gave her
enough forward momentum that she couldn't deviate from
the course once she'd committed. He held his footing until
the absolute last second, then dove for the arena floor, tucking
and rolling into the space she'd abandoned.

A high, wild viola and its army of violins mimicked the
estries's savage twists and turns. The low, powerful double
bass and accompanying cellos answered as the instruments
danced, calling and responding in their freeform interpretation of the opening moves.

"He understands her timing," I said on an exhale, breathing for the first time.

Silas understood wings. He was unfairly bound, yes, but
he was no hapless pedestrian. He knew birds of prey, of their
course, of their pitfalls, whether animal or fae. If anyone
could take a winged nemesis, it was an angel.

He was on his feet without missing a beat. Despite the
evidence of his mistreatment, he moved with no limp. He

held his ground as if he were in peak fighting condition, brandishing his sword as he faced her once more. He moved his head slightly, shaking the dust from his hair.

The flicker of a smile flashed as she registered his evasion. The estries channeled her fury into her spin as she rounded on the angel.

She looked at him for a moment before setting off into the sky, hovering with several powerful backbeats of the wide, stretched leather of her membranous wingspan. A chorus of violins created harmonies and fierce counter-harmonies as they paced themselves with the hovering flaps of her wings, every bow in the string section working to mirror the fear she instilled with as she treaded air just above him.

Silas took a few careful steps until he was directly below her. She cried out as she sliced through the air, committed to the death of her prey. This time, Silas didn't roll, but spun with his sword outstretched in a slicing downward arc. He evaded her with the expert timing of someone who was no stranger to battle. The cello cried out with deep commanding notes as the violins trilled and fell.

Perhaps the estries was unrestrained and her bloodthirst was stronger, but it seemed she'd been away from war for a long, long time.

His sword wasn't sharp enough for the clean slice he might have hoped, but the blunt force of the blade crunched as it connected with a hollow primary bone in the wings she'd failed to fold in time. He rolled as she hit the ground, unable to recover from the blow before it was too late.

Silas took the barest of seconds allotted by her downfall to take the sword to his restraints, but cried out in unmistakable frustration as the blade was too dull to cut even the ropes that bound him. The audience understood at the same moment as he, that Silas held little more than a long metallic club.

The orchestra responded in kind. A deep drum joined as Silas's musical companion, the instrument creating impact with each swing.

Between his bound wings, his useless weapon, and the metallic cuff that caught the spotlight and contained any power he might hope to wield, he was little more than a well-trained human facing an estries in her full glory.

My eyes watered, dry and begging for me to blink, but I couldn't look away.

He abandoned his attempt at his restraints and readied himself for another round as she grunted. She'd managed to maintain hold of her weapon as she'd hit the ground, wing clearly impaired by his successful blow. She didn't bother to wipe the dust from her face as she got to her feet and snarled. Her teeth seemed sharper, somehow. Her eyes were brighter. Her sword glittered with more might.

Anticipatory, vibrational strumming rang through the opposing instrumental parties as they waited to clash once more. The fight would have been horrible in and of itself, but the dramatic intensity of the music made it unbearable.

I wondered if fear had begun to take on hallucinogenic properties. My heart thundered. My vision struggled to stay fixed on the man I'd come to see not only as a savior, but as a friend. A bastard who'd been reluctant as fuck to save me, but he'd still saved me, and helped me, and healed me.

He'd given me his angelic poppet, not because he'd been forced to, not because I'd been bound to him, not because I belonged to Heaven, but because he'd chosen to help me. He'd entered a god-catcher in Bellfield and answered my call when I'd called out to him. And he didn't deserve to die. Not bound and sabotaged. Not taking the fall for a crime he hadn't committed. And not because he'd helped a human who he had no loyalty or allegiance to. Not like this.

The estries cocked her head, braided ponytail flicking to the side like a whip as she goaded him forward. She brandished her sword.

Silas was not just quick on his feet, but quick to adapt. The audience responded to the way in which he'd shifted his grip on his sword once he understood it was little more than a bat. He switched to a two-handed hold, both on the pommel. He accepted her goad, but not in the way she expected. The estries grinned as he sprinted for her, drums matching his every thundering step, waiting until the last second to leap into the air so he might miss.

I gasped, my intake of breath audibly shared by the Nordes at my side.

A creature of the sky himself, Silas had anticipated as much. The moment she jumped, so did he. The estries leapt upward, intent on evasion. The angel lunged forward, wielding his metallic club toward her knee. The blunt rod connected with loud crack, shuddering against her shin. If we hadn't heard steel on bone, the agonizing shriek that tore from her would have been unmistakable enough.

The estries dropped from the air like a bird of prey felled by an arrow. The violins scarcely had time to switch to the rushed, panicked high notes I'd expect to hear if Norman Bates approached me in the shower with a knife. The audience cried out as their champion tumbled.

Silas advanced on her, undoubtedly with the knowledge that he had a tiny window wherein she was blinded by pain to strike. He sprinted to the estries, the enormous, brown–black expanse of her wings shielding the audience from seeing her full fallen form. We heard the impact of metal before understanding what had happened. Her wings shuddered in response and I looked to Caliban, then to Fauna.

Both were glued in frozen, motionless shock at the battle.

I opened my mouth to speak, but Caliban anticipated my demand.

"He's got it," he whispered.

From the orchestra pit, the cellist must have had a vantage point, for he did not quit. His powerful bass notes continued to intertwine with the violin as they saw something we could not.

I was drawn to the center of the ring with horror as the estries's wings did not wilt in defeat, but flexed inward as new fight filled her in a way that blinded the audience. Onlookers cried out in support, in disappointment, in hope, in anticipation as everyone waited to see who would emerge from the wall of wings.

A flash of metal.

A woman's scream.

An agonized cry.

The estries's own razor-sharp blade sliced through her wing, leaving a gaping window of just their faces. Her weapon soared toward the audience, clattering to the earth and kicking up a cloud of sparkling dust just short of the seats as everyone cried out in surprise. The murmurs of unrest were quelled only by the intensity of the fight as, through the punched hole in the wing, I was scarcely able to discern the two-handed grip the estries had on the blade. Its steel chewed into her palms, crimson streams running from her fingers down her forearms as she cowed in submission. Silas held it parallel to the earth, forcing it downward toward her throat.

Stars danced before my eyes. I hadn't taken a breath in more than thirty seconds. He'd won. My heart swelled as I stared down at the angel. Relief and pride wrestled one another as my eyes lined with inexplicable tears. He'd overcome the impossible. He'd gone toe to toe with—

My hope died the moment the cellos took the lead, the deep reverberations of the standing double bass carving a musical path for Silas. Its commanding strokes overpowered the violins as he fought.

I couldn't be certain what had happened. It was wind and spirit and horror all at once as what remained of her wings, her legs, her very essence swept up the dust around them in a flurry of legs and limbs. It was as if a storm had descended on the arena, concentrated to their fight alone.

"Hey!" Caliban snarled at my side, jumping up in indignation.

I waited for this to be it—this to be the moment he would stop the fight—but the battle went on.

Just above him, Dorian was on his feet, hands in the air as he shouted at the injustice.

I told myself I didn't understand what was happening, but in my gut, I knew: Silas had been stripped of his wings, his sword, *and* his supernatural power. The estries had been allowed to keep all three. It was the third she wielded at long last.

If I needed any further confirmation, I had it. It wasn't just the initial soloists and the duets and trios that had been born from their accompaniment, but new instruments, new notes, new highs and lows added to emphasize the estries. Cellos abandoned their allegiance with his music as they symbolized her usurping power. She was given a symphony. He, a drum and the relentless bass notes. He was alone. She had it all.

Caliban had said he would start a war for me. He'd promised me he wouldn't let Silas die. I yanked at his arm, pleading with him to do something.

This time when he answered, it wasn't with words.

Like Fenrir, like the cave, he spoke into my mind.

"Trust me."

I was so startled by his response that I stumbled into Fauna. She braced for my impact as we watched glittering, sooty dust fill the stadium. Coughing was something I'd imagined would be below the gods, but even they were not spared from the sparkling, unholy winds of malice that caked the arena.

When the cloud of wind and fury subsided, I wiped the debris from my eyes to see two bat-like wings pointed straight into the air, strenuously flexed as they mirrored the corded muscles and tendons of her body. She was no longer smiling. A vein popped from her forehead. Her fangs were bared for blood and animalistic need rather than any pleasure. Her arms, her neck, her legs were tensed in a total-body commitment to smiting the life below her.

Something in the gust of power had knocked Silas's sword from his hands. He was flat on his back, forearms crossed above

324

him as he held on to what he could of his strength against the powerful vampiric succubus. He grunted, the gloss of his sweat catching in the light as it covered any bit of face that wasn't caked in dust. His lips were peeled back, teeth bared as he mirrored her expression, his of strenuous, grunting desperation.

Silas was losing.

This time, I shouted to him in my mind. "Caliban, he needs our help!"

"Wait," came the silent response.

She beat her wings to help counteract any weight he might hold against her. She could force herself down on him if she tried. She would get her teeth into his neck, suck him clean, leave him an empty shell—a symbolic, bloodless sacrifice where an angel once had lain. Her battle cry chilled me as Fauna and I joined the others on their feet.

I felt so helpless. I wanted to tear through the audience, to sprint across the arena floor, to shove my weak mortal arms between them. I had no power. I had *nothing*. Just blind faith that my demon had a plan.

What if he didn't?

Was I willing to gamble with Silas's life?

I forced myself to keep my eyes on Silas no matter how desperately I wished to look away. I clung to every one of the cellist's notes, absorbing the winces, the reddening shade of his face, the shaking of his limbs as he fought with everything he had to keep her at bay.

Caliban carried the guilt, the pain of everything that happened, everything my demon, the Prince, blamed himself for. I was not cowardly enough to avert my eyes. If Silas was to perish, then I was to earn the shame, the ghosts, the misery that haunted me. If he fell to the fangs of the estries, it would be me who was to blame, and it would be me who would never forget it.

The drum—*his* drum—made the sadistic choice of mimicking his dwindling life, representing his heart as he ticked away on borrowed time.

Another flap of her wings and she was closer.

My hand flew to my chest, clutching at my own heart through my gown as if to hold it together to keep from bleeding out.

His arms trembled. His body was giving out. He had nothing on his side. No weapons. No wings. No magic. He was on unfamiliar territory, in a kingdom that wanted him dead. His elbows buckled, and the audience gasped. Perhaps some had begun to root for him—whether because they wanted a longer fight, or because they viewed him as a worthy opponent, who was I to say? All I knew was that I would not be a coward.

If Silas died, part of me deserved to die with him.

Another beat of her powerful wings, grit and debris kicking up around her.

The orchestra was hers to command as the swelling crescendo sang her impending victory.

We lost our collective breath as we had in the moment before the fight began.

Another beat.

His eyes changed, and I knew I couldn't be the only one who saw it. He'd lost whatever hold he'd had on his upper body strength. Surely, he had to be thinking what we were all thinking. The cards had been stacked against him from the start. They'd never intended to give him a fair fight.

His drum slowed. Slower, and slower, and slower as it scored his death.

The moment I saw resignation in his eyes, a strangled, teary sound escaped me. Fauna began screaming obscenities. I was certain I heard even Poppy and Ella in the protests, but they were so muddied by the celebratory cheers that it was impossible to tell.

"Caliban! You promised!"

Silence in return.

"You swore! You said he wouldn't die! You told me to trust you! You—"

Everything screeched to a halt as a powerful woman's voice rang through the stadium.

"Stop!"

Estrid was on her feet. The booming voice belonged to the valkyrie, sacred chooser of the slain. Her command was louder than Silas's cry, than the estries's hungry howl, than the shock and excitement of the onlookers. Dissonant murmurs rippled through the crowd.

The world moved in slow motion as Ella swung to grab for her. Fauna's hair moved in a blur as her head whipped to watch the horror unfurl. As I curled toward the Nordes, I saw Poppy's wide eyes and Dorian's clenched jaw from my periphery. Caliban's hand was at my back. The world turned to regard the valkyrie as she stood against Baal.

"They call me valkyrie, as I know who has earned Valhalla. I was once known as Göndul, the wand-wielder, chooser of the slain. I was created by Odin to deem those worthy to live and die in battle, and I cannot stand idle as you cast a death sentence on one who has earned his life."

Chapter Thirty-Two

A LL EYES WERE ON US. THE AIR HAD BEEN SUCKED FROM THE stadium. Even Silas's eyes were trained on the crowd.

"Stop."

Into my mind, I heard a single cautioning word. "Love…"

He'd fulfilled his end of the bargain. I didn't know how he'd done it, but I knew he was the reason the valkyrie intervened. Perhaps he owed her a favor now, too.

It wasn't enough.

"I have something to say."

I hardly realized I was speaking to the audience before it was too late. I was committed. Caliban released the fabric of my dress as I joined Estrid on my feet. Even Estrid was caught off guard by my interjection. The crowd buzzed with hushed disapproval. I was human. The least important. The lowliest. I had no place here.

Baal looked to Estrid, then to the Prince. Caliban stood and slipped his hand around my waist. "She's entitled to speak her piece."

He had no idea what I was about to say. He had no way of knowing if I would help the cause or ruin it irredeemably. But a house divided could not stand. We were better united in ruin than divided so one might save face. And either he trusted me enough to not make a fool of us all, or he was ready to stand by me as I burned it all down.

"Hold." Anath barked her cold command to the estries. The vampire flapped again, lowering herself inches closer to the angel. I watched in horror as the creature, beholden to her bloodlust, did not listen.

Anath threw out a hand and the estries was hit with an unseen blast that shot her from where Silas remained on his back. She hit the ground with a smack, but wasn't down long. In the second it took for her to get to her feet and start in on Silas, Anath extended her arm, hand in a cupping motion. The estries gagged on invisible chains as she was throttled from afar. "I told you to hold," the goddess said. "Obey your goddess."

The estries was able to do little more than close her eyes in acknowledgment of the order. When Anath dropped her stranglehold on the vampire, her lips remained pulled back in a sneer at the prey she'd been denied.

Silas was safe, at least for the moment. I didn't expect him to stay that way.

I looked down at Fenrir. In my mind, I said, "I'm going to tell them why we're really here."

His gaze locked with mine. "You speak to the highest deities of their pantheon. It is not the same, human. Hades wars against those with names, with titles in his own realm. He joins you for the downfall of the Grecians in rule. The Nordes beside you fight because they are unequal with the highest Nordic gods."

"And you?" I asked.

We weren't just here for ourselves, or for the freedom of angels and demons. Our attendance was in the name of something bigger.

He looked at me for a long time before closing his eyes in silent acknowledgment. I looked up at Baal and said, "Who is your enemy?"

Electricity crackled around the storm god. He scoffed.

"I've stood in opposition to Heaven since before man etched the first of our legends into tablets. Their god has mocked us in our own land amidst our own followers. He's played us for a fool one time too many."

I threw my hand toward Silas. "And is *he* Heaven? This angel who rescued me, a demon prince's bride. He a subjected foot soldier—a messenger, one whose loyalties might be swayed to sympathetic sides—of your true nemesis."

Baal's eyes flashed with warning. "Human —"

Fauna cleared her throat. "The *Prince's* human."

Baal's eyes darkened. "You truly mean to stand against Heaven?" And then, as if considering our ensemble for the first time, he looked at Caliban, at Dorian, at Poppy, at the Nordes. His eyes drifted to the angel.

"There's more," I said.

The hairs prickled on my arms and the back of my neck as the air filled with static, just as it did before lightning struck.

It was a game of poker, and I had a winning hand. If ever there was a time to lay down my cards, it was now.

I gestured to Fenrir. He dipped his head, then looked back at the Phoenician god. "This is Fenrir, Odin's adversary, the harbinger of Ragnarök. He has joined us for one reason."

The Lord who straddled titles between the Phoenicians and Hell trailed over us with a shocked gaze, but no one contradicted my words. I felt the firm, reassuring pressure of Caliban's fingers at my back. Fenrir nodded his head before speaking into the minds of everyone in the audience.

"It's true. I'm prophesied as the Twilight of the Gods. I've deemed this human worthy in her cause, as she promised me one thing, and on this one thing I'm certain she can deliver."

It was Anath who spoke next. Her eyes were wide, but shoulders back, voice calm, as she said, "And that one thing is?"

I held her gaze, balling my fists as I said, "I may be a human, but Hell is on our side. Nordes and Grecians have joined our cause. An agent of Heaven fought to save me,

330

Hell's bride, and is here because of us. Don't stand against us. Be our allies as we share a common enemy."

Anath stared me down. "Name the enemy."

"Those in power. Those who've claimed the public consciousness. Those who've claimed the titles of masters and rulers while the rest of us wait in the shadows. Join us. Topple those in power. Be the reason we usher in a new era."

"And that era?" It was Baal's question, this time. The prickled hairs on my arm relaxed. The static dissipated. The same amusement I'd seen on his face played across his features just as it had the first day of the banquet.

"Dominos, Lord Baal. If one goes down, the others will follow. Fenrir is here because he was promised anarchy. Help me deliver on that promise."

Anath regarded Baal's contemplative expression before looking at me. "And what would you have us do, human?"

My mouth was so dry. Adrenaline burned through me. I didn't look away as I said, "If we have any hope of winning this war, we can't kill or wound those who might fight with us. I'd ask that you pardon both Silas of Heaven and Azrames of Hell. Absolve them of sins of the past so we can focus on the future. Let them leave this realm with us. And that you ready your people for the final war. Because whether those who've sat on their thrones know it or not, war is coming. You can stay in your realm and watch, or you can use your power and might to help us turn the tide."

Caliban's fingers flexed against my back encouragingly. His voice boomed. "The war between Heaven and Hell *is* your war. It's everyone's war. We topple their kingdom, and we free the mortal realm from two thousand years of one god's iron grip on public consciousness. Once we overthrow the King of Heaven, the rest of us stand a chance to make a new world. One where gods cannot toss us into the Underworld, mock us in front of our prophets, or chain us to rocks and leave us to die. This victory is the first step against every god who lords power over us."

I looked to Dagon, hoping he might weigh in with support given what I'd done to free him, but he seemed merely curious as to what the others would do. I looked for a sign, a signal, that they might be leaning in one direction or the other. My ears began to ring. My chest ached as my heart threatened to escape its cage. My palms were slick from the panic I tried so hard to conceal.

Anath was watching Baal closely. It appeared Caliban's reference to his Old Testament competition with the King of Heaven struck a powerful nerve. She arched a testing brow as she awaited his reply.

Amusement blossomed into something else entirely as the high lord of the Phoenician realm exchanged glances with Caliban. Pride. He was...*proud*...of me?

My concentration was broken by a loud, unholy shriek as the estries on the ground snapped. Clearly, she'd had enough of patience. If the gods weren't going to decide, then she'd show them exactly where she stood on joining sides with a lone angel as she scooped up the sword and sprinted for Silas. Her great bat-like wings folded for speed as she sprinted toward the angel.

An aching shock shot through me as I realized Silas couldn't block a blow. He didn't have his blade. He had nothing to stand against an armed estries. He—

A sickening crack echoed through the arena. The estries froze in her advance, sword aloft, mouth open, lips pulled back, but something was terribly, terribly wrong. She no longer faced the angel. Her chin jutted out at unnatural angle, neck horribly bent, mouth open in a silent cry. Her eyes remained peeled back in horror as she dropped to her knees, the sword we hadn't realized she'd retrieved before it was too late clattering to the ground. Her wings cascaded around her, blanketing her as she collapsed onto the dirt.

I looked at Silas, but he was not watching the vampire. His gaze was fixed in the stands, watching Anath.

"I said," came the loud, commanding answer through

gritted teeth, "obey your goddess." Then to the sea of shell-shocked onlookers, guests and gods alike, she arched a brow. "I, for one, would like to see Heaven fall. The *other* gods have waited long enough for the world to see our power. Who's with me?"

Chapter Thirty-Three

MY BACK POPPED, RIBS CRUSHED IN AN ALL-ENCOMPASSING hug as Azrames swept me up. His joy was a thick, tangible cloud. Relief, appreciation, and genuine giddiness filled the enormous room, which was particularly contagious when juxtaposed against his raw, masculine strength.

We'd waited anxiously in the palace atrium—well, Fauna and I had been anxious; the others wore masks of warrior-like stoicism—for the prisoners to be brought to us. Each step had filled me with tangible release as we walked through door after door, escorted past the seals and beyond the traps that had contained us. I didn't have to ask. I knew full well why our reunion was to take place beyond the seals.

We were free to go.

"Marmar." Azrames released me, holding me at arm's length as he looked at me with wide, grateful eyes. "How the fuck—"

"Stop hogging him," Fauna said, ducking between us. She wrapped her thin, freckled arms around him, intent on tucking her head against his chest in a hug. Her temple never made it to its resting place. He slipped a large hand into her coppery waves and gripped just firmly enough to force her chin up for a kiss. I barely had time to wiggle away from being an unwitting participant in a threesome as they behaved as if they didn't have a small audience of Nordes, Grecians, Phoenicians, and the Prince.

I giggled both at the intimacy of their very public display, and to work through the nerves of my insanity. Caliban caught me before I was able to put too many steps between us.

"Love," he breathed, silver eyes sparkling.

"I don't know what came over me," I said, each word sucked into an inhalation. I searched his face to discern the emotion behind those eyes. He cupped my cheek, fingers brushing just over my ear as he wove them into my hair. My hand went up to meet them, pressing his cool palm into my face.

"Fortune favors the bold," he said. "You were incredible."

I choked on the word. Stammering to pull something intelligent together, I said, "Not bad for a demon's pet, right?"

His brows furrowed for a moment. "Pet? Is that what you...?"

Our reverie was broken as Silas was led into the atrium. Shoulders back, chin level, he remained the picture of a warrior, even though he fooled none of us. He was in pain.

The guard escorting him undid his shackles, only the silver cuff that bound his magic remaining in place. I met his golden eyes as the chains dropped. I took a step toward him, Caliban relaxing his hold slightly, but not releasing me entirely as I positioned myself near the angel. Estrid intercepted us. She took the place the guard abandoned, offering Silas her hand.

Silas cleared his throat and took it with a firm, grateful shake. Emotion laced his words as he managed to say, "Thank you."

She dropped her hand. Ella approached her on the opposite side, touching the lightning bolt scars on Estrid's opposite arm lightly before looking at Silas. "I hope you understand what an honor it is that she deemed you worthy in battle."

Whether or not he attempted to quell the tears that lined

his lower lids, it was impossible to tell. He dipped his chin in acknowledgment. "It's the honor of my life," he said, and there was no question as to his sincerity.

"Well." Dorian clapped his hands. "I hate to break up this precious moment"—Poppy attempted to smack him, but he snatched her hand out of the air and interlaced her fingers with his before continuing—"but would any of you like to get out of here? We've shown our cards rather spectacularly. And, while I appreciate Merit's gumption, we all know that no kingdom is without its infiltrators. It will be a matter of days, if not hours, before word spreads of our involvement."

"Because of her." Caliban looked at Dorian with casual assertiveness. I'd always known he was tall, but seeing them stand eye to eye, it was impossible to tell if one had a single hair's width over the other. Perhaps the Greek god of the Underworld outranked him in the technical titles of the realms and their pecking orders, but I'd never forget what Azrames had said about Caliban when we'd first met. Az killed humans. Caliban killed gods. "We have an entire pantheon on our side."

"We do," Poppy confirmed with calm gratitude. "And we'll need all the numbers we can get."

"Unfortunately..." Dorian took a step closer to Caliban, which elicited an easy smirk from Caliban. I almost would have described his expression as casually amused as the powerful Grecian advanced. Dorian went on, "Nothing comes for free. She bought us quantity at the expense of time. There's no use crying over spilled milk. What's done is done. But we're going to need to move fast."

"He's right," Estrid agreed. She stepped toward the men, causing them to open their standoff as the warriors of the group—at least, the fighters who didn't still wear silver cuffs—triangulated for discussion. "Ella and I will see who we can stir up among the Nordes. She has a few strong connections with the Celts as well, as does Fauna."

Fauna, still breathless from her passionate kiss, lifted a

woozy thumbs-up in confirmation. "Leave the Celts to us," she agreed.

Estrid turned to Fenrir. "Your fate is your own, but you are more than welcome to remain with myself and Ella."

"I'll join in the amassing," he confirmed.

Dorian chewed on his cheek, lost in thought. "Pops, you have a far better standing with the Greeks and Romans than I do."

"I have a much better standing with *everyone* than you do," she countered.

He winked. "Not with the Slavs. I've got a few connections that have been looking for a war for a while. But the clock is ticking. For all we know, a little estries friend is already making a beeline for Zeus and Odin to tattle on our meeting. Silas." Dorian turned to the angel. "Do you have the pulse on any other defectors?"

Silas's lips parted silently.

"I—" I stuttered. I didn't have the courage to maintain eye contact as I said what I needed to say. "I may have exaggerated his willingness to help us."

"You didn't," Poppy breathed, horrified.

"Merit." Ella paled as she whispered.

Fauna positioned herself between me and the others. Caliban remained at my side, but I felt the temperature of the room change as everyone else realized I may have advocated for the freedom of someone who might turn us over to the King of Heaven.

"Silas has saved Marlow's life time and time again," she said. Her happy love bubble had popped as she evaluated the others with utter sobriety. "I've known Silas for a long time. He didn't deserve to die in there. And he won't betray our cause." She looked up at the angel, her gaze both challenge and threat as she locked eyes with him. "Right?"

"Right," Silas agreed quietly. The glossy sheen of a swelling black eye caught in the torchlight that filtered through the atrium.

"Go," Caliban said. "Work your contacts. Be in touch. I'll remain in the mortal realm. Find me there if and when you or our allies need me."

Dorian wasn't much for ceremonious goodbyes. He clicked his tongue while giving me a two-finger salute before tucking Poppy against him. They were gone before I had the chance to breathe.

"We need to be on our way as well," Ella said carefully, looking between Estrid and the others. "Dorian is right. If the clock is ticking..."

"When you hit the Celts—" Fauna began.

"Don't worry. I know to leave your boo for you." Ella grinned. Estrid nodded at the rest of us while Ella wrapped her arms around the valkyrie's neck. Again, without so much as a dramatic poof of air, they were gone.

"And then there were five," I said. The high black ceilings of the palatial atrium seemed far too large for such a small group. The guards remained at their posts at the doorway. I knew that we were free to leave at any time, but suspected Caliban wanted to speak with the gods before we departed.

"I'll be grateful to get this thing off," Azrames mumbled, rubbing at the silver cuff on his wrist. "I've never felt so bound in my life. Is this what it feels like to be human?"

He looked at me as if I might even have the capacity to understand the question. I grimaced to express my regret.

His mouth pinched as he considered. "You know that feeling when a word is at the tip of your tongue, but just out of reach?"

"Oh, I hate that feeling."

He nodded once. "It's that, but with power, with thought, with the abilities as familiar as limbs. They really know how to keep a guy from having a good time. But I don't need to tell you about that, do I?" he asked, opening up his stance to include Silas.

Silas looked between his cuff and the demon. "It is miserable. But I've been through worse."

Fauna laughed. "Worse than being kidnapped by a rival pantheon, beaten, restrained, and nearly murdered while everyone watched?"

I recognized the flash of feeling on his face. I knew it from the mirror, from the years I'd stayed within the confines of the church, from the time I'd still counted my mother as my very best friend. I didn't know what the King of Heaven had done to him that could be worse than his time with the Phoenicians, but my stomach ached at the thought. It also spiked with a clear and distinct worry. The captor bonding that happened when an abuser forged a loyalty with their underlings was not to be underestimated.

"Silas." I said his name carefully. "Now that the others are gone, can you tell us what you plan to do? When you're free?"

He took a half step backward, which only hurt me more. He didn't feel secure with us. With the Canaanites. In Heaven. I wondered what it would take to make him feel safe.

Before he had the chance to answer, the doors opened and Anath entered the atrium, Baal at her side. Her oil-slick dress trailed behind her with the iridescent shimmer of a raven's wings. She flashed a brilliant smile as she approached.

Much to my surprise, she came to me first, taking my hand into her own. "The human who sat in a fertility clinic, infiltrated a terraformed realm, murdered a goddess, wooed a demon prince, befriended an angel, and won rebel hearts to her cause. Your allies took my sister from me, but you stand to repay me with something so much greater. I may never forgive you for what you've stolen, yet a good goddess of war knows when to make an allegiance for the sake of victory. Please accept my regrets for underestimating you." She stepped away to regard the others. "Now, who will be our liaison?"

"Do you have any connections who might support you in an uprising?" Caliban asked.

"Of course," said Baal. "The Egyptians and Sumerians

have remained friends. Though I expect with the Egyptians…"

Anath's eyes narrowed. "Popularity is not a problem with them. Many of their gods thrive, as they stay on the hearts, tongues, and altars of their people. Fortunately, I know a few who are as interested in inversion as we are."

Fauna dared a comment. "Dorian shared something that I think we should keep in mind."

Anath looked the nymph up and down. "Go on."

Any uncertainty melted from her as she rose to meet the occasion. She was a deity in her own right, and she was their guest, not their prisoner. "It would be unwise to believe that everything said in the arena will stay safe in your realm. Word will travel. We won't have the element of surprise on our side."

Anath's grin was practically feline as she said, "Oh, way ahead of you."

I would have been surprised by her modern use of language contrasted against Dagon's and Baal's, but I supposed she'd been alongside her sister in Bellfield for more than two centuries. For all I knew, she was an expert in all facets of social media and fluent in slang.

"The arena's on lockdown. They'll remain fed and entertained as we commence…exit interviews."

"They'll be tagged," Baal explained.

My eyebrows lifted. I wasn't alone in my expression.

"You'll tag your own people?" Fauna asked.

Anath's face made it apparent she didn't appreciate the derision. "This is war. It's my area of expertise. How about you save your opinions unless we have a deer to summon?"

I knew in that moment that Azrames was ready to throw hands against a major deity in the name of Fauna's reputation. His energy went cold, his entire body shifting, fingers flexing at his side as he said, "I'd expected a goddess to be wiser than that."

Her eyes flashed.

"Likability isn't your specialty, so I'll offer some friendly advice. Don't make villains out of your allies, Anath."

I thought I was going to pass out. Azrames had barely escaped by the skin of his teeth. He was still in their kingdom. He wore their cuff. He—

"Set these two free for me so I can get them out of your kingdom," Caliban said. He wasn't willing to condemn Azrames, nor make an enemy of the Canaanites I'd risked it all to rally to our cause. If he felt any tension, I wouldn't have been able to tell from the effortless tilt of his brow, inclination of his head, or easy smile as he waited for Anath to oblige.

With control and smooth diplomacy, Anath allowed us all to see the barest edge of her disapproval before she beckoned Silas to her side. He approached and extended his arm. She grabbed him by the elbow, yanking him just off his footing. She looked into his eyes and said, "Don't fuck us over, angel. Remember who spared you."

The cuff unlocked as she grazed his forearm. He sucked in a sharp inhalation the moment he was released as his powers came rushing back. I wondered how many words had been waiting at the tip of his tongue, or whatever comparison Azrames had made, only to come crashing in now. She said nothing as she turned her back on Silas and extended her hand for Az. He gave it to her, but the two remained in a proud stalemate. Whatever tension they'd established had not dissipated. They'd be allies in war, perhaps, but it didn't appear to be in the cards for them to be friendly.

If Silas's intake of air had been alarming, it was nothing compared to the utter bloodlessness of Azrames's stunned expression the moment his cuff was removed. I had no idea what could make a demon assassin afraid, but the moment his powers returned, looking at my friend was like looking into the face of death.

"Az?" Uncertainty was replaced by the cold ice picks of fear as I continued to stare. Fauna extended her hand, then hesitated.

Anath and Baal were still here.

Whatever it was, he didn't want to speak it aloud in front of them.

If I hadn't spent my life staring in wonder at the too-beautiful imaginary friend who'd filled my heart, my home, and my bed, then I might have missed the minute feathering of his jaw. He saw. He understood. Alert and endlessly charming, Caliban extended his hands for goodbyes with the highest gods of the pantheon. I was sure he was thanking them for their hospitality, exchanging formalities, and whatever it was gods did, but I heard nothing aside from a muffled, high-pitched buzz. I couldn't look away from Azrames's face. He hadn't so much as blinked.

What must it take to terrify a demon?

Situation be damned, Fauna wrapped her fingers as far around his bicep as she could. She gave him a squeeze, gently shaking him, pleading with him to look at her. He remained utterly frozen.

The moment the room cleared, his eyes snapped to Caliban. "I need help."

"Tell me."

The column of Azrames's throat worked. "It's Betty." He turned to Fauna, absorbing the pain in her eyes as her face fell. "I think it's Heaven."

"Go," Fauna said hoarsely. "I'll explain. Go!"

He disappeared without another word.

"Heaven is attacking his practitioner?" Caliban took a step toward her as he reiterated the situation. He didn't know either of them well enough to understand the urgency, but I did. I knew what the witch and demon did together. I knew the bond they held. I also knew that Azrames would never have asked the Prince unless he truly believed it was necessary.

"Listen," Fauna said, dropping all decorum as she grabbed on to Caliban as if he were any man on the street. Desperation dripped from her voice as she dug her nails into his forearm. "She's immensely important. Not just to me and Azrames, but to the world. She's powerfully psychic, she's deeply warded, and she's spent centuries working with Azrames to clean the world of its trash. If Heaven is onto us...if they're onto Marlow, or you, or me..."

The severity registered with him, but not with me. What would Heaven do to a wonderful woman who helped the disenfranchised?

I stammered, "She helps women. She has nothing to do with me. She—"

"*Listen* to me," Fauna repeated. "Heaven needs to goad the Prince into showing his hand. Now that they know you're his human? The best way to attack him is through you. And before they can attack you, they need to eliminate your strongest resources. Betty is the most powerful witch I know. She's Azrames's link to the mortal realm. With her gone—"

"I'll help him." Caliban's voice was firm. "Take Love with you."

"No!" Fauna tightened her grip on his arm. He looked down, as did I. I half expected to see blood where she clutched him with feral intensity. "I'm going with you."

"I can't leave her—"

"Silas will take her!" Fauna relinquished a single hand to throw it out to the angel. She didn't wait for his nod in acknowledgment. "Caliban, we have to go, *now!*"

The flames in his gaze shot to meet mine, but I could do little, save for reiterate their panic. "Go! If I wasn't safe with Silas before, he now owes me a life debt and doesn't have a choice. I'll meet you at the apartment. Go, now."

Worry creased his eyes, jaw hard as he gritted his teeth and walked them both into nothingness. Silas and I were alone in the wake of whatever unfathomable turmoil they were about to encounter.

"Marlow?" he said carefully, extending his hand for me.

"Let's get the fuck out of here."

Chapter Thirty-Four

PURPLE, YELLOW, AND GREEN DOTTED HIS SKIN. SILAS WAS A bruise stitched together in the shape of an angel. Despite his numerous wounds, it was Silas who grabbed me to keep me upright as I stumbled through the ether and into my living room. He stopped me from smacking my shins against my coffee table. After my rather traumatizing experience with Richard and the shattered glass table, I'd replaced it with a minimalist concrete design. While far harder to damage, it was also more likely to crack my bones if I were clumsy enough to run headlong into it. He ensured I was steady on my feet before he groaned, sinking to the floor.

I was so disoriented. I couldn't tell if it was the realm-hopping, the jarring sense of incongruous time, or the murky purple twilight filtering in through the windows over the river that made it so challenging for me to gather my bearings. The elaborate dress that had seemed so glamorous in the arena was now a mockery of a realm I'd left behind when contrasted against the mundanity of the apartment. I needed to change, but something told me that turning on a lamp would make me nauseous, so I allowed the gloom to overtake me. I'd need to check the date, but I had to wait until the room stopped spinning.

He began moving his hands over his more obvious injuries, a subtle, glittering glow emanating from his palm as they disappeared beneath his touch. I recalled him healing my bruised knees in this very room as I examined him.

"Silas?" I slumped onto the table, shoulders hunched with exhaustion I hadn't realized I was carrying. I snatched the golden poppet that had escaped with me from Bellfield and rested in my living room as a literal guardian angel. I turned it over in my hands, looking between the figurine and the man as I said, "Your wings are missing."

He looked up from his task. "Mmm," came the barest of acknowledgments before he returned to healing the visible wounds. He pressed his hand to his stomach for whatever internal injuries I couldn't see. While I'd never known him to be particularly chatty, something seemed off.

"Where are the others? Are they okay?" I continued to squirm. I couldn't stop picturing the panic on Azrames's face. Fauna had lost all pretense and clawed at Caliban to get him to help. Whatever it was, it was bad.

"There is absolutely nothing you can do to help," Silas said. "Though I do suspect a few are hoping you might show up, which is exactly why you can't go."

"Can't," I grumbled, the word sour on my tongue. It was the angst I needed to push off from the table. I felt his eyes on me as I moved through the living room and entered the bedroom, stepping out of the otherworldly gown and grabbing cozy clothes that rested in the everlasting "too clean to wash, but too dirty to hang up" chair near the bed. I wasn't sure if I was dressing for bed, or for pacing back and forth in my apartment, but the gray sweatpants and loose black crop top would probably suit either need.

Silas ignored me as I reentered the living room, now looking obscenely underdressed compared to the battle-worn heavenly host in my living room, but that was par for the course as of late. I was far too anxious to resume sitting while we waited for word. I'd rather he talk about the weather than leave me alone with my thoughts. Remaining on my feet, I took a stab at eliciting a reaction.

"What's your favor count now?" I asked. "Caliban called in a tier-five favor, and you cashed it in for Bellfield. You rescued me twice from parasites. You returned to help him fight at the clinic. He worked with Estrid to get you out of the Phoenician realm. Why didn't you tell the Phoenicians that you didn't do it? Why did you take the fall for him?"

His mouth twitched, but it wasn't quite a smile. "You can't tell me that you genuinely believe in *innocent until proven guilty.*"

I cut to the heart of the question lingering between us. "Where do we stand with who owes who what?"

I wasn't sure if I cared about the answer. The bargains had never seemed important to me, even though I realized I was alone in my line of thought. The torture, the abuse, everything he'd been through in their realm had been because of me. He'd suffered indescribable traumas, and I had no idea how to make it better.

"You never owed me anything, Marlow," he said quietly, still fixed on his task. "And my wings aren't missing. You just can't see them in the mortal realm. Even with your sigil hack, we're still in human packaging."

"Because biblically accurate angels are all wheels and eyes and feathers and fire, right? Are you a flaming circle of eyeball wheels?"

He stopped long enough to look up at me with a deadpan expression. I cracked a smile, and despite his best efforts, I caught the way his lip turned up at the corner before he controlled it once more.

A thought struck me.

"When your cuff was removed, did you get input from Heaven? The same way Azrames got it from Betty?"

Silas said nothing.

I stiffened. "You did, didn't you. Silas, is Betty okay? Is Heaven—"

Whether or not he'd finished with his injuries, I'd never know. He got to his feet. From where I sat on the coffee table, he looked seven feet tall standing in the mundane gloom of my living room. He stretched out a hand and waited.

"What?"

There was a sorrow to his slow, deep exhalation. "There's something you need to know, and this may be my only opportunity to tell you."

I leaned away from his hand like it was a snake. I glared up at him. "About Betty?"

"No. This is so much bigger than Betty. Her role has everything to do with you. The clock has been ticking from the second they left me alone with you. I have moments to show you the truth, if you want it."

"Is this...?" I hedged. "Is this a trick?"

"How can you ask that?" Pain darkened his eyes, if only for an instant. "When they get back, I won't be able to tell you what's really going on. I just fought a death match to protect..." His sentence trailed off, leaving the barest edges of his thought unspoken.

My hand ached to touch his, to comfort him once more, but I fought the urge as if battling my own estries.

He said, "I fully embraced the consequences of being on your side. Now, before you say something that makes me regret my decision: grab the poppet. Don't leave it behind again."

I crossed my arms, hugging myself defensively as I took a half step away. I looked between the golden figurine and the angel. "I haven't done anything to Betty. You haven't either, right? Is it what Fauna said? They're antagonizing the people close to me in order to lure Caliban out?"

He looked down at his hand, crestfallen as he said, "You have no clue why everyone reacts the way they do to hearing that you're the Prince's human. You have no idea why everyone wants a piece of you, why they've been so receptive to your presence, what role you play. But you should. We all

347

deserve to understand whether we're the game maker, or the pawn."

My brows pinched. "I...I understand the power of name -dropping. There's an upward mobility that comes with dating well. As a human, I'm a no one. Attach me to a royal title, and they lend me their ears."

He laughed, dropping his hand. "They wouldn't give a shit if you were a human toy. You're not dating. You're not even..."

"I'm not even what?"

He rubbed at his eyes. "When this is over, I will have repaid you for saving my life."

Every moment that passed, every evasion, every cryptic change of the subject only heightened my wariness. I shifted my weight until I was on my feet. I didn't want to look defensive, but I also wasn't willing to play this game sitting down.

"I was already in a life debt. You rescued me—"

"Please," he said. He reached for me and my breath caught on his nearness. I felt as though he were coming in for an embrace before his hand stretched beyond me, snatching the poppet from the table. He slipped a finger into the band of my sweats, sending a jolt of electricity through me as he pulled me closer in order to force the poppet into my pocket. His gaze burned into mine as he said, "You deserve to know."

No air remained in my lungs as I asked, "Know what?"

He ran his fingers halfway through his hair, stopping at his crown in frustration. "Why everyone is willing to follow you into battle, Marlow. Why Fauna showed up. Why everyone is so giddy about your fae blood in this cycle. Why people treat you the way they do. You deserve to know why you're a key player in this war."

"Because I'm—"

Silas grabbed for me before I could complete my thought. I tried to jerk away, but he maintained his hold as my apartment disappeared. We were no longer inside. The time changed. The very *air* changed as I drank in humidity. My skin prickled with sweat as Silas and I slammed onto concrete. Once again, he kept me from falling over as my eyes widened. I spun uncertainly as I drank in the skyscrapers, the luxury vehicles, the tropical plants. The signs were in English, but as the distant electronic advertisement swirled, the messaging changed into Spanish. The air was too still for a breeze, but I could taste the roast beef of empanadas in the air, the spices hot on my tongue.

"We're in Argentina," I breathed.

"Watch." He nodded, jerking his chin toward a girl with muddy-brown hair at a bus stop.

I practically tripped backwards when she turned. It was me. I was looking at myself. Her forehead glowed with a subtle sunburn. She adjusted the bag on her shoulder and stepped out of the shade just long enough to see if the bus was on its way, then tucked herself beneath the protective awning once more.

"No one can see you," he said. "We're in your memories. We're in…an unveiled version of your memories."

"That's Taylor," I said, ignoring him. I'd never forget the chunky Louis Vuitton boots that had made her nearly my height. Except Taylor had been alone that day. I didn't recognize the woman with long black hair who accompanied her. She kept a hand on Taylor's lower back, guiding her to the bus stop. I gaped at the disturbingly beautiful stranger, noting the arch of her ears, the enormity of her irises, and the waifish way in which she seemed to step without the hindrance of gravity. The woman planted herself firmly in our path, then leaned in to whisper in Taylor's ear.

"I remember this day. I remember all of this. We were alone," I said.

"You were, and you weren't," he said. "Taylor doesn't know the woman is there, either. Taylor can't see the fae influencing her. Most humans have no cognizance of the guides who steer them in the mortal realm."

The woman pulled away after whispering. She pointed

to my hand and waited for Taylor's face to light in interest at the sight of my sun and moon tattoos. She watched encouragingly as Taylor introduced herself.

"She invited me to her villa in Brazil. She introduced me to..." I looked up at the angel, stopping myself before mentioning my life in sex work. It seemed like it might not be the kind of thing I'd want to speak with an angel about. "You can let me go," I said, jerking my hand slightly. The sticky, tropical climate had created a sweat-slick discomfort where his palm firmly encircled my wrist.

"No," he said, "I can't."

I understood why in the next instant as the glass and steel of Buenos Aires melted into a swirl of Caribbean blue. The vortex of colors and temperatures and scents made my stomach roll as if I'd been stuck in a blender. We crashed onto the street and I tumbled into him. I struggled to make sense of my surroundings: crowded streets, tin roofs, steep hills, and the shocking turquoise stretch of the ocean just beyond the cliff. I looked for familiarity in the faces, but saw none. I looked for a road sign and spotted a weathered shop hand-painted in careful French.

"What are you doing to me? Where are we?"

"Not just where. *When.*"

"We're in...Haiti." I tried once more to step away from him.

"Two cycles ago. Look." He gestured through the crowd to a young woman in a blue dress with long, tightly woven braids. There was a golden undertone to her rich, dark skin. She laughed at something said by another—a friend, a sister, a companion. "That's you."

I looked up at him and squinted. He blocked the sun, and its rays created a golden halo around his head and shoulders as it backlit him. He was distinctly apologetic as he said, "It's 1914. One year before the American occupation."

I wasn't sure if I was struggling against the statement, or from my utter lack of understanding. The more I tried to fight him, the harder he gripped me.

350

"Do you know what happens when soldiers invade, Marlow? Do you know how military men have historically treated the women in the countries they colonize?"

"I didn't even know America invaded Haiti," I said honestly. I was too stunned to see this as real. This was a horrible, immersive nightmare. It was like stepping into a live-action movie rather than experiencing a past life, though I supposed I didn't know what that was supposed to feel like. I struggled as I watched her happy laugh. The sky, the sea, the energy were as blue and clear as the bright, beautiful sound of her joy—*my* joy. I caught a flash of white just beyond the alley and squinted after the shape. Logic told me I'd spied a stray cat, but visions of a sleek white animal scratched at my childhood memories. I wrenched my gaze away from the gaps between textured walls.

"What are you saying?" I asked, horror taking my attention away from the creature.

He forced me to look at her again. "That you were beautiful, Marlow. That U.S. Marines invaded Port-au-Prince and occupied Haiti from 1915 to 1934."

"I don't—"

The blender swallowed me whole.

There wasn't time for me to ask anything further before we slipped out of the island paradise into the biting teeth of winter. I squinted against the bright monochrome wash of snow and ice as I chafed my arms for warmth The twilight gloom had painted the streets, the buildings, the world with its bluish brush, making it difficult to distinguish one shape from the next, but there was something peculiar about the buildings. It was too dark for me to understand what I was seeing, but an enormous honeycomb structure loomed in the distance. There were unfamiliar scoops and curves to the roofs around me. I wished I could see more, but I couldn't fight the urge to bring my shoulders to my ears, huddling like a turtle into myself against the unbearable temperature.

I gripped myself tightly, fingers burning from the cold,

teeth chattering. Silas tried to put his arm around me and I jerked away.

"For warmth," he said.

"Stay away from me!" I stuttered, jaw clenched. I'd trusted him. I'd rescued him. In return, he was dragging me through incomprehensible terrors. The arctic air burned my throat and lungs going down. I hoped my eyes looked as dark as they felt. I didn't know why he was doing this to me, but I hated every second of it.

Quick as a cat, he reached out to snatch me. He muttered something under his breath that I couldn't discern as he pinned me to him. I attempted to skid out of his reach, but my muscles had already seized up from the sub-zero temperatures. I'd been in the snow with boys before. I knew their tricks. There was no warmth in body heat unless we were both naked beneath the sheets. I expected to be annoyed by his touch, and the well-intentioned reach of an unwanted arm. The moment he placed his hand on me, ice melted from my skin. Warm honey replaced my blood as my shivering stopped.

"Well," I said, "we sure as hell aren't in Haiti."

I'd meant for it to come out bitterly, but the warmth took the sting out of my words.

"Well observed," he said quietly. He began to walk forward, and I had little choice but to follow. As reluctant as I'd been to let him touch me, now I knew what frozen misery awaited me if he left my side. He led us to the top of a flight of stairs just before the stone steps led down into a what may as well have been a dungeon.

I had a guttural aversion to the stairs without understanding why. I shook my head so hard I made myself dizzy. "Don't make me go down there. I don't want to go in."

"We don't have to," he said. "You're about to come out."

A heavy door at the bottom of the stairs opened, and with it, a new color broke through the night. A warm crimson glow spread from the opening. A hooded figure cast a shadow as they cut through the reddish light. A moment later, the smell hit me.

Tobacco. Ammonia. Acrid, bitter, spicy...

I recognized the scent. I'd smelled it twice before. Once with friends on a backpacking trip through the mountains in Southeast Asia. A second time, in a client's home. He'd been a collector of rare antiquities and had a certain hyperfixation on *mysteries of the orient*, as he'd called them. I'd never seen such an extensive personal collection of things that belonged in a museum. He'd passed me a silk robe and lit a bowl.

I'd put on my best Maribelle smile and worked hard for the money that had lined my purse when I'd left.

"It's opium," I whispered. I looked up at Silas, but his eyes were still fixed on the figure. She shut the door before her and ascended the stairs. She was a full foot shorter than me, but I couldn't discern much more from the strange, purple-blue hour until she was right in front of me.

"We're in China," he said quietly. "It's 1850."

"And I'm..." I watched the figure brush past us in thickly lined robes. "I frequent opium dens?"

"You aren't a patron," he said.

My heart twisted and wrenched as I watched the shadow disappear down the road. I wasn't sure where she was going, but I doubted it was home. No one who worked in the dens went home to kiss their parents good morning. Women in dens were responsible for keeping customers comfortable, happy, and spending their money.

The bitter, tar-like smell lined my nostrils. I inhaled sharply to try to clear them to no avail. Watching the speck of gray disappear down the road, I asked, "Why are you showing me these? Why do they matter?"

"You'll see in a moment."

Something in the weight of his words put a heaviness in my gut. My brows puckered, lips parting in a question when I felt the world tip. It was like falling backward only to realize there was no ground to catch me as I spun and spun and spun.

Ice and blue and winter melted into a shadowed gloom that smelled of stale hearth and smoke.

No longer under the threat of arctic chill, I tore away. Silas was unable to catch me as I used the movement to break free of him. My knees hit a wooden floor, hands chafing as I slid through the dirt in a small candlelit room. I blinked through vibrant spots that blinded me as my eyes struggled to adjust from the violet hour to the nearly pitch-black darkness of the windowless space.

A sound drew my attention before I was able to discern much more. It was the quiet snap as the busks of a corset were unhooked. I struggled to understand the pale hands, the long, golden hair, the pink, downturned lips of the silent, frowning maiden. It was as if I'd stumbled into a classical painting. The room was too cold to be undressing. She was too sad to be painted. I got to my feet just as she reclined on the low bed.

I didn't see the second presence until then.

A man stepped out from where he'd lounged in the shadows. He may have been her father, or grandfather, for the age that gapped between them. The barest yellow hint of a smile cut through the gloom as he slipped out of his overcoat. The boards creaked beneath the weight as he approached the bed.

"Get me out of here," I said, panic and urgency lacing each word. I trusted my gut this time. I had to leave, *now.*

"Marlow—"

"Get me out of here!"

He grabbed me and jerked me from the horrid painting, but I was not met with relief. I had not escaped the blond, youthful woman. She'd merely relocated. No longer was she in the dark on a bed, but had the fuller, youthful roundness of someone not quite twenty. She had a milkmaid quality, from the blush on her cheeks to the country simplicity of her layered aprons and skirts. A brisk fall breeze wasn't the only thing sending a chill through me as I searched for understanding. I struggled to soak in the thatched roofs, the wooden homes, the clucking chickens, the rolling hills. Someone called out in a language I didn't understand. It may have been vaguely German, but I spoke a smattering of German, and nothing registered as quite right.

"Spot the fae," Silas said softly.

My neck ached as I continued shaking my head. I was pretty sure I hadn't stopped the dizzying movement since looking down the stairs to the opium den. I didn't want to play this game. I grabbed on to his arm and yanked it, hoping he'd jolt me somewhere else.

"*Look*," he pushed. I winced, scarcely able to peek through my squinting eyes as I watched a handsomely dressed older woman assess the milkmaid from across the way. At her side was someone who, compared to the chaste fabrics of the day, may as well have been naked.

I saw her, and I hated it.

"What is she?" I asked, watching the older woman and the willowy entity that accompanied her.

"It doesn't matter," Silas sighed. "She's the entity following your friend in Argentina. She might as well be Fauna, for all intents and purposes. She's another god or demon or fae about to lead a madame—a human woman who has no clue what role either of you play in this game—to your doorstep so they might steer your path."

"Steer my path toward..." I flashed to the dissociative sorrow on the milkmaid's face. "Silas, what the fuck. What the *fuck*! Are you telling me that I've been a goddamn whore in all of my cycles? Is this why I'm here? Fuck you. Fuck you for doing this to me. Get me the fuck out of here." I ripped myself free of his grasp despite knowing I needed his help. I tore for the woods near the house, dry leaves crunching underfoot. I needed to put as much space between myself and the milkmaid and whatever fate awaited her as I could. Rough oaks and the browns and reds of brambles promised shelter, calling to me as I rushed from the village. I'd scarcely rounded the house when I stopped short in front of the unmistakable form of a perfectly still arctic fox. The ice-white creature was crisply outlined in autumnal orange, stark and unmistakable.

It didn't look at me, for I was not there. It had eyes only for the milkmaid.

The statuesque creature's head dipped slowly, as it looked down at its paws. Inky fear punctured me, filling me with sloshy black horror. First my heart submerged in the chilly waters within, then my lungs. I couldn't breathe. I couldn't move. I could only stare at the fox.

Brittle leaves broke underfoot as Silas approached. He stopped at my side, joining me as we looked into the past.

"What is this?" I whispered. I swallowed, struggling for volume. "What the hell is this? Are you trying to say Caliban did this?"

He extended a hand to touch my arm, then thought better of it, easing away as if I were little more than a skittish animal. His hand remained extended, though he did not touch me.

The darkness weighed down my feet, my fingers, my very soul. I could scarcely shake my head. "No. I don't want to go anywhere with you. Not until you tell me what the hell you're doing. Why would you show me this? Why would you show me this…?" By the second repetition, my demand caught in my throat.

"He didn't do this," Silas said.

"He's here," I choked. "He was there in Haiti. He was—"

"You knew as much, right? You've known he's been with you for endless cycles."

I bristled. I couldn't sort friend from foe. The prickly anger provided something I could latch onto. I grabbed the fury and pulled myself out of the slippery horror. My gaze darted between the fox and the angel. I gritted my teeth and asked, "Then what? He stood by and watched?"

"Marlow," he said sadly. "Fae have been pushing you—not other humans, not demons, not everyone, not just some poor girl, but *you*—toward this path in every cycle. Whenever a pantheon identified the Prince's human, it was only a matter of time before some fae, demigod, or spirit arrived to flex their persuasion. In some cycles, you were resistant. In one, you were a practicing witch. Your clairsentience was far too strong to fall for another fae's influence. In fact, the Prince was able to have this conversation with you himself in that life cycle, and you were informed enough to decide it wasn't something you wanted."

I hadn't even realized I was crying. Anger and confusion were a sickening cocktail as they boiled through me, abandoning my eyes and cutting hot lines over each cheek.

"In this cycle, in the one where you're called Marlow, where you write, where you live in your modern, flashy apartment and run with packs of gods," Silas said sadly, "everything has happened so fast. You scarcely had time to recognize the world behind the veil as a reality before you were thrust into it. This time, you have fae blood. While Taylor may have had someone else guiding her to you, Fauna was able to show up in a very prominent way—a way in which the pantheons never have before. And they care because..."

"Because I'm the Prince's human?"

"Gods have loved and lived with humans since the first sunrise. No other pantheon has cared to intervene. None of the Orisha stepped in to watch out for Zeus's lovers. There are no Shinto deities looking out for women godspoused to Loki. You know why this is different."

"I don't."

Silas looked away. He took a few calming breaths, but when he spoke again, he could barely hold my eyes. "Come on, Marlow. You know this lore. I've seen it in your memories. You've read it. You've heard it. You grew up in the church. You have to understand why fae would flock toward forcing the Prince's human—the *demon* Prince—toward sex work, cycle after cycle. Especially now, Marlow. Now that you're collecting gods. You're leading a rebellion. You're planning the toppling of kingdoms."

"No." Heat spread through my cheeks.

"Who is Fauna, Marlow? Why did she know where to

find Fenrir? How was she able to free him? Who is she, *really*, and why would that goddess need *the Prince's human*?"

"No!"

"Tell me you understand what role you play as a pawn. Tell me you understand why everyone reacts the way they do when they learn who you are. Why Heaven has sent agents to intercept you. Why they are involving your mother, and trying to lure you out by attacking close to the heart."

Rage burned through me. My skin was on fire, I could barely see through the blur of furious tears that clouded my vision as I stared defiantly at Silas's steady, pitying gaze. I looked into the golden halos within his eyes and hated that he was an angel. I hated that he was a servant of Heaven, that I'd grown up in the church, that I'd been raised under the watchful eye of baby Jesus and the Virgin Mary and...

Every thought emptied from my head, draining from my ears and dribbling onto the ground. I went perfectly still, eyes unfocused as the trees around the medieval village rustled in the breeze. Leaf-shaped shadows dappled Silas and I as we remained beneath the shade of the forest rimming the unsuspecting community. I looked over my shoulder, searching for something I knew I'd find, even in a small town.

The only stone building in town had an iron cross anchored to the steeple above its door. And just beyond its walls sat the Prince of Hell and his human.

I was a tin can as Baal's mysterious amusement clanged through me.

I owe you gratitude, both for what you've done, and for what's to come.

He'd known who Fauna was, and who they all expected me to become.

I understood her true name in that moment, and it broke my heart.

"Because," I said, voice so disconnected that it felt like it came from someone else entirely. "Jesus was born from a virgin. The lore says the antichrist will be born of a whore."

Chapter Thirty-Five

W HY DID YOU SHOW ME THIS?" THE QUESTION SOUNDED
every bit as hollow as I felt. We remained amidst the
trees.

"I just told you—"

"No," I stopped him. There was a clarity to my thoughts
and feelings that cut through everything that had overwhelmed
me moments before. "Why did *you* show me? It wasn't
Fauna, it wasn't Caliban, it wasn't Azrames. Everyone knows.
Heaven knows. And *you* were the one who told me. *Why*?"

Silas tilted his head back and looked through the ember-
colored canopy at the spots of blue. Bars of light filtered
through the leaves, kissing him with their golden warmth. He
pulled in another in a long line of slow, deep breaths. "Angels
and valkyrie have a lot in common," he said. "We know we
were made to blindly serve our creator. We answer every call
to battle and we facilitate wills that are not our own, because
our will *is* the will of another. If an angel starts to think differently, they're cast out—fallen. A defector. Estrid lives among
the Vanir as a defector from the Aesir. But at least we understand the roles we play, and we knew the consequences of
abandoning the paths set out for us. Humans are meant to
have free will."

"It's sort of our thing," I said bitterly.

"Famously so," he agreed with dry humorlessness. He met my eyes and held them. "And the gods have their fun. They push, they manipulate, they draw their power from their worshippers, they bless, they curse, but they stay in their lane."

"And what lane is that?"

"The gods keep to their people."

My eyes twitched as they narrowed into slits. "Everyone plays with their own toys?"

"More or less," he said. "Except all gods have their toys, and one—a popular kid, a bully, one with more power than he knows what to do with—is playing with a bomb. And everyone on the playground pokes and prods to see if they can get the bomb to blow up in that god's face. Because if it does…"

"Then king of the playground is up for grabs," I finished for him.

He extended his hand once more. "I was commanded to offer to bind myself to you. It would have done little more than press pause once more. You and your role as the bomb would be off the table for yet another cycle. I'd have kept you safe, of course, not because I cared about you, but because the longer you stayed on this earth under Heaven's care, the more time we'd buy to delay the explosion."

"And if Heaven can't keep me from giving birth to hellspawn?"

"Then we kill you."

"Thanks." My stomach roiled. Acid burned my throat.

"Heaven can't let Hell have their champion. They fuck with your fate, just like every pantheon who can get their hands on you fucks with your free will."

"And Caliban just lets it happen." I wanted to lie down on the forest floor. I wanted to be left in this memory to die.

"Yes and no. He went on the sort of killing spree that ancients wrote ballads about. His hands are stained with the blood of gods and fae and men across the realms and throughout time. Accords were struck. Promises were made. The pantheons went on urging you to become a whore so that the two of you could usher in the end of the world. Some got away with it, if they were subtle. Others played with your fate knowing their lives were forfeit."

It was the least of my problems, but the word stung. I couldn't help the quiet ache as I whispered, "Don't call me a whore."

His eyes looked as wounded as I felt. "I didn't want to play any role in this war. I don't want to manipulate you. But when the order came down, I wasn't given a lot of options. You and I both know what happens in my kingdom to angels who express free will. And when Fauna arrived, it became perfectly clear how much higher the stakes were in this cycle. This was what she was born into the world to do."

"She saw her shot at fulfilling her destiny. I'm so fucking fragile and broken that all she had to do was trick me into thinking she cared about me."

"I went on a date with her once, you know."

My laugh was bitter. "I know. Let me guess: you were trying to persuade her *not* to end the world."

"My job has always been to keep the ship on course. I knew things were bad when Fauna arrived, but suddenly it wasn't just the three of us. You were fucking with the Phoenicians. You were plotting with the Greeks. You're barreling toward a prophecy without even realizing the role you play in this war. And that's not fair to you, to anyone."

The now-dry remnants of salty tears itched. I wiped at where the evidence of emotion stained my face, using the motion as an excuse to look away. My hand stayed on my face as I frowned into my palm. "But you don't care about me."

"I *didn't* care about you."

I looked up at him once more. The sun hit the gold of his eyes in a way that set them on fire. They were the brightest things in the woods. Silas extended his hand once more.

"And?" I asked. "We leave here, and then what? What do I do with this information?"

"Now that you know? You do whatever the hell you want."

"And Betty?"

He swallowed. His fingers flexed slightly as if to withdraw his offer to take me away from the memories, but he forced his hands open once more. "Heaven is not your ally, even if I am. Our orders are to end you and your Prince. This is the time to take our shot. They're going to be coming for anyone you care about, starting with taking out the most powerful witch on your side who may have posed a problem. No better time to strike than while her demon was unavailable to help."

I sucked in a breath so fast I went lightheaded.

He didn't wait for my consent this time as he grabbed my hand. "Let's go."

Chapter Thirty-Six

I KNEW WHERE WE WERE THE SECOND I HIT THE CEMENT. I FELL to my side, skidding across the hot, dirty pavement on my arm before Silas could catch me. I looked up from my dizzying place on the ground and watched a car roll by just beyond the alley. The aged brick, the narrow walking paths, the rusted back-alley doors told me we were in the arts district. I knew that if I walked out onto the sidewalk and turned to the building's front, I'd find the aged wooden door and a window with the words *Daily Devils* neatly printed across the front. I knew there'd be brown, green, and blue glass bottles containing muted liquids, oils, powders, leaves, and herbs. I knew a kindly woman who worked with demons, advocated for women, had freed a selkie, and who loved chocolate-covered strawberries would be inside.

"Are the angels—"

"I wouldn't have brought you here unless I knew it was safe. No one from Heaven is here. Not anymore."

Silas's hands were balled into fists. Tendons and veins stood out prominently as they protruded from his arms and over the tops of his hands. His eyes were squeezed shut, face turned away from the gut-wrenching sound that wafted through the rusty door. The high, grieving wail could only belong to one person.

I winced against the pain of my impact, nose wrinkled at the faint city smells of urine and refuse as I planted my hands on the baking ground. I slowly got to my feet and moved toward the door as if pulled forward in a nightmare. Shrill ringing stuffed itself into my ears. The edges of my vision went fuzzy as I felt my way forward. My hands wrapped around the metallic handle, thumb pressing into the latch. I didn't have room for surprise as it opened easily. It didn't even squeak as I stepped into the dark room. My eyes struggled to adjust from the bright afternoon sun to the dim back room. I stumbled step after step, bumping into wall, then a desk. I blinked past the sooty blotches that dotted my vision and focused on the desk with its candles, sigils, and offerings. I'd seen this altar in the back room of the shop once before.

I followed the jagged, horrible cry.

My mouth was sticky and dry. I tried to swallow but couldn't. I moved with robotic, disconnected listlessness as my palm wrapped around another handle—the final handle. Betty's shop would be on the other side. Candles, books, crystals, and incense would meet me. There would be thick, bundled curtains. A cabinet of curiosities would serve as the counter.

Fauna would be there.

I'd recognized the anguish the moment I'd slammed into the pavement. Her pain forced me to twist the knob, to push open the door, to put one foot in front of the other. She'd held me as I'd suffered. She'd gone to Hell with me and back, quite literally. I had to find her. I had to look her in the eye and hear the truth for myself.

But when I opened the door...

The shop was a galaxy of sticky, confusing glitter. I gagged on the scent of frankincense, so overpowering I could no longer breathe through my nose. Gold glinted off the glass, dripped from the curtains, pooled on the floor. I struggled to look at any one thing as gem-like puddle after starlit drop forced my eyes to bounce from one place to the next.

The moment her sobs resumed, I spotted her.

Fauna and Caliban were on the floor. Fauna was kneeling over Betty, one arm under her back to support her. Caliban had her head in his lap, but there was nothing calming about his posture. Hands dripping with golden, shimmering liquid, he held her head firmly, eyes closed, jaw clenched as his lips moved, speaking to no one.

Azrames saw me before I saw him.

The metallic glitter splattered across his monochrome features was the most color I'd ever seen on him. My breath caught as I spotted the glinting, spiked ball of a meteor hammer in his hand, chain clenched tightly in his fist. I didn't know where he'd gotten it, but then again, I didn't know much of demons, or much of anything. I took a half step backward before I realized he wasn't looking at me. He snarled, fangs bared as he lifted his fist.

"Move, Marlow!" he growled.

It took me less than a second to understand Silas was behind me. I lifted my hands. "Az, wait."

"*Move,* or make the Prince clean up your blood next," he snarled.

Those were the magic words. Everything happened at once. Caliban was between Azrames and I before I could blink. Fauna's crying stopped as she called out in panic, begging Caliban to return. Her hysterics were hoarse as she commanded Azrames to stand down. I didn't understand her urgency. I knew only confusion, alarm, metallic gleaming, and the sickening scent of... I recognized the scent. It was similar to the thieves' oil and myrrh smell every time Silas entered the room.

Angels.

I looked at the shop with new, wide eyes, understanding the gold at long last. This was angel blood.

"I can help," came Silas's voice from behind me.

"Your death is the only help I need," came Azrames's hateful reply.

When Caliban ordered Azrames's halt, I witnessed a fraught battle between mind and body. His hands lowered. His weapon clattered to the ground. Loathing for Silas, for Caliban, for the command, for the world pulled his lip up in a venomous snarl, but it was with god-like power that Caliban commanded his subject. Azrames could not disobey.

"He's right," Caliban said hurriedly, eyes fixed on Az. "His people committed this violence. The angel has the power to undo what his kind attempted. If you let your logic outweigh your rage, you'll let him try."

"He won't get anywhere near her."

"Az!" Fauna's desperate, furious word came from the floor. I realized she was not smeared in gold, but in red. Her crimson-soaked dress clung to her, face pale, teeth sharp with her glare as she snapped at him. I'd never heard such malevolence in her voice before now as she bit, "This isn't just the end of her cycle. They came to smite her. If you are the reason Betty doesn't make it, Azrames, then you are fucking dead to me. If you don't let him help, I will *never* speak to you again."

Whatever hold Caliban had over Azrames ended. I saw it the moment his body relaxed as if released from an invisible fist. I remained in a shocked state of speechlessness. I couldn't watch the horror unfold on the ground. I couldn't focus on anything. It was all too much.

"I healed her physical wounds," came Caliban's voice at my side. I knew I should look at him but couldn't bring myself to meet his eyes. "There's nothing paramedics or an ambulance could fix that I haven't already knit together. I can work with the body, but if it's an angel who ended the soul..."

Azrames said, "She is warded against this. No angel should have been able to cross her threshold. Her spellwork is unbreachable. She—"

"Heaven lost two just to break her protective barriers," Caliban said. "Bringing down the only witch on your side who might pose a threat was important enough that they were willing to sacrifice however many it took."

Azrames looked away from his Prince. His eyes darkened as he stared into the depths of me. "Why are you here?"

I knew from the bitterness in his voice that he wasn't asking about me alone.

Caliban rested a hand gently on my arm and stepped to block Azrames from my line of sight. Gold shimmered on his cheek, on the side of his face. The reek of frankincense smothered his forest-fresh scent. His silver eyes softened as he reiterated, "Why *are* you here?"

I looked at his pale hand on my shoulder, then up at his face once more. I stepped away, breaking his hold on me. His expression changed in an instant. Gentleness became warning.

Fauna's cry of relief cut through our standoff. With a firm yank, Silas dislodged the curtains from the ceiling, bringing snowy bits of plaster down with him as he bundled up the thick velvet to create a pillow for Betty's head. Her chest rose and fell on its own as Fauna held her. I remained silent, unsure of what to say, what to do.

My world had changed.

Reality had shifted the moment I'd understood Caliban was real. Silas and Fauna had broken down all of the protective walls I'd built in my mind to convince myself that he'd been a coping mechanism, a trauma response. I'd opened wide and swallowed the supernatural whole, accepting gods and fae and demons as I'd trusted Fauna to lead our dance. She and I wanted the same things, if for different reasons. We had wanted Caliban free. We had wanted our friends back. We wanted...

It had all been a lie.

I wanted to cry at the sight of Fauna's now-smiling face. Her smattered freckles folded into the dimples on her cheeks. Tear-soaked joy beamed through her as bright as the glistening blood around her. She and Betty were on the ground of a battlefield, and Betty had survived. I'd thought Fauna and I were on the same team. I'd believed we loved each other.

I looked from her to Caliban and took another step backward.

"Love?" he asked, voice catching with true concern.

Free from his soul-saving endeavor, Silas took a few careful steps to position himself beside me. Caliban's gaze flickered from the angel to me. Behind him, Azrames's eyes stayed on Silas.

"He told me," I said simply.

I watched as concern transitioned into confusion, then worry, then fear. The column of Caliban's throat worked. His eyes flared with almost imperceptible alarm, the sort of dread I knew deep in my gut that anyone else might miss, as he fixed his stare on Silas.

I looked at Caliban. "You knew who Fauna was when you met her."

He stared back. He didn't disrespect me by giving me some bullshit about the Phoenician realms or listening walls. He could have told me Fauna's true name in the cave. He'd chosen not to.

Caliban looked away from me. For now, he had eyes only for the angel. "What did you do." His tone was flat. Even in the pandemonium-laden freefall of the moment, I knew the question wasn't *What?* but *How could you?*

"She deserved to know," Silas replied, voice terse.

Caliban took a step forward. When I took a half step back, placing my body partly behind Silas's, I saw the pain on his face, then in his entire posture. "I've never kept anything from her," Caliban replied. Then to me, he said, "I've told you many times. I'd tell you again. I've spent lifetimes protecting you, Love. I've slaughtered thousands for you. I risked my kingdom to keep you safe in this cycle as I have in the last and will again in the next."

No. Don't put this on me. Not now.

Darkness comforted me as my eyelids fluttered shut. I

blocked out the room, the slaughter, the pain. I couldn't carry the weight of his emotions. Not until I understood my own.

"And what?" Caliban asked. I looked up at him as he worked through a controlled smothering of his anger. His eyes flitted from Silas to me only once, boring into me as he said, "Now you trust the angel over me?"

I couldn't help the truth of the words that came out next. "Not you, Caliban. But...right now? Yes. He's been more honest with me than any of you."

I looked at Fauna, whose smile faltered. Her eyes left Betty and met mine. Her face folded into an unrecognizable emotion. I returned my gaze to Caliban, though I was acutely aware of how Fauna carefully rested Betty's sleeping form on the ground before moving to stand beside Azrames.

"Every one of you knew. Caliban, maybe you would have told me. But, Fauna..." I fixed my sights on her once more. "I've stood beside you as you've wielded *the Prince's human* time after time to further your cause. You knew what you were telling everyone. You knew precisely what you were leveraging. And most importantly: you knew I didn't understand what you were actually saying, because I had no idea who you were."

"Mar..." Her delicate fingers lifted toward me, then folded over her heart. For once, there was no witty sarcasm, no irreverent playfulness. She was blood-soaked and broken.

"I know your name."

The color drained from her face.

"Angrboda." I said the name, voice laced with venom. "The bringer of chaos and destruction."

The room remained silent. The bloodied reek of slain angels choked me as I struggled to look her in the eye.

"There's only one sentence about you in the Poetic Edda. Some lore said you were married to Loki. Some say you had children with him—but you gotta fuck a centaur for the plot sometimes, isn't that what you said? All of the stories underscore your one and only purpose."

Her words were strangled. "That's not—"

I couldn't breathe. "You aren't denying it. That's how you knew where Fenrir was. That's how you were able to set him free. Some lore says you're his mother, but the other stories got it correct, didn't they? You were his *keeper* until the end times."

"I swear, you don't know what you think you know. Please, listen to me!"

I neither saw nor heard her through the blinding rage. "You were designed for Ragnarök. Your *one* line. That's why you exist, right? To bring about the end of the world. And here I am, with Nordic blood. Lucky you. At long last, Fauna found her golden ticket, a use for her apocalypse dog, a conduit for her motherfucking chaos."

Tears flowed freely as she pleaded with me. "Marlow—"

"No!" My ears rang. My eyes stung. My cheeks were hot from the pain. "You know how hard it is to make a *whore* feel used? Congratulations. You used me. I thought you loved me. I thought we…"

Azrames was in no mood for pity. Clearly, he didn't give a shit about Fauna's true name or her role in the end of the world. He'd undoubtedly read the Poetic Edda and the theories surrounding his beloved. He loved her for being wild and free, and probably loved her all the more for being the goddess destined to usher in the end of the world.

Azrames had calmed now that Betty was safe. In place of his anger and vitriol was something blank and purposefully expressionless. Maybe he'd cared about me. Maybe that much was real. But he'd known precisely who she was, and what she was doing.

They'd made me a victim without giving me a choice.

Venom remained in his throat as he scoffed. "So, what, you stand with Heaven now?"

I looked into his dark eyes and saw no trace of the friendliness I'd come to know and love. He was drenched in the gilded blood of those who'd tried to slaughter Betty, not only in this realm, but at her core. Of everyone in the room, his emotions were the only ones I understood. He had every right to feel betrayed by me. Azrames had never lied to me. He'd loved Betty. He'd fought for her, and for me.

"No," I said firmly, looking solely at him. "I will never stand with Heaven. I am on your side now and forever, Az. But Silas isn't on Heaven's side, either." The angel hadn't said so, but I saw no other outcome. He couldn't share my history, Heaven's role, how they shuffled us as pawns, and how he'd chosen to tell me anyway, without facing consequences. "Azrames, believe me when I tell you that your enemies are my enemies. But…"

"But," he repeated, unyielding.

"But my enemies may be more numerous than yours," I said quietly. "At least you know Heaven is your foe. I thought Fauna was my friend."

The way her fingers clutched at her fabric, one might have thought I'd stabbed her. Her lips remained parted in silent pain.

"I'm beginning to wonder if I've ever truly had an ally."

Caliban remained statue still, carved from the very marble he resembled. I couldn't bear more than a glance at him before my eyes fell to my shoes. He'd loved me in every lifetime. But he'd hurt me, and I had no idea how to move forward. I grappled with timelines, forcing myself to remember that I'd sent him away long before he'd met Fauna or had any opportunity to intervene in the bond she and I had already formed.

But he'd had so many opportunities to tell me in the Canaanite pantheon, and he'd remained silent.

"And Silas is your ally?" Azrames demanded. His question sounded every bit as betrayed as I felt.

"I don't know." My voice dropped. So much of my fury evaporated upon seeing Caliban's heartbroken face. I closed my eyes and said, "I know that Betty is breathing right now, soul safely in her body because he helped. I know that he told me the truth and showed me my memories when no one else had. I know that he's informed me of Heaven's plans even at the expense of his own kingdom. And"—I looked up at Silas, waiting for him to look over his shoulder at me—"I know he'll come with me when I move to protect my friends."

"Kirby and Nia," Fauna choked out. "You don't think Heaven…"

"They will," Silas said definitively. "They started with Betty because she was the strongest. She had more at her defense than anyone else. But if they think they have leverage with Marlow's found family, then no one is safe."

"Could they already be there?" Caliban asked, still looking at Silas.

Silas shook his head. "I haven't heard anything from Heaven. I assume it's because you've slaughtered every messenger. Did anyone escape?"

Caliban moved his head once. No. There had been no survivors.

"I'll be cut off from Heaven the moment they know," Silas said to Caliban.

Fauna pushed him from behind. Caliban was a pillar, unmoving. His jaw clenched, eyes flashing slightly, though only I could see.

Her voice bubbled in an angry cry from behind him. "Do something," she begged, anger burning redder than any other emotion. "She's going to leave with him! You see it!"

I had no rebuttal, because she was right. I was going to leave with Silas. And Caliban knew it. I recognized it in his face, in the way he held his shoulders, in the movement of his knuckles as he flexed and unflexed his fingers at his side.

Fauna's voice kicked up into a distressed octave as she pleaded, "You can't let her go. You can't let your obsession with free will get in the way of keeping her from walking into a bear trap!"

Caliban closed his eyes. A tendon in his neck flexed as he kept his voice controlled. "She's had every right to turn away from me in any cycle she chooses, including this one. She always has the choice."

Fauna scrambled to her feet. She tore through the air, fist wound with the full intention of punching Caliban, had Azrames not dashed between them to catch her wrist. She struggled toward the Prince of Hell as she barked, "But this isn't other cycles, and you know it. This is *the* cycle!"

I wasn't sure what reaction was acceptable for one in my position, but I felt only an empty and bottomless sorrow. Fauna continued talking about me as if I wasn't there. She confirmed everything I'd feared, everything I'd refused to accept. I was a pawn she, like many fae from countless pantheons before her, had shuffled. She saw opportunity slipping away, and pounded her fists against it.

She wrestled against Azrames, twisting to me just enough to gasp, "Marlow, I love you. I meant what I said. I was ready to betray Heaven and Hell to bind with you! I would have done anything for you. I—"

"You didn't love me," I said, eyes on the floor. "You loved what I represented."

I'd been brokenhearted before. I'd felt pain, and rejection, and loss. I'd been wounded by death and abuse and neglect. Whatever protective shell encased my heart had splintered. Nothing poured in. Instead, whatever I'd held leaked out. Trust, love, intimacy, moments, memories hissed into the space between us as a newly fallen angel and I positioned ourselves against two demons and a nymph.

"I have to go," I said.

Fauna lurched toward me. Azrames kept his hold at first, but released her at her rallying cry, her free fist coming down against his forearm, body twisting from his grasp. I didn't even see her move as she covered the space between us. She gripped my shoulders, blood and gold joining the copper and silver of her hair and freckles. The whites of her eyes were too wide as she searched mine. "Please, look at me."

Tears spilled freely, but silently. I pulled in a ragged breath.

She attempted to pull me into a hug, but I pushed back. My forearms created leverage between us before she closed the gap. I pushed against her soft form, forcing her away from me.

"Mar," she begged. "You have to hear me: I *love* you."

"I thought you did," I said through the watery cloud that blurred my vision. "I wanted to believe you, because I loved you."

"No, please—"

I shoved away from her. This time when she lurched for me, it was Silas who stopped her.

"The thing is, Fauna," I said, voice thick with emotion, "if you had told me...if *any* of you had told me...it would have been hard to hear. I would have made a scene, or cried, or been human with my reaction. But I would have been glad to hear it from you. I would have made my decision. I would have taken the metaphorical pills, no matter how difficult they were to swallow, and I would have chosen you. But no. You didn't just manipulate me, or exploit me. You betrayed me."

"Mar..." Fauna's voice was fragmented, clawing against her breaths, against rejection, against whatever she knew I'd say next. She grabbed Silas's arm in an attempt to push past him, but he held firm.

"I would have chosen you," I said first to Fauna, then to Caliban.

It wasn't shame on Caliban's face, though the expression was one I couldn't quite place. It was as if, despite the wounds it caused him, he'd expected this. His shoulders straightened.

"Fauna." Caliban said her name quietly. "You have to let her go."

"No!" she screamed. A new ruby rage flooded her as she attempted to claw past Silas. I flinched at her advance, but it was out of emotion rather than fear. She likened herself to many deceptive things—nymph, skosgrå, forest deity—and perhaps some of those things were true. There wasn't much about her in the Edda beyond the throwaway sentence that led to my undoing. And if she was what she claimed, there were no plants, no wildlife, no wood or thicket or creature here for her to summon at her behest. She had no power here beyond what her pain did to my heart.

Caliban moved past them both. I wasn't sure if Silas allowed it, or knew he couldn't stop it. He took several forceful steps toward Azrames, risking his own exposed throat at the expense of returning Fauna to him while she struggled to get to me. I couldn't watch them. I couldn't expend what remained of my energy on them. My focus blurred, unable to look at the ones I'd loved so fiercely. My gaze drifted to the pool of glittering angel blood as it crept toward my shoes. I hadn't even realized Caliban had crossed the room to me when my hands were suddenly swept up in his.

"Love…"

"Betty's okay?"

He nodded. "She'll be okay."

Lead weighed down my eyelids, but it didn't stop the tears from escaping, one after the other. "Then I have to go. Nia…Kirby…"

"There's something I need you to know," he said. It took me a moment to accept the bid for attention. When I obliged, his face was collected. "Be angry. I honor it. If you tell me that you renounce me in this cycle and every cycle moving forward, I will go on loving you. If you tell me to leave you, I'll continue to protect your friends, and everyone around you. If you force me not to be with you, I'll pave a path for your employers, your family, your road in every life moving forward. You can send me away, Love, but in ten centuries, my heart will still belong to you."

My knees buckled.

He pulled me against him, holding my head to his chest. "You aren't the only victim of this prophecy," he murmured into my hair. I nearly cried out when he released me. The absence rushed between us like icy water as he stepped away.

Caliban looked at Silas, who had returned to my side.

375

"I understand that I'm taking her life as much as I'm saving it," said Silas.

"I'll take it off your tab," came Caliban's dry, broken response.

Behind them, Fauna had slumped into Azrames.

"I didn't do this, Azrames," Silas said to the still-feral demon, Az's pewter eyes etched with hate.

Azrames turned away, burying his face in Fauna's russet hair.

"You'll keep her safe?" Caliban asked, looking at Silas. And while some part of me wanted to be angry, wanted to make a comment about agency, about keeping myself safe, about my soul and my autonomy, I understood that this was bigger than my human life.

"I'll die trying," Silas promised.

Because I didn't know what to say, I could only voice the words that clanged through the tin husk of my heart. With hushed brokenness, I looked at Caliban and said, "I love you."

Mercury-colored tears lined his eyes as he replied, "I've always loved you."

Chapter Thirty-Seven

"P ICK UP, PICK UP, PICK UP," I MUTTERED INTO THE COMPUTER screen. My fingers tapped restlessly on the coffee table of my apartment. I had no phone, as I'd fallen into a pattern of abandoning every smartphone to the gutters or grassy plains of realms to which I didn't belong. I'd tried Kirby four times, but they hadn't answered. On my third call video call to Nia, relief flooded me as the chime of confirmation pinged and her face flooded the screen.

"Marlow!" she gasped in surprise. I looked up at her chin as she moved quickly down whatever fluorescent-lit corridor illuminated her path. Her screen was all whites and grays apart from the bits of her neck and hair. I heard the bar-click of a double door before daylight sun hit her face. "You'd better be dying."

I blinked at her in open-mouthed dismay. "Are you okay?"

"I'm in a meeting! I have ten minutes left in my workday. Aren't you supposed to be going on some grand escape or getaway or something with your mysterious friend?"

She might as well have hit the mute button. I was rendered speechless.

"Mar!" Nia demanded. "My boss is going to have questions, and I'm sure I won't have a good answer. I came into work hungover and am leaving a meeting early because my phone wouldn't stop going off."

I attempted to summon saliva but failed. I looked up to Silas, who must have understood my nonverbal plea, as he quietly fetched a cup and filled it with water from my kitchen sink. He'd barely set it down before I asked, "Why are you hungover?"

She smacked her lips. "Did you not have as many piña coladas as the rest of us last night? You lucky bitch. Now, how long are you going to be gone, and why couldn't you wait twenty minutes for me to finish work before you told me." Her tone was more accusation than question.

I didn't know where to start piecing together the nonsensical information, but supposed it didn't matter. The baffling nonexistence of time would have to go high up on the shelf above the reality of estries, the activity of angels and demons, the ruling gods, and the bits and pieces of some Christian folklore that had damned me to be little more than a marionette strung by puppeteers throughout the centuries.

"Nia, I need you to listen to me carefully."

Any sisterly irritation she'd possessed evaporated. She leveled the camera as she looked into my eyes through the screen. "Tell me."

I took a steadying breath. It had been so long since I'd been at their barbeque. I had no idea what day it was supposed to be, or what either of them should have been doing. I could have sworn we'd met on a Sunday, watched the news, eaten shish kebabs, gotten drunk on piña coladas, and watched my doxxing over national news on the Lord's day, but I couldn't be sure. If today were Monday, then Kirby would be at work. Their schedule was unpredictable, as it fluctuated with the veterinary hospital. "I need you to get Kirby to your house as soon as possible. Whatever it takes. Create an emergency. Lie. But get home, get them there, and I'll meet you."

I didn't know what was common of friends, as I'd never truly had close ones before them. I also wasn't sure what was expected of siblings, though I'd seen Nia interact with her brothers. Whatever we had between us, it was better. It was purer. It was chosen.

Nia didn't hesitate for a moment.

"It'll take me three minutes to get to my car, and fifteen minutes to get home—twenty depending on traffic. If they're in surgery, I'll call the front office and fake a death in their family."

I wanted to cry, but couldn't spare the time. "And Darius?"

"Working from home today," Nia said. Her breath quickened, afternoon light filtering into the camera lens from behind her and making it difficult for me to see her face. "Marlow, are you safe?"

I looked up at Silas, then back at Nia. "Honestly, I don't know. But I'm not the primary target right now." I couldn't settle between Silas's creased, worried face and Nia's. I thought of Caliban's final words as I asked, "Nia, I know you're not religious. Will you do something for me, no questions asked?"

She made a disconcerted noise as she reached her car. It took a few fuzzy motions of her positioning her phone onto its dock somewhere between her vents and dashboard before she shoved the key into her ignition and the engine purred to life. "Aren't I already doing that? How much weirder can it get than leaving work and lying to Kirby?"

"A lot," I said solemnly.

Nia had put the car in reverse. I'd heard the shift. I'd watched how she'd put her hand onto the passenger's seat and looked over the shoulder. The gravity in my voice forced her to relax her arm. She put the car into park and looked at me once more. Sweat beaded on her forehead as a long day of the car baking in the sun pressed in on her. She settled into her seat and looked through the camera and into my soul.

"Tell me."

"Nia, it's going to sound—"

"Tell me," she repeated.

I resisted the urge to look back up at Silas. I knew Azrames and Fauna were furious with me. I knew the world was in shambles. The pantheons were in upheaval. The first of the dominos had been pushed, and the others would continue to fall, whether we acted or not. Maybe the others hated me, but even if I'd hurt Caliban, even if I'd left him there in the metaphysical shop to clean up the debris and bloodshed, I believed him. He said he loved me. He said he'd protect my loved ones. And no matter how much turmoil or pain or confusion I felt, I clung to that like a drowning swimmer might grip a life raft in a storm.

"I know you grew up going to Sunday services," I began. Her amused sound was encouraging. She and Darius were Christmas and Easter churchgoers, only to appease her mother. Perhaps I would have said the same if my parents and I had been on better terms. "Nia, I'm about to say something truly crazy. Crazier than anything you've ever heard. And I need you to believe that as soon as I get to your house, I'll explain it all. But you have to listen to me, no questions asked."

Her mouth formed a flat, serious line. She dipped her chin, unblinking. The whir of her air-conditioning was the only sound between us.

"Pray," I said.

She blinked in rapid surprise.

"I need you to rebuke angels, and pray for demonic protection."

True shock plastered her face. "Marlow—"

"I *promise* you that I understand exactly how insane it sounds. I swear to you that as someone who grew up with crosses mounted on my wall and Jesus fish bumper stickers and hymns on the radio, I know how terrifying it would be to hear this from anyone. And I could get into a lot of things. I could get into how mysteriously my life has turned out. How my writing career took off. How I've lost time where no one has heard from me. How a wild, freckled woman too beautiful for this world smoked a bowl on your couch and said far too many peculiar things. I can, and I will. But I need you to trust me on this, at least in the time it takes for me to get from my apartment to your house where I can be with the three of you. Nia, please. I love you more than family, because you're the family I chose. I will keep you safe at any cost. Tell me you trust me."

The vibration of vents was the only sound between us for five seconds, then ten, then twenty.

"Nia, please—"

"Okay."

I looked at her with an amalgamation of skepticism and hope. My mouth pinched, teeth chewing on my lips from the inside to prevent myself from screaming at her in urgency, but the panicked need in my unspoken words wasn't lost on her. I saw her sift through the information. I watched her mouth flatten, her brows gather, her eyes set before she took in a short, affirming breath.

"Demons," she repeated, tone impressively neutral. "Anything specific?"

I smacked my lips in a grateful gasp, mouth and eyes dry as I struggled under the love and trust. "Caliban," I said quickly. "Caliban and Azrames. Ask them to help you. Welcome them into your car, your home. And again: rebuke any angels." I knew those weren't their true names, but I believed they'd come. Caliban would answer because he loved me, and I loved him. And Azrames, despite his rage, was my friend. I trusted him. And I knew he understood what it was like to watch someone you loved suffer when they were innocent.

Nia, Kirby, and Darius had no wards. They had no train-ing. Betty had done so much to set up her shop and home against any and all attacks, but Heaven had waited until her heavy hitter was out of the picture. The infernal wrath that would always answer her call for dark divinity had been detained at her time of need. Caliban and Azrames would not fail a call again.

"Caliban and Azrames," Nia repeated back to me. She gearbacked out of her space with more speed or caution than any normal human would hope from a parking lot. She looked into her phone once more before saying, "I'll keep trying Kirby. You'd better be at my place when I get back."

She tapped the screen and her face disappeared. The chime of disconnection underlined her departure. I looked up at Silas. "Can you keep her safe on the highway?"

He grimaced. "No."

Disgust splashed through me. I clutched the couch and coffee table alike as I got to my feet, facing the angel standing in my kitchen. I wasn't sure whether to be terrified or enraged as my only resource, my lone ally, turned down my first and most important request.

"I have to stay with you," he clarified. "I'll get you directly outside of Nia's front door, though she'll have to see me and invite me in by name if she's truly rebuked angels. But I can't leave you alone. Not only for your safety, but for mine."

My brow furrowed.

"I've fallen with no net, Marlow. I betrayed Heaven and Hell in one fell swoop. There's nowhere for me to go. Heaven wants you dead. Every other realm is invested in your survival. If I stick with you, I might survive, too."

"How noble." I narrowed my eyes.

It wasn't a coldness that entered the room, but a pain. Not a deep, penetrating betrayal, but a cut I recognized. It was the hurt of someone who'd never come to expect anything different. It was in his eyes, the sinking of his shoulders, the softening of his face. It was the hollowness that followed rejection.

I'd seen it in the mirror. Someone who hadn't felt love, nor believed themself deserving of it. His wounds were shallow, because this was the only love he'd been shown. He'd been used and cast aside before, as had I. It was no one's fault. It was just our role in the world as secondary players.

"Silas." I moved toward him. This time it was me who extended my hand. He looked down at the offer and frowned without taking it. I left it outstretched. Maybe it was because

I'd already lost my mind, or because I was so overwhelmed by demons and pantheons and deities that I truly had no filter. I spoke from a deep-seated place, telling him what I'd always needed to hear for myself as I said, "You are sovereign in and of yourself. Your existence has meaning. Not because anyone else grants it to you, but because you deserve it. And maybe that's a journey we're both on." I made a few more beckoning motions with my hand, measuring the uncertainty, the kicked-dog energy in his tension as he looked down at my hand. It took a long while for him to slip a few reluctant fingers into my palm.

I latched onto them, gripping his hand fully. He looked at the hand holding his, then up at me.

"You're an angel without a kingdom," I said quietly. "I'm a girl caught in a myth. Maybe we're both orphans. But right now, I need you as much as you need me."

His fingers tightened around mine. Fear pulsed through him as he squeezed my hand. "I don't know what to do, Marlow."

I laughed a low, short, desperately sad laugh. I wasn't shocked in the slightest when the burst of emotion resulted in the prick of impending tears rather than a smile. "Neither do I. But we can figure it out. And it starts with making sure that a few innocent souls aren't slaughtered in the crossfire. If you're my friend, you'll help me protect Nia and Kirby. And if you don't..."

"Then I'm no more your ally than the ones who lied to you," he agreed quietly.

"Can you see other things?" I asked. "Can you see Nia and Kirby? Can you see if—"

I was cut short as he closed his eyes. A hypnotic effect overtook him as his eyes moved rapidly beneath his closed lids. It took him the barest of moments to provide an answer.

"Caliban is already with Nia," he said, eyes still closed. I wasn't sure how he saw them, but I believed him. I wanted to cry with relief knowing that no matter how crazy Nia thought I was, she'd prayed. She'd done exactly as I asked.

"And Kirby?"

Silas nodded. "It's not the same. Nia asked for protection by name. I can see them so much more clearly. It's meant to be a shield against us crossing certain thresholds. But with Kirby—"

"They don't know to ask," I said breathlessly. "Silas, can you get me to them?"

He opened his eyes. "They're in the middle of surgery. They're elbow-deep in the guts of a horse. If we—"

I broke free from his hand, staring up at him. "Would angels stop? They can't be seen by human eyes. Would anything prevent them from bursting in on Kirby? Heaven's soldiers came for Betty. They're coming for anyone close to me. Betty is a witch. She's the most powerful human I know. But if we don't arm Kirby with information, then they're more vulnerable than they've ever been. Tell me Heaven won't hit them next."

Silas looked at me helplessly.

"I wish I were wiser," I said honestly. "I wish I had answers. All of you—Fauna, Az, Caliban, you—you've been alive for forever. You're drowning in answers, in rationale, in time. I can only tell you what I know right now. I know that I love those on the immortal plane, and those in the mortal realm. And right now, it's those on the mortal plane that need my help. Nia and Kirby don't deserve to die in my crossfire, just like no angel or valkyrie deserved to fall in battle because some supreme god commanded their bloodshed. My friends are innocent."

Silas attempted to rub the back of his neck with his hand, but I caught it before it landed. I squeezed it and forced him to look at me.

"We need to be on the same page."

"And what page is that?"

My smile flickered weakly. "You see me here, in my human form. As far as I know, you've never dealt with me before this cycle. I trust you with who I am right now in this lifetime. That includes the friends I have right now, the loved ones I have right now. You've poked through my memories, but this is the only life you've interacted with, right?"

His golden eyes dimmed ever so slightly. "You're the only version of you I've ever known."

"I agree with Fauna," I said. "This cycle is *the* cycle, but not for the reasons they think."

He looked down at the small hand still clutching his, then back up at me, raising his brows skeptically. He was too big for my apartment, too glimmering, too powerful for the modernity of the clean lines and sleek furniture. The clock on the microwave behind him clicked forward another minute, heightening my anxiety. Despite all of that, he remained too small for me. He may have been centuries old, but his age matched that of my inner unhealed child. I squeezed his palm more tightly, which only stirred the hurt on his face.

"This cycle matters more than any other because my eyes are fully open. Not just for me, but for all of us. No one is in the dark this time."

His mouth twisted. "None of us," he repeated, feeling the liberation in his words.

"Come with me as someone free. Someone who doesn't have to do what they're told. Someone who wants to help the world be better. But please, start with two innocent souls who do not deserve pain incurred by powerful forces over which they have no control."

"And what?" he said quietly. "Help you give birth to the antichrist?"

I would have chuckled but didn't have it in me. I waited for his crown-gold eyes to meet mine before I said, "I know you realize how many realms are at stake. Help me save my friends. After that, it isn't just Heaven and Hell that hang in the balance. It isn't the realms and their individuality. Something so much more precious is on the line, and I wouldn't have understood it if you hadn't showed me my past lives. We're

385

positioning ourselves against the highest gods for the most valuable thing of all."

His nostrils flared as he sucked in a long, slow breath. His chest expanded, eyes settling more deeply on mine. "And what is that?"

"Free will," I responded.

The clock on the microwave changed again. Then again. Anxiety took me as I thought of Nia in her car, assuaged only by the inside knowledge that Caliban was in her car without her knowing how divinely protected she was. My mouth worked against the urge to shout out as I thought of the remaining players in the game. Azrames, despite his anger, would not ignore Kirby if they called on him. If their arms were deep in the intestine of some horse, we truly gambled on who would answer the call sooner: Heaven, in the knowledge that their angels had been slain, or us.

"Okay," he said at long last. "We save your friend. Because we know what it is to be used in the war of realms against our will."

"First, we save them," I said, giving his fingers a final tense squeeze. "Then, we figure out what the hell we're going to do with the realms."

He chuckled humorlessly. "The lore always said the antichrist would be born from a whore."

I fought the urge to drop his hand, to elbow him in the nose until his face was bloodied, to storm from the room and deal with it myself. But I knew he was my key to fast travel, if I hoped to reach Kirby in time. So instead, I said, "It will be."

He looked up at me skeptically.

"Get ready, angel," I said through clenched teeth, squeezing his hand. "The antichrist is the catalyst for the end of the world, and I'll be damned if I've been shoved into being the vessel for a goddamn baby. Consider this my rebirth. Here the fuck I am."

·CHARACTER DRINK ORDERS

DORIAN

COFFEE   ITALIAN MACCHIATO

ALCOHOL   ALE CAPONE
- WHISKEY
- VERMOUTH
- CAMPARI
- ORANGE TWIST

POPPY

COFFEE   MATCHA LATTE
WITH OAT MILK

ALCOHOL   PINK LADY
- GRAPEFRUIT GIN
- LEMON JUICE
- ORANGE LIQUEUR
- SIMPLE SYRUP

ELLA

COFFEE   TOASTED MARSHMALLOW
MOCHA

ALCOHOL   CLOUDBERRY COCKTAIL
- WHITE RUM, ROSÉ
- CLOUDBERRY, LIME JUICE
- SIMPLE SYRUP, ORANGE PEEL

ESTRID

COFFEE   DRIP, WHOLE MILK,
TWO SUGARS

ALCOHOL   ALE

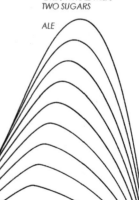

Acknowledgments

Rough ending, right?

At this stage, it feels appropriate to thank my radical evangelical religious trauma for turning enough of a profit to compensate for the hundreds of hours in therapy. I contemplated acknowledging my childhood pastors and Sunday school teachers by telling them to go to Hell, but I'm going to be there, and I don't think I want to share it with them. Thank you to the bit of problematic end-times folklore about virgins and "whores" that inspired the series. And thank you to the corner bodega man who supplied my chardonnay-fueled writing binges. I couldn't have done it without you.

My beloved editor, Letty Mundt, has been so kind and patient (particularly as my brand of neurodivergence demands a ten-page explanation of every comment) in helping me turn each rough draft into the best possible version of itself. I am eternally grateful for the brilliant, talented Helena Elias for her stunning cover art and character art. My agents, Alex D'Amico and Carolyn Forde, are so hardworking, mindful, and supportive for believing in me when I don't believe in myself.

The acknowledgments section is a wild exercise in

gratitude; as I list so many people who've helped me, I feel like the luckiest gal in the world. My long-suffering loving, hype-besties—Haley, Lindsey, Kelley, Allison, Cera, and Bela—have read each draft in its least readable forms, sending reactions to each plot twist and strongly worded feelings about each character while holding my hand every step of the way. Thank you to Glory, Meg, and Arrow for being there for me whether or not this book sells a single copy.

Thank you to the Other Gods.

About the Author

Piper CJ, author of the bisexual fantasy series The Night and Its Moon, Villains, and No Other Gods, is a photographer, hobby linguist, and French fry enthusiast. She has an M.A. in folklore and a B.A. in broadcasting, which she used in her former life as a morning-show weather girl, hockey podcaster, and in audio documentary work. Now when she isn't playing with her dogs, she's binging cartoons, studying fairy tales, or disappointing her parents.

Website: pipercj.com
Instagram: @piper_cj
TikTok: @pipercj